CUT ADRIFT

CUT ADRIFT

Chris Simms

First published in Great Britain in 2010 by Orion Books,
an imprint of The Orion Publishing Group Ltd
Orion House, 5 Upper Saint Martin's Lane
London, WC2H 9EA

An Hachette UK Company

1 3 5 7 9 10 8 6 4 2

A CIP catalogue record for this book is
available from the British Library.

ISBN (Hardback) 978 1 4091 1107 8
ISBN (Trade Paperback) 978 1 4091 1108 5

Typeset by Deltatype Ltd, Birkenhead, Merseyside

Printed in Great Britain by Clays Ltd, St Ives plc

The Orion Publishing Group's policy is to use papers that are natural,
renewable and recyclable products and made from wood grown in sustainable
forests. The logging and manufacturing processes are expected to
conform to the environmental regulations of the country of origin.

www.orionbooks.co.uk

To Ken and Hil – by taking care of the real-world stuff,
you've allowed me to do the imaginary.

In blood and death 'neath a screaming sky,
I lay down on the ground,
And the arms and legs of other men,
Were scattered all around.

'A Pair of Brown Eyes',
The Pogues

Prologue

Graceful and white, the sheet of sea water rose above the bow of the ship and was shredded by the wind. Instants later the haze of droplets struck the windscreen of the bridge, filling it with a sound like wet cement hitting the inside of a mixer. All visibility momentarily lost, the vessel continued its sickening lurch and the man gripping the metal railing felt the same fear as when his torturers' footsteps used to halt outside his cell.

Then the wiper swept the sliding layer of liquid from the glass and he glimpsed sky again. He lifted his fingers to the network of thin scars that encircled his throat. The skin had been left to heal badly, the tissue so heavily puckered in places it seemed to drag the corners of his mouth down to expose a jagged row of lower teeth. 'How far west do you intend to go?'

Keeping both hands on the ship's wheel, the master glanced at the radar screen. 'As far as I need to avoid that whore of a storm.'

To their right, a black anvil of cloud pressed down on the horizon. Snakes of foam had begun to streak the sea around the ship and every time a crest formed, its tip appeared to smoke in the gathering gale.

The man's fingers lowered from his ruined throat. 'And we're already six hours outside the shipping lane?'

'At least.'

'So this will cost us a full day, maybe more?'

'Better that,' the master replied, 'than we sail into the vicious bitch over there. See? There is already movement on the containers up on deck. I can't afford to have any go over the side.'

Cursing, the man braced himself as the ship now began to roll sideways. They'd been delayed by almost two days getting through the Suez Canal. Now this. The people in America who awaited their arrival would not be happy.

A chair, broken free of its restraining clips, rolled across the gleaming floor to bump into the backs of his legs. He kicked at it, sending it crashing over on its side.

Below them, sea water that had been sloshing aimlessly around the deck began streaming to starboard as the heel of the vessel increased. But, before it could pour from the ship's deck, another wave hit. Vapour exploded up then was whipped towards the bridge as if being sucked into the vent of a monstrous machine. Their view of the forty-foot metal containers lined up across the deck disappeared. Then, as the wiper swept back across the glass, the man blinked with astonishment. He could see two women. Wearing jeans and thin tops, they clung to the corner of a container, hair whipping about as they waved frantically at the bridge with their free hands.

The man's thick eyebrows bunched, forming a solid line across his brow. 'What ...?'

Beside him, the master's face turned white.

A mass of cardboard boxes appeared from nowhere and began washing about the deck. A third woman appeared from one of the narrow gaps running between the rows of containers, this one clutching a suitcase. Several of the wooden pallets on which freight was placed inside the containers glided into view, followed by a mass of yellow objects. Ducks. Hundreds and hundreds of grinning plastic ducks.

'The doors to one of the containers must have come loose.'

'Come loose?' The man turned to the master, fury thickening his voice. 'How many people have you got down there?'

'Me? They're not mine.'

'Whose, then?'

'Mykosowski. He gave the instructions.'

'Mykosowski?' The man thought about the ship's owner, probably sitting in his London office and contemplating how much money he'd make this month. The stupid, greedy bastard. 'How many?'

The master's cheeks puffed out momentarily, air escaping from his lips with a fleshy pop. 'Just under fifty.'

'In one container?'

'Two. About twenty women in one, all the men in another.'

'This was to be a clean ship. That was the condition. No risks, nothing illegal.' He shook his head, cursing under his breath. 'Where did you pick them up?'

'Karachi.'

'Pakistan? They were already onboard when you docked at Umm Qasr?'

The master nodded. 'Once we were clear of Iraqi waters, they were moved to a pair of containers up on deck.'

'Where are they going?'

'The deal is to drop them off the British coast before we dock at Felixstowe.'

Bottom teeth exposed in a silent snarl, the man glanced down once more. The deck was now completely covered in a bright yellow layer of ducks, dozens cascading into the sea, boxes and wooden pallets following them. More heads were now peeping from between the rows of containers. Arabs. Possibly Chinese. A man wearing a Pakistani shalwar stepped forward, waving a lit distress flare above his head.

Nervously, the master of the ship ran a hand over his mouth. 'They've opened the other container. Shit.'

Several cardboard boxes had split open, leaking bunches of skipping ropes. They washed about among the ducks like the tentacles of ocean creatures seeking prey.

The man slammed a fist against the side of an anglepoise lamp, sending it swinging on its hinge into the console. The bulb inside shattered and shards of glass fell onto the master's chart. 'Drop them off in what?'

'There's a lifeboat in each container. No markings, nothing to link them to this ship once we set them down. After we were well clear, they were meant to light those distress flares—'

'That's not going to happen.'

'What?'

'Are there any other ships nearby?'

The master examined the radar once again. 'No. We're on our own out here.'

3

'Slow the ship down and bring her round.' He turned to a shaven-headed man who had, until that moment, been standing silently by the door to the bridge, back pressed against the wall, knees slightly flexed in readiness for the ship's roll. The top of one of his ears was missing. 'Marat, get the others. Put your wet-weather gear on and meet me on the forward deck.'

The master raised a hand. 'What are you doing?'

'Getting rid of them,' the man with throat scars replied.

'What?'

'We lock them back in their containers and dump them overboard.'

'You cannot.'

Still looking at his colleague, the man motioned with his chin. 'Marat, go.'

'Wait,' the master blustered. 'I am in charge here. I will not let you do this.'

The edges of his charts began to flap furiously as Marat stepped out into the gale. Once the door had clicked shut, the man turned to the master, eyes sliding contemptuously over the insignia on the shoulders of his white shirt. 'Your rank means nothing to me.'

'I am master of this ship!'

The man took a step closer and the open collar of his khaki shirt parted slightly, showing more of the ugly latticework of scars that enmeshed his throat. 'You answer to Mykosowski, same as me. My orders are to ensure that nothing puts the delivery of that container below deck at risk. Nothing.' He glanced down at the huddles of people clinging to whatever they could find on the deck below. 'Not them. Not any pirate ship off the African coast. Not even you.'

'But you can't just throw them overboard,' the master whispered.

The man stepped closer, his bottom teeth showing like points. 'You want maybe to join them?'

The master's eyes dropped and he turned away without another word.

One

Sixteen days later

Using the main blade of his penknife, Oliver Brookes worked at the tablet of driftwood. The machinations of the sea had worn its edges smooth, salt water had bleached and softened it. He prised a rusty nail out, shaved the burr from the rim of the hole and then looked into it. An eye. The hole would make a good eye.

He held the piece of timber at arm's length, looking beyond the flow of its faded grain to the very nature of the thing. It was a turtle, he decided. That was the shape trying to get out. Tomorrow he would pare the extraneous wood away and watch the animal gradually emerge.

In the corner of the room, an ancient-looking radio played soft music. There was no television, computer or phone. There was no electric toaster, microwave or coffee-making machine in the narrow kitchen off to the side. No halogen lights, stereo system or burglar alarm.

Every available surface was covered by driftwood sculptures. Dolphins, basking sharks, hermit crabs. Gulls and puffins and kittiwakes hung from the roof's low beams. Shoals of sea bass, herring and mackerel milled in the corners of the flagstone floor.

The front door was open, allowing a breeze to blow in off the sea just beyond. He placed the piece of wood on the table to the side of his tatty armchair and stood, feeling the stiffness in his hip bones as he did so.

The sun had almost set and the brine-filled draught swirling round his front room now carried with it a pinch of cold. Time to shut the door, draw the curtains and climb into bed. As usual, he paused in the doorway to survey the bay that curved away on each side of his cottage. To the right, the nearest sign of human life were the twinkling lights of Combe Martin, a good mile along the jagged coast.

He was just about to pull the wooden door closed when he spotted a dark form in the shallows. His eyes narrowed. A moment later there was movement as the whale raised its fluke in a futile wave. To Oliver Brookes it was a beckoning; a plea for help.

Leaving the door open, he walked straight through to his bedroom, yanked the eiderdown from the bed and peeled the sheet from the mattress. He reached down and removed a second, folded sheet from the drawer built into the base of the bed. Leaving them on his armchair, he stepped into the kitchen where he dragged out the bucket and hurricane lamp from below a trough-like sink. Then he marched back through the cottage, dumping the sheets into the bucket on the way.

His front garden was crowded with larger sculptures, some of driftwood, others incorporating the flotsam and jetsam regularly washed up on the beach. Gnarled lengths of rope, plastic containers of all shapes and sizes, fragments of sack bearing the remnants of foreign words. He removed a large shovel from the stone shed that held his supply of wood for the winter, slipped through the waist-high gate and was immediately on the strip of grass that bordered the beach. He stepped down the gentle bank and on to the expanse of coarse yellow sand.

After ten strides he reached the band of seaweed deposited by that afternoon's unusually high tide. Stepping across the spongy bed, he reached sand again and walked slowly towards the stranded whale, the fast-retreating tide now two metres behind it.

Its slender body was about five metres long and dark grey in colour. The fluke moved again, the pointed tips gouging deep ruts in the sand. The sea water filling them was red with blood. He examined the hooked dorsal fin set far down its back, the white band on the upper side of each flipper and the fringe of porcelain white which he knew covered its underside. A young minke, just a few years old.

Putting his things down, he slowly approached the head of

the animal, gaze moving along the ridge that stretched from its blowhole down the head to the midpoint of its upper jaw. A mass of dents and nicks covered the animal's shiny blubber, reminding him of the bodywork on a battered car.

An eye, so small for such a large creature, stared at him without blinking. He looked into the black pupil, barely darker than the iris which surrounded it. What places you've been, he thought. The crushing silence of lightless depths. Air exploded from the animal's blowhole and moments later he felt a few specks of moisture settle on his face.

'Calm now,' he cooed in a deep and gentle voice. 'Shush.' Slowly, he extended a hand and placed it on the smooth, warm flesh above the animal's eye. 'I'll not hurt you, my friend. I'll not hurt you.'

The eye slowly closed and he felt the creature had somehow understood him. Brookes straightened up and looked out to sea. The sun had now almost dipped below the horizon and he knew the tide would not return for another twelve hours. He turned to the distant lights of Combe Martin, the hill called Little Hangman looming high above the village. To get there involved climbing the steep cliff path, walking through wooded slopes and then following sheep trails across empty heathland. By the time he had made it to the village and persuaded whoever was in the Focsle Inn to help, the whale would be dead. Looking back at the creature, he sighed at the enormity of the task before him.

He walked round to the fluke, quickly spotting the small lacerations to the right-hand edge. He knew the blood was mixing with sea water, making the bleeding appear far more serious than it actually was. Still, the object causing the wounds needed to be removed. Ready to move back at the first twitch of the tail, he reached into the crimson water and quickly felt around. His fingers closed on a thin, jagged lump and he dug around it, pulled the thing out then scrabbled clear. It was slate, common to that stretch of the north Devon coast.

After flinging it far away, he picked up the bucket, walked down to the shallows and tipped the sheets into the water. Once they were soaked he fished them out, walked back to the whale, lifted one up and tore a hole in its middle. He draped it over the whale so the dorsal fin protruded through the slit. The other sheet he draped further up the animal, positioning the corners of the dripping cloth over the fins. That left only the head exposed, along with the areas around the creature's eyes and blowhole.

He trudged back up the beach, scooped an armful of damp bladderwrack, carried it back to the shrouded whale and began stringing it across the creature's head. An eye opened, following the movements of his arms before more air burst from its blowhole.

'I know,' Brookes murmured. 'As wigs go, it's not fooling anyone.'

He stepped back then looked at the spade. Have I got the strength to do this on my own? He put his hands on his hips. You've got no choice. There's no one else to help. He stooped to pick the tool up.

By the time the eastern sky began to lighten, Brookes was sitting by the whale, arms resting on his knees. His head lolled slightly as sleep momentarily took him. The whale's breathing had grown more and more ragged as the night wore on. Now it coughed and Brookes' head came up. He looked at the blowhole, saw the lumps of white phlegm sliding down into the wreath of seaweed that circled it. The animal didn't have long left.

He studied the pit he'd dug round the creature then examined the channel, flanked by piles of sand leading down the beach. At last the tide had turned: water was starting to creep into the far end of the channel. Turning his head, he saw the eye watching him.

'Soon, my friend, soon. Are you feeling a bit dry, there?' He picked up the bucket, stepped down into the pit and filled it with brackish water. 'Here you go,' he said, smoothing his wet palm around the animal's eye. Slowly, it closed, allowing him to dribble water over the lids. He walked round, moistened the creature's other eye then sluiced the remaining water across its back, worried at how hot the animal had become.

By now a tongue of sea water was pushing up the channel.

Lumps of sand were beginning to collapse into it, leaving behind a light froth which was then carried towards them. 'Come on, come on,' Brookes whispered.

A few minutes later, the sun cleared the crest of the moors behind him, bathing the pale sand in a golden glow. Water had begun to fan out into the pit, trickling around his bare feet. Five minutes later, it had reached his ankles. He splashed his way over to the animal and rubbed gently above the whale's eye. Slowly, it opened. 'Now, you have to try. I can't shift you.' He pointed to their right, towards the open sea. 'That way, OK? That way.'

Water was now sloshing at his calf muscles, lapping at the whale's belly. The creature's fluke moved. Brookes lifted off the damp sheets and threw them onto the mound of sand behind them. He swept the seaweed from the whale's head.

Slowly, he walked backwards to the top of the channel, water pushing at the backs of his knees, soaking the turn-ups of his trousers. He clapped, beckoning the creature towards him, watching as the level of water inched over its flippers, then up to its eyes. Soon just its dorsal fin and upper back were showing.

He clapped louder. 'Come on! Come on! To me, to me, to me!'

Water churned and the fluke broke through, thrashing from side to side as the creature struggled to swing itself round in the shallows.

'Yes! Yes!' Brookes roared, slapping the waist-high water with his palms, trying to guide the animal from the circular pool.

The dorsal fin inched towards him, fluke struggling to power the whale forward. He stepped to the side and reached out a hand, trailing it along the animal's smooth side as it sensed the deeper channel and began nudging its way down it.

'Go!' he shouted tiredly, wading along beside it and weakly punching the air. 'Go!'

The animal made the sea proper, and with its fluke finally able to work freely, quickly disappeared beneath the waves. About thirty metres out, it resurfaced, blew a cloud of vapour into the air then sank from sight once more. Hands on hips, Brookes waded backwards out of the sea, eyes continually scanning its surface. Minutes later, his face broke into a smile as the sun lit another cloud of vapour, this one rising about two hundred metres out to sea.

As he turned to retrieve his things from the rapidly encroaching tide, something bumped against his ankle. He looked down and saw a yellow duck bobbing its way past him. He spotted another, looked along the shoreline to his left and realised there were perhaps a dozen more of the things being washed up on the beach. Stiffly, he bent down and picked it out of the water.

The yellow plastic had been bleached by the sun and the blue paint at the edge of one eye had come away, giving the thing a cross-eyed look. It grinned up at him. Frowning, Brookes turned it over, feeling the faint rattle of droplets within. He studied the lettering stamped on its underside. Trademark and copyright stamps, then lettering: Kyou Inc, Made in China. No surprise, he said to himself. Everything seems to be made there, nowadays. He stepped clear of the water, dropped the duck into his bucket alongside the hurricane lamp, scooped up his sheets and spade then trudged slowly back up the beach.

Two

Jon Spicer leaned back in the hot water. A bath after work, he thought. Never in a million years would I have believed this would become a regular habit. But since Alice had kicked him out the previous year, retreating into a small room and lying there in silence somehow felt right. He listened to sounds as they lost strength and blurred in the steamy air. The high tones of a siren somewhere close by in the city centre, the noise of a band rehearsing in the renovated warehouse behind the apartment building he was in, muted voices from the television in the next room.

The song which carried across the narrow alley separating the two buildings suddenly collapsed, drums being the final instrument to fall silent. Shit, that was me. Sorry. Sorry. The female vocalist's voice. Jon imagined the woman to be somewhere in her early twenties, a mess of dyed hair held back by a brightly coloured band. Maybe a piercing through a nostril or her upper lip. OK, let's go again from the start, a male voice announced and the keyboard started up an instant later.

As usual, he tried to straighten his legs so the warm water covered his knees. No chance, he thought. The baths in these new-build city-centre apartments weren't designed for someone well over six feet tall. Instead he pressed his chin into his sternum and watched the coating of black hair covering the thick muscles of his chest shift and sway beneath the surface. A drip slowly detached itself from the tap at the other end of the bath, hitting the water with a delicate noise.

He thought about his life and the now-familiar sense of not being able to control it. Despite all his promises to change things, Alice had refused to allow him back. Even if he gave up the job.

She'd shaken her head with a sad smile when he'd offered to do that.

'And what would you do instead?'

'I don't know,' he'd replied. 'Retrain as something. Boiler technician – I saw an ad by British Gas the other day. They pay for you to do the course. You end up with your own van, covering a set area.' Even as the words were coming out of his mouth, he could tell they sounded absurd.

Alice didn't even meet his eyes. 'It's your fortieth later this year. You're a policeman, Jon. It's all you've ever wanted. Anything else would leave you miserable.'

'Not if it costs me my family.'

He watched another droplet slowly swell, the bulb of water stretching a fraction before it fell. He sighed, mind moving to giving evidence the next day. He and his partner, DS Rick Saville, were due in court at two fifteen. A rape case with all the potential for the attacker to walk away because, at the end of the day, it was his word against hers.

He hoped his part in the agonisingly slow court proceedings wouldn't take up too much time. It was Friday the day after tomorrow and he had his daughter, Holly, for the night. He needed some time to prepare: buy in some of her favourite foods, visit a toy shop and get her some stuff to play with.

In barely two weeks it was her fifth birthday. Where had the years suddenly gone? Nearly five and she was showing anxiety-related behavioural problems. He shifted slightly, his body pushing out a little wave that rebounded off the side of the bath then hit his shoulder with a quiet slap. For the past few months he'd had to endure the fact his daughter spent more time in the company of Mummy's new boyfriend than with himself.

Dr Phillip Braithwaite. Jon felt his jaw grow tight. Maybe if the man applied some of his psychiatry skills to Holly, he'd realise that his presence in the house was part of Holly's problems. A short burst of air escaped his nostrils. Why couldn't the twat just piss off? Fat chance. The bloke was ingratiating himself, easing his way deeper and deeper into their lives.

The knock on the door caused him to flinch and he almost

sat up, the instinct to cover himself strong. The door opened, dragging steam out with it, and Carmel Todd, thirty-year-old crime reporter at the *Manchester Evening Chronicle*, stepped into the tiny bathroom. 'Brought you a brew.'

Jon lifted his eyes, took in her long, willowy figure and smiled. 'Cheers.'

She lowered the lid of the toilet at the side of the bath, sat down and then placed the mug of tea on the corner. Jon leaned back, trying to appear at ease with being naked in front of her. How bloody ridiculous, he thought. You've been sleeping with her for weeks. What's the big deal about her wandering in when you're having a bath?

Her fingers began to caress the cropped hair covering his head. A thumb strayed down, brushing lightly over the thick scar that bisected his left eyebrow. 'Which musical feast are we being treated to this evening?'

His eyes flicked towards the frosted glass. 'Sort of Pink Floyd, but a bit faster.'

'Any good?'

'A bit ambitious. The singer keeps losing her thread halfway through.'

Her hand worked its way to the side of his head and a finger began stroking his ear. Don't, he wanted to say. I can't stand my ears being fiddled with. Instead, he stopped the movement by raising a hand to give her fingers an affectionate squeeze. She returned the pressure and he raised himself up slightly so he could reach for the mug. 'What are you watching on the telly?'

'Oh,' she said half-heartedly. 'Channel Four news. A special report about human-rights abuses in China. Your boxes are still by the stereo. You're allowed to unpack your stuff, I hope you realise?' A playful tickle at the back of his neck. 'Especially if Holly's sleeping on the sofa this weekend.'

'Yeah, sorry. I'll try and do it later.' He thought about his last attempt to sort out his collection of albums and films. The way he'd packed when leaving the family home amounted to little more than scooping the uppermost DVDs and CDs off the shelves, placing them in a couple of old cardboard boxes then putting the remainder of his collection on top. As a consequence, music he hadn't listened to in years was now uppermost in the untidy stack.

Looking inside a few days before, the first album he'd seen was *Rum, Sodomy and the Lash* by the Pogues. Fond memories had immediately surfaced. Alice and him drinking in an Irish bar on Oldham Street as the album was being hammered by a group of laughing lads who spoke with the lilting accent of southern Ireland. They kept returning to the jukebox and selecting 'A Pair of Brown Eyes', roaring delightedly along to the words, Guinness sloshing in their glasses as they waved them about.

He could hear the exuberant banjo, uilleann pipe and drums, taste the fug of cigarette smoke in the air. At some stage during the evening, he'd walked unsteadily up to the jukebox, slotted in a coin, selected 'Dirty Old Town' and then stood in the middle of the pub, pint raised to Alice as the song described kissing by the gasworks wall and dreaming dreams by the old canal.

Later that night, they'd walked along beside the Rochdale canal as it wended its way through the centre of Manchester, derelict mills and empty warehouses rearing up around them. He'd paused to lift Alice so she sat on the crumbling wall bordering the towpath and, faces level, kissed her as the song played on in his head.

'It'll be going cold.'

'What? Oh, yeah.' He lifted the cup and took a sip of tea. She's forgot the sugar.

'Nice?' she asked.

'Perfect, thanks.'

'Good.' She got to her feet. 'And another thing ...'

He turned his head to see her gaze sliding slowly down the contours of his torso. With one hand, she swept her mane of blonde hair over a shoulder. The gesture was just a little too contrived and he had to concentrate on maintaining his unsuspecting expression. 'If Holly's staying over this Friday, we should get some action in tonight.'

He raised an eyebrow, while picturing the yawning expanse of her bed. The platform on which he'd have to perform, yet again. God, I'm getting old. 'I'll get this down me, then.'

Once she'd closed the door, he sat back and replaced his half-finished drink on the rim of the bath. What the hell, he thought, am I doing here? He let his eyes close. What other options did I have?

For the first few weeks after Alice had asked him to move out, he'd kipped in the spare room of the cramped flat his younger sister, Ellie, owned. But with his irregular hours, the impracticalities of it soon became apparent. After that was a room in a cheap hotel. But, even with a discount for booking by the month, the cost was too high to maintain on his wage.

Buying property was completely out of the question, so he'd begun looking at renting somewhere near the city centre. But prices had rocketed in the past few years. He remembered driving around the slightly cheaper areas near Withington one Tuesday afternoon. Students ferrying crates of bargain beer back to their flats. Clusters of uncollected bin bags in unkempt gardens, litter dotting the pavement. Bikes with their front wheels missing chained up to railings. The idea of living there was ridiculous.

When Carmel made a move on him one evening after work, a night of no-strings sex was too good to refuse. A little to his surprise, there was no hint of awkwardness the next morning. The arrangement grew in frequency until, a few weeks before, she mentioned that he may as well move in. Sharing the bills and rent would save them both a bit of money. Things would also be easier, she reasoned, if he didn't have to go back to his hotel most mornings to throw on fresh clothes before heading into work. Unable to see any major drawbacks, he'd agreed.

The skin on the tips of his fingers had begun to pucker and the bathwater was growing tepid. He leaned forward, yanked the plug out and looped the chain round a tap. The plastic nail file which had been floating between his knees began to turn, slowly making its way to the far end of the bath. He felt a slight tickling on his ribs as the level of water gradually dropped. Now the nail file had begun to rotate on the spot directly above the plug, tilting upwards as the vortex of water gathered strength beneath it.

Soon it was almost vertical, the speed of its revolutions growing faster and faster until its tip finally made contact with the plug itself. It shook and trembled and eventually keeled over as the last remnants of water vanished.

Three

'Twelve thousand US dollars? How many containers? And what's the cargo? Flat-packed garden sheds? Export Cargo Shipping Instruction and Standard Shipping Note? And it's cash they're offering? OK, then make up a Bill of Lading and take it.'

Silence as the person at the other end of the phone spoke.

'The fridges? What about the fridges? If they wanted a time-definite delivery for their fridges, they should have booked their fridges on a liner. Or put up the money for a time charter. They didn't. They booked their fridges on a tramp service, so their customer gets the fridges when you show up with them. And that will be after you've dropped those garden sheds off in Melbourne.'

Slavko Mykosowski cut the connection, tapped a few details into the computer on his desk, then looked up. 'These people.' He glanced at the phone. 'That idiot. He calls me any time he likes, not thinking if it's night or day here in London.'

On the other side of the room was a sofa. The man sitting on it ran a forefinger over the thin loops of scar tissue encircling his throat. His cheekbones now jutted painfully through the stretched skin of his face and his eyes appeared a little too large for his head. He stared at the platter of food on the low table before him.

Mykosowski gazed across at him for a few more moments. 'Come on, Valeri, eat.' He patted his ample stomach, leaving the hand resting on an expensive-looking pale blue shirt. 'God knows, I don't need it.'

The man with the throat scars surveyed the spread. Caviar, smoked salmon blinis, potato salad, pelmeni, kulich. He waved a hand over the items. 'Slavko, all I do is eat. And still this hunger will not leave me.' Almost reluctantly, he forked a dumpling into his mouth and started chewing.

Mykosowski shrugged, turning to look out the window at the Thames stretching away below. Evening was settling in and light from the strings of bulbs stretching between lamp-posts had started to catch on the river. His gaze was dragged, as usual, to the circular shape of the London Eye. 'You had an unfortunate experience. Little food for over a week, it's no wonder you're hungry.' He paused to sneak a look at the other man. 'I told you on the phone, I feel bad – really bad – about what happened. It was the rules, though. The master of the ship couldn't turn back.'

Valeri held up his fingers to halt the flow of words. 'There's no need. Delivering the container took priority over everything. I knew that.' He sat back, continuing to chew on his food. But you, he thought, jeopardised the delivery, didn't you? You broke the rule by taking those migrants on board. And we wouldn't have been out on deck when that monstrous wave hit if it wasn't for that. He remembered the unstoppable force of water sweeping him over the side, one of the lifeboats falling just metres from his head. Then the impact, salt water filling his nostrils, mouth and throat. Gasping and coughing as he resurfaced, ducks and people all around him, looking up to see one of the containers slowly toppling over the edge of the rapidly receding ship, screams of the people trapped inside mixing with the wind. Beneath his skin, the ridged cartilage of his throat ratcheted up then slid back as he swallowed.

'So,' Mykosowski announced, one hand going to his mouse as he checked something on the screen. 'Our phone calls have been rushed. You and your team were swept overboard. You drift for days before the fishing trawler finds you. Tell me what happened after that.'

Valeri let the memory of the trawler's appearance form in his head. The joy they'd felt when they knew for certain it had seen them. The fishermen had pulled the four of them onboard then spooned thin soup into their mouths as they lay on deck, too weak and exhausted to move. 'It took us back to land, the port called Liverpool.'

'I know it; many of my ships call in there.'

'They must have contacted the authorities while still at sea because there were ambulances and a couple of police officers waiting at the dock as we arrived. None of us had the strength to try and escape. I told everyone we would have to seek asylum, claim we were dumped from a container ship out at sea. It was the only way to buy time until you could sort something out.'

Mykosowski blinked nervously at the comment. 'Then what?'

'The ambulance took us to hospital and a doctor checked us over.' He thought about that night. The sensation of lying in a clean bed and feeling it shift with non-existent waves. One staff member, a Russian girl originally from Moscow, had taken pity on her compatriots, sneaking them chocolates and biscuits from the gifts left at the nurses' station. 'Next day, immigration officers arrived to drive us to a big building near the river.'

'All five of you?'

'Four. Marat, Yegor, Andriy and myself.'

'I thought you had four others in your team.'

'There were,' Valeri answered, seeing the knife once again as he plunged it into Sergei's neck. 'One didn't survive.'

Mykosowski's face dropped. 'I am sorry, Valeri.'

He shrugged. 'We were taken for screening, that's what they called it. We were given numbers and sent upstairs to this big interview room. Your number showed on a panel and they asked you for your name, date of birth, nationality.'

'You had no documents?'

'Nothing.'

'And you said you were Russian?'

'Yes.'

Mykosowski gave a cautious nod. 'Go on.'

'Then I was photographed, fingerprinted and asked more questions. Why are you claiming asylum? Where did you live in Russia? Who are your relatives? How did you travel here? Things like that.'

'What did you say?'

'That I was a political activist, from Moscow. No family.

Caught a ship from St Petersburg after the FSB came for me. Dumped in a lifeboat and found by fishermen.'

'And the others?'

'Same sort of stuff. The officer who questioned me wanted to know if we knew each other before getting on the boat, but I'd already instructed them to say we were strangers. At the end of the day we were driven, with about a dozen others, to a new place for the night. Next day, vans started taking us all off to other accommodation.'

'Other accommodation?'

'Flats. Rooms in tower blocks. Places where asylum seekers wait for news about their claim. I couldn't stay in mine. They took my fingerprints, remember? I don't know where that information goes. Interpol? Maybe further. So I came here as soon as I could.'

'Which means they'll be looking for you,' Mykosowski murmured.

Valeri laughed. 'They will. Here and in half the other countries on this planet.'

Mykosowski rubbed at his temples. 'This is a mess. What about the others? Where are they?'

'I've no idea. Somewhere near Liverpool, I suppose. Before we were separated, I gave them orders. They were to wait a few days then phone here.'

'Here?' Mykosowski looked horrified. 'Contact me?'

Valeri's voice hardened and the tips of his lower teeth showed as he spoke. 'They're sitting in shit-hole flats with nothing. Vouchers for food. That's it. I served in the Russian army with those men. Marat? We did three tours in Chechnya together.'

His mind went back to an incident on their second tour. Their patrol had walked into an ambush, a tripwire triggering an explosion that sent shards of shrapnel slicing through the air, one of which took off half of Marat's left ear. Then came the firefight. With all their comrades dead or unable to fight back, the two of them had held off the advancing soldiers long enough for helicopter support to arrive.

He reached into a pocket and flicked a credit-card-sized piece of plastic on the table. On it was a small photo of his face. 'We've all been given these identity cards. Soon, our stories will be discovered. If they're still sitting in those flats, they'll be arrested and taken to a detention centre. Marat's got a wife and two kids back in Russia. I've bounced the little things on my knee, read them stories. Andriy has a fiancée waiting for him back in St Petersburg. They're your responsibility.'

Mykosowski placed both palms on the table, took a deep breath and lifted the tips of his fingers a fraction. 'OK. When they ring, I'll get their locations and you can take some cash to them.' He thought for a moment. 'How much do they know?'

'About the ship?'

'Yes.'

'They were aware the container we were guarding was for America.'

'They don't know what was inside?'

Valeri thought about the final, desperate, days at sea before the fishing trawler found them. Lolling in the heat, thirst driving them mad, his colleagues demanding to know why the ship didn't turn back. Why they had been left to die. I shouldn't have been weak, he thought. I shouldn't have told them what was in that container. He shook his head. 'Of course not,' he lied. 'Where is the *Lesya* now, by the way?'

Mykosowski joggled his mouse then studied the screen. 'It cleared the Channel the day before yesterday. It's now a couple of hundred miles out in the Atlantic.'

'Only yesterday morning?'

'That storm caused a lot of damage. It had to wait a week for new parts for the radar system. After Felixstowe it made a delivery to Rotterdam. That's done and now it's headed for America.'

Valeri could hardly believe his ears. 'You accepted a delivery to Rotterdam? That wasn't on the itinerary.'

'It's a tramp ship. We get an opportunity to take on freight, we take on freight.'

'And there were no questions asked at the two ports?'

'What? About missing crew?'

Valeri nodded.

'The regular crew are all onboard. You and your team weren't even officially on that ship, remember?'

'What about missing containers?'

Mykosowski's belly shook as he chuckled. 'Valeri, do you know how many shipping containers are lost at sea every month? Hundreds? Thousands? Who knows? Customs officials only care that the containers being offloaded in their port have the necessary paperwork. They don't check ship manifests. That's my responsibility.'

Valeri crossed his arms. 'That cargo – which was the whole point of the voyage – is out in the Atlantic without my team to guard it.'

'Valeri, don't worry. Next stop is Baltimore. We unload the container there and our part in this is over.'

In fact, Valeri thought, once that cargo hits American soil, the entire mission will be over and we all get paid. The people so anxiously waiting will finally have what they want. Valeri's eyes dropped to the floor, an uncomfortable feeling creeping over him as he considered what they'd do with their precious delivery. It's not my concern, he told himself. It's nothing to do with me. He looked up at Mykosowski. 'How long until it reaches Baltimore?'

The other man tilted his head to the side. 'Eight days, at most.'

Eight days. Valeri prayed nothing else could go wrong in that short amount of time. 'And the master knows what's in the container?'

'Kaddouri? He follows whatever orders I give him. And his orders are to go nowhere near the thing.'

Valeri glanced at Mykosowski. The ship's owner was studying his screen once again. You have no idea, he thought, about the people in America you're dealing with. The power they wield. He wanted to jump up and tell Mykosowski that the fact they were on the other side of the Atlantic from them meant nothing. These were people who could reach out anywhere in the world and make other people disappear. Christ knew they did it often enough. Instead, he reached for his coat, feeling the Bounty bar in his side pocket. Sweets, chocolate, junk food. When will my cravings for the stuff pass? 'OK. Let me know as soon as all my team have called in.'

Once outside, he took the walkway that led alongside the Thames. The riverside restaurants and cafes were busy, people chatting at tables placed out in the evening sun. He looked at the plates of food. Fish and chips, earthenware pots of unshelled prawns, steaks sizzling on platters. He thought about their last desperate days at sea and what they'd finally resorted to. Queasiness stirred in his gut.

Off to his left, a small wooden jetty stretched above the exposed gravel and rock which bordered the greyish-brown water. He paced the battered planks, stopping at the jetty's end to gaze across the river at the Houses of Parliament.

His mind went to the slow drag of days before the lifeboat he and his team were on had finally been separated from the raft carrying the last two refugees. The woman on it was still alive, he was sure. Such a tiny thing, he thought. Those deep-brown, almond-shaped eyes. Eyelashes so thick she seemed to be permanently wearing mascara or eyeliner or whatever it was women did to arm themselves with a glance that could make a man's mouth go dry. Yet the femininity of her eyes was balanced by the squareness of her jaw and the set of her lips – they lent her a determined look. Defiant, even. The fact she was still clinging to life when so many others on the raft had died didn't surprise him.

What was her name? Amira, that was it. Amira Jasim. She never let go of her little plastic bag with the notebook and pen sealed inside. Every few hours she would take it out then scribble away, writing God knew what. Ripping the pages out, ramming the little notes into those cursed ducks and dropping the things back with the masses that floated alongside them. After eight days at sea, she was unable to stand. But still she continued to write. Surely, he told himself, she couldn't have survived for much longer after their lifeboat and her raft had drifted apart.

He leaned on the wooden rail to watch the river. A squat

cruiser was making its way towards Tower Bridge. Crowded beneath the curved canopy on its upper deck was a mass of tourists clutching electronic devices to their faces. Phones, cameras, camcorders. Flashes continually lit up the inside of the glass. Slowly, he turned the mobile Mykosowski had given him over in his hand, tracking the river's currents as they curled and slid away before him.

After the huge wave had swept all of them overboard, they'd survived two more nights of storms. During that time, they'd prayed for the ocean to calm. Then they'd got what they wished for: days spent motionless on its flat surface, slowly baking under the sun, desperate for movement of any kind. A ruffling of the water, a murmur of breeze, even a cloud floating across the sky.

He thought about the freight ship, now halfway across the Atlantic and him standing on a jetty, unable to watch over the cargo that was his duty to guard. And he wondered if, by breaking his promise to the people in America of running a clean ship, Mykosowski had signed a death warrant for not only himself, but everyone with any knowledge of what lay below the deck of the *Lesya*.

'Give me the name of this website.' Mykosowski sat up, mobile phone pressed against a cheek that carried the imprint of a sofa cushion. In the corner of his apartment the live feed to a porn shoot somewhere in Albania still filled the grotesquely sized plasma screen. Now, two young girls were being filmed. They were kneeling between a seated man's legs, guzzling away as if their lives depended on it. Which, judging from their ages and the types of tattoo visible on the man's lower arms, it probably did.

Realising he must have fallen asleep within seconds of logging on the previous night, Mykosowski lifted the remote and cut the connection. Then he dragged his laptop towards him across the coffee table, one shoulder hunched, phone now wedged against his flabby jaw. After typing in a couple of words, he growled, 'Got it,' staring at the screen as he hung up. He read through the story slowly and thought for a few moments. God, this wasn't happening. When he rang Valeri's number, there was a crystal glass half-full of cognac before him. As the phone started to ring, he took a large sip. 'Valeri, where are you now?'

'Waiting for the train. I'll be back in Manchester late morning.'

Mykosowski nodded. The three men in Valeri's team had all called in the previous evening. He'd taken their addresses and passed them on to Valeri, giving him instructions to supply each one with enough money to disappear. 'I think we have a problem. My client who lost his consignment of ducks. He's been searching about on the internet and came across a news story. A woman, walking her dog on a beach in somewhere called Minehead. She says she found some yellow ducks washed up on the sand. In one of them was a note.'

'A note?'

'Yes, she removed the plug in the base of the duck. There was a note inside.'

'What did it say?'

Mykosowski ran the back of a thumbnail down his heavy cheek. 'I wouldn't believe it was real, but for one thing.'

'What?'

'I'll read it to you.'

Once he was finished, he swivelled in his chair to look at the dead grey TV screen. '"The man with the throat scars is a naval soldier?" Valeri, I think it is you this man is describing.' All he could hear was background noise of the station. 'Valeri, are you there?'

'It is a woman, not a man.'

Mykosowski cocked his head to one side. 'Explain.'

'She was scribbling in this little book the whole time. Tearing out the pages and sealing them inside those ducks.'

'How many notes?'

'A lot.'

'And this woman. She was from inside one of the containers?'

'That's right. Iraqi woman, called Amira. Early twenties. She spoke good English.'

Mykosowski raised his chin, eyes scanning the immense painting of a white stallion on the far wall of his apartment. A few tiny beads of sweat now showed on his brow. 'What happened to this woman?'

'I don't know. She was on the raft with the refugees. I was in the lifeboat with my team. We became separated.'

'Could she have survived?'

'I doubt it. She was inches from death when the wind blew us apart.'

'But you can't be sure.' Mykosowski traced a finger down the side of his laptop. 'You know, if more of the messages this woman wrote are found, we are vulnerable. The *Lesya* is still seven days from the American coast. What if you mentioned the name of the ship and she heard it? What if that's mentioned in a note?'

Valeri thought of the other things he had talked about with Marat, Yegor and Andriy as they aimlessly drifted for day after day. *Thank God we spoke in Russian. Even if our words carried to her across the water, she couldn't have understood.* 'We didn't,' he lied. 'I'm almost certain of that.'

'Almost? And you said there are more of these notes?'

'Yes. But thousands of ducks poured from the ship when the containers broke open. Who knows if any more carrying notes will make it to shore? What about the ducks themselves? Could they be traced back to the *Lesya*?'

Mykosowski reached for his cognac and took another sip. 'No. They were listed on the manifest as bathroom items, nothing more specific than that.'

'What about the person who had paid you to ship them – the one who found this story?'

'He won't talk, I can assure you of that.' He tapped a nail against the rim of his glass. 'But this woman? What was her name?'

'Amira Jasim.'

'Amira Jasim? I think you should check the hospital you were taken to. See if she also was taken there. And if she was, deal with her.'

'OK.'

'And we need to talk about your team. They worry me. If the authorities somehow make the link, I'm afraid they might talk.'

'I'm on my way to see them right now. Once they have cash, they'll just vanish.'

'And if they're picked up as they try to leave the country?'

'You could make sure they get out safely. On one of your ships.'

'It's not that easy. Not in the ports of this country. Valeri, I think they'll have to be dealt with, too.'

The line remained silent.

'They could put the delivery of the container at risk. Valeri, you know it's the only way.'

Four

Jon's eyes travelled slowly up the pillar, his head starting to tilt back as he took in the white girders and frames of the glass atrium high above him. Somewhere below, a series of electronic beeps echoed as a person passed through the security gates inside the entrance to the Crown Court.

He heard coins and keys rattle in a plastic tray, the murmur of the guards' voices, then the click of heels on the tiled floor of the hall. He glanced over the balcony. A young female solicitor, walking quickly towards the rear of the building, hair in a tight ponytail. They always wear their hair in tight ponytails, he thought, as she passed from sight.

Turning back, he examined the carpet at his feet. Little circles of cream-coloured dots floated on a sea of turquoise fabric. They stretched away in perfect diagonal lines to the chunky wooden doors leading through to courts seven and eight.

'This is a joke,' he sighed, glancing down at his watch. Two hours sat here waiting for the court doors to open and the usher to call us in. He tried to search for a positive. At least the rest of their workload was relatively clear: they would surely be part of the investigation into who had bludgeoned, burned, stabbed or shot the next corpse to show up in the city.

Jon glanced across at his partner, taking in his trendily messed-up hair and well-proportioned profile. Rick's eyes were glued to his mobile, thumb moving over the scroll button. Jon sighed again. Bloody things were destroying the art of conversation. Holly would be wanting one soon. 'What are you looking at, anyway?'

'Scanning surf reports. Looking good down in Devon for next week.'

Jon reflected for a moment on Rick's new hobby. 'Oh yeah, you've got holiday booked, haven't you?'

'Yup – from Saturday. Three days' worth. We can't decide between the West Country or somewhere closer. We've got Zak – so it'll probably be somewhere closer.'

Zak, thought Jon. The eight-month-old infant created from sperm Rick had donated to a lesbian couple.

'Seen this?' Rick was holding his mobile out.

Jon squinted, trying to make sense of the dense type packing the screen. 'What?'

'Newspaper article. Found it among the surf reports in the *North Devon Messenger*. These ducks have started getting washed up along the Bristol Channel, probably fallen off a container ship somewhere out in the Atlantic.'

'And?'

'A woman walking her dog along the beach at Minehead found a note in one. The *Messenger* got hold of it and they've printed the thing word for word.'

'What does it say?'

'It's probably all a hoax, but here, I'll read it you.' Rick held the screen a little closer to his face.

LETTER THREE
Nothing to eat and no rest for last night and all this day. Warm sun for three hours and our clothes are drier. Many look to the horizon, but still the ship has not been seen.

Others have been busy, making good the raft and gathering all possible from the sea around us. A man from the crew with many scars on his throat thought to gather all the ducks close to us and push them in the space between the top and bottom of the pallets. The raft is now higher, though water still reaches to our ankles, so we cannot sit.

Another man, Ali, who is also from Baghdad, swum out to bring back many more of the children's ropes. He and the man with throat scars have used some to secure the raft more firmly. Other ropes they have tied to the edges of the raft. Everyone now can hold a rope and so people do not fall when the raft is made to move suddenly by the sea.

I am ashamed for when I need the toilet. All the women help to hide each other when it must be done.

This afternoon two plastic drums were recovered, one containing many packets of dates. The other was empty.

The man with the throat scars is a naval soldier? He has given each of us a number. There are on the raft twenty-one of us. Unlike in the containers, people talk to each other now.

Six of us are from Iraq. Myself, Ali and two men, Khadom and Qais are all from Baghdad. Two women — Sura and Zainab — are from Basra whose husbands were trapped in the container that sank. There is a Kurdish woman, Sheren, and her boy of ten years, Jîno. His father also did not survive the fall when the wave washed us from the ship. Qais asked why I fled from Iraq alone. I dared not tell the truth — even here, I fear it could cost me my life.

The two men who first built the raft are Mehdi and Parviz. They are brothers from Iran. Seven are from maybe China, five men who stay together and an older couple. The man has a beard and wears a white headcap. His wife has a headscarf of bright red. They do not speak the same language as the five men. They have been passing little sweets to Jîno.

There are three men from Pakistan and last person is the crewman. He asked that everyone place their food and drink in the empty drum. Eventually we all agreed. The crewman then called each number out and every person received three biscuits, eight dates and a small amount to drink.

Sometimes today, while working to save ourselves, I felt hope. A ship must surely pass close by soon. But now I see only waves, endless in every direction. It is getting dark and the wind is growing stronger again. Our lives are no more than candles, flickering.

Jon sat forward, looking suspiciously at Rick's phone. 'So they're on a raft and someone's written a note, put it in a plastic duck and chucked it into the sea?'

'Exactly. Message-in-a-bottle style. And remember, the letter said it was number three. So there are two earlier ones somewhere.'

'And maybe more to follow,' Jon murmured. 'You reckon it's for real?'

Rick shrugged. 'Who knows? They're just scribbled on scraps of paper.'

'How many of these ducks are being washed up?'

'Hundreds, apparently.'

'The things could have been floating for days – weeks – before making the coast.'

'Yeah – the report says the ducks look like they've been in the water for some time. That's what the editorial is asking. If the note is real, what's happened to the poor bastards on the raft?'

Jon sat back. 'Someone's having a laugh.' He crossed his arms and directed his eyes towards the doors opposite them. 'Been round to Alice's recently?'

From the corner of his eye, he saw Rick look at him.

'Don't start this again, mate. Please.'

'What do you mean?' Jon kept his gaze straight ahead. 'I'm only asking. Holly's staying over tonight, I'm just wondering how things are at home for her.'

'They're fine. I dropped by the other day. Everything seems fine.'

Jon tried to keep the sourness from his voice, but he heard it creeping in. 'Nice to hear.'

Rick and Alice had become good friends over the years. In some ways, Jon reflected, Rick was closer to Alice than he'd ever been. Since Jon had been forced to move out of the family home last year, his work partner was now his main source of news about his wife and daughter. A reluctant go-between, who'd finally rejected that role when the messages he was asked to relay became more and more acrimonious.

'What were they up to when you called round?'

'You know, usual stuff. Getting Holly ready for bed. Trying to drag her off the Nintendo.'

'She's got a Nintendo?' Jon knew his voice held an accusatory note. Alice and he had agreed to try and keep their daughter away from computer games until she was at least eight. 'Braithwaite bought it for her, did he?'

Rick looked away. 'Not my business.'

Jon felt his teeth pressing together. It would have been him. The prick. 'Trying to buy her, that's what he's doing.'

Rick sighed. 'Jon, the bloke is trying to do the right thing. He's not steaming in there looking to take over. He knows it's a sensitive area.'

Jon turned to his partner. 'What? Trying to replace me as Holly's father? Yeah, I suppose that is a sensitive area. It's what the arsehole's trying to do, bit by bit. The worm.'

'I'm not getting into this, Jon. Not if you're just going to wind yourself up.'

'I'm not wound up.' He realised that, beneath his folded arms, his hands were bunched into fists. He flexed his fingers. 'I don't like the bloke. There's something wrong about him.'

'He's a psychiatrist,' Rick murmured.

'So what?' Jon hissed. 'That automatically gives him saint status? Rubbish – and you know it.'

'I'm not getting into this. The bloke's genuine.'

Yeah? Jon thought, looking down at his feet as his mind went back to the Sunday night from a few weeks before. He'd nipped out from Carmel's to pick up a curry from her favourite place near Ardwick Green. The short drive took him down to Piccadilly station and then along Fairfield Street, a dimly lit road that was well known as a spot where prostitutes plied their trade.

Waiting for the lights to change at the junction behind the train station, he was surprised to see Braithwaite, in his distinctive maroon-coloured Saab convertible, cut across the junction from the opposite side. He's come from the direction of Heaton, Jon had thought. Where Alice lives. What's he doing in town at this time of night?

The lights went green and Jon took the turn on to Fairfield Street, quickly spotting Braithwaite's vehicle as its brake lights glowed red. It slid into a narrow side road. Jon turned in as well, passing the Saab as it began to execute a three-point turn. He's gone wrong, Jon had concluded. He pulled over, watching in his rear-view mirror as the man who was now regularly sleeping in the same house as his wife and daughter didn't rejoin the main road and retrace his route back to the brightly lit junction behind the city's main station.

Instead, Braithwaite parked at the top of the road and turned the Saab's engine and lights off. Jon felt his eyes narrow, gaze fixed on the barely visible shape of Braithwaite's head as he sat in his darkened vehicle, staring at the girls out on the main road.

Blondes, brunettes, black-haired girls. Most somewhere in their twenties, some far younger. Gathered in twos and threes, they'd break off from their conversations with every change of the lights and turn their gaze to the procession of passing cars, hands on hips, breasts pushed out.

Drivers would come to a stop, prices would be agreed, girls would climb into passenger seats. After almost twenty minutes, Braithwaite's car came to life. He pulled out, indicated right and headed slowly back towards the station.

A second incident had taken place less than a fortnight later. It was after ten on a Tuesday night when Jon had finally closed his computer down and called it a day. Mind dulled by fatigue, he'd driven on autopilot, only realising he'd returned to where he used to live once he was halfway along his old road. Bollocks, he'd cursed, calculating that it would now be best to drive past Alice's house and take the A34 back into the centre of town to where Carmel's apartment was located.

As he'd neared his old home, Braithwaite's Saab had set off in front of him. Slowing, Jon glanced at his dashboard clock. Ten twenty. The decision had obviously been made that he wasn't staying over tonight. Eyes sweeping across the red-bricked terrace he'd lived in for so many years, Jon saw Alice's bedroom light go off.

But when their cars reached the A34, Braithwaite didn't indicate left to join the southbound lane which would lead him away from the city's outskirts towards his big house in Hale. Instead, he indicated right, joining the northbound traffic heading for the city centre.

Pulse beating slightly faster, Jon trailed him straight back to Fairfield Street. Once again, Braithwaite parked in the side road, turned his lights and engine off and watched the girls going about their business. From his vantage point further down the dark street, Jon waited. Please, he'd thought. Please make a move on one. What a result nicking you would be. But after half an hour the man restarted his engine and drove away alone.

From outside the courts came the muted screech of a tram as it passed on its way to Piccadilly station. Through the vertical rows of windows in the double doors before them, he saw several figures quickly approaching. Were they talking or was that sobbing he could hear? He narrowed his eyes, recognising Sarah, the eighteen-year-old rape victim who was meant to be in court testifying.

The doors burst open and she stumbled out, eyes wild and face blotched with red. The woman from witness services managed to get an arm round her, directing her off down the corridor. Jon began to stand, eyes on the pair of them. The woman from witness services held a hand out, palm down, waving it back and forth. Oh no, Jon thought. It's game over: our victim's gone bandit on us.

The barrister and CPS lawyer emerged through the doors and Jon waited for the victim to disappear into the witness suite before speaking. 'What happened in there?'

The CPS lawyer, a lady in her mid-twenties, looked to the barrister without speaking. He brushed a hand down his black gown and shrugged. 'She went to pieces on the stand. I don't think we should ever have let her testify in open court.'

Jon cursed. It was always a fine call whether to use the special measures granted in the 2003 Sexual Offences Act to allow your victim to testify from behind a screen or via video link. But nothing could beat the impact on a judge like Terence Atkins of seeing a young, fragile woman coming face to face with the person accused of her rape.

'She started coming apart straight away,' the barrister continued, sounding more like a Shakespearean actor. 'You do realise she alluded to a previous psychiatric episode? Not letting something like this push her into another breakdown, or words to that effect?'

'You what?' Jon looked at the CPS lawyer. 'She never said anything about mental-health problems when we asked her.'

The CPS lawyer sighed. 'The defence were on it in a flash. Atkins has adjourned for psychiatric reports.'

Jon sat down. That's tomorrow's workload right there, he thought, knowing the file preparation he'd been doing over the last few months now hung in the balance: the victim's statements, the evidence collected by the Nightingale Officer – the specially trained policewoman who'd first seen Sarah – the forensic evidence gleaned from Sarah's person, the head of her hairbrush covered in the accused's fingerprints, the witness statements, the CCTV footage showing the accused following the victim off the night bus, the soiled clothing recovered from his flat. Jon thought about the hours he'd spent interviewing the bloke. The tape transcripts he'd prepared to pinpoint the man's repeated shifts in story.

When they'd presented the case to the CPS's RAFA unit, it had all seemed so tight. Now an earlier, unrelated, episode of mental instability in the victim's life could bring the entire thing crashing down.

The barrister had wandered solemnly away, leaving them in shocked silence. After a couple of seconds, the young CPS lawyer looked around then leaned down. 'He spooked her,' she whispered.

Jon looked up. 'How?'

'I saw it – just. Before she even got in the witness box. He licked his lips at her. Really quick, but he did it.'

Jon wanted to slam a hand down on the empty seat next to him. A key piece of forensic evidence had been a sample of saliva from the accused which had been swabbed from Sarah's inner ear. He had, according to her statement, repeatedly licked it during the assault. True, no semen had been recovered from the scene. But it wasn't unusual for sexual offenders to be incapable of ejaculating while actually with their victim.

So that was it, then. The accused back on remand and an

eight-week delay, minimum. During which time the defence would, no doubt, work up a new angle calling into question the reliability of the victim's entire account. Suddenly the fact Sarah had been in town drinking before the attack took place would become an issue. He could see this one going completely pear-shaped. 'Tell Sarah to hang in there,' he announced, glancing towards the witness suite. 'We'll work round this, OK?'

The CPS lawyer nodded, looking unconvinced as she hurried away.

Jon and Rick set off down the stairs leading to the entrance hall. 'Well,' said Jon, trying to push the prospect of defeat from his mind. 'On the plus side, we get out of this place early.'

'True,' Rick replied, transferring the folder with all their notes to under his other arm.

As they cleared the bottom steps, Jon paused, mind weighing up the chances of a successful prosecution. Face it, he thought, it's not looking good. The bastard had licked his lips. There was no way, Jon decided, I'm letting that one go. He made his way over to the head of security, a squat bulldog of a man he used to play rugby with at Cheadle Ironsides.

'Finished for the day?' the man asked, white short-sleeved shirt gleaming, faded naval tattoos visible on both forearms.

Jon gave a resigned look. 'Victim couldn't testify. Just a young lass. The sight of the bloke was too much.'

'Nasty one, was it?'

Jon nodded, lowering his voice to a whisper. 'Very. He couldn't actually get it up – so he used the handle of her hairbrush on her. Ripped her insides to shreds.'

The man's lips had curled in disgust. 'Sick bastard. Which court was that in?'

Jon stepped towards the exit. 'Seven,' he answered, knowing that information would now trickle down to the guards in the cells below the courts. When carried back to Strangeways, it would ensure the accused suffered a very unpleasant next couple of months.

As they stepped out onto the stone steps leading down to Minshull Street, Jon could sense Rick looking at him.

'That was naughty,' his partner said under his breath.

Jon shrugged, thinking about the courts behind him. The sheer flood of people passing through. Trials for burglary, robbery, assault, affray, rape and threats to kill. His gaze swept across the tram-tracks to the derelict Department of Employment building opposite. The boarded-up windows on the ground floor were plastered with fly-posters, the window frames on the floors above dark and empty. At the top of the building a bedraggled flag lay collapsed at the base of its pole, red cross barely visible on its grime-covered folds.

Somewhere, Jon reflected, there's an irony in that.

Five

As he walked up to the front door of the house he used to live in, Jon scanned the modest garden for anything different. The patch of grass had been mown and a potted shrub placed to the side of the front door. He leaned down to examine the tag still attached to the lowermost branch. Camellia. He looked at the shiny green leaves. A gift from Braithwaite, no doubt.

He knocked at the door then stepped back onto the path, wondering who would open up. The lock clicked and the door swung in to reveal Amanda, Alice's mum.

Great, Jon thought. The viper's come to visit. 'Hi, Amanda, how are you?'

Looking down at him, her thin lips stayed together as she gave a tight smile. 'Fine.'

He waited for her to ask after his health, but no question came. Glancing over her shoulder, she called into the house. 'Holly, time for you to go!'

Jon looked at her carefully arranged hair, dyed light brown and shot through with streaks of ash. 'Is Alice here?'

She turned back and raised her plucked eyebrows. 'Phillip's taken her away for the night. A gastro pub, somewhere out in the Yorkshire Dales.' Pleasure suffused her voice. 'It's got a Michelin star, Phillip says.'

Does he? Well, thought Jon, let's hope he doesn't choke on his foie gras. Holly appeared behind her grandmother's knees, peeping cautiously round them. Alice had decided to have their daughter's hair cut in a bob and the style emphasised her delicate, elfin features. Seeing her lack of confidence made something shift deep inside him. She never used to be like this, he thought sadly. 'Hello, princess!' he beamed, crouching down with his arms held out.

She smiled, stepping forward so he could sweep her up. Turning away from Amanda's disapproving gaze, he planted a huge kiss on Holly's cheek. Then he leaned back, drinking in the sight of her. 'How are you?'

She smiled uncertainly. 'OK.'

OK, he thought, aware of a slight tension in her torso. 'Ready for some fun?'

'Yes,' she giggled.

'Good.' He swivelled back to face the house aware that, having spent the day trying to prevent the rape case from going down in flames, he hadn't found the time to buy toys or anything else to keep Holly entertained. 'Now, have you got a bag?'

Amanda reached to the side and slid a small pink suitcase onto the top step. A glossy image of a Disney princess was emblazoned across its front. 'She's got a change of clothes in there. Plus an absorbent bed sheet, in case of accidents. And there's some Junior Calpol in her washbag.'

'Great, thanks,' Jon replied, reaching for the plastic handle, eager to be away as fast as possible.

'Oh!' Amanda exclaimed. 'Don't forget your Nintendo, Holly. I'll get it.'

'No,' Jon cut in. 'We've got plenty of stuff.'

'Have you?' Amanda's eyes were on Holly. 'Are you sure you don't want it?'

Jon stepped away, keeping his voice bright. 'We'll cope somehow, don't worry!'

'Well,' Amanda said, 'I'm looking after the house while Alice and Phillip are away. Just call when you set off to bring her back. Lunchtime tomorrow, yes?'

'That's right.' He tried to walk away.

'Kiss for Na-na, my darling!'

Bollocks, Jon thought, reluctantly moving back to the front door and holding Holly up so Amanda could lean down. As she placed a kiss on Holly's cheek, the scent of her perfume clogged his nostrils.

She kept a hand cupped on Holly's cheek. 'Fish fingers for lunch, tomorrow! With my special mash!'

Just shut it, Jon wanted to say as he set off down the path, resenting how the woman was jumping ahead, laying out future treats to undermine the time he had with his daughter.

They got to his car and he opened its rear door, dumping the suitcase on the floor before strapping Holly into her car seat.

'Bed by seven o'clock, Holly!' Amanda called out. 'You know Mummy's rules.'

But you don't know mine, Jon thought, shutting the door and scooting round the vehicle to jump in the driver's seat. He slammed the door with a sigh of relief. 'Right, sweetie. You want to watch a film tonight?' he asked as the engine came to life.

'Which one?'

'I don't know.' He glanced at the house and saw Amanda still on the top step. 'How about *Snow White*? With the evil hook-nosed old crone?'

'*Jungle Book*!'

The injection of enthusiasm in her voice caused him to grin. 'Oh, I'm the king of the swingers,' he began to croon. 'A jungle do-bee-dee ...'

'Daddy! You can't sing!'

'Can't sing? Can't sing? Oh yes I can.' He started up again. 'I've reached the top and had—'

'You can't!'

They found a space outside Carmel's flat twenty minutes later and Jon led Holly up to the entrance. The sound of arguing could be heard coming from round the corner of the NCP car park opposite.

'A fucking taxi, Ron!'

'Bus,' came the slurred reply.

'Fuck's sake!'

Jon glanced over as the couple came into view. In their fifties, her stick-thin, him way too fat, the pair of them staggering from booze. The shopping bags hanging from the woman's hands were leaking water. Jon knew the score. Into town to find some cheap frozen food in the Arndale, then – on the spur of the moment

– a cheeky one in a nearby pub. Probably the King on Oldham Street with its deals on spirits and mixers. A few hours later and they're both off their faces, the food they came into town for in the first place now defrosted in its packets.

'Taxi!' she snarled at him.

'Got no money for one,' he burbled in reply.

Fuckwits, Jon thought, keying the code for the door then ushering Holly through as soon as it started to roll back.

'The shopping.' The woman had realised the bags were leaving a trail of droplets behind them. 'It's gone to shit.'

Jon glanced down, hoping Holly hadn't caught the exchange. 'So,' he said, 'see those little doors?' He pointed to the panel of lockers lining one side of the lobby. 'That's where the letters for the people who live here get delivered. Lots of people live here, not just Carmel.'

He stepped across and pointed to one on the middle row. 'Number fourteen, that's Carmel's post box. She's so excited you're coming to stay.'

Holly's eyes moved uneasily around the lobby. Garish flyers for nearby takeaway places had been blown behind the pot of a large palm tree in the corner.

'Let's get the lift, shall we?' Jon suggested, jabbing a thumb at a silver door.

She nodded and he pointed out the button so she could press it. 'How cool is this?' he announced. 'Catching a lift up to your front door.'

A few seconds later the lift opened, and to Jon's relief, the interior was clean. 'OK, floor two, that one there.'

Holly pressed the button and the door closed.

'I wonder what we'll be having for tea,' Jon mused, anxious to keep any silence from enveloping them. 'Maybe pasta?'

'Yuk.'

'Baked potato?'

'Yuk.'

'Worms, with dead flies on top?'

'No!' she squealed with delight.

The doors opened and Jon led his daughter across to Carmel's door. Up until now, Holly had only met his girlfriend in neutral places – cinemas, parks or restaurants. He knocked on the door and when Carmel opened it moments later, the smell of pizza wafted over them.

'Hello, you two!' she exclaimed a touch too cheerfully, beckoning them both inside before bending down to address Holly. 'I'm so glad you've come to stay.'

Jon looked down at Holly as she pressed herself against the side of his leg. He placed a hand on the top of her head, trying to wordlessly reassure her everything was OK. 'Holly, this is Carmel's flat. Nice, isn't it?'

Holly said nothing, a hand now hooked round the back of his leg.

Carmel stood up, eyes bouncing uncertainly off Jon's as she did so. 'Who would like some crisps? Tea's not quite ready yet.'

'Sounds good. Come on, Holly.' He tried to move her towards the sofa, but her feet seemed stuck to the wooden floor. He realised his daughter was saying something in a voice so quiet, he had to crouch down. 'What was that, sweetie?'

Carmel was also looking at Holly, eyebrows raised encouragingly.

Holly's eyes, so huge in her little round face, moved from Carmel to Jon. 'Mummy says we don't eat snacks before tea.'

Shit, thought Jon. She's right. We never eat snacks straight before a meal. He took a breath in, preparing a line about how it would be OK, just this once. The rules and routines which provided stability in his daughter's life were beginning to slip. No wonder the poor little thing had started wetting her bed.

'You're right, Holly,' Carmel intervened. 'That's a bad habit. How about we do something else?'

Jon glanced up to see Carmel looking round her apartment. Not a toy or activity in sight. Damn it, he thought, I should have brought that Nintendo.

'Some drawing, maybe? I've got some paper here.' Carmel motioned towards her workstation and the printer at its side.

Jon pictured all his daughter's colouring books, pens and pencils in her bedroom at home. I should have just asked Amanda,

42

he cursed. 'I know,' he said. 'Can you help me unpack a box? You could line my CDs up on the shelf.'

Holly gave a little nod, so he led her over to the shelf units on the far side of the room. He knelt down in front of the two boxes and started trying to scrape away the brown tape which sealed one of them shut. 'Daddy's got no nails. Can you do it?'

Holly sat down and started picking at the corner of tape. Behind her, Carmel raised a thumb and stepped into the galley kitchen.

Jon lifted the flaps of the other box he'd previously opened, peered at the stack of CDs inside, then lifted half a dozen out, trying to remember the last time he'd listened to any of them.

Rattlesnakes, Lloyd Cole and the Commotions.

Stanley Road, Paul Weller.

Hatful of Hollow, The Smiths.

T.B. Sheets, Van Morrison.

Central Reservation, Beth Orton.

Rum, Sodomy and the Lash, The Pogues.

His fingers stopped moving as The Pogues album caught his eye. Remembering the letter which the paper claimed had been found inside a rubber duck, Jon looked at the painting of the raft on the cover with renewed interest. He studied the scene of utter desolation as a handful of survivors, surrounded by corpses, waved frantically at the merest hint of a sail far off on the horizon. Jesus, he thought, I've never really seen the painting for what it is, never noticed its horror.

'Daddy?'

He blinked, as the present obliterated the thoughts in his head. 'Yes, honey, that's right. You put them there, so the writing points out towards us. Good girl.' As Holly continued sliding his collection of albums onto the shelf, Jon sat back and opened the CD case, searching for details about the painting itself. There in the small print, he found it.

Cover painting Le Radeau de la Méduse by J.L.A. Géricault.

'Carmel,' he called out. 'You speak a bit of French, don't you? What's Le Radeau?'

She poked her head round the corner. 'The raft, I think. Why?'

The Raft of the Medusa, he thought. 'Just something to do with an old album cover here.'

'One of your weird bands from way back when?' She grinned.

'Something like that,' he smiled, eyes drawn to the image once again. The horizon was set so high in the sky, the sombre spectacle seemed to draw him in. To stand before the actual painting, he imagined, would put you right there on the sodden timbers.

An ugly buzzing noise started from his jacket and Jon looked up, suddenly aware that he was sitting on the floor of someone else's home, his daughter obediently lining up his music collection on an empty shelf. A sense of profound regret pulled at him as he reached for his mobile.

'Jon here.'

'DI Spicer, Sergeant Innes.'

Innes, Jon thought. A supervisor from the station's radio control room. His eyes closed with the knowledge of what was coming next.

'Got something for you, Jon.'

He sighed, turning away from Holly. 'Don't tell me no one on the night shift is available.'

'You've hit the nail on the head. Friday night and they're a team short, apparently. You're top of the list for cover.'

'Graham, I'm not coming out unless it's a body. Anything else, leave it with the uniforms attending and I'll get on it tomorrow morning.'

'Sorry, mate. It's a body. Head only just hanging on, but a body nonetheless.'

Shit, Jon cursed. 'What do you mean, only just hanging on?'

'Someone's cut through the guy's throat, I gather.'

Jon rubbed the palm of one hand briskly across the top of his head, noticing Holly staring at him uncertainly. Guiltily, he looked away. 'Whereabouts?'

'Grimsville, I'm afraid.'

Grimsville, Jon thought. That could be several of Manchester's more deprived and decaying boroughs. 'Anything to narrow that down?'

'Old block of flats in Lostock.'

'Stretford way?'

'Yup. Drop off the M60 just before the Trafford Centre, then head back towards the city along Barton Dock Road.'

'I know it,' Jon replied, picturing the wasteland of warehouses, depots and trading units stretching away on one side of the road, the maze of drab streets and run-down housing stock on the other. 'What are these flats called?'

'Sunlight Tower. I presume the architect was having a little joke.'

'Victim?'

'Foreign national. The block is one of those properties the Home Office have leased. You know, the ones they use for housing asylum seekers.'

Valeri waited outside the entrance to the Royal Liverpool University Hospital's Accident and Emergency. Earlier, as a man with a blood-soaked bandage pressed to one eye had been guided through to the waiting room by a mate, he had glimpsed her behind the front desk before the outer doors had slid shut.

He'd made a note of her name the evening she had smuggled sweets and biscuits to them as they'd waited to be wheeled through to a ward for the night. Yulia. A kind girl. He hoped what he was going to ask of her wouldn't mean that she would have to die.

He gave a small shake of his head. If only the duck carrying that note had been washed up after the *Lesya* had off-loaded the cargo at Baltimore. None of this would have been necessary, then. Where, he wondered, would the ship be now? Probably just a few hundred miles off the American coast, drawing a little closer with every hour that passed.

A while later, she emerged from the side doors used by ambulance crews to wheel their gurneys in and out. He made sure his turtleneck top was properly covering the skin of his throat, then, keeping close to the wall, slowly approached as she said goodbye to a couple of colleagues before setting off across a poorly lit parking area. Once he was sure she was alone, he jogged after her, dismayed at how quickly physical exertion drained the energy from his limbs.

'Yulia!' he called out breathlessly, while still a few metres behind her.

She looked back, the expression on her face showing partial recognition.

Careful to keep his distance, he smiled then said to her in Russian, 'I was in the hospital last week. You brought me chocolate and other things to—'

'Vladimir!' Her face relaxed as she remembered him. 'How are you? Are you OK?'

'Yes, fine. Thank you.' He placed a hand on his stomach. 'Getting better. Eating. Always eating. My strength is returning now.'

She was frowning slightly. 'That's good.'

They looked at each other and he waited, deliberately letting her ask the next question.

'So,' she said, glancing towards the bus stop on the main road nearby. 'What about the other three?'

He let his eyes become sad. 'They separated us. The immigration people gave us accommodation in different places. I haven't seen them since.'

'Oh, that's a pity.' Her eyes cut to the main road again.

'You're catching a bus? Can we talk while you wait?'

'OK.'

They walked in silence between two rows of parked cars. A gap in the side railings led to the road. He noticed, with some relief, that no one else was at the bus stop. 'I worry for them,' he announced. 'We haven't been made to feel welcome here. It's not easy.'

She nodded. 'Give it time. Have they allowed you to stay?'

'My claim is being processed. I have another interview in a few days. I think they will have decided by then. But maybe they don't need someone like me in this country. Someone who only knows how to help run a trade union.' He paused, making a show of building up to something. 'Did you hear what happened to us?'

Gaze shifting to beyond his shoulder, her eyes made small movements as they scanned the approaching traffic. 'The ship which carried you from Russia put you down too far from the coast.' Her eyes connected with his. 'It was several days before another boat found you.'

'Yes,' he replied, bowing his head. In the periphery of his vision, he saw one of her feet move forward. A hand pressed lightly on his shoulder.

'I think you will be successful. Your ordeal is obvious.'

He kept his eyes lowered as he spoke again. 'I didn't tell the immigration officers something. There were others on the ship that took us from St Petersburg. Including a woman. I'm afraid for her safety.'

'A woman? From Russia?'

He raised his head. 'No. She was fleeing from the trouble in Iraq. I don't know where she had paid to go. But if the ship's crew left us out at sea, maybe they did the same to the others.'

'How many were there?'

'Seven or eight. The woman spoke English. She was a good person, Yulia. A doctor, I think. I got to know her a little.' He pursed his lips, trying to give the impression of anguish. 'Her name was Amira. Amira Jasim.'

Yulia's frown had returned. 'Amira Jasim? And she is a doctor?'

'I believe so. Could you check the hospital computer? I only want to know that she is safe.'

Yulia nodded. 'Yes. That's simple enough if she has been admitted here.'

'It's likely. There are only two screening units for people seeking asylum. Here and somewhere called East Croydon, near London. But I don't think our ship was going near there.'

Her eyes widened slightly and her hand shot out to the side. 'My bus. How can I contact you if I find her name?'

'Here.' The piece of paper he handed her had his mobile number and Amira's name already written on it. 'Thank you, Yulia.'

'That's fine,' she replied, reaching into her purse and removing a bus pass. 'I will call you if I find anything.'

He nodded, moving away before the vehicle pulled up and anyone inside it saw him talking to her.

Six

When the glowing domes of the Trafford Centre came into view, Jon switched off the flickering blue light mounted behind the car's radiator grille. He took the slip road leading from the M60 and drove down to the roundabout under the motorway flyover.

Hugging the car to the roundabout's tight curve, Jon half-turned towards Rick. 'You OK with that, then? I really can't stay long.' He thought about having to leave Holly, knowing his daughter already had a thing about Daddy walking out on her. As he'd retreated towards the door, her chin had developed its dimple: a sure sign she was fighting back tears. They'd found the DVD of *The Jungle Book* at the bottom of the second box, tucked in between copies of *Raging Bull* and *Heat*. But the film, pizza and the promise of a treat when he got back couldn't alter the fact he was leaving her alone in what amounted to a near-stranger's flat.

'Of course, mate,' Rick replied. 'I'll get a lift back to town in a patrol car.'

'Cheers,' Jon sighed, eyes catching for a moment on the panel of store names running down the illuminated sign on the other side of the road.

Selfridges. Next. River Island. Game. Monsoon. The Pier.

What a place to dump penniless asylum seekers, he thought. Right next to one of the biggest shrines to shopping in Europe. He turned onto Barton Dock Road, immediately spotting several high-rise buildings to his right. Concrete clad, with paint peeling off wooden balconies, many of which were festooned with lines of washing. Semaphore to passing traffic, he thought: we can't afford a tumble dryer in this flat.

He pulled up behind two patrol cars and a white van. Seeing the Greater Manchester Police crest on its side, he announced, 'Scene of Crime Unit's here already.'

Rick nodded. 'Least we won't be hanging around waiting for them to show.'

They climbed out of their vehicle and approached the officer standing guard at a gap in the crime-scene tape. At the corner of the building another uniformed officer faced a huddle of men, all with cigarettes in their hands. Jon wondered how, exactly, the men's clothing immediately marked them out as from somewhere else. Non-branded trainers, tracksuit bottoms, tight stone-washed jeans, plain dark trousers, baggy shirts or tops with American words emblazoned across the chest or down an arm. Teamster. Varsity. New York. Ed's Gym. Jon imagined the grim, Third World sweatshops where the garments had been manufactured, doubting the poor bastards who'd actually done the stitching would ever come close to the United State's coast.

The men were answering the officer's questions quietly, risking the odd glance, but never making eye contact for more than a moment. The officer at the rendezvous point saw their warrant cards and raised his clipboard.

'DI Spicer, DS Saville,' Jon announced. 'Who's in charge?'

'Sergeant Moore,' the officer replied, adding their names to the form then speaking into the handset clipped to his tunic. 'Boss? MIT are here.'

A minute later, a trim-looking man of about forty with short brown hair emerged from the lobby of the building. 'Evening, Detectives.'

'Evening,' Jon replied. 'DI Spicer, DS Saville. How long has the Scene of Crime Unit been here?'

'Thirty, maybe forty minutes. They're just getting started. Home Office pathologist has also showed.'

'Really?' Jon replied. 'That's keen. Who is it?'

'Richard Milton.'

That figures, thought Jon with a nod of approval. A couple of years back, Milton had worked with him on a case involving a burned-out church with a body in it. The man knew his stuff, even if his sense of humour was a little twisted. 'So, what have we got?'

The sergeant looked around. 'As you can see, this place isn't among your most sought-after rental properties. Used by the Home Office, mostly, for asylum seekers.' He gestured at the group on the corner. 'We've started asking questions. They're pretty keen to help, with waiting on their asylum applications and all.'

'Anyone see anything?' Rick asked, looking across at the group.

'One spotted a man he hadn't seen before in the lobby. Possibly from India or the Middle East, but the bloke kept his head down.'

Great, thought Jon, sensing the tangled investigation coming their way. 'And the victim, he doesn't appear to be British?'

'No. White Caucasian, though he's come from somewhere hot. Judging from the state of his skin, he wasn't using sun cream.'

Jon raised an eyebrow in question.

'Nasty case of sunburn, remains of a few blisters on his scalp. Must have nodded off on a beach for a good while. Shall I take you up?'

'Why not?' Jon replied, thrusting his hands into his pockets: an automatic reaction to the prospect of approaching the crime scene itself.

The sergeant led them into the lobby, where only a single strip light appeared to be working. The concrete walls had recently been painted, but traces of earlier graffiti still showed through. 'Needless to say,' the sergeant announced, voice echoing slightly, 'the lift's out.'

'Surprise, surprise,' Rick murmured. 'Which floor?'

'Five,' the sergeant stated. 'Guy in the next flat was trying to borrow some matches. Walked into a horror movie instead.'

Reaching for his phone, Jon hung back as the other two men started plodding up the stairs. 'Carmel, it's me. How's it going?'

'Hang on. Holly, I'm just going into the kitchen, OK?' A rustling sound as Carmel got up. 'She's not saying a thing, Jon.

Quiet as a mouse. Hasn't moved a muscle since you left.'

In the background, he could hear the rise and fall of a song. Kaa, the snake, urging Mowgli to trust in him. 'Listen, I'll be back soon. Another hour, tops.'

'OK, I'll see if she wants hot chocolate or something.'

'No, she doesn't like it. Try her with a bit of cold milk. Thanks, Carmel.'

'What is it, by the way? A murder?'

Jon smiled. 'Can't resist, can you? Give us a break, Carmel. I've not even seen the body yet.'

'Anyone from the *Chronicle* there?'

'No.'

'Other papers?'

'No. And don't you dare put a call in, Carmel. It's dodgy enough that we're seeing each other without photographers from your paper miraculously turning up at murders within minutes of my arrival.'

'OK, OK. My lips are sealed.'

'Cheers.' He cut the connection, then jogged up the flights of steps. Rick and the sergeant were waiting for him halfway along the corridor of the fifth floor.

'Down here,' Moore called out, pointing at a doorway with a ribbon of police tape stretched across it. Someone had opened a window somewhere and cool air washed over Jon's face as he set off towards the two men. As he neared them, an unpleasant aroma began to hit him.

'Which one of you two dropped that?' he asked light-heartedly. 'Rick, doesn't smell like one of yours.'

Moore nodded at the open door. 'Victim shat himself.'

'Lovely,' Jon answered, knowing it was a common occurrence in suicides where the chosen method was hanging. The body's muscles giving out in the last throes of death. He peered into the dingy flat. A couple of arc lamps had been set up at either end of a small sofa, the back of which was facing him. Jon could see the top of a man's shaved head tilted back against the pad-ded material. A scene-of-crime officer, head to toe in a white oversuit, was filming the body on a hand-held camcorder while

Dr Milton, dressed identically but a good foot taller than the other man, spoke softly into a dictaphone.

Returning his hands to his pockets, Jon leaned through the doorway to better examine the rest of the room. The walls were blank, shelves empty except for a couple of crumpled magazines and newspapers. Aside from the sofa, he could see only an armchair and the corner of what appeared to be a coffee table. No television, or even anything for playing music.

The dictaphone clicked and Richard Milton turned a slightly piercing stare in his direction.

Jon gave a little lift of his chin. 'Dr Milton. DI Spicer, we met—'

'How are you, Jon?'

'Good, thanks,' he replied, shoulders relaxing. 'Yourself?'

'Busy, busy, busy. Been a while since I've had one like this, though.'

'How come?'

'Slip on an oversuit and I'll show you.'

A few minutes later, Jon was lifting the tape across the doorway then ducking under to step onto the first of three metal footplates that led to the sofa. As he straightened up, more of the scene was revealed.

He felt his stomach tighten and the paper-like layer of the oversuit suddenly seemed to be trapping the heat of his body. Pressing the edges of the face mask tight against his cheeks, he took in a deep breath.

Milton was beckoning eagerly from the other side of the sofa, seemingly oblivious to the smell. 'As you've probably gathered, the victim's bowels evacuated during the struggle. Also, whatever was looped round his neck ruptured his carotid, quite possibly his jugular, too.'

Jon looked at the fine plumes of red dots which coated the coffee table and carpet beyond. Speckles of blood had even reached the skirting board and lower parts of the wall on the opposite side of the room.

He stepped onto the second footplate, more of the body coming into view. The man's head was at an unnatural angle, alarm frozen in his bloodshot eyes as they stared at the ceiling. More blood coated his lips and chin, pools of it were gathered in the folds of his T-shirt and jeans. Jon craned his neck. 'What's happened to his left ear?'

Milton looked at it for a second. 'Lost the top half of it, somehow.'

'In the struggle?'

'No. It's an old wound. A good few years, I'd say.'

Jon looked back down at the victim. The section of sofa visible between his outstretched legs had changed from a pale green to a dark, glistening purple.

'There won't be much blood left in the body,' Milton stated, eyes bright with something that looked suspiciously close to excitement. 'Not with his head hanging half off. Come round my side and you can see the extent of the laceration.'

Jon lowered the zip of the oversuit, then tugged at the material to try and circulate some air within it. 'You're all right, cheers. I'll look at the photos later. Any pertinent details I should know, now?'

Milton shrugged. 'You're missing out. I've not seen one like this before – and I've seen some corkers, believe me.'

You have, Jon thought. And your fascination for them never seems to dim. 'Go on, then. What makes this one special?'

'Well.' Milton gazed down at the corpse. 'The killer approached the victim from behind, just in front of where you're standing now. He obviously caught the victim unawares to loop a length of something over his head.'

'Garrotted him?' Rick asked from the doorway behind.

'Correct. You're familiar with the technique?' Milton asked.

'Only from films,' Rick replied. 'Luca Brasi in *The Godfather*, wasn't it?'

'I believe you're right,' Milton mused. 'My guess is our killer had his arms crossed when he got the wire – or whatever it was – round the victim's neck. Then he uncrossed his arms and pulled apart, effectively closing the loop. You see the back of the sofa? Those two dents in the top edge? I imagine they were made by the killer's forearms or wrists.'

Jon looked at the scene-of-crime officer.

'Don't worry,' the man replied. 'I've checked. One hair, already bagged-up.'

'By crouching down,' Milton continued. 'He would have gained extra leverage, pinning the victim in his seat and allowing the exertion of some serious pressure. It would also have had the added advantage of keeping him clear of any arterial spray.' He cocked his head at the ceiling.

Jon glanced up and saw the fine mist clinging to the peeling paint above him. He looked back down. The coffee table had been kicked askew during the struggle, scuffs in the cheap-looking carpet where the victim's legs had thrashed about. 'He put up a bit of a fight.'

'Yes,' Milton replied. 'But it was game over the moment the garrotte went round his neck. Actually, he got one hand up. Managed to hook the tips of his fingers under it.' Milton leaned down and lifted a hand. The middle three fingers had been cut through to the bone. 'He's wearing a wedding ring,' the pathologist continued. 'So there's a wife – and possibly kids – somewhere.'

'How long would it have taken him to die?' Jon asked.

'The noose would have cut off the supply of blood to his brain, so about ten seconds or so to lose consciousness. Death another twenty seconds to half a minute after that.' He waggled the victim's thumb. 'No sign of rigor in the extremities, yet.'

'Hour or two ago, then?' Jon asked.

'With this heat? He could have been here a while longer than that. I'll take his rectal temperature as soon as we get him back to the MRI.'

Jon pictured the mess inside the man's trousers. 'Rather you than me. What was it, then – wire, you reckon?'

'Something thin and very strong. Many man-made fibres would be up to the task. Perhaps silk, I'm not sure. Looking at the wound, whatever it was cut through his sternocleidomastoid.' Milton's head turned and he ran a finger down the ridge of muscle curving from behind his ear to his collar bone. 'This one. It's a tough muscle. Has to be to support the weight of your brain. But, of course, you're really looking to cut off the supply of oxygen – and the garrotte has done that, all right. It's also gone through the thyroid cartilage of his larynx like – well, to use a cliché, like a knife through the proverbial butter.'

Looking to his left, Jon could see into the small side kitchen. 'I don't suppose,' Jon said, 'there's a cheeseboard in there, the wire for it all covered in blood?'

Milton smiled. 'The thought had occurred. Nothing, I'm afraid.'

'Would have been too good to be true,' Jon murmured, now studying the scene before him, trying to picture the sequence of events that had unfolded in the small, spartan room. Did he manage to creep up on him? Was the victim asleep? Or were they discussing something and the killer sidled round the sofa to catch the victim by surprise? 'Rick. No sign of a forced entry, I presume?'

'Nope,' Rick announced from behind him. 'Peephole in the door, too. Unless it was already open, our man has been let in.'

Which suggests a familiarity between killer and victim, Jon thought, tapping a forefinger against his thigh through the lining of his trouser pocket. 'Doctor, someone was sitting in that arm-chair, judging by the impression on the seat.'

Milton looked to his left. 'Yes.'

Jon weighed up the length of the small sofa. The victim was seated in the middle. No, Jon thought, trying to place the killer. You wouldn't squeeze on to it as well. Not if the armchair was free. 'They're both in here, probably talking, then our killer gets behind the victim one way or another. Weird dynamics there, don't you think?'

'How so?' Rick asked.

Jon stepped back on to the first footplate. He held a hand towards the armchair, his middle and forefinger walking in the air. 'Circling round the back of someone. Something like an interview, doing that. One man giving the questions, the other sitting there – looking straight ahead presumably – and providing answers.'

'Or he was making out that he was getting something,' Milton remarked. 'There's a cabinet just to your left.'

Jon looked behind him. The battered-looking item of furniture in the corner had various letters and forms spread out across the top. Snapping on a pair of latex gloves, he slid a footplate towards the cabinet, stepped onto it and peered down at the assorted pieces of paper. The uppermost was titled *IS96*. Jon skimmed over the first few lines, seeing it was about being granted temporary leave to stay in the UK. Next to it was a small, purplish-coloured plastic card. Words across the top read *Application Registration Card* and next to it was a Home Office stamp. He flipped the card over and saw a gold chip embedded in the plastic, identical to the one on his own cashpoint card. Turning it back over, he examined the front more carefully, seeing a passport-style photo of the dead man alongside the words, *Not permitted to work*. Last was a name and country of origin. Russia. Jon spoke over his shoulder. 'Rick, we'll need to get on to the Border Agency. Find out what the score was with Mr Marat Dubinski here.'

Seven

'Don't worry,' Jon said, lowering himself onto one knee so he could look his daughter in the eye. 'Carmel doesn't mind. None of us do, sweetie.'

Holly's eyes were on the washing machine in the corner of the galley kitchen. Inside, her bed things churned slowly round and round.

'Your dad's right, Holly.' Carmel lifted a dripping bowl and placed it on the draining board. 'It all washes out. Now, you'll come back and stay again, won't you?'

Holly nodded hesitantly, her little suitcase standing on the floor next to a plastic bag containing her still-damp pyjamas. Jon thought about the previous evening. By the time he'd got back to Carmel's, it was almost half past nine. *The Jungle Book* had finished a while before and he found the two of them sitting in silence, half a cold, burned pizza on the table in the corner, an abysmal game show limping towards its concluding round, canned laughter filling the flat.

From the way Holly had failed to get up from the sofa, he could tell she was distressed. More and more she dealt with her emotions by simply withdrawing into a shell. Carmel had shot him a concerned glance and nothing he said could reassure Holly that Daddy wasn't about to disappear back out the door.

Halfway through the night, he'd heard her stifled sobs, and on walking through from Carmel's bedroom, had discovered his daughter had wet the bed they'd made up for her on the sofa. He'd stripped everything off, realising he'd forgotten to lay the absorbent pad down that Amanda had packed. A damp patch was showing on the suede-like surface of the sofa itself.

Once Holly was enveloped in one of Carmel's spare nighties, he'd laid some towels down and tried to tuck her back up. But she'd clung to his neck and the high-pitched whining sound coming from her throat made him want to cry. He'd spent the rest of the night cuddled up with her on the sofa, cold air where the duvet didn't cover his back keeping him awake.

Jon glanced at his watch. He didn't have to drop her off until lunch; that gave them two more hours together. 'Shall we go to the park?'

Holly gave a nod and he straightened up, one hand lifting the suitcase and bag, the other searching out his daughter's fingers. 'What do you say to Carmel?'

Holly breathed the word, lips hardly moving.

'That's all right,' Carmel smiled, drying her hands on a tea towel. 'It was lovely having you to stay. See you soon.'

Jon led her out into the corridor, closing the door to Carmel's flat behind him.

The boiling weather had lasted for a fortnight now and people had become accustomed to spending their weekends outside. He looked at the park's cafe: packed full. Scrapping his idea for sitting down with a cup of strong coffee, Jon wandered with Holly round the perimeter of a small lake, his daughter shunning all his attempts at small talk. This, Jon thought, is what worries me most. Her silences.

People stood at the water's edge, adults tearing up slices of bread and handing the pieces to small children. The chunks were then hurled at a flotilla of bored-looking ducks, geese and swans. Jon peered into the murky shallows and saw bloated crusts and crumpled cans coating the bottom. An elderly woman held out a plastic bag and dumped the best part of a loaf into the water, the child in the pushchair at her side idly kicking a foot as the mound of slices slipped slowly below the surface.

As they walked across the yellowing grass to a smaller expanse of water, Jon looked at the clusters of motionless sunbathers around them. They were laid on blankets like fatalities, arms and legs akimbo as the sun slowly roasted their flesh.

The lake had a few men and children standing at one end. As they got closer, the hum of little motors grew in strength and he could see that many of the people were holding control consoles in their hands.

Out on the water, an assortment of boats went through their manoeuvres, tiny wakes trailing behind them. The motor of a red speedboat suddenly whined and faint curls of blue were left clinging to the surface as the vessel surged forward.

Jon's mind drifted back to the crime scene from the evening before. The victim had probably made enemies in his home country. Shagged the wrong woman, stiffed the wrong business associate. That sort of thing went on in Russia all the time, didn't it? Jon realised he was making assumptions, unfair ones at that. The man could have supported the wrong political party or written an article containing embarrassing information. The murder could be about something a whole lot more serious than some petty grievance or wounded honour.

Voices to his side.

'It's not working, Grandad, it's not.' A boy of about ten was looking round at the elderly man on the bench just behind him.

'Bring it here, sonny.'

The boy kicked impatiently at the ground then thrust the controls at the old man.

'Well, it's not the batteries. We've got power, here.' He pointed to the glowing red diode in the handset then looked across the boating lake. Out in the middle a miniature yacht drifted aimlessly on the grey water.

'What will we do?' the boy asked.

'Well,' the grandfather replied slowly. 'Wait for some wind?'

The boy looked about, forehead wrinkling. 'There isn't any.'

'You're right, there. How else could we get her back?'

The boy stared at the boat, motionless and forlorn on the flat water. Around it, other vessels buzzed and whirred. 'You could wade out,' he eventually announced, face lighting up.

'Against the rules. Park warden would have our guts for garters.'

The boy's face fell. Jon had started looking round for an extremely long branch when he heard Holly's voice.

'Another boat could push you.'

The old man turned to her and Jon looked down, unsure if it was really his daughter who had spoken.

She pointed. 'One of those.'

'A tugboat? Good thinking,' the old man grinned, giving Jon a wink and then turning to his grandson. 'Ben, which boat shall we ask for assistance?'

The boy strode to the edge and started surveying his options.

Jon bent down, sensing an opportunity to coax his daughter into conversation. 'Would you like a boat like one of those?'

She shook her head.

'What would you like for your birthday, any ideas?'

She shrugged, her flow of words now dried up.

I know what you'd really like, Jon thought. A return to normality. Me living at home with you and your mum. 'Well, why don't you think while you eat your ice cream.' He waited for the comment to sink in and eventually his daughter raised a questioning look. 'You know. The one waiting for you in McDonald's.'

The faintest of smiles appeared on her face.

The counter in the fast-food restaurant was crowded with customers and Jon looked about, spotting many other men just like him. McDads: indulging sons or daughters with treats before returning them back to the homes of ex-wives or partners.

He examined the garish menu board with its emphasis on child-friendly fare. What did they say about this place? One of the world's biggest toy retailers. To get one, all you had to do was stuff a crappy kid's meal down your throat.

'Yes, sir?' The young woman behind the till beamed.

Jon raised his eyes to the ceiling hanging splashed with a photo of the latest dessert. 'One of your ice-cream things with all the bits on top, please. And a black coffee for me.'

'Any food with that?' she asked without breaking her smile.

'No. You're all right, cheers.'

She rang it in, and after taking his money, turned to get the order ready. Jon glanced round, looking for a spare table. In a sectioned-off area to the side a kid's birthday party was in progress, a dozen children shouting at a staff member as she tried to organise some sort of game.

He turned to the opposite side of the restaurant and spotted a couple of free stools at the wall counter. Their tray was slid across. 'Thanks,' Jon said, picking it up. 'Come on, Holly.' He was halfway across when his eyes were drawn to a familiar figure sitting at a nearby table with two spare chairs. No, Jon groaned to himself. It's Dad. The older man was sipping at a drink, Jake seated beside him.

Jon looked at the little boy from the corner of his eye. Despite the fact he now lived with two loving grandparents, the son of his dead brother still had a sickly air about him. Testament to developing in the womb of a heroin addict who'd pursued her habit through virtually the entire pregnancy. The usual thought flashed up. Where the hell is Zoe now?

Since she'd disappeared the year before, he'd heard from her only once: a postcard from Dublin. She'd said she was heading over to Galway, trying to find an Irish friend called Siobhain who, while living rough in Manchester, had also been forced into working for the pimp called Salvio. Zoe didn't know when she would be back, but the postcard ended with a row of kisses for Jake.

Jon wondered whether to join his dad. But he knew how it would play out – polite small talk for the benefit of the kids, but that curious mix of defiance and guilt never leaving his father's eyes. Emotions, Jon guessed, that would probably be showing on my face, too. Why, he asked himself yet again, can't we both just admit to our parts in the mess the Spicer family has become?

To his relief, they made it to the stools without Jake clocking them. But, as soon as he'd helped Holly up, she spotted her cousin. 'Jake!'

The little boy's head swivelled on his scrawny neck. 'Holly!'

Feigning surprise, Jon looked across, catching his father's eyes flickering over them.

'Hello there, Holly.'

'Grandad!' She squirmed down off her seat and hurried over to Jake's side. 'What's that?'

'I got tiger.' Triumphantly, Jake held up a plastic toy.

Aware he couldn't sit apart, Jon lifted the tray and sidled over. 'Alan.'

His father inclined his head in reply.

'How's Mum?'

'She's fine, yes. Taking part in a concert, so I'm looking after the little man, here.'

'What's she up to?'

'Oh,' he waved a hand. 'A choir concert in the Hidden Gem.'

Jon nodded. The Catholic church tucked unobtrusively down a side alley off King Street. The outside gave little hint of the interior's splendour. He searched his mind for something to say, but unspoken issues had robbed him of the ability to make conversation. 'Jake seems well.'

His dad's gaze settled affectionately on the young lad, who was now demonstrating to Holly how the animal's jaw opened and closed. 'He's grand.'

Jon looked at him, too, thinking of the hovel of a flat he and Rick had rescued the boy from, over a year before. Finding his nephew might have saved the boy from death, but doing so had cost Jon his own marriage.

'We'd better go,' Alan announced. 'Jake? Grandma will be home soon, time to go. Holly, you'll come to play soon, won't you?'

Jon stepped back as Alan got stiffly to his feet.

'Yes,' she replied. Jon saw her begin to pick at the seam of her pink trousers, as more members of her family started melting away before her.

'Come on, princess. Your ice cream is turning gooey.' Jon placed it in front of her then reached over to ruffle Jake's hair. 'See you about, mate.'

Just over an hour later, Jon was back at the front door of his old house, Holly standing silently at his side.

The catch clicked and the door swung open to reveal Alice. She was wearing a fitted black shirt and brown trousers with a subtle check pattern, neither of which Jon remembered being in her wardrobe when he'd lived in the house. Her blonde hair had been cut short, barely to her collar. She looked well, skin smooth and radiant. Even the fine lines he'd noticed beginning to creep around the edges of her eyes during the months before he'd moved out seemed to have disappeared.

'I've missed you!' she exclaimed, dropping to one knee and stretching out both arms.

Holly stepped into her mother's embrace, leaving Jon behind. He watched as the two of them rocked slightly back and forth, cheeks pressed together, eyes closed. He felt his fingers twitch with the urge to wrap his arms round the pair of them, just as he used to do.

A figure appeared in the hallway behind and he looked up to see Phillip. The guy was in a suit, angular frame making its shoulders jut out. Revulsion rose at the back of Jon's throat and he forced it back down with a smile. 'All right? Good hotel?'

'Wonderful, thank you.' A second's silence then he gestured weakly towards the kitchen. 'Just need to ...'

Yeah, Jon thought, watching the other man retreat from sight. Make yourself scarce. You're as welcome in my house as a gas leak.

'So,' Alice said, finally breaking contact to look into Holly's eyes. 'You had a nice time?'

Holly's head dipped for a moment.

'What did you have for tea?' Alice asked brightly.

'Pizza.'

'Pizza?'

'Yes, but Carmel forgot it was cooking.' She gave Jon a look, the type of one she used before announcing a newly found fact from school. 'The food had gone to shit.'

Alice flicked a furious glance at Jon.

Bloody great, he thought, remembering the drunken couple who'd staggered past the entrance to Carmel's apartment block. 'She got that from these two—'

'Holly,' Alice said in an admonishing tone. 'That's not a nice word!'

'Which word?' she said, voice immediately beginning to wobble.

'The one that began with "sh". You're not to say it. Do you understand?'

'Yes,' she whispered.

'So,' Alice's voice had regained some cheer. 'Did you watch a DVD?'

'Yes, with Carmel.'

'Just you two?

'Yes. Daddy ...' She looked at him again, words petering out.

'Daddy what?'

'I got a call,' Jon cut in to put an end to his daughter's predicament. 'Had to pop out for a bit. Fine though, wasn't it, Holly?'

Her eyes slid to the floor. 'Yes.'

Alice stood up, crossing her arms as she did so. Here we go, Jon thought.

'Holly, why don't you see what we brought you? It's in the kitchen. Mum will be inside in just a minute.'

Holly now looked like she was on the verge of tears as Jon crouched down. 'I'll see you soon, princess. OK?'

'Yes. Bye.'

They hugged briefly and she walked tentatively back into the house.

Alice pulled the door shut behind her. 'You left her alone in a stranger's flat? Burnt bloody pizza to eat?'

Jon paused, knowing a placatory response would be best. But anger surged through his arms, causing the palms of his hands to tingle. Fuck it. 'Stranger's? In that case, you're doing the same thing, right now.'

'Don't be so bloody stupid. This is her house – not some dodgy flat in some squalid part of the city centre.'

'If Carmel's a stranger, so is Phillip.' He flipped the final syllable off the end of his tongue like it was a gob of phlegm.

'I am standing on the front step,' she hissed. 'Not off somewhere else. Work call, was it?'

Jon toyed with the idea of lying. He knew it was the job that had forced them apart. A wedge that had worked its way so deep into their marriage, it could never be prised out. But even that might not have caused Alice to finish things. There were the broken promises, too. The way he repeatedly failed to give priority to his home life. His refusal to accept Alice's claim that the deaths he investigated often grew more important to him than the lives of his family. 'I had my mobile on the whole time – which was all of an hour or two.'

'Hour or two.' Alice's voice was scathing. 'Since when do your bloody work calls ever last just an hour or two?'

'Since I make them,' Jon snapped back.

Alice's fingers drummed against her upper arm, eyes moving to the plastic bag by the suitcase. 'What's in there?'

'Her pyjamas. We washed them, but Carmel's tumble dryer isn't working.'

'She wet herself?'

'Yes.'

Alice stayed silent for a couple of seconds. 'Have you thought any more about the divorce?' Slowly, her eyes turned to his.

Jon shook his head. 'I won't let you do it. Not on unreasonable behaviour. I'll fight you every inch. I was never unreasonable.'

'That's open to debate,' she whispered, looking off to the side.

Jon found himself staring at the side of his wife's face; her eye, the corner of her lips, the strand of hair hanging over her ear. He shook his head. How did it ever come to this? 'I was only ever doing my job, Ali. Locking up shit-heads. Finding the person who killed my little brother. Helping his son have a life that won't end like his dad's did. That's all.'

She kept her eyes fixed on something further up the street, but he could see the skin at the side of her neck becoming red. 'You weren't there for me, Jon. When I needed you ...'

No, Jon thought. Please don't put me through this again. She took a sharp intake of breath and he guessed she couldn't summon the will to dredge up those particular memories, either.

She sighed. 'I haven't the energy for this. Not again.'

Jon stepped back. 'I won't let you end our marriage, Ali. You can't place all the blame on me.'

'Fine. So we go down the living apart for five years route.' She brushed something off the cheek he was unable to see. But when she lowered her hand, he saw moisture on her knuckle. 'More uncertainty for Holly, as if she needs any more of that in her life.'

Or, Jon thought, angrily setting off for the garden gate, you could kick that shifty bastard out of my house and give me another chance.

The four people approached a little unsteadily, all speaking at once, their voices loud and cheerful. Jon glanced at the clock on the dashboard. Ten past eleven. Pub closing time.

Earlier, after spending the afternoon on the sofa watching telly with Carmel, Jon had glanced at the clock. 'Bollocks. I have to bob back into the office.'

'What, now?' Carmel had asked.

'I know. Crap, isn't it? But the uniforms will have completed initial witness statements for that murder in Stretford by now. They need to be checked over and anything significant given to the indexers for putting in HOLMES.'

'I thought you said it wasn't urgent.'

'Well, not in the sense of an innocent kid or pregnant housewife being butchered. But initial actions still have to be completed. It's protocol.'

She'd hauled herself upright. 'How long will you be? We're meant to be going for a few drinks later.'

'Not long. I can always catch you up, though. Circle Club, wasn't it?'

The two couples were now almost adjacent with his parked car. He kept still, knowing that only by moving would his presence in the vehicle's dark interior be betrayed.

'Sal, he's always been a tight bastard.'

'No—'

'Exactly! Biggest duty-free shopping centre in the world, isn't it?'

'No—'

'So what did he bring you back?'

'Not even a bottle of perfume.'

Three of them dissolved into incredulous laughter and the last member of the group finally got to speak. 'No, bollocks to that. It's a change of planes for me, that's all. Not a bloody shopping expedition.'

'He always says that,' the girl with her arm around his waist complained, light-heartedly. 'Never a moment to spare. Poor Terry, racing down causeways. Dubai, Singapore, Hong Kong, his feet hardly touch the ground.'

Their voices were getting fainter now as they moved further down the street. He watched their progress in the rear-view mirror then turned his eyes to his old house. In the seconds he'd been watching the group, the light in the bedroom he used to share with Alice had gone off. Now every window of the property was black. Braithwaite's maroon Saab convertible was parked on the other side of the street, and as Jon waited on the slim chance the man was about to emerge through the front door, he gazed at the window of Holly's room.

The curtains were tightly drawn, not even a hint of the night light he knew would be on showing round the material's edges. A couple of minutes later and the front door still hadn't opened. That's it then, thought Jon. He's staying over. No drive back to his house in Hale, no late-night diversion to Fairfield Street.

He studied the psychiatrist's car, reflecting on how he'd recently run the registration through the work computer to see if it had shown up as a nuisance vehicle in any of Manchester's kerb-crawling spots. Nothing. Despite the distinctive model and colour, none of the girls he'd spoken to were familiar with the vehicle either. None had noticed it prowling around or had been approached by a man fitting Jon's description of Braithwaite. He considered his next move. Strangely, the Saab was still registered in Braithwaite's estranged wife's name. From what Jon had been able to glean, the couple had separated a year or so before and she'd moved into a posh little apartment in the middle of Wilmslow.

Why had the marriage hit the rocks? Jon wondered. He could understand why Braithwaite had stayed in the house: the annex was used for the man's private practice. Jon had watched the expensive cars swinging in and out of the wide driveway. Wealthy Cheshire-types trying to cope with the stresses and strains of their high-pressure lives. Poor things.

He scratched a nail against the steering wheel, thinking of Carmel. Probably in The Circle Club by now, chatting to her media-type mates about the punishing hours her boyfriend in the police worked. The knowledge of his deceit made him wince. The same lies, he thought. The same bullshit you fed Alice, using the demands of a non-existent case to let you roam around on your own private missions.

He thought about Carmel's friends. Overly made-up women in expensive clothes. Skinny blokes in designer glasses, hair either a meticulously arranged mess or completely shaved off. He'd have to sit there, fending off their requests to hear about the dark and depraved goings-on in Manchester's underworld. When no juicy stories were forthcoming, they'd bemoan how dangerous it could be in the city. The hassle of avoiding low-lifes looking for trouble. The desperate people, seeking respite from their shit lives through cheap pints and pills. Sad, they'd conclude, pushing aside their bottles of imported beer and heading off to the toilets for a quick sniff of coke.

Deciding he'd better show his face, he looked Braithwaite's car over one last time then started the engine and began to pull out. It was now a total of three times he'd followed the man as he drove into the city centre for his late-night, passive observation routine. The guy, Jon thought, was building up to an approach. He could easily afford the services of any escort, but no. You want something else, don't you? Domination, maybe. A sordid car park liaison with a malnourished addict. As Jon drove away, he glanced up at his old bedroom window, unable to prevent the picture of Braithwaite in bed with his wife. When you finally make your move, my friend, I'll be there, dragging you out of your vehicle and bringing your world crashing to the ground.

Eight

Walking in from the car park, Jon nodded to some of the night-shift boys making their way home. 'Morning, Dave. Busy night?'

'Mad start then a piece of piss once we got past midnight. Just a suicide on the M60 near Denton shortly before five. A witness saw him jump from the flyover. We had all the lanes open again well ahead of rush hour.'

Suicide, Jon thought. Nice and easy. No suspicious circumstances there.

'Oh – and thanks for picking up that job. The asylum seeker one over in Stretford.' The man glanced back to the building. 'Curtis off with a bad back, Heywood on holiday. We were stuffed when that one was rung in. What was the score with it?'

Jon grimaced. 'Someone nearly took his head off with a garrotte.'

'Unusual.'

'Yeah, we're following up on it this morning. Nothing else for us?'

'Phones haven't gone for over two hours.'

'OK. See you.' He carried on through the doors, down the corridor and up the stairs. Just after eight on a Monday morning and the main office was quiet. His eyes swept the unmanned desks and files stacked in trays. Reports and actions waiting their turn. Trace, interview and eliminate this person from the investigation. Check that statement again. Process this evidence. Close this case because a fresh incident will be in any minute. Sometimes, he reflected, this place is just like any other factory.

Rick was already at his desk and in the side office Jon could also see their boss, DCI Mark Buchanon. Jon made his way across. 'All right, Rick? Been in long?'

'Twenty minutes? I thought I'd get the psychiatric assessment requests started for the rape case. Lindsay over in RAFA said she had some time later this morning.'

'Great,' Jon replied, taking his jacket off.

'Well, you know,' Rick replied. 'This asylum seeker one is going to be a runner, I reckon.'

Jon hung his jacket on the back of his seat. He could see a dozen witness reports waiting in his in-tray. He sat down, switched on his computer then started leafing through the sheets as his machine booted up.

Three reports contained reference to an unidentified male seen leaving the scene. As was usually the case with visual recollections, the descriptions varied wildly. This one had him with black hair, going thin. The other two maintained his hair was brown and cut short. Average build in two reports, muscular in the other. At least each statement had him wearing a dark top and trousers, possibly jeans. They all also concurred on his skin being light brown. One thought he was from India, one from the Middle East and one thought he was Caucasian, with a sun tan. None had seen the man actually leaving the victim's flat. Jon sighed. 'We'll need to get these guys in, go over their statements in more detail. What's the wait on forensics?'

'Six to eight days. I asked if there's any way they could squeeze in the hair from the back of the sofa a bit sooner. There was a multitude of prints from the frame of the front door, too. Stands to reason when you consider the transient nature of the residents.'

'True.' Jon sat back. Their contact with the Border Agency had borne little fruit. The Liverpool office was closed at weekends and the person they'd spoken to in the head office down in London had informed them a claim from a Marat Dubinski had gone on the system the Monday before. The case owner processing it was due in the Liverpool office first thing Monday morning. All Jon and Rick could do was send the guy an email, saying his workload had just got one applicant lighter and that they needed to talk. 'What time did we tell the bloke from the Border Agency we'd be showing up?'

'Before ten.'

'Right, we'd better let Buchanon know what we're up to and get over to Piccadilly station. It's an hour to Liverpool on the train.'

Forty minutes later they were seated in a half-empty carriage of a Transpennine Express as it skirted the edge of Manchester's centre, trundling slowly round the back of the Palace Hotel with its exterior of intricately carved reddish stone. Soon after, they crossed the Manchester Ship Canal into Salford, a freight storage area in the industrial park to their left.

Metal containers, mainly in shades of orange, green or blue, were stacked high. The building blocks of a young giant, Jon thought, studying the lettering on their sides. China Shipping. Hapag-Lloyd. Maersk. Yang Ming. Norasia. Cosco.

My own father used to work these docks, he thought. And how many times did I hear him complaining that those standardised boxes were crushing his job – and those of thousands like him around the world? Now freight ships delivered the containers to ports where cranes waited to lift them clear and lower them directly onto the beds of specially adapted railway carriages or the backs of lorries. Apart from officials checking the paperwork, people hardly played a part in the process. The old maritime centres like Liverpool had died on their arses while modern ports like Felixstowe couldn't grow fast enough.

They now were passing a series of industrial units and Jon let his eyes rove over the yards which backed up to the railway line's fence. The waste-ground was home to forklift trucks and the cars belonging to those working inside the buildings. In the corners were squat columns of rubber tyres, skips overflowing with rubbish, untidy stacks of wooden pallets, mounds of dull-grey gravel, stray bollards and unwanted coils of plastic piping.

A rail company repair shed slid slowly past, a spur of track leading to a solitary carriage, paint stripped off to expose pale metal. A phantom, returned to haunt the depot where it had been dismantled.

He thought again about his family. Mary and Alan in their house, looking after Jake. Ellie, still single and now fretting she'd never find someone to have children with. Alice and Holly, Braithwaite lurking at the edge of their lives. Punch, his Boxer dog, also banished from the family home because Alice didn't have the time to look after him with everything else that was going on. The animal was being looked after by Senior, the gruff old rugby coach from Cheadle Ironsides. Christ, Jon thought, how many days since I've rung? As he took his mobile out, he noticed Rick's questioning look. 'Just calling Punch.'

His partner glanced about, a look of dread on his face. 'Here?'

'Yeah, why not?'

Rick sank lower in his seat. 'There are other people in this carriage.'

Jon shrugged, keying in a number. 'Senior, you old git! It's Jon. How's things?'

'All right, mate, all right. Where are you? On a train?'

'Yeah, heading over to Liverpool.'

'Keep an eye on your wallet.'

'Will do.'

'Pre-season training's started.'

Jon sighed. He'd hung up his boots two years ago, but it didn't stop Senior from trying to tempt him back. 'I'm nearly forty, mate. Give it a rest.'

'And I'm nearly sixty. Doesn't stop me from playing.'

Jon pictured the ex-Marine trundling round the pitch, packing down against props a third his age. 'Yeah, but you're not normal.'

'You'll be wanting a word with your dog, then?'

'Please.'

'And you're saying I'm not normal.'

Jon grinned. 'Where is the brainless thing?'

'Lying right here, next to Bess. Took them for a runaround first thing this morning.'

'I bet,' Jon replied, thinking of Senior's dawn runs and imagining his exhausted Boxer stretched out alongside Senior's Labrador. 'Let's have a word then.'

Senior's voice went faint and Jon knew the phone was being held to his dog's ear. 'It's your useless owner, Punch. Don't worry, I'll hang up on him in a minute.'

Jon raised his voice. 'Punch, it's your daddy! Punch, it's me!'

He listened as a suppressed yelp came down the line. Grinning, Jon spoke again. 'Punch, it's Daddy! Where's your daddy? Where's your daddy?'

A succession of barks and excited whines. Laughing, Jon fell back in his seat. 'Good boy, Punch! Good boy!'

More barking and then Senior's amused voice. 'Happy? The bloody thing's going bananas now.' The line went dead.

Chuckling, Jon placed his mobile on the table and looked at Rick. His partner's face was bright red.

'You are so embarrassing. Do you know that?'

Jon peered down the aisle, spotting several people's heads turning back round. 'Any more news on those letters? The ones in the rubber ducks?'

Rick put aside one of the witness statements spread out on the table between them. 'Do you not read the papers?'

'Not if I can help it.'

Rick shook his head. 'Another note was found on Sunday, this time at Lyme Regis on the coast of Dorset and, when I checked the internet this morning, another had been discovered on a beach in south Wales.'

'What did they say?'

Leaning to the side, Rick looked down the aisle. 'I'd have thought it would be in this morning's papers. Here you go.' He leaned across and removed a discarded copy of the *Metro News* from an empty seat.

Jon looked at the paper Rick dropped in his lap. It was open on the business section: a story about opposition in the fledgling Iraqi parliament to plans for awarding no-bid contracts to major Western oil firms. Many Iraqis feared the deals would allow the corporations to gain dominance over their country's vast reserves. 'So what am I looking for?'

'Try page three. It's where they usually run the quirky human-interest stuff.'

Jon leafed to the front of the paper. On the third page a bold headline declared POOR MOLLY GOES FOR A SPIN. The accompanying image showed a cat held in the arms of its owner who was kneeling before a washing machine with a partially open door. He flicked through the rest of the pages until he reached the business section once again. 'Can't see anything.'

'Odd,' murmured Rick. 'I thought every paper would have picked up on it by now.' He raised his mobile phone, pressed a few buttons and then handed it to Jon. 'Here you go.'

'Oh for God's sake,' Jon muttered. 'How does it work?'

Rick grinned. 'Just scroll down using the silver wheel above the buttons. Both new letters are there.'

Hunching over the tiny screen, Jon extended a finger and revolved the wheel through a few clicks. The introductory paragraph shunted up to reveal a mocked-up image of curling parchment prepared by the paper's graphics department. Jon squinted. They'd even printed the lettering in a loose, handwritten style.

LETTER TWO

We were abandoned yesterday at sunset. Two men near me in the water used children's ropes to secure some of the wooden pallets in the sea around us. These we held on to during the night. Many others were crying out around us in the dark as the storm grew more angry.

With daylight, the sea calmed. Many have not survived. The two men have tied many more pallets to our raft and we are able now to stand. We are most wet and cold. Surrounding us are the yellow ducks. There are many thousands of them. Beyond is only open sea.

Others from the ship have now swum to us, some with bags. There are now twenty-one of us. These numbers are too many for our raft. It has been pushed almost below the water, and the waves now wash over our knees.

It seems ... storm ha ... passed. Others believe the ... return.
I am not ... certain.

Jon looked up. 'What's happened to the last bit?'

'Water damage, apparently. She could well have named the ship at that point.'

Jon continued to click the wheel until the second letter filled the screen.

LETTER NINE
Last night was free of storms. The old lady moaning and her husband talking to himself disturbed us all. In the blackness, the boy saw balls of fire floating above the sea. He believed they were witches. To calm him, I said they were ships, searching for us. I heard Parviz praying.

At dawn, the old Chinese man told us he was getting help. He stood up, but I was too weak to reach out. He stepped from the raft and was gone.

Our numbers are now only six. Ali said to use the pallets from the ends of the raft to make a higher area in the middle. The man with the throat scars agreed. Clothes and some plastic bags have been laid across, so little water passes through. At last, after four days, we can lie down without getting wet.

Hunger has woken us all. Cruel and sharp, it never tires. After our noodles, Ali and I lay down and talked of how Abu Nawas Street was before the Americans came. Strolling along beside the river, choosing a restaurant to sit and eat muskof. The smell of the fish as it roasted slowly beside the coals. Amba, the spicy mango sauce, and sweet, smoky tea, flavoured by the pot being left on the glowing embers. Such memories!

Ali spoke of bache, the lamb flavoured by dried lemon pieces. I spoke of sipping yoghurt, mixed with water, salt and ice. He answered with watermelon, cool from the fridge and I begged him to stop.

At sunset, a family of dolphins surrounded us, chasing under our raft, leaping from the sea. They are the masters here and we are nothing. When they left, I cried. Who will save us?

Saying nothing, Jon scrolled back to the top and read the stories again, more carefully. 'This is ...' His words trailed away. 'Christ, in letter two, written on the first day, there's twenty-one of them. Then it jumps forward three days and there's only six left. What the hell went on out there?'

'I know,' Rick replied. 'That first letter found on the beach at Minehead describes Iraqis, Iranians, Chinese or somewhere, a few from Pakistan and a crewman.'

Jon stared out the window, the Géricault painting vivid in his mind. 'They were on their feet for four days, it sounds like people were beginning to hallucinate. Where's Abu Nawas Street, anyway?'

'Baghdad, according to what I read. The foods are all Iraqi dishes – muskof is something you only find in the city. A fresh-water fish they roast at the edge of beds of embers. Sounds quite nice.'

Jon slid the phone across the table. 'Do you reckon they were rescued?'

'Surely something like that would have made the news. Apparently more and more people have started searching the beaches, looking for notes. The ducks have been washing up everywhere – from the Lizard right up to Portishead in the Bristol Channel and Portsmouth on the south coast.'

'Can no one find out where the ducks are from? I mean, they must have fallen off a ship. Someone, surely, will have noticed half their cargo is missing?'

Rick shrugged. 'There's writing and a serial number on each one. They were made in China, apparently. I imagine there'll be journalists rushing to find out where.'

'Well,' Jon said, watching the countryside rolling past. 'There's at least six more letters to be found. That should make interesting reading.'

They lapsed into silence and Jon gazed at the green countryside beyond the glass. West of Manchester. Land of the woollybacks; places like Wigan, Warrington, Widnes and Leigh. Old textile towns, the inhabitants of which once trekked to market, bowed beneath sacks stuffed full of cotton. He thought of the people and their fierce love of rugby. So many Saturdays spent in these parts, leading Greater Manchester Police's team out to do battle on pitches which had to be cleared of crushed cans, broken bricks and dog shit before the match could kick off. Trading blows with the bastards and, further towards the coast, with mouthy gits from Liverpool itself. He realised he'd started touching the scars and lumps which dotted his hands. His reflection showed in the glass, the bump in the bridge of his nose where it had been broken, then broken again. God, he thought, how I loved those days.

Nine

'More coffee, Amanda?' Phillip Braithwaite was looking over his shoulder, eggs sputtering in the frying pan before him.

'I can get it,' she answered, starting to rise from the table.

'No – you relax.' He flicked a dishcloth over his shoulder and plucked the octagonal-shaped espresso maker from the stove top.

'That's such a wonderful gadget,' Amanda beamed, as he re-filled her cup. 'I've never tasted coffee so good. Where did you get it, again?'

'Milan,' he replied. 'But, worry not. I'm sure I'll be able to find you one next time I'm in Manchester.'

'Oh.' Her face reddened. 'I wasn't trying to ...'

'Amanda,' he smiled, 'it will be my pleasure.' He replaced the espresso maker on the gas ring, lifted the frying pan and expertly flipped the eggs into an oven tray that already had half a dozen rashers of bacon inside it. Then, using the dishcloth to protect his fingers from the hot metal, placed the tray in the centre of the table. 'Tuck in, everyone.'

On the other side of the table, Alice felt herself smile. Smooth bastard.

He sat down and laid out a copy of the *Telegraph* so it formed a bridge between the edge of the table and his bony knee. 'Spotted a curious story on the internet yesterday. About a duck. But it doesn't seem to have made the papers yet.'

Alice broke off from buttering a croissant and glanced across. 'What sort of a duck?'

'A plastic one, washed ashore at Lyme Regis.'

'Down in the West Country,' Alice replied.

He gave a slight cough, as if preparing a formal address. Perhaps a talk to a newly qualified group of medical students. 'Yes, Dorset. You know *The French Lieutenant's Woman*, the film?'

Alice looked slightly sheepish. 'I don't think so. Holly, do you want some jam on this?'

Next to her, Holly shook her head.

'How about some of that nice apricot conserve?' Phillip asked.

Holly shook her head again.

Amanda raised an eyebrow. 'Holly! Phillip has been very kind buying us all these nice breakfast things. What do you say?'

Alice found herself almost giggling. The plummy accent her mother put on in Phillip's presence was truly absurd.

Holly's fingers sought refuge beneath the crooks of her knees. 'No, thank you,' she replied, voice small.

'That's OK,' he replied with a smile, turning back to Alice. 'You've not seen *The French Lieutenant's Woman*? Superb adaptation. John Fowles wrote the novel on which it's based. There's a famous scene with Meryl Streep standing on the stone jetty. Are you sure you haven't seen it?'

Slightly flustered, Alice handed the croissant over to Holly. 'Must have passed me by.'

'Oh.' The word was pitched slightly high, a suggestion of disappointment, even disapproval, contained within it. 'We should hire the DVD. Anyway, according to the report, these plastic ducks are being washed up along the coastline there. Someone had already found a note inside one on the beach at Minehead. I'm not sure exactly what it said. Then this second one was discovered on the beach at Lyme Regis.'

'What did it say?'

'A kind of diary entry. It appears to have been written by some poor soul who'd gone overboard – from a ship out at sea. Along with a load of yellow ducks, by the look of it. It described how this person, and a few other survivors, fashioned a raft from wooden pallets floating around them. Twenty-one people, standing in water up to their knees.'

'That's terrible,' Alice murmured as Phillip reached for a rasher of bacon.

'Oh, come on,' Amanda admonished, cutting into an egg. 'It was off the internet. It won't be genuine, for goodness sake.'

'How do you know?' Alice asked.

'Well,' she widened her eyes. 'Abandoned at sea? Not in this day and age. They'd have been spotted. The ship would have reported them missing or something.'

'Mum, what if they were stowaways? If the crew found them while they were miles out at sea ...' Aware Holly was beside her, she stopped speaking, preferring to let the other two adults absorb the implications of her comment.

'Phillip, what do you think?' Amanda asked.

His bottom lip turned down. 'Hard to say. It wouldn't surprise me if it turns out to be some sort of marketing gimmick by the duck manufacturer.'

The phone started to ring and Amanda picked it up from the table beside her. 'Hello? No, it's her mum. Yes, she is. One moment.' She cupped a hand over the receiver. 'It's Martin, from that refugee place.'

Refugees Are People, Alice thought. The charity organisation she'd been helping out at now for over two years. 'Martin, hi. Everything OK?'

'Sorry to ring you this early on a Monday, Alice. I'd take care of it myself, but ...'

'What's up?'

'It's Nathaniel. You know – the gentlemen from Zimbabwe who's been living in the Moss Side flats?'

'Yes, I know who you mean. Nathaniel Musoso.'

'The police picked him up in a distressed state early this morning. He was wandering the streets. He's been self-harming. Lacerations to his forearms.'

'Where is he now?'

'They dropped him off at Sale General. He's been admitted back onto the mental health unit.'

Alice bowed her head. They'd been working with Nathaniel for over four months, offering support as his claim for asylum was slowly processed. Sometimes he seemed to be coping fine.

Then memories of what had happened in Africa returned to torment him.

'A nurse called here just now. He's asking for—'

'Sudoku.' Alice completed the sentence for him, thinking about the informal arrangement between the hospital and the charity. When an asylum seeker with no friends or family ended up on the ward, a member of RAP would go in and offer support that could involve anything from bringing in supplies to arranging contact with community groups originally from that person's country. With the pressure the nurses were under, it sometimes included helping out with non-clinical paperwork, too. 'Rolling tobacco as well. Am I right?'

'Spot on. Is there any way you could ...'

'Leave it with me. I'll take some things in for him.'

'Thanks so much, Alice. Keep any receipts, won't you?'

'Will do. I'll call to say how he's doing.' She hung up and looked guiltily at Holly, knowing how her daughter hated it when this happened. 'Mummy's got to pop out, sweetie. I won't be long. Is that OK?'

Holly's eyes dropped to the table and she started sliding her spoon back and forth.

'Is that OK?'

Holly gave a faint nod. No, it's not, Alice thought sadly, turning to Phillip as she stood. 'A client's shown up at Sale General's MHU. Nathaniel Musoso?'

Phillip looked blank.

'He's been admitted before. Are you due to do a ward round soon?'

He nodded.

'Great. Look, I'll check what meds they've got him on. But last time he was in, I don't believe he was properly assessed. Maybe you could take a look at him? You know – perhaps a Hopkins Symptom checklist? He's definitely got post-traumatic stress disorder.'

He raised his eyebrows and fixed her with a look.

Hastily, she corrected herself. 'Well, in my opinion, he has. You know how busy the nurses are in there.'

82

He glanced at his watch then folded the paper. 'Alice, you shouldn't fret.' A smile was playing at his lips. 'There is an assessment system in place. The nurses are fully qualified.'

'I know,' she said, suddenly aware she was offering advice to a consultant psychiatrist when she had yet to qualify as a counsellor. 'I'm just saying ... well, you know. If you can give him some time, I'd really appreciate it. He's been through so much.'

Phillip had turned back to his plate. 'I'm sure that won't be a problem.'

'Thank you. Sorry to rush off like this, Mum. Are you OK looking after Holly for a bit?'

'Yes.'

Phillip gestured to Amanda. 'Try some of the dry-cure bacon, it really is delicious.'

'Hello, Mary,' Alice smiled, walking across the lobby to the security desk. 'Here to see Nathaniel Musoso. He was admitted earlier this morning.'

'Ah, yes,' the middle-aged lady replied, examining the computer screen. 'He was. Guy – can you do the check, please?'

Beside her, a large man with the word Security stitched onto the breast of his dark blue jumper was flicking through the *Sun*. With a hint of reluctance, he looked up, saw Alice and quickly stood. 'Morning,' he mumbled, a blush creeping beneath the black skin of his face.

'Guy.' Alice tried not to smile at the man's futile attempt to mask the fact he fancied her. She racked her brains for anything she'd recently read about Manchester City in the local press. 'Is that Wright-Phillips a good signing, then?'

The man's eyes lit up. 'The prodigal son returns! Hughes has signed us a player there.'

She held the bag open. 'Just a Sudoku puzzle book, some tobacco and papers and a bottle of Ribena.'

'Yup,' he replied, after glancing in. 'You're all right.'

Alice signed her name on the form, then Mary pressed the button that opened the outer doors. Alice stepped through, hearing them clamp shut behind her. She walked the twelve feet to the inner doors and pressed the buzzer, hating every second she was trapped in the airlock.

A long-haired nursing assistant wearing faded jeans and a purple T-shirt was at the desk just beyond the doors. Twenty-two years old, at most, Alice thought, buzzing again. He spotted her looking at him through the glass, reached under the desk and released the lock. The doors slid apart.

'Morning,' Alice said thankfully, quickly stepping through.

Down the corridor to her left she could hear noise from a television. Most of the patients would be in there by now, she thought, slumped in soft chairs, eyes glued to the screen. A sharp, salty smell lingered in the air. Bacon. Cooked hours ago and then left in the heated food trolleys, slowly stewing in its own juice.

'Hi, there,' he replied. 'Who are you seeing?'

'Nathaniel Musoso.' Alice glanced at the nurse's room immediately to her right. As usual, the door was firmly shut. She pictured them all inside, desperately trying to prepare patient files ready for the ward rounds the next day. 'Busy night?'

'Better believe it,' the assistant replied. 'That Nathaniel was kicking off big time. We've got another in the isolation room and two more are on their way in. That'll be us full, again.'

An overweight man of about fifty was shuffling down the corridor towards them. Alice caught sight of the unlit cigarette in his hand.

'Can you let us out?'

'Hang on, Tony,' the assistant replied.

'You said that twenty minutes ago. I need a smoke.'

This is the disaster, Alice thought, of the government's recent ban on smoking in public places. Patients on mental health wards were notorious for smoking like chimneys – and now they had to get a member of staff to accompany them out for every single cigarette.

'I'm sorry,' the assistant replied. 'Someone will pop out with you soon.'

'Now! I want to go now!'

'Tony, do you think you should be going out at all, if you're all worked up?'

'I'm not worked up. I wasn't worked up. It's you who's doing it to me. Just fucking let us out, will you?'

'Tony, you want me to write this up? Ward round's tomorrow and this can go in your file. It's not a problem for me.'

'I just need a smoke.' His voice dropped to a whisper. 'Please.'

The nursing assistant looked at Alice with a triumphant glint in his eye. 'He's in bay three, I think.'

'Thanks.' Alice took the corridor which led straight ahead, past the women's section. The threat of a write-up, she thought. Amazing the effect that can have. Phillip – or whichever psychiatrist doing the rounds – would periodically sweep in and review each patient's notes from the previous few days. Compliance with taking medication. Ability to get on with others. Willingness to eat and wash. And any episodes that weren't in keeping with what the world beyond the sliding doors deemed as acceptable behaviour. Like talking to imaginary people or answering back to those in authority.

One by one, each patient would then be ushered in to a room where Phillip and the care coordinator would be waiting. The system confused her. It was the nursing assistants who had by far the most actual face-to-face contact with the patients. Yet their input was reduced to a few observations which, depending on time pressures, the qualified nurses may, or may not, add to the patient's file.

She continued along the corridor, passing three bays on her right, each of which held six beds. Prints of famous paintings were screwed to the wall at regular intervals. Constable's *The Hay Wain*, Monet's *Water Lilies*, Bruegel's *Hunters in the Snow*. Shame, Alice thought, that they wouldn't put up anything by Van Gogh. A lot of his best work, she reflected, had been done while inside a mental institution. A few fragments of plaster on the floor caught her eye and she spotted damage to the wall. Something had been thrown at it pretty hard.

The corridor turned left, past the stretch of single-occupancy rooms reserved for those too vulnerable to share with others. At its midpoint the corridor became the men's half of the ward. A few more single rooms and the corridor turned left again, leading past the three men's bays. After that, the corridor turned left a final time to complete the square. The TV room, dining area and visitor rooms were all on the final stretch of corridor which led back to the nurses' desk and the doors to the outside world.

Alice was passing the final single-occupancy room for men when the door opened. She glimpsed a thin, hollow-cheeked youth propped up in the bed, scabs covering his bald head.

The woman closed the door and turned round. Her arms were at her sides, and for a moment Alice wasn't sure if she was a nurse or a visitor. Then one hand moved, allowing Alice a glimpse of the identity card and panic alarm attached to her belt. 'Hi, there. I was wondering where Nathaniel Musoso is?'

The woman pointed. 'Bay three. He's calm, now.'

'Is he on meds?'

She nodded. 'Sedatives and some antipsychotics.'

'Antipsychotics? He wasn't psychotic, was he?'

'He was hearing voices. Engaging with them.'

'That's—' Alice stopped. That's not psychotic behaviour, she wanted to say. Where he comes from, it's normal to address your dead ancestors, especially in times of distress. Too late now. 'Bay three, thanks.'

She found him sitting up in bed, bandages covering both forearms. 'Nathaniel,' she announced, pulling up a chair.

He stared back with deadened eyes.

'Got your Sudoku puzzles. And some tobacco, too. Is this type OK? Samson?'

'Thank you.'

'And Ribena. None of that sugar-free crap, either. You'd like some?'

He gave a faint smile. 'Crap. You should not use such language, Alice.'

She adopted a Mary Poppins voice. 'You prefer it when I speak like a lady?'

'That is better, yes,' he nodded, smile taking hold properly.

'Well, I'm a northern lass, Nathaniel. So bollocks to that.' Grinning, she added some juice to the plastic beaker of water on his bedside table. Then she turned to face him, taking his hand in both of hers. 'What happened, Nathaniel?'

He raised his other hand and rubbed at the greying curls on his head, sleeve sliding back as he did so. The bandages went right up to his elbow. 'My application to stay here has been turned down. They will call me back to Dallas Court, Alice.'

She thought about the anonymous-looking reporting centre tucked away among other windowless units on an industrial estate in Salford Quays.

'And when I go,' Nathaniel added mournfully, 'I will not come back out.'

Ten

They approached the ticket barrier at Liverpool Lime Street, warrant cards at the ready.

'All right there, lads.' The ticket officer waved them through.

Jon heard the way the man's tongue rolled over his 'l's. Scouse, he thought. Bloody horrible accent.

The signs for the taxi rank directed them off to the left. They crossed the shiny floor and emerged from a side exit to a line of black cabs bumper to bumper in a tight turning circle.

'Reliance House, Water Street, please,' Jon announced as they climbed into the vehicle at the front of the queue.

The driver gave a knowing nod, eyes on them in the rear-view mirror. 'Business, is it?'

'Yup,' Jon replied, trying to find his seat belt as they pulled away.

'You don't look like the usual crowd outside that place. Not with ties on.'

The taxi swung out on to the main road, the towering row of Roman columns which formed the front of St George's Hall dominating the view. The cab then turned down a slightly sloping side street. They passed another grandiose building, this one with a dome similar in style, Jon thought, to Manchester's central library. He reflected on the fortunes of the two cities – the factories of Manchester making the cotton and the port of Liverpool controlling its shipment. Until, that is, tens of thousands of navvies had been recruited to dig out the Manchester Ship Canal. The cities had never been the friendliest of neighbours, that was for sure.

The road continued on a downward slope and Jon spotted the tarnished copper birds perched atop the Liver building up ahead. Beyond it, he glimpsed water. The Mersey, its pinched surface sliding sideways, a relentless flow of silver emptying into the Irish sea.

'Reliance House.' The taxi pulled to a halt.

After collecting a receipt, Jon climbed out, leaving the door open for Rick and turning to examine the building on the opposite side of the road. Its anonymous-looking front lacked the Gothic styling of the Liver building or stately appearance of the other buildings which lined the street. Stone steps led up to the main doors, above which chunky metallic lettering spelled out Reliance House. The queue of people stretched down to the pavement.

Skirting round them, Jon and Rick stepped through the glass doors and into a lobby area dominated by two airport-style metal detectors. The smell of carpet-cleaning fluid mixed with the aroma created when too many people were crammed into too small a space. They approached the white-shirted security guards, warrant cards in their hands.

'All right, mate?' Jon announced.

A guard glanced at them suspiciously. 'Yes?'

'We're here to see a Derek Marlow.' Jon held his ID up. 'He knows we're coming.'

They were waved through a side gate and directed up some more steps to an inner desk, where a couple of other officials were chatting. One was wearing white rubber gloves with the words Front Desk written across the back. They introduced themselves and, as one of the men made a phone call, Jon examined the headline of the poster pinned to the door which led into a large waiting area.

> Ali* didn't give his real name during his interview.
> Giving false information to us can result in
> your arrest and imprisonment.

The remainder of the poster was made up of a series of panels, each one filled with words of a different language. The asterisk featured after every first word and Jon searched out the English small print at the poster's base.

*This name does not refer to an actual person who is claiming asylum.

A minute later a door marked Staff Only opened and a tall man with greying brown hair stepped out. He was wearing grey trousers, a white shirt and a navy tie. An identity card was attached to a red ribbon around his neck.

'DI Spicer, DS Saville?'

Only a faint Liverpool accent, Jon thought with relief as he stepped forward with a hand out. 'Morning. I'm Jon Spicer. Is it Derek Marlow?'

'Yes.'

'My colleague, Rick Saville.'

Once they'd all shaken hands he turned round, swiped his card through a reader to the side of the door and opened it up. 'There are locks throughout this place, so I'd better lead the way. We're heading straight up the stairs.'

'Is it always this busy?' asked Rick.

He grunted. 'When we moved into these offices, they were considered palatial. But the numbers just keep going up. We'll have outgrown this place pretty soon.'

'Why the increase?'

'I wish I knew,' he replied wearily, 'then we could stop it.' He glanced over his shoulder and gave a wink.

'Too many countries can't take care of their own, surely,' Jon said. 'So they come looking for a better life here.'

'Actually,' Marlow replied, coming to a halt and considering something for a second. 'You won't hear me saying this in the main office, but you want a more accurate reason?'

Jon raised his eyebrows.

'Foreign policy. And I'm talking about our government's. A few years ago, the numbers of Iraqis and Afghans we had turning up here was relatively low. Now, they're arriving in their thousands. We invade their country and destroy their homes: they come here to find new ones. You reap what you sow, as they say.'

Jon exchanged a look of surprise with Rick. Not quite in keeping with the government's stance on the issue, he thought.

At the top of the stairs, Marlow ran his card through another reader. The door gave access to a narrow office, tiers of desks running along its length. Blue files were piled up on each one and the people who weren't sitting down filling in forms were ferrying paperwork round the corner at the far end of the room.

'I sit halfway down. Tea, coffee?'

'Coffee, thanks. Black, no sugar,' Jon answered.

'Tea, just with milk,' Rick added.

He passed the order on to a young woman busily typing at the workstation in the corner then led them to his desk. A small bronze cast of a horse in full gallop was the only personal touch: most of his work surface was taken up by the ubiquitous blue files.

'So,' he said, dragging over two extra chairs then sitting down and reaching for the file at the centre of his desk. 'The man calling himself Marat Dubinski. He's dead?'

'Yes,' Jon replied, taking a seat. 'That's not his real name?'

Marlow shook his head. 'I started on his background checks – and knew within a few hours he'd spun me a yarn. Suspected as much during his interview, to be honest. Next time he checked in at Dallas Court he was to be detained.'

'What's Dallas Court?' Jon asked.

'Our reporting centre for asylum seekers placed around Manchester. From there he would have been taken to Harmondsworth Immigration Removal Centre,' he fluttered his fingers in the air, 'and back from whence he came.'

Jon leaned an elbow on the edge of the desk. 'I've not come across Dallas Court before.'

'Salford Quays? Near the Theatre of Dreams?'

Jon registered the mocking tone in the man's voice. Theatre of Dreams was how supporters of Manchester United described their football stadium. Bollocks, he thought. We're going to have to go through all this shit. 'Who's your team, then? Liverpool?'

'Liverpool?' He scoffed. 'I'd rather scoop my eyeballs out with a blunt spoon.'

Everton, then, Jon thought. The city's other team, separated from Liverpool's ground by a short stroll across Stanley Park. From the corner of his eye, he could see Rick's attention had already started to wander. His partner's head turned so he could peer at the noticeboard next to a heavily laden coat-stand on their right.

'I take it you're a red?' the immigration officer asked in a guarded tone.

Jon shook his head.

'Blue, then?' Marlow stated, referring to City, the other major football club in Manchester.

'Neither.' Jon paused, wondering how long the other man could hold his nonplussed expression. 'Sale Sharks.'

'Aaaah.' Marlow's eyebrows dropped with something close to relief. 'Rugby. Fair enough.'

Jon grinned at the customary reaction then, seeing Rick was still a million miles away, saw an opportunity to stitch him up. He nodded at his partner. 'Don't ask him, though. He's from down south.'

Grimacing, the officer turned to Rick. 'Not Chelsea, I hope?'

Rick realised the comment had been directed at him. 'Sorry?'

'Chelski. That Russian billionaire's plaything. You don't support them, do you?'

Failing miserably to hide his look of boredom, Rick replied, 'I don't really follow sport, to be honest.'

Jon stifled a laugh, knowing the reaction the comment would have on a man like Marlow. You had to support someone in these parts. If not a football club, a team from another sport was just about acceptable as an alternative. But to not support anyone? That was unnatural. Freakish.

Marlow swivelled in his seat and Jon knew Rick was now as good as invisible. 'How did our man die?' Marlow asked.

'Gruesomely. He was garrotted.'

'You mean strangled?'

'Basically. But through a wire or something similar being looped round his neck.' He glanced at the file. 'What do you have on him?'

Marlow placed both hands on the blue folder in readiness to open it. 'Well, considering his story's false, not a lot. Photo, fingerprints. That's it, really.'

The cover of the file had the same passport-sized photo of the dead man Jon had seen on his Application Registration Card. Alongside it was the letter D and a line of numbers.

'D is for Dubinski,' Marlow explained. 'That and the seven digits form the Home Office reference. Though we'll soon be having to increase it to an eight-figure number, at this rate.'

'So what happens?' asked Jon, looking around. 'You interviewed this man somewhere in here? Where did you take his fingerprints?'

Marlow stood. 'Why don't I walk you through the process? It'll make things a lot clearer.'

'Please.'

He led them over to the door by the side of the noticeboard. Jon glimpsed a piece of paper titled *The White List*. Below were two columns made up of countries' names. Marlow swiped his card and pushed the door open.

Jon followed the immigration officer through and found himself in a large waiting area. To their left, rows of seats stretched to the back of the room. A sea of faces stared at them. Trying not to catch anyone's eyes, Jon registered several large beards and a bewildering array of head-coverings. Scarves, dainty little lace caps, brightly coloured wraps of material, turban-like coils of faded cloth, satin veils.

On their right, the room ended at a glass screen. Modest partitions divided it into ten or so booths, each one with two stools bolted down into the pale green carpet. A row of Border Agency officers were jotting things down or asking questions of the people sitting on the other side of the glass. On the wall above each booth was an electronic board. Different numbers glowed red from the screens.

'So,' Marlow announced. 'They come in downstairs and go into the main waiting room there. Numbers are allocated and they're brought up here in batches. When their number flashes up, they proceed to the allocated booth. At this point we're just taking basic information. Name, date of birth, nationality, brief details of how they entered the UK, details of any previous applications for asylum or visas.'

A child's laughter. Jon glanced to the corner of the room where an African girl of about five was tickling the rounded belly of what he presumed was her younger brother. The boy writhed on the floor, brown eyes open wide as he sought to stop the fingers burrowing beneath his T-shirt.

'That information,' Marlow continued, 'is fed into CID, the Case Information Database. The Home Office reference is then generated with all information given ready-populated in the appropriate fields on their file.'

The little boy had struggled to his knees, and now shrieking excitedly was trying to escape from his sister by crawling across the floor. An ache suddenly blossomed in Jon's chest. Holly. God, I love you. He thought about waking her in the morning, gently turning her over so he could press his lips against the cheek made hot from being in contact with the pillow.

Marlow held out a hand, forefinger directed downwards. He began circling it round as if trying to remove coffee stains from the base of a cup. 'Whose are these? Can you please keep them quiet? We're conducting interviews here.'

A man wearing long flowing robes of white quickly stood. 'Sorry,' he said, scooping the boy up and hissing strange words at the sister.

Marlow walked over to another door. 'Next is fingerprinting.' He swiped his card and they stepped into a hospital-style room. The hard, grey floor sparkled with silver flecks, and staff members wearing latex gloves bustled around several large white machines.

'Their prints are scanned electronically,' Marlow pointed to the apparatus in the corner, 'and then interrogated against EuroDac. Thirty minutes and we know if they've gone through any other border within Europe before arriving here. Thirty-five grand for that bit of kit. God only knows how much the computer it's linked to cost.'

Rick coughed. 'Does it give access to other countries' databases for criminal offences?'

Jon waited for Marlow to respond, but the other man didn't appear to have heard. 'Derek? Do you get to see if the asylum seeker has a criminal record elsewhere in Europe?'

Marlow shook his head. 'Nope. Only previous asylum claims. We also photograph them for their ARC.'

Jon thought about the card in the dead Russian's flat. 'Application Registration Card?'

'Correct.' Marlow reached towards a large machine bearing a Lexmark logo. From the side tray, he plucked out a blank card with the familiar gold chip embedded in its corner. 'All their data – including the biometric stuff – goes on here. Then it's back into the main waiting area for the full screening.'

He proceeded across the room and led the way through another door which took them back into the office. Sitting at his desk, he picked up the cup of tea that had been left by his phone and took a sip. 'Just right. Thanks, Natalie!'

Jon sat down and reached for the black coffee. 'How did this Dubinski character strike you?'

Marlow opened the blue file. 'I was a little wrong-footed by him, to be honest. He didn't speak much English, so it was all coming via one of our interpreters. For the full screening, you ask them the reason for their asylum claim. Religious, political or some other form of persecution – just to categorise it at this point. We go into background: family, names of siblings, the area they're from, what their address was. His answers all seemed fine.' He ran a finger down the page to a large box. 'He didn't enter the country as a clandestine. Said he'd been dropped off near the coast, brought to shore by a passing fishing trawler. That all checked out with the authorities who met the boat at the dock.'

'Is that usual?' Rick asked. 'To be set down at sea?'

Marlow kept his eyes on Jon. 'It's not unheard of. Far more common for our southern European neighbours. I read a memo the other day – twenty-four thousand have landed so far this year on the Italian island of Lampedusa. Plus you've got the ones making it from North Africa to the Balearic islands. And those are the successful crossings. No one knows how many don't make it. People arrive here all sorts of bizarre ways. Frozen to the landing gear of aeroplanes, sometimes. As if you're ever going to survive something like that. Anyway, he had that look. Someone who didn't touch down while seated in the first-class section of any plane.'

'And is Russia a country we get many asylum seekers from?' Jon asked.

Marlow shrugged. 'It's not up there with Iraq, but it's not on the white list either.'

'White list?'

'Countries deemed as having no overt risk to their citizens. Like Jamaica, for instance. People flying in from there trying to claim asylum are generally super-fast-tracked straight down to Harmondsworth and put on the first flight back.'

Jon thought about the Yardie problem. Manchester had seen a fair few shootings linked to Jamaican gang members vying to get a slice of the drugs trade. Innocent school kids caught in the crossfire. Real victims. People whose murder merited a proper investigation. 'This Dubinski seemed like a genuine case?'

'Not genuine, no. But the detention centres are chock-a-block at the moment. That swung it for me, really. He was destitute, too – so he went off with the day's lot to Greenbank.' Catching Jon's questioning look, he elaborated. 'Overnight residence. Ex-student halls or something the Home Office purchased. A bus takes them there at five. They're fed, watered, seen by a doctor if necessary then shipped on to initial accommodation the next day.'

'Which, in Dubinski's case, was Sunlight Tower, in Lostock,' Jon concluded.

'Indeed.' Marlow sat back and sipped more tea.

Jon tapped a finger on the rim of his cup. 'What's next then?'

'First reporting event. We try and conduct it within two days of their arrival. If they're being housed in the Manchester area, it takes place in Dallas Court. As case owner, I explained to him the process of how his claim will be handled and then set a date for his substantive interview. That's when we go into the meat of the claim – proper detail, all cross-checked.'

Jon sat forward. 'And by this point you'd realised his story was fake.'

'Didn't even get to the substantive interview. Just my initial checks which had shown that no Marat Dubinski lived in a town called Kolpino just outside St Petersburg or worked as a journalist for the *Peterburgsky Metropoliten* newspaper. I was in the process of calling him back to be detained in Dallas Court when you emailed.'

Jon finished his coffee. 'I don't suppose we can have his finger-print scans? It could be worth checking them on the criminal databases we have access to.'

Marlow tipped his head at the ceiling. 'Upstairs will have to give the go-ahead for that. If it was me, you'd be welcome to the whole file. One less for me to deal with.'

Jon sensed a drawn-out bureaucratic process. 'No problem. His body's in the morgue at the Manchester Royal Infirmary. I can get prints off that. Anything else you think is worth us knowing?'

Marlow shook his head. 'Can't think of anything.' He picked up his pen and turned to the last page of the file. 'Not sure what to class this as. Claim withdrawn, I suppose.' He ticked a box and closed the file. 'Good luck. I wouldn't want to be trying to solve this one.'

'Cheers.' Jon checked that Rick had also finished his drink then stood. 'Not sure if I want to be, either.'

It was almost ten at night when, with his car's indicator making a faint ticking sound, Jon turned into his old road. The street was deserted. He crawled along in second gear, scanning the parked cars on either side. Streetlight had rendered them all in similar, drab, shades and he struggled to make out any maroon among them. His house came into view, lights still on in the downstairs windows. He slid the vehicle into a space on the other side of the road and turned his engine off.

The evenings were now drawing in, making it possible for him to observe where he used to live a little earlier each week. In less than two months, he thought, the clocks would go back and it would be dark by late afternoon. He nodded to himself, liking the idea of taking up his position before Holly went to bed. Perhaps he'd glimpse her through a window.

As the engine's ticks slowed to nothing, he stared across at where she slept. Something thick and gristle-like rose up and caught at the back of his throat and he had to lower his eyes. Bits and pieces filled the storage tray by the gear stick. A packet of Polo mints, a pound for the shopping trolleys at the local super-market. An old parking ticket had attached itself to the cover of The Pogues CD. He peeled it off and looked once again at the Géricault painting on the album's cover. The light in the sky was rapidly fading, stormy clouds blowing in at the right-hand side of the painting. Wind tormented the rag one of the survivors had raised above his head and the lurching ocean was made up of cold, grey tones.

He took the CD out, slotted it into the dashboard player and skipped through to track seven. The sad notes of the harmonica began to stretch themselves out, and when Shane MacGowan's ragged voice joined the lament, the night with Alice all those years ago came hurtling back. He felt the fabric of the car seat brush against the back of his hand as it fell limply at his side. His fingertips traced circles in the carpet as he remembered holding Alice close, her warm lips closing over his. Gone. My wife is gone, drifting further and further from my reach, taking Holly with her.

Light shifted and he realised his eyes were closed. He opened them to see another car approaching. The maroon Saab convert-ible pulled up a little further down the street and Braithwaite got out, a bottle of wine in one hand. Jon felt like jumping out of his car, racing up to his front door and hammering on it, warn-ing Alice not to let Braithwaite in. He isn't the nice guy you think he is. The other man stepped away from the car, and as its hazards flashed twice, he paused, key fob still held out. His eyes seemed to settle on Jon's car. Impossible, Jon thought, shrinking down in his seat. You're almost thirty metres away and sitting inside a darkened vehicle. The bloke hasn't seen you.

Braithwaite walked round to the pavement and opened the front gate. He transferred the bottle to his left hand and lifted his right to the door. You've got your own key, Jon thought. He wanted to moan. Your own key. Coming and going as you please, like you live in my fucking house. His fingers dug into the carpet, knuckles pressing against the hard plastic base of the seat. Don't get used to it, you bastard. It's not going to last, you can be sure of that.

The song died back down, until the wavering note of the uilleann pipes was all that remained. Then it too dried up and silence filled the car. Fuck this, Jon thought, starting the vehicle and racing off down the street.

He was in Wilmslow twenty minutes later, finger raised to the bell of Braithwaite's estranged wife's front door. Christ, he thought. What are you doing? His hand lowered a couple of inches and he stared at the frosted panel of glass. Think, Spicer, this is stupid. But the image of Braithwaite returned. The way the bloke had casually let himself in without even knocking. Jon took a deep breath and pressed on the bell.

Seconds later, a light came on in the hallway. It's not too late, he thought. Ten steps and you could be round the corner and out of sight. But as a blurred form approached, his feet refused to move.

The door half opened and a glamorous-looking woman peered out. There was a sharpness in her eyes. This is bloody stupid, Jon thought, even as he held his warrant card up. 'Miranda Braithwaite? I'm with Greater Manchester Police. Would it be possible to have a word?'

She opened the door more fully, eyes moving momentarily to Jon's identification. When she looked back at him, he detected a trace of irritation in her eyes. Jon was used to the reaction from people like her; normally, they only talked to police when they had called for them. This was an unwelcome break from the status quo.

'Is there a problem?' Her voice was crisp, the words clearly pronounced.

'Nothing serious. Could we talk inside?'

She considered the request for a second then stepped back. 'The kitchen is straight ahead. Would you like a drink?'

'No, thank you. I appreciate it's late, so I'll be as quick as possible.' He walked down the short corridor, a row of recessed halogen lights dotting the ceiling above him. The carpet was beige and felt luxuriously thick. 'Nice place.'

'How can I help?' The words sounded like they'd come out of barely parted lips.

The kitchen was small and immaculate. A set of knives, the blades and handles forged from a single piece of metal, were stuck to a band running above the hob of a range cooker. A Dualit toaster. One of those expensive flip-top bins with an Italian name. Jon positioned himself by the breakfast bar, one hand resting on the cool granite surface.

She crossed the room, raised a glass of red wine and looked at him in silence.

'It's in relation to a maroon-coloured Saab convertible. Our records indicate the vehicle is registered to you.'

Her eyelids fluttered slightly. 'Yes.'

'Do you use it on a regular basis?'

'Not really, no. It's actually more my husband's. We live apart.' She tilted her glass a fraction. 'One of several things we haven't got around to sorting out. Why?'

Jon couldn't gauge anything about the state of their relationship from her reply. Cautiously, he proceeded. 'Do you ever use the vehicle, Mrs Braithwaite?'

Her eyes narrowed and he could sense she didn't appreciate her question being answered with another. 'No. At least not recently.'

'As in the last few weeks?'

'Yes.'

'So your husband would be the main user?'

'As far as I know.'

'You don't have much contact with him, I take it?'

'As I said, we live apart.'

'Could I ask the reasons for that arrangement?'

Light suddenly caught in her eyes, causing them to glitter coldly. 'What's this about, please?'

Jon forced out a cough to let her know he was about to broach an awkward subject. 'We've been conducting an operation recently in the Fairfield Street area of the city. Residents have been experiencing some problems in relation to working girls using the neighbourhood for the purposes of solicitation.' He searched her face for any kind of reaction. Movement of the eyebrows, a pursing of the lips: anything to suggest a familiarity with the implications of what he'd just said. 'Many local women have complained about being approached by kerb-crawlers.'

She crossed her arms and a tiny movement in the muscle of her jaw told him her tongue was moving around inside her mouth. Her lipstick suddenly seemed too harsh and he realised the blood had drained from her face.

'In your relationship with your husband, did he ever give you cause for concern ...'

She swallowed and her eyes finally dropped. Jon imagined what might have taken place between them. How did she find out about his habit? An unannounced visit like this? Money inexplicably spent? Perhaps an infection, the sort that could only be passed on from sexual contact with another?

'Were there any incidents that might have suggested he had an involvement with the type of scenario I'm describing?'

'You mean, did he use prostitutes?' Disgust made her voice sluggish and hoarse.

Jon lowered his eyes. 'I'm very sorry to place you in this situation. A maroon Saab,' he glanced at his notebook and read out the registration. 'It's been spotted several times in the area, often late at night. The driver is described as tall with a thin build, dark brown hair, glasses.'

'Is he there now?'

Jon blinked. 'Sorry?'

'Was he there just now? Cruising around? That's why you've turned up at my house at this time of night?'

Jon closed his notebook. 'It was earlier tonight, yes. A resident rang, giving us the vehicle registration.'

'I'm sorry, but where my husband chooses to drive is no longer my concern.'

'Of course. It was more about what – if anything – you could tell me about your estranged husband's conduct when you were together.' The shutters are coming down, he thought. She's not going to give me anything. How can I provoke something from her? 'Several of the females are very young.'

Suddenly her eyes were boring into his. 'He's approached young women?' Anger was now in her voice. 'Prostitutes or people who have to live there?'

'I'm only saying some of the prostitutes are very young. We don't know if he's actually approached any.'

'But you just implied ...'

'I'm sorry if I led you to believe that.'

She gazed at him for a second longer, the muscle in her jaw twitching once again. 'I can't help you. Isn't it the normal way to talk directly with the person you suspect of ... of a crime?'

Jon half nodded. 'We will probably do so in due course. But with the confusion over who's actually using the car, I wanted to check things over with you first.'

'Well, it seems like a very odd approach to me, officer ...?'

'Detective Inspector.' He replaced his notebook and turned to the door.

'Detective Inspector?' She sounded surprised at his rank. 'Sorry, I didn't catch your name.'

That, Jon thought, is because I avoided giving it to you. She was waiting. 'Spicer.'

'Spicer.'

He could almost hear the information being filed. 'Obviously, I'd appreciate it if you could treat this conversation as confidential while we look into the allegations. We hope no formal action will be necessary.'

'I see.'

Is that a yes or a no, Jon thought, hesitating in the doorway.

'Do I need to show you out, Detective Inspector Spicer?'

Eleven

Jon pushed his chair away from his desk and hung his head forward. *What was I thinking going to Miranda Braithwaite's house? And what was going through her head when I left?* She had obviously been riled by my visit. But, he wondered, how much of that anger had been as a result of my presence in her kitchen and how much the result of what my questions had implied? It was the questions, Jon told himself. They had really pissed her off. Touched on something that was sordid or embarrassing enough to leave her trembling.

He lifted his head and refocused on the typed sheets of the forensics report before him. Nothing usable had shown up. The lab had managed to take a look at the hair removed from the back of the sofa, but it had no follicle attached, so a meaningful DNA analysis was impossible. All the technician could say was that it belonged to a Caucasian. No forensics. No witnesses. Jon closed his eyes. This case was rapidly grinding to a halt. The dead man's fingerprints hadn't pinged up with anything on the Police National Computer, so all they could do now was cross their fingers and send them to Interpol and the authorities in Russia.

Meanwhile, his emails that morning had contained a message from the Home Office. They needed the flat in Sunlight Tower for another asylum seeker, cleaners were ready to go in as soon as Jon gave permission. He looked once more at the forensics report. 'You want to check the flat of Marat Dubinski again?'

Rick sat back. 'Why? Forensics drew a blank, didn't they?'

'Yup.'

'No need then. Buchanon's looking for someone to get across to Castlefield. Body of an elderly male found under the railway arches.'

'Hang on – haven't we got enough on with trying to sort out the rape case?'

Rick visibly sagged. 'Shit – I forgot to say. Her solicitor called, she's decided not to press charges.'

'What? She's backing down?'

'Afraid so.'

Jon looked at the shelving unit to the side of his desk. He had the sudden urge to pull the file out and drop-kick it at the nearest bin. Instead, he placed an elbow on his desk and pressed his knuckles against his lower lip.

'What are you thinking?' Rick asked.

Jon said nothing for a few seconds then lowered his hand. 'He'll do it again, you know.'

'Why do you say that?'

'Because he was too casual. You don't enter someone's flat and do what he did without practice. He'll have built up to it over several attacks, mark my words. If we could have prosecuted this, other victims would have started coming forward, I know it.'

'You're probably right. But what the hell can we do about it?'

'There is something,' Jon replied, picking up his phone. 'Log his style with the Violent Crimes Unit, especially that licking the ear business. We get those details with the VCU and, next time they crop up in an attack, we'll be banging on the bastard's door within hours.' He sat back and grinned.

'That guy. He'll be cursing you on his deathbed.'

'I hope so.' After making the call, Jon turned to his computer and tapped out a reply stating they had no further need for the flat in Sunlight Tower to be preserved as a crime scene. He pressed send. That was it then. Unless a fresh witness came forward or they received an anonymous tip, there wasn't a lot more they could do.

His phone started to ring. Two short notes, denoting an external call. 'DI Spicer.'

'Detective Inspector Spicer?'

Jon frowned. The voice had the type of accent an actor might use when playing Dracula. 'Morning, how can I help?'

'The Russian man. It was me. I killed him.'

Jon relaxed his shoulders. 'Really?' He didn't pick up a pen. 'And your name is?'

'Ivan.'

'And would you like to come in and sign a confession, Ivan?'

'Yes. And I will write it with his blood. Ha, ha, ha, ha!'

Jon looked around the office, quickly spotting a detective in another syndicate beaming in his direction, a mobile phone pressed to his ear. Holding up a middle finger, Jon replaced the receiver on its cradle and turned to Rick. 'Word's obviously got around that the Russian case is a cul-de-sac.'

As Rick glanced across the room and also held up a finger to the detective, Jon reflected on the structure of the Major Incident Team. It was made up of eight syndicates, each one under the charge of a Detective Chief Inspector. The top brass claimed the arrangement wasn't designed to instil a sense of rivalry between each syndicate, but a whiteboard dominated the end of the room and listed on it was the status of every syndicate's current jobs. Jon's eyes settled on the entry for the Russian case and its label of undetected. Not meant to create competition. My arse, thought Jon. Everything's a bloody competition – life, everything.

He looked at his partner. 'What did the uniforms say about this elderly guy out at Castlefield?'

'Just an old boy in his sleeping bag. No obvious signs of trauma, but the body looks like it might have been rolled.'

'My money's on a heart attack. Makes them jerk about a bit, sometimes.' He'd stating reaching for his car keys when his phone went again. 'You want to tell Buchanon we're taking it?'

'OK.' Rick began to tidy the sheets of paper on his desk into a pile.

Jon checked around the room to make sure no one else was on a mobile before picking up his receiver. 'DI Spicer.'

'Morning, Jon. Richard Milton.'

The Home Office pathologist. 'Hi, Richard. Forensics didn't find anything usable on the Russian guy. Nothing much I can tell you.'

'Oh—'

'You may as well put him in storage until we can work his identity out.'

'OK. I'll bag up his intestinal contents, too. Could be something in there to indicate the region of Russia he came from, if we get really desperate.'

'Assuming he's even from Russia.'

'True. I was actually ringing about something else.'

Jon stood and removed his jacket from the back of his chair. 'Fire away.'

'I've just had a call from a colleague in Oldham. We run a thing called Chart Toppers. A top ten of the most unusual or bizarre ways people have been recently ... well, topped. I'd proposed our Russian guy for the new number one, but some miserable sod was contesting it with an—'

'Sorry, Richard,' Jon interrupted, seeing Rick had stood up to try and spot if Buchanon was in his office. 'We're just on our way out.'

'Right. I'm rambling. My apologies. Oldham. A body's just shown up there. My colleague says it's identical to the Russian.'

Jon started clicking his fingers at Rick. 'Identical?'

'Yes. Head hanging half off.'

His eyes were on Rick as he spoke into the mouthpiece. 'You mean another garrotting?'

Rick froze at the mention of the word.

Jon sat back down and turned to his computer. 'Is it on the system yet?'

'No. The locals are just assigning it a Force Wide Incident Number now. It'll show up any minute.'

'OK. Where in Oldham is your colleague?'

'It's a place called Hedley Court. A complex of flats, apparently.'

'Flats? Home Office-owned by any chance?'

'Yes. Used for housing asylum seekers.'

The local radio provided a backdrop of noise as they moved rapidly along the M60, this time heading in an anticlockwise direction, passing Ashton and continuing towards Oldham.

'More on the mystery notes turning up along the south-west coast,' the announcer said. 'Sam, you've been following this?'

'You mean the ones people have been finding in those rubber ducks?' the DJ's female sidekick replied. 'That story is ker-ray-zey!'

Rick glanced at Jon then turned the radio up.

'Spot on, darling! According to this report, it's the fourth letter our mystery writer has penned. It describes how six more of the poor souls stuck on the raft didn't survive the night. Check out the full letter on our website. In the meantime this, listeners, is the latest from Elbow. And we love it.'

As the track started up, Rick was already pressing buttons on his mobile phone. 'Come on, bloody connection speed on this thing can be shite. Here we go ... latest headlines ... shipwreck: new letter found.' He double-clicked and raised the screen closer to his face. 'Shall I just read it out?'

'Go ahead.'

'OK,' Rick replied.

LETTER FOUR

Last night was far more hateful than our first. With darkness, the wind became very angry. Many cried in terror as waves raced at us out of the night. Never have I known such blackness, only the white foam showed as the sea fell on us. All staggered as waves swept from one end of the raft to the other. I held on to my rope and many times I vomited sea water I had swallowed.

When sun showed on the horizon, the winds finally lost strength. More have not survived the night. The two women from Basra are gone and also the men from Pakistan. Sheren, the Kurdish mother has been drowned – her legs trapped in a gap between two pallets. She lay with her face beneath the water, her shivering son clinging to her back. As I cared for him, the man with the throat scars pulled the mother's legs free, so she could be rolled from the raft.

When the crewman gave us numbers for rations, he counted fifteen. With less numbers, everyone received an extra biscuit. Thankfully, the sun is warming us.

Parviz saw a ship just now. It was very far off. Many shouted until their voices became cracked. Slowly, it passed from our sight.

It is almost two days since we have been standing in salt water. The skin is coming from our feet and ankles. Everyone has removed their shoes. The pain is like many cuts from a knife.

We are so low in the water, I fear that is why the ship did not see us. I thought to attach the mirrors from Sura's and Zainab's bags to make a signal. Ali and the man with throat scars have made a mast with some long pieces of plastic and the mirrors are now tied to the top.

'For fuck's sake,' Jon murmured, glancing uneasily at his partner. 'I've got a horrible feeling this thing is for real.'

Rick nodded. 'I agree.' He scrolled down. 'It lists related pieces in the *Telegraph*, *Guardian*, *Independent*, *Mail*, *Express* and *Sun*.' He blinked. 'Most-read article on the website of *Al-Jazeera*, that Arab news service. The story has, as they say, officially broken.'

'She's smart, though,' Jon stated. 'Resourceful. Thinking to use the mirrors to reflect sunlight at any passing ship.'

'Yeah,' Rick replied. 'She isn't giving in, that's for sure.'

Ten minutes later they were pulling into Hedley Court, a confusing cluster of three-storey flats, each angular building positioned slightly askew to its neighbours so the concrete path connecting them zigzagged back and forth.

An elderly lady wearing dark grey robes and a shawl over her head was sitting on some stone steps, tossing fragments of bread to a group of fussing pigeons. Her head was turned away from the birds, as if she was afraid her act of charity might cause them some embarrassment.

They got to the block containing flats 61 to 80, where a uniformed officer stood at the door.

'DI Spicer, DS Saville,' Jon announced. 'Major Incident Team.'

Their names were added to the list and the officer stepped aside. 'Floor above. You can't miss it.'

As they reached the first landing, a familiar smell became

apparent. 'Bloody hell,' said Jon, twitching his nose. 'What is it about being garrotted?'

'Might just be a blocked toilet,' Rick replied hopefully.

'Now you're talking crap.' Jon grinned, pushing the door to the first floor open. Further down the corridor, a scene of crime officer was crouching before the type of box fishermen favour for storing tackle. For a moment, Jon thought it was Nikki Kingston. Things were still a little awkward, even though the pass she'd made at him was now several years ago. But then he caught sight of the woman's profile and realised he didn't know who she was. The door to her right was open.

'Any spare face masks?' Jon asked as he approached.

She looked over her shoulder then held a couple up. 'Be my guest.'

Jon clamped one over his nose and mouth before examining the door frame. No sign of forced entry. He peered into the flat. Another SOCO was inside, this one wearing the full white suit. Kneeling near the body on the sofa was the pathologist. She was shining a small torch into the gaping slit that was once the victim's throat. Jon's eyes bounced away from the glistening wound, trying to seek something normal to look at. Fine specks of blood seemed to have settled like dewdrops around the room. He ended up closing his eyes. 'Chart toppers got a joint number one, then?'

He heard a rustling sound and an exhalation of breath. When he looked again, the pathologist was standing. 'DI Spicer?'

'Correct.'

'Richard said you'd probably be here soon. Same as your last one?'

'Appears so. Did Richard ask you to check for hairs along the top of the sofa?'

She navigated the line of footplates leading back to the door. 'He did. Two indentations, but no hairs this time.'

Jon sneaked another glance at the body. Both legs were thrust straight out, one arm draped across his lap, the other hanging limply at his side. 'Any damage to his fingers?'

'None. Caught him completely by surprise. Whoever did this is a very nasty piece of work.'

Jon looked down the corridor. 'Would you hazard a guess when he came to visit?'

The pathologist stared at the corpse. 'With this hot weather, it's hard to say. I don't know if his heating has been on.'

'Let's assume it wasn't: he's destitute. Living off vouchers.'

'Late last night, then?' the pathologist ventured. 'Best I can say at this stage.'

Probably when I was getting filleted by Braithwaite's wife, Jon thought. 'Who found the body?'

'The person in flat sixty-five.' She looked at the SOCO. 'What was he? Eastern European, I should think.'

'One of those countries,' the man replied. 'He'd arranged to play chess with the victim at the local community centre. The uniforms have taken him off for statementing.'

'Hill Square nick?' Jon asked, picturing the big station next to Oldham's law courts.'

'I think so.'

'OK. Did the uniforms recover any ID?'

'No. They had a peek then shut the door and called it in.'

'Could you have a quick scout round? He should have something called an Application Registration Card. Same size as a cashpoint card, pinky-bluish colour with a little photo on it. There'll be the Border Agency logo at the top.'

The SOCO inside the flat raised a hand. 'I saw some stuff. Hang on.'

Jon had just snapped on a pair of latex gloves when the officer reappeared. 'These were on the bedside table.'

Taking the pile of letters, Jon examined the uppermost one. An IS90 granting temporary leave to stay in the UK. Below it was another detailing a date for his substantive interview at Dallas Court. Home Office reference T8471988. Jon scanned the letter for a name. 'Here we go. Yegor Tsarev. Russian. Just like the other one.' He flipped the sheet over for details of who the case owner was. 'Well, well, well.'

'What?' Rick asked, craning his neck to see what the letter said.

'Case owner for our man, here. A certain Her Majesty's Inspector Derek Marlow.'

'His caseload just keeps getting lighter,' Rick snorted.

'Doesn't it?' Jon replied, retrieving his notebook and phone. He turned to the page where he'd jotted Marlow's details down. Moments later, his call was answered. 'Morning, Derek. DI Spicer here. We talked the other day about a murder investigation?'

'Yes, morning, Jon. I've just sat down at my desk with a brew. A moment's peace before the doors get thrown open.'

Jon pictured the mass of people waiting outside the screening unit. Flotsam and jetsam looking for a home. 'Well, you can cancel the substantive interview you had lined up for a Yegor Tsarev at Dallas Court this Friday.' He glanced at the letter. 'At two forty.'

Silence. 'Two forty? Sorry, my brain's not quite in gear, yet. I'm interviewing who at that time?'

'Yegor Tsarev. Or you were. I'm looking at his body. Someone's almost taken his head off.'

'He's dead?'

'Oh yes. Very.'

'Gosh.'

'Listen, can you make sure you're free in about an hour's time? Dig out everything you've got on him, we're setting off for your office now.'

'No problem. DI Spicer, when you arrive, head round the side of the building. There's a staff entrance there. Saves you battling through the queue at the front.'

'OK, cheers.'

Alice stood in the airlock of the mental health unit, eyes fixed on the surface of the inner door. Come on, come on, she thought, stamping down on her mounting sense of unease.

The nursing assistant finally finished what he was writing then released the lock without even looking up. Alice stepped through into an aroma of tinned tomatoes and scrambled egg. 'Farts.'

The nursing assistant glanced up. 'Pardon?'

Alice's hand shot to her mouth. 'Did I say that out loud? Sorry.'

He smirked good-naturedly. 'Just slipped out, did it?'

'Yes. It was meant to be silent.' They grinned at each other for a moment. 'How's things?'

'You know. Busy as ever.' His eyes went back on the form he'd been filling in. 'Three referrals, no beds.'

'Familiar story. I'm here to see Nathaniel Musoso. Is he ...?'

The young man waved to the empty corridor. 'In bed, I think. That's where you can usually find him.'

Probably because of all the bloody sedatives that have been shoved down his throat, Alice almost replied. 'Thanks.'

She set off, eyes straying into the female bays as she passed them. A woman sat slumped in bed, staring mournfully at the doorway. Alice nodded but the woman didn't seem to see her. She turned the corner, passing the row of single-occupancy rooms and crossing into the male half of the ward.

Nathaniel was lying on his side and from the shape of him beneath the sheets, she could tell his knees were drawn up to his chest. Every other bed in the bay was empty and she saw his bottle of Ribena was almost gone. 'Nathaniel.' The back of his head shot off the pillow. 'It's me, Alice.'

'Alice.' He settled again. 'Hello.'

Seeing that he wasn't going to sit up, she moved round the bed so she could see his face. 'How are you?'

'I am sad.'

She gave a small smile. 'Are you feeling less anxious now?'

His eyes half closed and he answered in a flat voice. 'They will send me back there, Alice.'

'That's bollocks, Nathaniel, pardon my language. We've contacted the Border Agency to express our concern. They're aware you've been admitted to hospital. Nothing will happen while you're here.'

He remained staring off into space.

'And, in the meantime,' she said, sitting on the edge of the bed and leaning forward, 'we'll be fighting your case.'

'You cannot fight them.'

She shook her head. 'That's not true.' She glanced at the bottle on the bedside table. 'You've got through that Ribena. It's almost vanished.'

'The other men took it.'

Her sense of dismay was quickly replaced by outrage. 'Which other men?'

His gaze moved and she saw how the whites of his eyes were tinged yellow at the edges. 'The big man who is in the corner.'

She glanced over. 'There's no one there.'

'He is watching television. He is the big man.'

She paused. 'Big man? He's large?'

'No, he's the big man. The one who is in charge.'

The big man, Alice thought. Most mental health units developed a hierarchy of patients, with one dominant personality at the top. Similar, she gathered, to prisons.

'He mocks me, sometimes. I think he took my tobacco, also.'

'Your tobacco has been stolen?'

'Yes.'

The shits, she thought. That was so unfair. 'Don't worry, I'll get you some more. You must keep your things in your locker, Nathaniel. Where they'll be safe.'

'OK.'

She placed a hand on his head and felt the wiry press of his sparse curls against her palm. The sensation conjured images of scrubland, parched dry by a pitiless sun. 'I'll also have a word with the staff for you.'

'OK.'

'Try not to worry, Nathaniel. You're not alone. We're here for you.'

'I know. Thank you, Alice.'

'I'll nip to the shop and get you some more things. Then I'll need to get going. Is that OK?'

'You are very kind.'

As she walked back round the corner, her feelings of anger stirred. This bloody place, she thought. It's the last place someone with mental health problems should end up. As she drew level with the first of the male single-occupancy rooms, she slowed down to glance through the small window. The young man she'd glimpsed on her previous visit was still inside, lying on his back, eyes closed. Alice's eyes lingered on the delicate bone structure of his face, the smooth curve of his skull. He looks so peaceful, she thought, continuing round to the reception desk.

'Excuse me,' she said gently, seeing a different nursing assistant behind it. 'My name's Alice Spicer.' She waited for her name to connect, and a second later the man's demeanour altered.

He looked at her expectantly, like a waiter hovering to take an order. 'How can I help?'

Amazing, Alice thought. And all because I'm seeing one of the consultant psychiatrists. 'Nathaniel Musoso has mentioned the theft of some of his personal items. Taken by the man in bed one, bay number three.'

The assistant sighed, reaching for a plan of the ward. 'Tony Garrett. We should fit a revolving door at the entrance. This is a second home for him.'

Alice thought about the Salford Tool for Assessment of Risk. Every person admitted on to the unit was assessed according to five categories: violence, self-harm or suicide, serious self-neglect, behaviour, exploitation and vulnerability. 'Surely Nathaniel scored highly for vulnerability on the STAR test?'

'Yes, he did.'

'Could he not be allocated a single room, then?'

The assistant chuckled. 'He can join the queue.'

Should have guessed, Alice thought. 'What's his care plan, by the way? Is he on much medication?'

'Antidepressants and selective serotonin reuptake inhibitors to deal with his PTSD symptoms.'

'He's been diagnosed with post-traumatic stress disorder?'

'By the on-call psychiatrist when the police brought him in. Emotional numbness, enhanced startle reaction.'

Alice thought of how Nathaniel had jumped when she'd said his name. It would help in their fight to stop him being deported. 'Cognitive behavioural therapy?'

'If he's here long enough. Psychiatrist rounds are tomorrow. In fact,' he continued, stumbling slightly over his words, 'isn't he under Phillip Braithwaite?'

He didn't mention that he was actually overseeing Nathaniel's care plan, Alice thought, making a mental note to broach the subject with Phillip. 'Oh – the single-occupancy room at the male end of the corridor. What's the score with the patient in there?'

The nursing assistant made a sour face. 'You know what? Your guess is as good as ours—'

The panel on the wall with the floor plan of the ward displayed on it suddenly started emitting a rapid series of beeps. The assistant peered at it for an instant. 'Staff member needs assistance in the washroom.' He started round the desk.

'How do you mean?' Alice persisted, stepping out of his way.

'File's been mislaid by the Royal Liverpool University Hospital.' He hurried off, talking over his shoulder as he went. 'That or it's been lost in transit. We're not sure which.'

Twelve

Jon half mounted the pavement of the road running down the side of Reliance House and slapped a police notice on the dashboard. As they got out of the car, a sudden shower started peppering the dry tarmac around them. Jon hurried across to the side entrance, feeling a pattern of cold dots spreading across the thin fabric of his shirt.

A couple of men stood within the doorway, cigarettes in their hands, looking up at the clear sky with surprised expressions.

'We're here to see Inspector Marlow,' Jon announced. 'Can we get in?'

'Doors are open,' one replied, glancing up once again. 'Where's that bloody rain coming from?'

'Wherever it is, I'll take it,' his colleague answered. 'My garden's more like the Gobi bloody desert.'

Jon pushed open the black glass door and they found themselves at the inner desk, the main waiting room immediately to their left. 'Hello,' Jon said to the security guard. 'We're here to see Derek Marlow. He's expecting us.'

The man nodded then reached for a phone. 'Derek?'

Jon almost winced as the 'k' rasped across the roof of the man's mouth.

'Couple of gentlemen to see you down here.' He hung up. 'He's on his way.'

A tiny man and woman emerged uncertainly from the entrance lobby, dark brown faces etched with anxiety. They stared at Jon and Rick in silence.

Jon stared back until he realised that they were awaiting instructions. He glanced at the member of staff, who noticed them for the first time. 'In there,' he jabbed a thumb at the doors to the main waiting area.

As the couple continued through, the door by the side of the desk opened with a loud click. Marlow beckoned to them. 'Hello again.'

Climbing the stairs to the first floor, the Border Agency officer glanced back over his shoulder. 'Do you think the same person killed the man you found this morning?'

Jon tilted his head. 'Same technique. Which is, to say the least, unusual.'

The inspector swiped the lock at the top of the stairs and they made their way back to his desk. 'Here's the file. Not a great deal more than on the first victim, to be honest. I'd processed him, set a date for his substantive interview and was just about to run a few background checks.'

'He said he was from Russia,' Rick stated, taking a seat.

Marlow nodded. 'He did.'

Remembering how Rick had been cold-shouldered on their previous visit for not supporting any sports team, Jon raised an eyebrow at his partner. Looks like you exist again. 'What else did he say?'

Marlow ran a finger over the top sheet. 'Yegor Tsarev. Worked for a business supplying equipment to one of the big gas companies out there. The owner of said gas company currently resides in a rather large flat in Mayfair. He has claimed political asylum and President Putin is currently demanding his immediate extradition back to Russia.'

Jon sat up. 'So the guy's story is actually true?' Finally, he thought. We've got something to run with.

Marlow gave a shake of his head. 'Don't get your hopes up. It's true the man resides in Mayfair, along with several billion dollars.'

'Something tells me,' Rick said, 'he didn't go through any screening interview in this place.'

A dry chuckle escaped Marlow. 'He probably flew in on a private jet and was waved straight through to his London residency.'

'What about Tsarev?' Jon asked.

'Well, the company name he gave me is real enough. But they have no record of a Yegor Tsarev in any department.'

'So, it's all bullshit,' Jon sighed, sitting back.

'Seems so. I was going to have him pulled too – next time he reported into Dallas Court.'

Jon picked at the corner of Marlow's desk. 'Anything show up on the fingerprint check?'

'No – if it had, I wouldn't have given him temporary leave to remain.'

Pressing his palms together, Jon ran his fingertips down both sides of his nose. Two Russians, two garrottings, probably within hours of each other. Someone knew the pair was in the country, along with their exact whereabouts.

'When did you interview these two men?' Rick asked. 'Was it on the same day?'

Marlow nodded. 'They were brought in together. From the hospital.'

'From the hospital?'

'Yes – that's where they'd been first taken when the fishing boat docked.'

'Hang on,' Jon said, sitting up again. 'Tsarev was also rescued by the trawler that found Dubinski?'

'Correct.'

'What was the story again?'

Marlow consulted his notes. 'An unidentified ship from St Petersburg set them down in a lifeboat. Somewhere in the Irish Sea, probably. But they'd had problems – the tide carried them away from the coast, not towards it and they'd drifted for several days before the trawler found them.'

'This sounds like the bloody story in the press at the moment,' Jon said incredulously. 'It was a lifeboat they were in, not a raft?'

Marlow smiled. 'No, a lifeboat. And no mention of rubber ducks, either. They were in quite bad shape though, I gather. Hence the overnight stay in hospital.'

'This lifeboat,' Rick said quietly, eyes on the floor. 'Were there any other Russians rescued from it?'

Jon glanced at Rick. Good point, mate. His eyes moved back to Marlow and he saw the other man had stiffened ever so slightly. The inspector's eyes dropped to the file and he tried to clear his throat. Jesus Christ, Jon thought, there were others, weren't there?

Marlow pored over his notes. 'Yes. Two others. Four were brought in by the trawler.'

Jon almost spread both palms in a gesture of incredulity. We ring you to say a second Russian claiming asylum has been garrotted. You didn't spot a pattern emerging here? 'Who are the other two?'

Marlow swivelled in his seat, punched a password into his computer and activated a drop-down menu. 'Sorry. This is hardly your run-of-the-mill event. It just didn't occur to me.'

'Don't worry about it,' Jon murmured, rolling his eyes at Rick.

'What's the date on Tsarev's file?' Marlow asked.

Rick leaned across and closed it so he could see the cover. 'Eighteenth of August.'

Marlow tapped on a few keys and the screen filled with names. 'We processed over two hundred and seventy that day,' he whispered at the screen. 'Easy to forget details. Now, sort by nationality. Russia. Here we go.' His voice became louder. 'Two more. Andriy Bal and Vladimir Yashin.'

Rick raised an eyebrow. 'Ten quid says they're made-up names.'

Marlow got to his feet and called across the room. 'Stewart, you picked up a case on the eighteenth. Reference number ...' He flexed his knees to examine the screen. 'B8471872. The B stands for Bal.'

A man of about thirty looked up, hair swept forward as if he'd been sticking his head under a hand-drier. 'And?'

'Could we have the file, please? It's urgent.'

The man started sorting through the pile on his desk.

'What about the fourth one?' Rick asked.

Marlow bent down to regard his screen once again. He straightened back up and surveyed the room. 'Is Jim Price in today?'

'Manchester,' someone called back. 'Substantive interviews at Dallas Court.'

Marlow turned to Rick and Jon. 'That's where the file will be. I'll bring up the copy stored on the system.' He sat back down, pressed a couple of buttons, frowned, then pressed them again. 'Has anybody else's computer ...'

A chorus of groans started to ripple across the room. Heads starting going up.

Marlow looked over to the young woman in the corner. 'Natalie?'

'I'm phoning them now,' she called back.

Marlow sat back down, palms slapping against the tops of his thighs. 'Every time the system crashes we have to ring a bloody IT company down in London. I think the government would contract out the supply of air in this place, if they could.'

The young inspector walked over, holding Bal's file before him like it was a drinks tray. 'Sir ordered a White Russian?'

'I could bloody do with one,' Marlow muttered, taking it from the man's hands and opening the cover. 'Let's see – he had his first reporting event already. Substantive interview scheduled for this Thursday.' He glanced up. 'What were your thoughts, Stewart?'

The man thrust both hands into his pockets. 'His story wasn't checking out.'

'No surprise there. On what grounds was he claiming—'

Jon cut in. 'Sorry – let's worry about that later. What I need to know is where the man is now.'

'Of course.' Marlow's face reddened and he bowed over the file once again. 'Not far away, as it happens. Runcorn.'

Runcorn? Jon pictured the succession of roundabouts connecting an industrial landscape. 'I didn't think anyone actually lived there.'

'Well, the Home Office has found some housing stock somewhere in the area,' Marlow replied, extending the file towards Jon.

'Where is Runcorn?' Rick asked.

'Next to Widnes,' Jon replied, writing the address down. 'Top of the Mersey estuary.'

'What do you reckon?' Rick asked, hands on knees in readiness to stand. 'Call for local support?'

Jon glanced to the windows. 'We could be there in the time they take to respond. Let's go for it.'

They both stood and Jon gestured at the door. 'Can we get out without a pass?'

'No,' Marlow replied. 'I'll have to escort you down.'

Rick flicked a business card onto Marlow's desk. 'My mobile's on that. Can you call your colleague with the other file? We'll need that fourth Russian's address as quick as possible.'

Jon and Rick sped along the A561, the Mersey glinting away on their right-hand side. The road took them inland, skirting round Liverpool John Lennon.

Jon stared for a moment at a huge sign for the airport. 'Wish they'd get over The Beatles.'

Rick frowned. 'World's most famous band.'

Jon pushed his bottom lip up. 'You reckon? Overrated, if you ask me. Scousers? They just cling to the past.'

'Surely you're not knocking them for celebrating the fact The Beatles came from Liverpool?'

'Do you get roads in Manchester named after Oasis?' Jon responded, provocatively. 'Joy Division? The Smiths? Happy Mondays? Stone Roses? Doves? Elbow? Those Scousers have even preserved that cellar where The Beatles used to play. Turned into some sort of shrine. Or grotto. Go down there and you'll find groups of fat fifty-year-olds who start blubbing every time "She Loves Me" gets played on the jukebox. Pathetic. Time they moved on.'

Rick shook his head. 'What is it with this antagonism? Two great cities, almost touching. Football teams, rugby teams, amazing music. You lot should be proud.'

Realising Rick hadn't detected the note of sarcasm in his voice, Jon fought back a smirk. But he knew plenty of people – Mancunians and Liverpudlians alike – whose main reason for living was based on a hatred for the other city. Which was ironic, he reflected, because they were precisely the people who would mourn most if the other city were to somehow ever vanish.

The road started to rise up, the pale green girders of the Runcorn Bridge rearing above them like the struts of a roller-coaster ride. As they crossed the Manchester Ship Canal where it emptied into the Mersey estuary, he glanced down at the dirty-looking water. 'Why do Manchester's toilets have such a strong flush?'

Rick sighed. 'Do tell me.'

'It's a long way to Liverpool.'

His partner managed a resigned smile.

Jon grinned, amused at how his partner just didn't get the rivalry between the two cities. 'Right, Marlow said to continue to the big roundabout and take the turn-off for Weston Point.' He nodded at the sprawl of chimneys, storage tanks and industrial buildings away to their right. 'That bloody huge eyesore, over there.'

The roundabout's curve took them almost back on themselves before a slip road allowed them onto a dual carriageway which led towards the massive chemical works. 'OK, take the first turning and then look for some sort of apartment building set off the main road.'

A minute later, a seventies-style block of flats came into view. 'Stanhope Road,' Rick said, pointing to the sign partially obscured by weeds springing up out of the heavily cracked pavement. 'This is it.'

Jon turned right and the road led them into the vast parking area which surrounded the building. Four cars were grouped near the main entrance. He looked across the empty ocean of asphalt to a row of five pine trees on the car park's far side. 'No cars. How the hell do the poor bastards get about?'

'Bus, by the looks of it.' Rick pointed to a shelter further down the road. Over a dozen people were huddled in its shade. Those who couldn't fit in were sitting on the kerb, staring across at their vehicle.

'Grim,' Jon said, pulling up beside a Mini Metro with a rear panel that was crumpled and scratched. He opened the door and immediately felt the sun beating down on his head. The shower which caught us in Liverpool must have passed this way too, he thought, looking at the rapidly diminishing remains of a puddle near the Metro's rear wheels. In its middle, the body of a pale and bloated worm bowed slowly back and forth. 'Come on, then. Flat forty-six.'

The lobby of the building was cool and gloomily lit. Jon squinted at the sheet of A4 paper stuck to the lift. 'An engineer has been notified. Looks like that's been stuck there for weeks.'

They started up the stairs and had reached the first-floor landing when the sound of quickly approaching footsteps caused Jon to slow. A man with closely cropped hair and wearing a black turtleneck top was bouncing down the steps towards them. Their eyes connected for a moment and his expression caused Jon to step aside. Once they'd reached the next flight, he looked back at Rick. 'Wouldn't like to bump into him at night in a dark alley.'

Rick peered down the stairwell. 'Didn't notice him.'

'Scary. Looked like someone had just given him some seriously bad news.' They continued up to the fourth floor and Jon pushed through the door into the corridor. The flat directly in front had the number forty on its door. 'Must be just along here,' Jon murmured, looking to his left and then flaring his nostrils. 'Can you smell …?'

Rick nodded. 'Definitely.'

Jon saw a door was slightly ajar further down the corridor and he hurried towards it, the aroma growing stronger with every step. Flat forty-six. Using his elbow, he pushed the door inwards, immediately spotting a man sitting on the sofa. His head was tilted back to expose the yawning wound that was his throat.

Jon retreated a step and turned to Rick. 'There's a body in there,' he hissed.

Rick peered round Jon into the flat. 'Christ. What do we do?'

Jon thought for a second. 'I'll lead. Keep your eyes on the doorways leading off from this room. Any movement, shout.'

Cautiously, he pushed the door fully open, and dipping his head, quickly glanced behind it. Clear. 'That guy's only just died,' he whispered, edging a step further into the flat and quickly checking the tiny bedroom and bathroom. Empty. Suddenly, a shrill noise rang out and Jon almost leapt up in the air.

Rick fumbled for his phone. 'DS Saville.' There was a slight tremble in his voice. 'Oh. Yes, Marlow mentioned you have a file – sorry? Right, that would be great, cheers.' He snapped his phone closed, unable to peel his eyes from the corpse. 'That was Jim Price. Marlow's colleague doing the interviews in Manchester.'

'Yeah? Well, he almost gave me a bloody heart attack,' Jon murmured, stepping lightly over to the galley kitchen and glancing in again. 'What did he want?'

'The fourth Russian, Vladimir Yashin. He failed to show up to his substantive interview. Price sent someone from Enforcement and Compliance to check his address. No sign of the bloke.' His phone pinged. 'This'll be his mugshot. The system's back up so Price said he was sending it.'

Jon was now examining the bedroom. Sheets were in a frozen cascade over the end of the single bed and a pillow was crumpled against the flimsy-looking headboard. He turned back to study the body. The man's eyes were actually still moist. There was surprise and dismay on his face. Jon extended a finger and held it to a blood-free patch of skin behind one ear. Minutes, Jon thought. He was killed minutes ago.

'Someone's been hitting this guy with the ugly stick,' Rick said in a muted voice.

Jon glanced over and Rick turned the phone so its screen was visible. He felt his eyes widen. 'The stairs! We just passed him on the stairs!' He bolted back out of the flat, sprinted down the corridor and starting bounding down them, left shoulder bouncing off the wall as he reached each landing. Seconds later he got to the lobby and raced outside. Bright sunlight hit him and he cupped a hand over his brow, eyes sweeping the car park. No movement except the shimmer of heat rising from the tarmac.

'The bus stop,' Rick breathlessly announced behind him. They jogged over. 'Hello, anyone speak English?'

The people regarded them in silence.

'We're police,' Jon said, holding his warrant card up. Shoulders suddenly hunched and faces looked down. 'Does anyone speak English?'

An elderly man with leathery skin got up from the kerb, the hook of his nose casting a shadow across his lips. 'I speak English.'

Jon gestured at the tower block. 'A man. Black top, short brown hair. Tanned. He came out of that building just now. Did you see him?'

The person frowned then spoke rapidly in Arabic to the watching group. A woman with a beige headscarf nodded, hand fluttering as she spoke. Her fingers looked like they were shooing off an insect.

The elderly man looked back at Jon. 'She says the man drove off. His car was red. The one next to yours.'

Jon looked across at his dark blue Mondeo. Next to it was a partial tyre track where the Mini Metro with the dented rear had reversed through the puddle. Like a row of dark hyphens, the damp imprints led across the car park, fading to nothing well before the exit.

Thirteen

The sun had just started to sink behind the row of five pine trees. Jon eyed their finger-like shadows creeping across the car park with suspicion, as if they were readying themselves to snatch the building and its crime scene away.

'Oh, and I brought you these.'

He turned to Marlow, thinking it was somehow strange to see the man outside of Reliance House.

The inspector fished two cans of Vimto from his shoulder bag. 'You Mancunians love this stuff, don't you? They're quite cold. I was told there are no shops anywhere near this place.'

Reaching out a hand, Jon took one and popped the tab. 'Cheers. And thanks for taking the trouble to bring us Yashin's file.'

'No problem. It's nice to get out of the office.'

As Marlow handed the other can to Rick, a van trundled into view, coming to a stop outside the front of the building. Jon watched as a uniformed officer hopped out and opened the rear doors, releasing the group who'd been waiting at the bus shelter. Earlier, they'd been taken away to give statements at a Liverpool police station.

The elderly man he'd spoken to earlier approached, the baggy folds of his pale cotton trousers flaring with each step. 'I am concerned,' he announced. 'We all are. Our interviews were earlier this afternoon. The police officers were not interested, but our asylum claims can be rejected because of this.'

Jon turned to Marlow. 'Can you sort that out for them?'

Marlow sighed then removed a notepad from his bag. 'Let me have all your ARC cards,' he said to the elderly man. 'I'll note your reference numbers down and contact your case owners to explain.'

'And our claims will not suffer?'

'They won't suffer,' Marlow replied wearily.

The man started relaying the information to group. Jon continued watching the old man. He had a certain air of authority about him. 'Could I ask,' he said, continuing to address him with exaggerated slowness. 'What were you back home?'

The man drew in breath. 'I was head of the economics department at An-Najah University, Palestine.'

Christ, thought Jon. And there's me talking to you like you're thick. 'Well, thanks for your help.'

He turned to his car, where Rick was sitting with the file on Vladimir Yashin that Marlow had just delivered. Jon's eyes lingered on the man's mugshot. Same guy as they'd passed on the stairs, absolutely no doubt about it. He looked off to the side, eyes snagging on the remains of the worm near his vehicle. The Metro must have reversed over it when Yashin had driven away. The sun had then dried the creature out, so the body now resembled a mangled rubber band.

So close, Jon cursed. So bloody close to catching him. 'Anything of use?'

Rick raised one shoulder then let it drop. 'Not really. He was destitute, like the three victims. And, according to Jim Price's notes, none of the information initially given checked out. All we've got is the photo and his fingerprints.'

Jon finished off his drink, placed the can on the roof of his car and looked wistfully at the block of flats. A white crime-scene van was parked by the entrance, along with two marked police cars. Despite an immediate call, no patrol had spotted the Metro on nearby roads. 'I don't suppose forensics will find much. Not if the other two crime scenes are anything to go by.'

'No. Probably the same story for Yashin's flat, too.'

'Where was he being housed?'

'Cheetham Hill. Buchanon sent a team over to check his accommodation.'

'Who?'

'Gardiner and Murray.'

Jon nodded. The two detectives were also part of Buchanon's

syndicate and both had years of experience handling crime scenes. 'I still want to have a look at it myself.'

'I never doubted anything different.'

A silver Passat pulled into the car park and Jon straightened up. 'Speak of the devil. Buchanon's here.' The vehicle eased to a stop beside them and Jon watched as their senior officer climbed out and self-consciously passed a hand over the tight crimps in his light brown hair. Why, Jon thought, do you bother? A hammer and chisel couldn't make an impression on your barnet. 'Afternoon, boss.'

Their eyes met for a moment, then Buchanon flexed his knees. 'Hello, Jon. Bit of a trek getting here.'

Jon caught Buchanon's odd expression and was trying to make sense of it as his senior officer glanced about. 'Strange place for a block of flats.'

Rick spoke up. 'It used to house workers for one of the industrial plants by the estuary. Long since closed down.'

'Hello, Rick,' Buchanon replied, a patch of sunlight catching in his hair as he regarded the building. 'Same MO as the other two, then?'

'Identical,' Jon replied. 'A length of wire or something similar looped round the neck from behind. Considerable force causing a laceration right through the cartilage.'

'I can't believe you actually passed him on the stairs.'

Jon felt the corners of his mouth curl down. 'I know. I'm gutted.'

'But you got a decent enough look at him?'

'Yes. No doubt it was the man using the name Vladimir Yashin. Short brown hair, wiry build, five ten or so. He looked like he'd just killed someone, too. Didn't I say to you, Rick? He had this look in his eyes. It made me step out of his way.'

Buchanon held a hand towards the group gathered around Marlow. 'Witnesses?'

'Well, they spotted our man leaving the building and driving off in a red Mini Metro.'

'Registration?'

Jon closed his eyes momentarily, searching the image in his

mind once again. He could still make out the individual dents in the car's bodywork. 'It ended in an X. That's all we've got.'

Buchanon sniffed. 'Get someone to check the stolen car list. He was living in Cheetham Hill without any means of transport. Chances are he took it from around there.'

'Will do.'

'Now we have his prints, we can recheck the other crime scenes more carefully. Ascertain if he was there, or not.'

'True,' Jon replied. 'We nearly lost the first one, sir. I'd just given permission for the Home Office to have it cleaned when I received word about the second victim.'

Buchanon crossed his arms. 'Well, maybe luck will be on our side. In the meantime, I'll get on to Interpol, Europol and the Russian embassy. I strongly suspect this guy will feature on a database somewhere.'

'OK.' Jon turned to the building once again, the sequence of events following their arrival replaying in his head. *Five minutes earlier and we'd have had this bastard.*

'One more thing, Jon. A quick word, if you don't mind.'

He looked at his senior officer who was now walking away from the car towards the middle of the empty car park. *This, he thought, explains the odd look when you arrived.* He followed the other man. The strength of the sun was finally fading and he could feel the warmth leaching back out of the dark tarmac beneath his feet.

'I've had a call from a member of the public. Not a complaint, but a concern,' Buchanon said quietly, coming to a stop and turning round.

Braithwaite's wife. It has to be, Jon thought. He felt his face flush and wondered if it could be attributed to the waves of heat rising up from the ground.

'A gentleman called Phillip Braithwaite.'

Shit, Jon thought. She went and rang him.

'He's the one now seeing Alice, is that right?' Buchanon asked.

Jon nodded.

Buchanon sucked in air through his nostrils then held up a

hand. 'I don't know what you're up to, visiting his wife like you did. And, seeing as the man didn't make an official complaint, I don't want to know, either. But whatever you're up to, Jon, it stops now. Understood?'

Jon concealed his surprise. *I turn up at his wife's house, pretty much accusing him of propositioning teenage prostitutes and all he does is express concern at my visit? That's not the reaction of someone with nothing to hide.* He gave a single nod.

'Good.' Buchanon went to step away then paused. 'Everything OK with you? I know it's not easy: you and Alice living apart.'

'Yeah – things are a bit shit at the moment.'

'Where are you living?'

Jon pictured Carmel. Buchanon certainly didn't need to know he'd moved in with the *Chronicle*'s head crime reporter. 'An apartment in the Northern Quarter.'

'Yours?'

'No – a friend. Kind of.'

'Well – if you need a bit of breathing space, we can assign this case to another team. It won't be a problem.'

Breathing space? Jon almost laughed. Are you joking? It's stuff like this that keeps me from going bloody mad. 'I'm fine, sir. Thanks. Hopefully me and Alice will sort things out between us.'

Buchanon held his eyes for a second longer. 'Well, the offer's there. I'll get back to Manchester. When are you heading in?'

'Soon. I just want to check everything once again. The fact he was actually here ... I don't know. There might be something in the crime scene we've overlooked.'

'Your shout. Let's speak later.'

Jon lingered as Buchanon's car pulled away. Once he'd turned the corner, Rick's head poked out of the Mondeo. 'What was that about?'

'Nothing much,' he replied, setting off for the block of flats. 'Just taking one more look. I'll be five minutes.'

Rick gave a resigned nod, leaned back in the passenger seat and tilted the can of drink to his lips.

★

Inside the building, Jon climbed the stairs two at a time, the smell of human faeces hitting him as he entered the fourth-floor corridor. The corpse was still sitting on the sofa and the phalanx of three SOCOs gathering evidence gave him a regal air. A king, attended to on his throne.

Hands in pockets, Jon stood in the doorway watching. He knew every crime scene began immediately to deteriorate with time. The presence of people, or mere currents of air caused by their movement, could lead to fragments of evidence shifting and the narrative they told being lost. This was the golden time, never to be regained. 'Can you dust for prints on the frame, here?' he suddenly asked, nodding to his left. In his mind, he imagined the man stepping up to the door. Did he lean a hand against the wall, listening for a moment before knocking? 'And the corridor wall immediately around it. Just the area between waist and shoulder height.'

He heard a door open further down the corridor and an over-weight black man stepped out, a mobile phone in his hand.

'Is the man really dead?' he asked in a sonorous voice.

Jon moved towards him, anxious to stop him from getting too close. 'He is. Can you use the other stairwell, please?'

Stepping back, the man drew in air between the spaces of his teeth before muttering to himself, 'He owed me money.'

Jon had half turned to the crime scene. He glanced back. 'Sorry?'

The other man held up his phone. 'He borrowed this to make a call. My credit is now almost gone.'

Rapidly, Jon closed the gap between them. 'When was this?'

'Five days ago? It is here in my call history. Six minutes and eleven seconds. Over two pounds fifty.'

'Can I see, please?' Jon asked, taking out his notebook.

'Yes. It is recorded here.' The man pressed a few buttons and showed Jon the screen.

4:15 pm, 21 August 2008. 6 mins, 11 se cs.

Jon looked to the next line of text. Oh, you beauty. The phone number was right there. Jon scribbled it down. 'What did the man say to you, when he borrowed your phone?'

'He did not speak English. He knocked on my door, making a telephone with his hand. Then rubbing his fingers to say he would pay. Which country is he from?'

'Russia.'

'Ah, Russia.' The man gave a knowing nod, as if it was common practice in that country to borrow phones and then avoid paying for the calls by being murdered. 'I should not have trusted this man.'

'And what is your name, please?'

He hesitated before replying in a low voice. 'Victor Labon.'

'And the number of your phone, Victor?'

Reluctantly, the man gave it.

'And has anyone tried to call the man back?'

'No.'

Jon rummaged in his pocket then handed the man a five-pound note and his business card. 'Here – a reimbursement from Greater Manchester Police. Anything else about this man, call me. OK? Anything you might hear about him from other people in this building, I'll pay you.'

The man grimaced, teeth a perfect white in the gloom of the corridor. 'The reason I am here is because I did such things in my country. Governments change, and soon the police and their friends are got rid of too.'

'Well,' Jon said, card and money still held out. 'Governments also change in this country. But us lot? We're not about to be replaced by anyone.'

With a sad smile, the other man accepted the two items. Jon headed for the stairs, eyes on the phone number in his book. It was a landline with an 0207 prefix. The code for central London.

The sea before Oliver Brookes was ribboned with long white crests, giving the appearance of shallow steps receding towards the horizon. He imagined walking up them, striding across the glossy surface until he reached the giant red orb quivering in the distance.

With a gentle sigh, another small wave toppled onto the coarse sand. He closed his eyes, savouring the last of the day's heat. When he finally opened them again, the sun had disappeared.

In his arms were another seven ducks, left behind by the high tide. As he trudged across the sand, he held each one to his ear and shook it. All were free of water.

He reached the gate to his garden and the wind chime he'd fashioned from some lengths of washed-up bamboo began to tock as a light breeze stirred.

The mobile he'd been creating from the ducks now dominated his front garden. A central strut rose ten feet high with thin arms radiating off at erratic angles. From the end of each one hung a wooden coat hanger. From each of these dangled several ducks, all wearing the same vacant grin.

He sat down and lined his latest harvest up in the grass. From his shirt pocket, he produced his penknife and several lengths of twine. He picked up the first duck and removed the white plug from its base. Then he turned it over and with the penknife's spike began to gouge out a hole through the centre of its back. Once it was wide enough, he fed the end of some twine through, pinching the thumb and forefinger of his free hand together, so he could reach into the empty plug hole and extract the string from the duck's belly. He then repeatedly looped the twine on itself until the knot was larger than the hole in the duck's back. As he drew the string back out and replaced the white plug, the noise of an outboard motor reached his ears.

Les, he thought. Out checking his lobster pots. He looked across the small cove, but the boat had yet to round its rocky point. He stood up in readiness to flag the old fisherman down. His sack of potatoes was almost empty. Tinned produce was getting low. Milk powder and biscuits were pretty much gone. He had an account with the small store in the village and Les would happily ferry him supplies, accepting only a wooden sculpture as payment.

The boat came into view, but it was an inflatable, lying low in the water with the weight of the three men inside. He watched the vessel, water furling against its blunt prow, a pair of whisker-like lines trailing behind it.

The three men were all wearing odd clothes. Inappropriate choices for a boat. A black leather jacket. A white tracksuit top. One was wearing a red baseball cap and none had a buoyancy aid on. They were all facing inland and he knew they had seen him. He was about to raise a hand in salute, when something made him change his mind. The skinhead at the front turned slightly to say something to his companions. They continued to stare as the boat slowly skirted round the rocks at the other end of the small bay. Feeling faintly uneasy, Brookes turned back to his garden and the tree-like structure festooned with dozens of ducks.

Jon pushed the armchair round so it was facing the windows then sank down into it, the case file for Vladimir Yashin on his lap. Breath escaped his lips as he stretched his feet out. The tightly packed buildings of the city's Northern Quarter filled his immediate view, most now completely bathed in darkness. Beyond, the structures of Manchester's taller buildings loomed, the red lights at the top of the Beetham Tower marring his view of the moonlit sky.

A solitary figure appeared in the deserted street directly below, hood up, hands dangling at his sides, knees flexing needlessly and shoulders rolling backward with each step: the triumphant strut of those who felt that the streets of the city were theirs. This is me, the gait said, and I do what I want.

Jon wasn't surprised as the man began looking into each parked car, checking for briefcases, coats or anything of potential value. He moved from sight to continue his nocturnal scavenging elsewhere.

Seconds later, a smaller, silent, form glided into view. A fox. Ears alert, it skittered nervously along, pausing to lower its nose and test the exact parts of the pavement the man had just paced. An anxious pet, Jon thought, fallen behind its master.

The soft music coming from the speakers at his side started up again, the easy cadence of the banjo accompanied by a slowly beating drum. I'm a man you don't meet every day. The lids of Jon's eyes lowered as his mind went back to the night he'd spent with Alice in that Irish bar. I've got to stop listening to this album, he thought. It's messing with my head. But he didn't reach for the stop button. Instead, he remained motionless, remembering his certainty that, as good as the evening was, it was only going to get better. The pints of Guinness, the smoke, the singing. Alice's smiling face. He held the memory, not daring to breathe in case it should disintegrate.

Somewhere, a car's horn started to beep, the urgent repeats like an agitated animal calling for its young. He opened his eyes, lifted the bottle of rum from the floor at his side and examined the label. Havana Club, Cuban Barrel Proof. He looked for the strength. Forty-five per cent. Good choice, Carmel. After pouring some into a small glass, he took a sip and tracked its fiery descent.

Carmel. He pictured her face, the way her eyes lit up before that infectious laugh of hers rang out. Weird, the difference an age gap of ten years makes, he thought. Another time and another place, I could have really fallen for you. God knows, before having Holly, all I wanted was to go out, drinking in bars and eating in nice restaurants. But now? He regarded his glass. A relaxed meal at home was fine. A decent bottle of wine, music on low.

A brief tattoo on the drum announced the start of 'A Pair of Brown Eyes'. The song had never sounded sadder. He crossed his feet, sinking further down into the seat, the glass perched on his near-horizontal stomach. It's all wrong, he thought, picturing his old home with Alice and Holly asleep inside. His dog, Punch, living indefinitely in the house of his old rugby coach. This distance between us all should not exist.

The dark windows before him suddenly brightened with a strip of reflected light. He looked round the backrest of the chair and saw Carmel standing in the bedroom doorway, the buttons at the neck of her nightie all undone. 'What time is it?' she squinted.

'Late,' he whispered, guilt at what he'd just been thinking immediately filling him. 'You OK?'

'Yeah.' She scratched her head. 'What are you doing?'

'Just mulling over stuff. This case. Is the music too loud?'

'No. Are you coming to bed?'

'In a bit.'

'We've hardly seen each other recently.'

He sat back in his seat, addressing her reflection. 'I'm sorry – it gets like this sometimes with work. Once this blows over, how about I take you out for a meal? You choose the restaurant.'

She smiled. 'Deal.'

'Good.' He placed the glass on the floor and opened the file. From the corner of his eye he could still see her reflection. She stayed there a few moments longer and, when she eventually stepped back and pushed the door shut, he couldn't help feeling relieved.

Fourteen

Alice turned the corner of the corridor. At the other end of it, a stick-thin man was handing a bottle of Ribena over to a more heavily built individual. As she approached, they caught sight of her and the bottle vanished beneath the larger man's Manchester City top. Tony Garrett, Alice thought. The MHU's Mr Big. He watched her, something like a leer playing at the corners of his lips. Suddenly Alice wished she had one of the panic alarms that hung from the belts of all of the unit's regular staff. Light from the fluorescent strip light caught on his bald head as his eyes slowly ran down her body. He's not going to move, she thought. He's going to make me brush past him.

She slowed to a stop, and realised she was outside the single-occupancy room that contained the youth. The name tag on the door read J Smith. With his file missing, she thought sadly, they don't even know his name.

Alice knocked, then opened the door and stepped inside. He was lying in the bed, brown eyes staring upwards, bare scalp covered in flaky red patches. Alice glanced through the window to the corridor beyond. Garrett was walking away, bottle of Ribena swinging from one hand.

Knowing she shouldn't be there, she turned uneasily to the figure in the bed. 'Morning, my name's Alice.'

He stayed perfectly still.

Alice stepped over to the bed and looked down. The sheets had been tucked up right beneath his chin, so only his head poked out. She looked at the remains of scabs on his lips, the high cheekbones and feminine eyelashes.

The doors to the narrow wardrobe behind her were ajar and she could see it was empty. You are one nosy cow, she thought, quickly crouching down to open the bedside locker. A washbag was the only item on the shelf. She unzipped it and examined the small amount of toiletries inside. Not a single personal item. After replacing it, she straightened up and leaned forward to bring her face directly above his.

'Can you hear me?' She lifted a hand, held it a few inches from his face and suddenly clicked her fingers. He blinked. So you can hear, she thought. You just prefer not to. What on earth happened to put you in this state? 'Are you thirsty? Can I pour you a drink?'

She thought his head moved the tiniest of fractions.

'You'd like a drink?' Alice sat on the edge of the bed and reached for the plastic beaker of water on the bedside table. 'Here, shall I lift your head?' She slid her hand round, fingertips passing across the bumps and nodules of his skull. Slowly, she tilted the cup to his parted lips. Some water went in and his throat moved. 'More?'

He closed his eyes and she guessed it was to signal no. So, Alice thought, you understand English. She replaced the beaker. 'Can you tell me your name?'

A tear welled up out of a corner of one eye.

'Hey,' Alice whispered, brushing it away with one forefinger. Her hand returned to her lap and she contemplated her next move. 'Would you like a mint? I've got some, somewhere. Though I warn you, they're a bit strong.' She removed the packet of Fisherman's Friends from her pocket. 'Here, try one.' She shook an oval-shaped lozenge out.

As soon as it neared his face, his nose wrinkled and his head thrashed to the side.

Hastily, Alice withdrew her hand. 'Sorry, sorry.' Bad idea, Alice, she told herself. She shoved the mint into her pocket and placed a palm on his shoulder, waiting for his breathing to calm. Jesus, she thought. What's the problem with mints? Still, at least it seems he understands me. A bit more care and attention and he may open up a little more. 'I'll pop in again, if that's OK? Maybe bring you something else. Biscuits. Some fruit juice, maybe?'

He kept his face averted and his eyes slowly shut.

'OK,' Alice whispered. 'You take it easy.'

Back out in the corridor, there was no sign of Garrett. She hurried round to bay three, reaching for the pouch of tobacco in her pocket. A white man with an unruly mop of red hair was in Nathaniel's bed. Realising she was staring, mouth open, Alice peeled her eyes away.

Garrett was sitting on his bed, one leg hanging over the edge. The bottle of Ribena was on his bedside table.

'Where's Nathaniel Musoso?' she demanded.

'Who?'

'The man who was in this bed.'

'The oonga-boonga with the slashed-up arms? Group 4 took him.'

Group 4, she thought. The private security firm the Home Office often used for enforced deportations. 'When?' She realised one of his hands had strayed down to the front of his tracksuit trousers. His fingers were probing around.

'Late last night,' he grinned.

Turning on her heel, Alice marched back round to the front desk. Just before it, she passed the door to the medication room. She noticed its upper half was open and looked in. Two nurses were inside, placing little pots of pills into the drawers of a trolley that was chained to the wall. Keys jangled as one of them unlocked a wall cabinet and withdrew a large box. 'Let's just put the diazepam in the bottom. We can dish it out straight from there.'

'Excuse me,' Alice announced. 'The assistant who let me in, he didn't say Nathaniel Musoso was no longer here.'

The woman slid the box into the compartment at the base of the trolley then looked up. 'Which one was he?'

'He was in bay three.'

'Oh, him. He was transferred.'

'Where to?'

The nurse straightened up. 'Yarl's Wood.'

Alice closed her eyes for a moment. The immigration removal centre in Bedfordshire. 'He wasn't well. How ... who the hell authorised that?'

The nurse was looking embarrassed. 'Erm, it was Dr Braithwaite. He signed the forms.'

Phillip? Alice swallowed, waiting until she could be sure her voice was under control. 'Could I use a visitors' room, please?'

'The one opposite the Games Room is free.'

Alice let herself into the windowless room, took her mobile out and called Phillip's number. 'How could you? How could you do that to that man?'

She heard him cough and his voice was muffled. 'Excuse me for a moment, I need to take this call.' His voice came back on the line, now much clearer. 'You're talking about Musoso?'

'He had PTSD. He was self-harming. You knew these things.'

'Alice, Yarl's Wood has its own mental health facility. He'll be cared for there.'

'Cared for? Yarl's Wood is a fucking prison. The solicitors' reports we have for cases of abuse and brutality by the staff there fills a bloody filing cabinet in our office. There's attempted suicides all the time. Cared for. Who are you trying to fool, Phillip?'

He kept his voice down, irritation underpinning each word. 'Who was paying for that man's care in our unit, Alice?'

'I don't know.'

'Well, I'll tell you. It wasn't the Home Office. It wasn't social services. And it wasn't the Local Authority. We were paying, Alice. Our Primary Care Trust. We do not have the money. The Home Office was prepared to take him, so I gave my consent.'

'He was in no fit state.'

'It was him or that J. Smith character. Derbyshire PCT pays for two beds in the unit, Alice. Cash up-front, each quarter. They needed one of them, so someone had to go. Musoso's claim has been turned down. So, I gather, have repeated appeals.'

Alice felt like she was about to cry. It was all so fucking hopeless. 'But he was ill,' she croaked.

'That, if I may say, is not a matter you're qualified to judge upon.'

'Oh, come on: it was obvious. You did assess him, didn't you?'

'I'm not getting into this.'

'Did you assess him?'

'I'm in the middle of a clinic at the moment.'

Yeah, Alice thought. Your private clinic out in Hale. Quids in there, aren't you? 'You didn't, did you?'

'We'll talk later. Goodbye.'

The line went dead and Alice turned to press her forehead against the wall. She thought about Nathaniel in the bed, knees drawn up in a foetal position. The poor man probably wasn't even in the country any longer. What would become of him? I'll probably never find out, she concluded, tears starting to well up. No, she thought, finding a tissue and dabbing at her eyes. You're no good to anyone like this. You lost Nathaniel, but there's someone else on this unit who needs your help. So stop the bloody crying.

Once she composed herself, she stepped back out into the corridor and returned to the meds room. 'Sorry to bother you again, but what about the other foreign national on the unit? The one in the last room?'

The nurse was attaching a printed sheet of A4 to a clipboard. She glanced up at the clock on the wall. 'We're still waiting for the file.'

'Still? Who's sending it?'

'Liverpool. The Royal University Hospital.'

'So why did this unit get the referral?'

'Luck of the draw – otherwise known as the National Dispersal Scheme.'

Of course, Alice thought. Government has the power to allocate asylum seekers all round the country. 'Well, they're taking their time with the file. Is there anything I could do to help? Maybe chase it up for you?'

The nurse was bowed over the list of names, double-checking the pills in each pot. 'Be my guest.'

Fifteen

'You won't believe this,' Rick murmured, eyes on the screen of his computer.

Jon looked across at his partner, his own computer midway through printing out a document. 'What've you got?'

'Two more letters have been found in ducks. All the major news providers are now reporting on them. First one follows on from the last one they printed, the other jumps forward a bit.'

Jon leaned back in his seat. Christ, we're meant to be looking into the murdered Russians and any links to the freight company in London the victim out in Runcorn phoned. 'Rick. Lloyd's Register of Shipping? What happened to that?'

'Oh, yeah. Sorry. I've found eight vessels owned by his company so far. But he's a sneaky bastard ...' He paused. 'You sure you don't want to hear what the latest letters say?'

Jon took a sip of coffee, ran his tongue across the backs of his teeth and swallowed. 'Of course I bloody do.'

Rick's eyebrow arched as he reached for his mouse. 'Thought so. Last letter to be found was number four, right?'

Jon nodded. 'Yup. Down to fifteen survivors from the original twenty-one, the best part of two days spent standing knee-deep in sea water.'

'OK,' Rick replied. 'So a letter marked number five was found on a beach near Salcombe yesterday afternoon.'

'Salcombe?'

'On the south coast, not far from Plymouth.' He took a deep breath and started reading.

LETTER FIVE
This, our second day after being abandoned, I have noticed the people are becoming into groups. The only language is English,

though the five men from the east do not speak any. They stand at the other end of the raft and they whisper and frown. I fear what is in their eyes.

In the group I am in, there is Ali, Khadom and Qais from Baghdad, Mehdi and Parviz from Iran. Also staying close to us is the old man and woman. He speaks a small amount of English. They are Uighur Muslims from the corner of China and the government destroyed their home. Last in our group is the boy, Jîno. He will not talk.

The man with the throat scars guards the drum.

Everyone is tired and little is said now. The sun often breaks through the clouds and there is only the sound of water as it surges and falls through the many gaps in the raft. Parviz explained this is its weakness and its strength. Though we always are wet, the raft cannot sink.

My feet hurt me all the time and I long to sit. Hunger and thirst are becoming worse. Writing these letters keeps my mind from black thoughts.

The eastern men demanded more food this afternoon, but our group refused. We cannot tell when a ship will find us and there is so little – some packets of noodles, dates, sweets and less than five bottles of drink.

Sunset and the wind has just blown strange jellyfish among the ducks which float around our raft. Their pale blue colour reminded me of the balloons in the soldiers' base in the Green Zone when there was held a party. One of the eastern men lifted one up, then screamed and dropped it. Everyone kept back until the wind blew the animals away. The man has very bad pain.

All day we drift with the sea, unable to know our direction. For those who are Muslims, there is no way to know which direction is Mecca for their prayers. Only now when the sun nears the horizon it is possible to tell. The wind is moving us north.

A passing detective, one hand clutching a sausage and egg sandwich, paused at their desks. 'Don't tell me you believe that shit?'

Jon glanced up at him. 'Hard to say.'

143

The man took a bite, his words distorted by the food in his mouth. 'Someone is pissing themselves with laughter over this. Notes in fucking ducks.' He chewed for a bit then pointed the remains of his sandwich at Rick's monitor. 'You know how the *Express* is offering a grand for every letter? Think I might scribble a few myself. I fancy a break in the Caribbean this year.' He placed the crust into its greaseproof wrapper and dropped it in Jon's bin. Shaking his head, he continued on his way.

Jon waited for him to go before turning back to Rick.

'The Green Zone? So she was working in Baghdad. You've got to go through all sorts of security checks to get in there. Surely they can—'

Rick cut in. 'No one knows her name because she doesn't sign the letters. The editorial here pointed out the same thing.'

Jon was gazing at a point above Rick's head. 'Didn't the ducks have a company name printed on them? Aren't the papers trying to trace it?'

'Yes. This report says there's a particular town in China where these sorts of items are made. The Kyou Corporation is located there. They made a batch of rubber ducks with the serial codes these ones have on them last year. But they failed to get a safety kitemark for sale in Europe and the States. Something to do with the paint used. The lot were meant to have been destroyed.'

'What does the next letter say?'

'It was found yesterday by some kids on Tramore Beach ...'

'County Waterford?' Jon interrupted.

'What?'

'County Waterford. In Ireland?'

'Yeah, it says Ireland.'

'These ducks are getting everywhere.'

'Wherever the currents take them, I suppose. Anyway, it's number twelve, so it jumps forward a bit.' He leaned closer to the screen and licked his lips.

LETTER TWELVE

Afternoon. The sea just broke into activity. Tiny fish, fleeing from a dark shadow below. Many leaped onto our raft in panic

144

and we fell on them, squeezing our cheeks full. More we wrapped in clothes. I saw Ali chasing one with his fingers, many tails sticking from his lips. I pointed at this and we laughed together at our luck.

Once we had eaten, Ali and I lay back down and talked of food once more. It's all we can think about. Ali described tashreab – the rich tomato sauce poured over two pieces of flat bread. I spoke of sha'ar benat – how the soft, pink lumps would melt in my mouth.

Ali told me they have this too in Great Britain. It is called candy floss. I am so desperate to make a new life there, to not be afraid all the time. I know they read Arabian Nights to their children, too. At Christmas they even have plays about Aladdin. Ali says they also keep pigeons, in cages on roofs, like at home. We smiled at memories of the birds, rising in the evenings over Baghdad, the whistles as the old men called them back.

I miss the sounds of birds. The bulbul's song. The Americans cut down all the trees, saying their enemies could hide in them. Their tanks tore up the pavements and knocked down all our traffic lights and street signs.

The edges of where Ali was bitten have grown angry and the wound bulges out.

Jon let out a long stream of air through both nostrils. 'They were heading for Britain. Their destination was here. If they weren't abandoned too far away, perhaps they made it.'

Rick shook his head. 'Those jellyfish she describes in the earlier letter? The paper reckons they were Portuguese men-of-war. Rarely found north of the Bay of Biscay, which is bloody miles away. Plus, the actual ducks look like they've been drifting for weeks, apparently. Face it, whoever wrote those notes is fish food by now. You heard what Marlow said, no one knows how many people trying to get here end up at the bottom of the sea.'

As Jon tilted his head back, he noticed the massed dots that seemed to be spreading like some form of mould within the casing of the strip light above. Moths, lured in by the fluorescent glow. He wondered briefly how long it had taken the insects to die. 'Fish. Maybe the poor bastards caught enough from the sea to survive.' He glanced at the bin where the other detective had just casually tossed his crusts. 'How much food do you need each day to survive? Surely someone would have spotted these people sooner or later?'

Rick nodded. 'You'd have thought so. I'm sure more notes will show up now they're offering a reward for them. They reckon all the ducks have been washed ashore now.'

Jon drained his coffee. 'So, what's the score with this freight company's ships?'

'Well, according to the person at Lloyd's I spoke to, it's common practice in the freight business to charter vessels to yourself.'

'Why?'

'Tax avoidance, circumventing government regulations, keeping the crews' wages down. Our man's company is registered in the Ukrainian port of Odessa, though his commercial office is in London.'

Jon crossed his arms. 'Carry on.'

'And he's doing business all over the world – I know that from the ships I've tracked down so far.'

'Whereabouts?'

Rick held up a hand and started counting off fingers. 'Pakistan, Hong Kong, Indonesia, Russia, New Zealand, the Bahamas. What you do is set up a corporation in each country and register a ship under that country's flag. You then lease the ship back to yourself, thereby avoiding all the costs incurred by operating as a foreign company in that country.'

'That figures,' Jon replied, picking up a printout. 'Especially since our man only offers tramp services.'

'Those being?' Rick asked.

'According to this government website a tramp vessel,' he turned to the sheet, '"operates entirely according to the demands of the freight shipments." It's an unscheduled service with no fixed itinerary. Basically, you want to shift a load of TVs to India? Contact this guy and he'll give you a quote. He also provides secondary services like customs clearance and inventory management as well as sorting documentation issues like Bills of Lading.'

'Bills of what?'

'Lading. It's a nautical term, mate.' Jon grinned, putting on a Cornish accent. 'You've got your Bills of Lading and your Consignor. He places the freight with your shipper. Then there's your Consignee who'll be waiting for his freight. You've got your deep-sea trade routes, your international waterways, your stowage and your dunnage. It's a whole different language, my hearty.'

Rick winced. 'Where did you learn all that?'

'My old man. From working on the docks.'

'Well, beam me up, cap'n.'

Jon rolled his eyes. 'When did we jump to bloody *Star Trek*? Anyway, it's "beam me up, Scotty". And it's "master" on merchant navy ships, not "captain".'

'Whatever,' Rick replied, head turned to his computer once again.

'How many ships did you say he's operating?' Jon asked.

'I've found eight so far. The *Adria*, *Baden Star*, *Hai Maru*, *King Olav III*, *Oxus*, the *Lesya Ukrayinka*, *Camito Princess* and *Karanchi*.'

'Sounds like the two forty at Epsom.'

Rick smiled. 'Could be more, too. It's tracing them back to his company where it gets tricky.'

Jon rested his hands on the arms of his chair. 'The murder victims claimed the ship that set them down had set off from St Petersburg, where one of them worked as a journalist. If it dumped them in the Irish Channel, as they claimed, where was it bound for? Cardiff? Liverpool? Dublin?'

'Could have been headed straight for the States. Caribbean, central America. Anywhere.'

Jon nodded. 'We could do with trying to map his ships' itineraries.' He opened up a new screen and stared at the introductory paragraphs of the Ukrainian's website.

> We have the honour to introduce you to Myko Enterprises.
> Just a brief perusal will allow you to ascertain the
> professionalism of our service – which allows for the quick
> dispatch of operations 365 days a year.
>
> We have an intimate knowledge of the world's major ports
> and renowned connections with container terminal officials
> therein. Consequently, we are confident of our position to
> secure agreements with officials to grant you a discount on
> your containers' fees.

Jon sighed. 'This company has dodgy written all over it.'

'You still want to meet the man in person?' Rick asked.

'Is there any other way?' Jon replied, getting up and stepping over to a nearby printer. He stacked the sheets of paper with the others on his desk and slid the lot into a perspex sleeve.

'Shouldn't we put a call into the Met? Let them know we're heading onto their patch to question a suspect?'

Jon glanced at his watch. 'No time. Our train leaves in less than twenty minutes. Besides, he's not a suspect – yet.' He picked his jacket off the back of his chair. 'Though I can't wait to see his face when I say a Russian-speaking asylum seeker called his office hours before almost being decapitated by a garrotte.'

Rick stood. 'Fair point. And he's there at the moment?'

'According to the woman who answered the phone.'

'What's his name again?'

Jon placed the perspex sleeve in a slim briefcase. 'Slavko Mykosowski.'

Sixteen

As the train approached Euston, the embankment walls on either side of the track grew higher until it seemed they were heading along the bottom of a narrow ravine. How old was I, Jon reflected, when I was down here last? New Year's Eve, sometime in my early twenties. He examined the patches of graffiti covering the lowermost blocks of grey stone. He realised that, as he read out the scrawled names in his head, it was with a cockney accent. Same as I did all those years ago. Craning his neck, he watched the strip of sky grow thinner until it suddenly disappeared as they entered the tunnel leading to Euston station itself.

The terminal building was packed with people, everyone cutting across each others' paths, jostling for the angle they wanted. Pickpockets will love this, Jon thought, hand going to his jacket to check the inner pocket holding his wallet was buttoned shut. 'How do you get into the Underground?'

'Tubes are this way,' Rick replied, leading the way.

'How long did you live down here?' Jon asked, trying to keep up with his partner as he deftly weaved through the throng.

'Years. Mum and Dad only moved out when I started at secondary school.'

You mean public school, Jon thought. That nice little place somewhere out in Kent or Surrey or somewhere, wasn't it? 'Where did you live?'

'Holland Park?' Rick glanced back.

Jon looked at him blankly.

'West London, basically. The office of Myko Enterprises overlooks the Thames, doesn't it?'

'Yes, near Waterloo. I've got the printout from Google Maps in my briefcase.'

'No need. We'll just go straight down the Northern Line. It's only five or six stops, I think.' Rick stepped on to the top of the escalator.

'Really?' Jon followed him. 'How long will that take?'

'Excuse me!'

Jon looked back to see a man in a suit behind him. 'Can I help?'

The man's look of irritation increased.

'Jon,' Rick said, tugging his partner across. 'You stand on the right.'

The man brushed past with an impatient sigh.

'How was I to know?' Jon replied. 'There was nothing saying that.'

'There are notices at the top,' Rick replied, suppressing a smile. 'But they are really small.'

'Small? Bloody microscopic.'

The underground station was now coming into view and Jon felt the sensation of being hemmed in growing. Low ceilings, artificial light, stale air. People were queuing three-deep at the barriers. We're rats, he thought. Let loose in a maze.

When they emerged back into daylight, Jon breathed a sigh of relief. Rick beckoned him along a walkway and suddenly the Thames was there before him. Relishing the sudden sense of space, Jon rested a hand on the trunk of one of the trees that lined the boulevard bordering the river. He felt his shoulders drop and, finally, felt a hint of what gave the city its lure. The massive structure of the London Eye loomed over him.

Beside him, Rick was looking up, too. 'Makes the one outside the Triangle in Manchester look like a bicycle wheel, doesn't it?'

Thinking how right his partner was, Jon shrugged. 'It's not that much bigger.'

'Yeah, right.' Rick laughed.

Glancing along the river, Jon spotted buildings that he was only used to seeing on television. He unzipped the front pocket of the briefcase and removed a piece of paper. 'Waterloo Tower,' he announced, holding it out to Rick. 'It's marked with an arrow.'

Rick examined the piece of paper without taking it. 'Somewhere along here.'

A couple of minutes' walk took them to a building clad in unnaturally smooth-looking beige stone, all of its windows tinted a faint purple. They crossed into a lobby that seemed to be entirely lined with marble. Shiny tiles stretched across the floor then up the walls to head height. They approached the front desk, behind which was a huge expanse of brass filled with plaques, each inscribed with a company name. Jon worked his way down the alphabetical columns. 'There you go,' he nodded. 'Fourteenth floor.'

Rick looked at the security guard, warrant card outstretched. 'Hello, there. OK if we head on up?'

The man examined the badge. 'Who are you here to see?'

'That's our business, I'm afraid.'

He slid a visitor book across the counter. 'Well, can you sign in, please? Just so we know you're here officially, like.'

They added their names and he tore the slips out and inserted them into a couple of plastic pouches with a fastener mechanism. 'Thanks, gents. Lifts are on the right.'

'Result,' Jon murmured, pocketing his as they strode across the lobby. 'He won't know we're here until we're stood in his office.'

The lift whisked them up, doors opening on a quiet corridor. A noticeboard was on the opposite wall.

'Third on the left,' Rick whispered.

They stepped out and Jon noticed the carpet felt thin underfoot. A yucca plant stood in a plant pot to their side. Stretching between two of the dry, yellowing leaves was a cobweb. At its centre there rested a spider's husk, brittle legs caught up in the folds as if it had fallen victim to its own trap. Eyes settling on the discarded Bounty wrapper at the base of the plant's trunk, Jon said, 'Not quite so flash away from the entrance hall.'

'Don't be fooled,' Rick replied quietly. 'Rents for this place will be astronomical.'

They walked along to the offices of Myko Enterprises and

Rick knocked on the door. The intercom made a clicking noise and a male voice with a heavy accent asked, 'Who is it?'

Rick leaned towards the perforated metal panel. 'DS Saville, DI Spicer. We're police officers.'

'Police?'

Jon bent down to the little box. 'Open the door, sir.'

Two seconds silence. Jon's palm was on the handle, and as soon as the lock buzzed, he pushed it open. No reception area or lobby. An overweight man in a pale blue shirt was seated behind a large wooden desk, straggly black hair hanging down to his shoulders. Floor-to-ceiling windows behind him gave an impressive view of the river.

Jon walked over, closing the distance between them as fast as possible, glancing to each side as he did. Strange, he thought. A woman answered the phone earlier. 'Slavko Mykosowski?'

'Yes.'

'DI Spicer, Greater Manchester Police. My colleague, DS Saville.'

'Manchester?'

Jon kept his gaze on the man. The mention of Manchester had caused something to glint in his beady eyes. 'If you have a minute or two, we have a few questions.'

Mykosowski tilted back in his seat, raised both hands up and started gathering his oily-looking hair into a bunch. For a moment, Jon thought he was about to produce something to tie it back with. But to his relief, the man let it fall back over his collar. 'Of course.' He gestured to the chairs against the wall. 'They are on wheels.'

Rick rolled a couple over and sat down. Jon remained standing, satisfied when he saw how it disconcerted Mykosowski. Deliberately, he said nothing.

The Ukrainian stared back for a second, turned to Rick, then looked at Jon again. A small laugh escaped him, high-pitched with nerves. 'We are playing who blinks first?'

Satisfied he had control, Jon lowered himself on to the edge of his seat as if he might spring back to his feet at any second. 'You are, I gather, in the business of shipping freight?'

'Yes.'

'What types?'

'What is this about, please?'

'Just background enquiries, sir.'

Mykosowski smiled. 'That doesn't tell me much.'

'Your company's name came up during enquiries into the dumping of contaminated waste in a freight yard near Manchester,' Jon stated, hoping the lie would be sufficient.

'I will transport most things, except hazardous materials. I do not have the necessary licences.'

Jon looked about. 'I called earlier and a woman answered the phone.'

'It is a serviced office. The receptionists are all located in the basement and route the calls up.'

'Where do your ships operate?'

The man hesitated and Jon could tell the way his questions kept changing tack was wrong-footing him. 'All over the world. My operation is global – as business is, nowadays.'

'Russia?' Rick asked, crossing his legs.

'Of course Russia,' Mykosowski replied.

'Were any of your ships off the north-west coast of Britain a few days ago?'

Mykosowski studied Rick before replying. 'Possibly. I have many vessels, it would be necessary to check.'

'Could you do that for us, now?' Jon asked.

'That information is commercially sensitive.'

'We wouldn't be passing it on to your competitors.'

'Even so, it's not something I'd like to share.'

'Anything set off from St Petersburg recently?'

'I'm sorry. I am not at liberty to say.'

'Russia. Is that where you're from originally?' Jon asked, standing up and moving towards the windows.

'Ukraine. I am Ukrainian.'

'But resident in the UK?'

Mykosowski twisted his neck, trying to address Jon as he moved behind his chair. 'I am not a British citizen, but I have a visa to live and work here for most of the year.'

'The Houses of Parliament,' Jon murmured, slowly circling him. 'What great views.'

Mykosowski looked over his right shoulder as Jon proceeded along the windows. 'Yes. This stretch of river, I never tire of watching it. Day or night.'

'"The sea reach of the Thames stretched before us like the beginnings of an interminable waterway",' Rick stated.

Jon looked at his partner with surprise.

'Conrad!' Mykosowski exclaimed enthusiastically.

'*Heart of Darkness*,' Rick replied. 'I studied it at school.'

'He was Ukrainian, you know,' Mykosowski smiled proudly, his posture easing slightly. 'English was his third language.'

'Incredible,' Rick nodded. 'It's a true masterpiece.' His eyes flicked to Jon. Go for it, the look said. Now.

Jon stepped over to the desk, the edge of it pressing against his thighs as he loomed over the ship owner. 'A man's body was found in Manchester. He called this office hours before someone murdered him.'

Mykosowski's legs stiffened and his seat moved back a few inches. 'Sorry?'

Jon placed both sets of knuckles on the desk. 'You heard me.' The other man's hand rose up to flutter protectively at his throat. I didn't mention how he died, thought Jon.

'Who was this man?'

'The name he'd given to Border Agency officials was Andriy Bal. Maybe you could enlighten us as to his real name?'

'Andriy Bal?' Mykosowski made an absurd show of considering the name. 'I do not know anyone called that.'

Jon straightened up. 'It wasn't real. As I said, maybe you could tell us his true identity.'

'Well, I deal with many callers. People ring with enquiries all the time.'

'No one's rung you since we've been here.' Jon sat back down and opened his briefcase. He extracted the Border Agency photo of Bal. 'Here he is on his arrival to the UK.' He placed an A4 image next to it. 'And here's the pathologist's photo after his head was almost severed. Excuse the blood, won't you. A familiar face?'

Mykosowski pushed away the photo of Bal with his throat rendered wide open. 'He is not someone I know.'

'He rang here. His call was connected for over six minutes. You don't stay on the line that long if you've dialled a wrong number.'

'Maybe he was making a freight enquiry. I would need to check my records.'

'He was a destitute asylum seeker. He didn't even have a suitcase. Why did he call you?'

'I don't recall speaking to any man called Bal.'

Rick examined the nails on one hand, not looking at Mykosowski. 'In another day or so, the phone company will have located the recording of that call.' He glanced up. 'Every word of it.'

Nice touch, thought Jon, knowing their application for that information was going to take three times that long to be approved. He sat forward. 'Does the freight you deal in include humans, Mr Mykosowski?'

'That is stupid,' he replied, waving a hand across the desk. 'I will not answer such questions.'

'He's not the only one to have been killed in this way.' Jon took out the pathologist's photos of the other two victims. 'This one claimed to be called Marat Dubinski, this one Yegor Tsarev. Both killed within a day of Andriy Bal. Please look at the photos, sir.'

'Why?' Mykosowski's eyes flashed. 'These names are not known to me.'

'Faces, not names,' Jon replied. 'I want you to consider the faces. You can tell so much from one, yours included.'

'I must return to my work.' He reached for his mouse and stared at the computer screen, eyes not moving.

'Or this man. Vladimir Yashin.' Jon placed the photo across Mykosowski's keyboard. 'Friend of yours, maybe?'

Using the tip of a finger, Mykosowski slid the photo back without looking at it. 'Please go. I will not answer any more questions.'

Taking his time, Jon gathered the photos into a neat pile. 'You know,' he announced casually. 'We're checking the records of the payphones in the accommodation where the other two victims were housed. Officers are knocking on doors, asking if either murder victim had borrowed a mobile phone to make any calls. What should we think if these other men had also phoned this office?'

Mykosowski stared at his screen in silence.

As they headed for the door, Jon called over his shoulder. 'Your name has been flagged with the Border Agency. So don't you be trying to go on any holidays now.'

Only once the door to his office had clicked shut did Slavko Mykosowski dare to look away from his screen. He stared towards the corridor, half expecting them to buzz again, march in and arrest him. A minute passed and still his posture was tense. This is all going so wrong, he thought. So completely wrong. Running a hand through his hair, he turned back to his computer monitor and selected the programme that displayed the current satellite locations for all his ships.

He typed in '*Lesya Ukrayinka*' and a screen opened up with a slowly flashing dot at its centre. He zoomed out slightly, and on the screen's left-hand side, the east coast of America came into view. There was the jagged fissure that was Chesapeake Bay. There, a little further inland, was the port of Baltimore. Mykosowski stared at the flashing dot with something like sadness in his eyes. So close, he thought. So close to offloading that cursed cargo.

Seventeen

The escalator disgorged them back into the terminal at Euston and Jon stepped clear of the stream of hurrying passengers to address Rick. 'So, we start trying to map the movements of his ships. That's a priority. What else?'

'See if we can hurry up the fingerprint search for the one called Vladimir Yashin. He has to link in with Mykosowski, surely.'

'I agree. What we really need, though, is something on our murder victims' identities. If we can trace a family member, they could put us on to who was paid to ship them over here.'

'How were Buchanon's enquiries with the Russian embassy going?'

'Not sure. Maybe he'll have something when we get back. How are we doing for time?'

Rick made his way across the terminal, eyes on the enormous departure board. 'There's one leaving in forty minutes. Let's see if there's anything sooner.'

Jon stood behind his partner, feeling like a boulder in a river as the current of people moved past on either side. A crop-haired man in a black body warmer and jeans was walking directly towards them, fingers flexing at his sides. Jon glanced to his other side and saw another male closing in from that direction. He raised a hand and was just about to warn Rick when he felt fingers on his shoulder. Instantly, he grabbed them and started to squeeze as he looked round.

A smartly dressed man somewhere in his twenties was wincing with surprise, long fringe flopping down to his eyes. 'Rick,' Jon said urgently.

The other two men's pace had quickened and Jon tensed his free arm in readiness to shove the nearest one away. Both were now reaching into their tops. 'Rick!' Jon barked. At last his partner looked round.

The man whose fingers he was crushing dropped his attaché case and reached into his jacket to produce a black wallet. He held it up to display the identity badge inside.

Jon saw the crown and portcullis with a dragon-like animal in the centre. The words *Regnum Defende* ran below the crest. He felt his eyebrows lift. MI5, he thought. Never seen one of those this close.

'Let go of my bloody fingers!' the man hissed.

Jon threw the man's hand aside, turning to glare at the other men. 'You two, as well?'

They flashed identical badges then quickly returned them to inner pockets.

'We need to talk,' the first man said, straightening the sleeves of his suit jacket before picking up his case and looking down at his fingers. Gingerly, he stretched them out and examined his knuckles before gesturing at the balcony pub on their left.

Jon shrugged. 'We're police, you realise?'

'I suspected.'

'So, what's this about?'

'Let's find somewhere to sit down, shall we?'

Their table overlooked the terminal and Jon stared down at the mass of humanity below. Spanish-looking student types sitting on the floor, rucksacks propped against the windows of a newsagent's booth. Commuters with their heads down, striding determinedly to their platforms. People wheeling suitcases with airline tags still attached to the handles. A black cleaner meandering through the throng, plucking up items of litter with long-handled pincers.

The staff member arrived with their drinks and Rick moved a half-finished glass of Coke to the corner of the table to make room for the tray.

'Black coffee?' the waiter asked, Australian accent unmistakable.

'Cheers,' Jon replied, taking the drink.

'Latte?'

'Thanks,' Rick answered.

The man placed the last drink before the suited man then disappeared back through the balcony doors.

'What with almost breaking my fingers?' the man from MI5 asked, tearing open a sachet of sugar and pouring it into his tea.

Jon felt his face redden slightly. 'I didn't know who the hell you were. For all I knew, you were a gang of pickpockets.' He glanced awkwardly at the other two men who were sitting in silence at a nearby table.

The young man smirked. 'Gorblimey, it's crawling with tea-leaves round these parts.'

Jon registered the mocking tone. I should have squeezed your fingers harder, he thought.

The man stirred his tea. 'What was your business with Mykosowski?'

'We're pursuing a line of enquiry,' Jon replied. 'A string of incidents up in Manchester.'

'You're with Greater Manchester Police?'

'The Major Incident Team. I'm DI Spicer, this is DS Saville.'

The man placed his teaspoon in his saucer and smiled. 'What type of incident?'

Jon sat back. 'I didn't catch your name.'

'I haven't given it.'

'Up north,' Jon replied, deliberately overplaying his accent, 'we get to know each other a bit before exchanging information. You know, chat?'

'I'm an MI5 officer.'

'So I gathered from your badge.'

'What sort of an incident?'

Jon sipped from his coffee, saying nothing.

The man looked at Rick, who stared back in silence. 'This is absurd,' he blustered. 'I make one call and this information will be sent to me – by your Chief Constable, if necessary.'

Aren't you the big fucking deal, Jon thought. 'You want to borrow my phone?'

The MI5 man raised a hand and swept his long fringe back into place. 'Bloody ridiculous. My name is Edward Soutar.'

Jon held out a hand. 'Jon Spicer.'

Looking bemused, the man shook.

'And this is Rick Saville.' Jon nodded at his partner.

'OK,' Soutar said, taking Rick's hand. 'All done?'

Jon turned to the nearby table. 'All right, boys? I'm Jon.'

One raised a finger. 'Alex.'

'Matt,' his colleague added.

Jon nodded then turned to Soutar. 'There. I feel at ease now.'

'Good. Slavko Mykosowski is under our surveillance. I can't divulge any details.'

'People trafficking, by any chance?' Rick asked.

The officer shot him a glance that hinted Rick was wide of the mark. 'Why were you questioning him?' he asked, looking back at Jon.

'Murder investigation.'

'Really? Who?'

'We don't know. Three men, all claiming to be Russians, have been garrotted in recent days. All were housed in Home Office-provided accommodation after having put in bogus claims for asylum.'

Soutar was now sitting forward, hands clasped on the table. 'Why bogus?'

'The case owners at the Border Agency had started looking into their claims. None of their names were even real.'

'They had no documents?'

'None. Arrived in only the clothes they stood up in. Picked up by a fishing trawler, having been drifting off the south-west coast for some time.'

'When was this?'

'Almost two weeks ago.'

Soutar produced a notebook and pen from his attaché case. As he started jotting things down, a wasp homed in on the torn sachet of sugar. He flicked a hand at the insect and it moved away, turning its attention to the glass of half-finished Coke. 'Have you got any photos of these three men?'

Jon nodded, reached into his own briefcase and extracted the Border Agency mug shots. 'This one,' he tapped the photo of Bal, 'had borrowed a mobile from a fellow asylum seeker. He called Mykosowski's office, staying on the line for over six minutes.'

'We've started looking into Mykosowski's freight business as a result,' Rick added. 'He operates tramp ships – vessels with no fixed schedule or ports of call – which travel all over the world. The three murder victims all spoke Russian. They said the ship which dumped them in the Irish Sea had set off from St Petersburg. Is Mykosowski trafficking people?'

Soutar glanced up. 'If he is, it's the least of our concerns.'

'So why are you watching him?' Rick asked.

Saying nothing, Soutar spread the photos out, and as he examined them, Jon watched the wasp.

Antennae seeming to bob with excitement, it reached the rim of the glass then attempted to walk down the inner side. Immediately it lost its grip and fell into the Coke. With ponderous movements, it began trying to free its legs from the meniscus, but lifting one limb only seemed to press its other ones deeper into the liquid. Soon, its abdomen had also become attached to the sticky surface. It buzzed its wings in frustration, the noise slightly amplified by the glass.

'Tell me,' Soutar said. 'These murder victims. Have you got a suspect?'

'We have.' Jon half extracted Yashin's photo from the file. 'There was a fourth man on the lifeboat they were all found on. He's since absconded. On our way to interview Bal, we actually passed the guy on the stairs. We got to Bal's accommodation seconds later and found him dead. Killed, literally, minutes before.'

'No sign of this fourth man when you tried to catch him up?'

'No. This is him. He used the name Vladimir Yashin.' Jon placed the Border Agency's shot on the table.

Soutar looked down at it and nodded. 'The dead guys. They weren't being trafficked: they were working with this man.' He held up the photo to the two men at the other table. 'Lads.'

Jon saw both men's eyes widen.

'He's done three up in Manchester,' Soutar stated.

The one with the short cropped hair whistled. 'Another day at the office. Were they garrotted?'

Jon turned in his seat. 'Yes. Wire, nylon or something – whatever it was, their heads were just about hanging off.'

'That's how he likes to do them,' Soutar replied. 'A brief struggle, a little noise, but no chance once the thing's round their neck.'

Jon stared at the younger man. 'You mean, you know who he is?'

'We do. I can assure you of this, DI Spicer, you do not want to come close to this man.'

'Who is he?'

'The devil, mate,' the crop-haired man spoke from the other table. 'Alive and well and striding the face of the earth.'

Jon remembered the look in the man's eyes as they'd passed on the stairs. A needle of ice traced its way down his vertebrae.

'They crossed paths on the way to one of the murder victim's flats,' Soutar said, a grin playing on his face.

His colleagues shook their heads.

'Two minutes earlier,' Jon said. 'And we would have caught him in there.'

'Two minutes earlier, and you wouldn't be talking to us now. Count yourselves lucky you were late,' Soutar replied.

'Who is he?' Jon repeated.

'Call him a jack of all trades.'

'I'll call him my prime suspect.' Jon placed his elbows on the table. This building-up of the man calling himself Vladimir was getting annoying. 'Do I call you agent?'

Soutar shook his head. 'I'm an officer. Like you.'

'Officer Soutar, you have information on a series of murders which I'm investigating.'

The younger man raised his bottom lip, nodding in acknowledgement. 'I do. But I also know this investigation is touching on something that relates to national security.'

'I'd appreciate you letting me know who the hell this man is.'

Soutar picked up a teaspoon, fished the drowning wasp from the glass and, with a flick of his wrist, deposited it on the table.

It crawled out of the puddle it found itself in and started trying to brush the moisture from its antennae with its two front legs. Soutar placed the spoon to one side, picked up the glass and lowered it onto the insect. Jon heard the crunching sound as its carapace gave way.

'You probably think the crimes you investigate up in Manchester rank as major incidents. But believe me, DI Spicer, this investigation is in another league. And compared to the scallies – as I believe you call them – up there, this person is an entirely different species.'

'Liverpool,' Jon said quietly.

'Sorry?' Soutar replied.

'Scally is a Liverpudlian expression. We prefer the term scrote in Manchester.'

'Fascinating.' Soutar lifted the glass and examined the pinkish jelly oozing from the split in the motionless creature's thorax.

Nice speech, Jon thought. Probably been practising that ever since you got the nod from MI5 at the graduate fair you went to at Oxford or Cambridge. He thought about his own years serving in the police, the endless investigations he'd worked on. 'Until my senior officer tells me otherwise, it's my murder investigation, Ed.'

Soutar looked up, clearly irritated. 'Tell me, Detective. Did you inform the Metropolitan Police that you would be here?'

Jon felt his nostrils flare as he took in breath. Shit, the little twat has got me.

Soutar's smiled gloatingly. 'I thought not. By the time your train has crawled back into Manchester, your investigation will be over, Detective.'

Jon replaced the photos in his briefcase and stood up. 'You reckon?' He reached across the table and flicked the dead wasp into the younger man's lap. Soutar's chair shot back and he jumped to his feet, tugging frantically at the seams of his trousers to dislodge the corpse.

As Jon made his way to the balcony doors, he caught sight of the crop-haired colleague turning away in an attempt to keep his grin hidden.

Less than four hours later, Jon was standing outside the door to Vladimir Yashin's flat. A notice headed with Greater Manchester Police's crest advised him not to enter. He thought about how, on their arrival back in Manchester, his suggestion to take a look round the Russian's accommodation had caused an expression of awkwardness to sweep across Rick's face.

'I'm meeting Andy,' his partner had said. 'We were going for some food in China Town.'

We'll probably be off this case in the morning, Jon thought. Last chance to get a handle on who our man is.

'It's almost half nine,' his partner had continued. 'We've been on the road since eight this morning.'

'No, you're right,' Jon had replied. 'You go for it.'

'What are you going to do?'

'I might have a quick peek.'

'You're making me feel guilty, now.'

'No – get some food. Murray and Gardiner have gone over the flat already. I'm only being nosy.'

'Why don't we both go first thing tomorrow?'

'First thing tomorrow, mate, we'll be dragged in to see Buchanon. You can be sure of that.'

'Come on, then.' Rick had started towards the cab rank at the rear of Piccadilly station.

'No. Have your meal. We don't both need to go.'

Rick's step faltered. 'You sure?'

'Yes. I'm only going because I've got nothing better to do.'

Jon opened the ziplock bag and removed the small keys from inside. Voices grew louder and a fire door further down the corridor opened. Two men stepped through, their conversation coming to a halt when they saw a white man wearing a suit in front of them. Jon nodded in their direction and they nodded back, skirting round him in silence.

Jon waited for their footsteps to die away then reached into the bag, his sense of touch slightly dulled by the latex gloves he wore. He released the hasp, removed the padlock then undid the door's main lock. It opened on a dark and airless room. He stood in the doorway, testing the smells. A citrus-type scent lay on top of the musty aroma of old carpet. He reached in and turned on the light.

The bulb in a round plastic ceiling shade stuttered into life and Jon found himself looking at a bare room, stripped clean of anything personal. Already knowing his search would reveal no tangible evidence, he stepped inside and walked to the centre of the faded carpet. A narrow sofa, a chair that would have looked at home in a doctor's waiting room, a flimsy table. Empty shelves ran along one wall, a small gas fire set into the base of another. He crouched in front of the sofa and placed a hand on the slightly dented backrest, picturing the man who'd sat there. The memory of him on the stairs returned. The hunch-shouldered descent, somehow full of barely controlled violence.

Jon stood up, walked over to the corner door and leaned into the tiny bedroom. Light spilling in from the main room revealed blankets and a pillow piled neatly at the base of the bed. Straight out of a barracks. The kitchen cupboards were empty, except for a single jar of pickled gherkins. Jon removed the lid and the sharp smell caused his nose to wrinkle. He screwed the lid back on and walked over to the window. On the sill was a can of air freshener, the yellow cap hinting at its lemon-scented contents. His eyes turned to the window. Off to the left was the Boddington's chimney, all that now remained of the city's famous brewery after its foreign owners decided to move production elsewhere. Away to the right was the imposing Victorian tower of Strangeways prison. Jon surveyed the rest of city, eyes moving over the massed lights. Where are you? he thought. Nearby? Or is your work done? Have you vanished back to whatever world spawned you?

He shook his shoulders and glanced at his watch. Just after ten. Still time to catch Braithwaite, if I'm lucky.

The psychiatrist's car was parked outside his old house. Jon batted the indicator lever down and pulled into a free space almost opposite it. Come on, you bastard, he thought. Make your excuses and head into the city. Please.

The living room was softly lit, and staring at the crack at the top of the curtains, he watched the strength of the glow rise and fall. They're watching something on the telly. He glanced at the dashboard clock. Ten twenty. Alice usually heads up at half past. If he's not staying over, he'll be making a move soon.

Ten minutes later, he became aware of a change in the darkness off to his left. Bending forward a little, he was able to see Belinda, the elderly woman who doted on Holly, at her front window. Funny time, Jon thought, to open the curtains and be talking on the phone.

She was gazing across over Jon's car, talking directly at his old house. A tingle of alarm went through him as he turned to look across the road. Fuck! The curtains of his old front room suddenly opened and there was Alice, phone pressed to one ear, trying to peer out. Jon started his car and began to pull away. In the periphery of his vision, he saw Alice hand the phone to Braithwaite and hurry from the room.

A black taxi was making its way towards him, parked cars on either side reducing the road to a single lane. His front door opened and Alice started running down the garden path. 'Bollocks,' he snarled, stomping on the brakes and trying to slam the car into reverse.

'What are you doing?' She was at his side window, pounding it with her palm. 'Tell me! Why are you out here watching us!' Flecks of spit hit the glass.

Headlights appeared behind him. No. This is not happening.

'Answer me. You have no right to be doing this!'

The driver of the car behind continued inching forward. Jon slammed a hand against the steering wheel. The stupid prick. He clambered across to the passenger side and jumped out. 'Back up, you fucking arsehole!'

'What are you doing here!' Alice screamed, pointing at him across the roof of the car. 'Answer me!'

Jon caught her eyes for a moment. Then he strode towards the car behind. Belinda was now on her front step, arms crossed over a dressing gown. The woman in the car looked like she was about to scream as Jon reached her vehicle. 'Fucking move!' he yelled, slamming a hand down on her bonnet.

She looked over her shoulder and the car began to zoom back, engine whining.

Braithwaite was now at the front gate. 'Alice, come inside. That's enough.'

'No!' she shouted, anger and confusion filling her voice. 'He won't answer me. Say something, you coward!'

He glared back at her, teeth clenched tight. I wish I bloody could. The curtains on the first floor moved and he saw Holly's pale face behind the glass. Her mouth was open and she was sobbing. 'Go to her.' His wife frowned and he pointed to the window. 'She's upset. Go to Holly.'

The sight of her daughter's distress caused Alice to retreat. 'I'm telling my solicitors about this, I bloody am.'

Jon stood looking up at his daughter. His sternum felt like it was splitting open as he raised a forefinger and placed it against his lips. God, I can't even go in there and give you a cuddle.

As Alice hurried through the front door, Braithwaite was struggling to close the catch on the garden gate. Once Alice was inside, Jon stepped over. 'I know what you're about,' he stated quietly.

Braithwaite stepped back. They regarded each other for a second. Then the other man suddenly seemed aware of the gate between them. Jon saw realisation in his eyes. You don't dare enter, his look said. Braithwaite's face relaxed slightly. 'I'm sorry?'

Jon raised his eyebrows in warning. He saw Braithwaite's expression change from alarm to pity. Slowly, the other man shook his head, turned on his heel and walked back to the house.

Eighteen

'Is she OK?' Phillip Braithwaite asked.

'I think so,' Alice replied, sitting down with a sigh. 'She's asleep now.'

He placed a cup of tea before her and took a seat on the other side of the kitchen table.

'I can't believe he's been out there, spying on us. It's frightening.'

Braithwaite crossed his legs and contemplated his bony knee for a moment. 'He went to visit Miranda the other night.'

Alice felt her mouth open. She resisted the urge to ask what he'd been doing talking to his estranged wife. 'What did he want?'

'It appears he's been following me home on occasions after I've spent the evening here.'

'Following you?' She looked to the doorway, picturing the street outside. 'Oh, Phillip, I'm truly sorry.'

He lifted his eyes and she felt a slight jolt. His look was so cold. 'It doesn't bother me.'

'Well, that's a relief. But even so – this all needs to go to my solicitor. I mean, why would he visit your ...' The word didn't want to come out.

Braithwaite tilted his head back as he breathed in. She saw black hairs massed inside each nostril. 'The Saab is still registered in her name, something we need to sort out. A few times after leaving here, I've taken a diversion and driven to the city centre.'

Alice frowned. That was the opposite direction to where his home was.

'A private patient of mine – a young lady – she recently left her family home in a fragile mental state. The father, who's a very

168

prominent public figure, has received word she's been working as a street prostitute in the area around Fairfield Street. Near Piccadilly station. She developed a drug habit while away at art college. It's all very sad. I've been hoping to locate her.'

Alice half nodded, unable to picture him showing that kind of concern with any patient in the NHS mental health unit. Chiding herself, she pushed the thought away. 'You should have mentioned it to me.'

'Why?'

'Well, I don't know ...' She realised she couldn't lay claim to his every movement. 'I'd assumed you were going straight home. That's where you said you were going.'

'It was a spur of the moment thing.'

'Right. I don't understand the significance of the car.'

'I think Jon was just using it as an excuse. He claimed the police had received complaints about a car with that registration hanging around in the area. You know, kerb-crawling. I think it was a story he concocted to question my wife about me.'

'He actually went into her house?'

Braithwaite gave a nod.

Alice stretched a hand across the table, but he picked up his cup of tea. Her fingers slid back. 'I'm so sorry. Jon gets fixated on things – usually investigations. But this ...' She shifted uncomfortably. 'What does your wife intend to do?'

'What do you mean?'

'Is she going to make a complaint?'

'She's pretty damned angry.'

'Of course. But could you talk to her – try and persuade her not to.'

Braithwaite looked taken aback. 'Why?'

Alice looked down. 'It's his life, Phillip. Doing that job is what he lives for.'

'I know. You said that's why your marriage went wrong.'

'It was.'

'Yet you're trying to protect him.'

'I couldn't stay married to him. That doesn't mean I want to see him destroyed.'

'I'm afraid I rang the police already. Just a quiet word, nothing official. I was hoping it would be enough.'

'You've contacted them already?' Alice heard the dismay in her voice. 'Why didn't you say?'

'It was a matter concerning Miranda. I didn't want to involve you. The whole thing is rather awkward, after all.'

'I wish you'd said something to me first.'

Braithwaite frowned. 'I didn't think you'd be so perturbed.'

'Perturbed? Well – there could have been a better way to handle this.'

'He used his status as an officer of the law to enter Miranda's home and question her.'

'I know. It was stupid.'

'It was an affront. Can we expect more behaviour like tonight's episode? It appears a quiet word wasn't enough.'

'If he gets something in his head, it's hard to make him give up on it.'

'Great. So, he'll continue harassing us. Has he always been like this?'

Alice took a sip of tea. 'I don't know. He's stubborn by nature. And very determined. Some would say they're qualities, I suppose. You know, in certain situations.'

His voice was sour. 'Qualities that attracted you to him in the first place?'

She glanced across at him, trying to read his eyes. Nothing showed on his face. 'Perhaps. A bit. I mean, it can be flattering if it's you that's the focus.'

'You liked it when you were the focus?'

His comment lay between them and she had the urge to move away from the table. Instead, she ran a hand through her hair. 'Why are we talking about this? We need to discuss what to do next.'

'I think it would be instructive to know about your early relationship with him. These are foundations on which the situation we find ourselves in tonight is built.'

He's analysing me, she thought. Like I'm a psychiatric patient. She didn't know whether to laugh. 'Look, Jon isn't a complicated person. He tends to see things very much in black and white. Maybe it's all those years in the police. But if he suspected there was something – something about this kerb-crawling business – his hackles would go up. He'll be … you know … defensive.'

'Defensive?'

'I'm not saying it's justified. But, you know, he'll be concerned about Holly and me. Our welfare.'

'What do you think there might be in your character to stir such behaviour in him?'

'Me?' She gulped back a sudden wave of nausea. 'My character?'

His eyes were now fixed on hers. 'When you left the house and approached his car, you were seeking a confrontation. You accused him of being a coward. His refusal to answer visibly angered you.'

She laughed incredulously, curious for the first time to know the exact reasons why Phillip's marriage had broken down. He'd always claimed they'd simply drifted apart. 'Phillip, I was annoyed. I wanted to know what he was doing, sitting out there. Surely that was reasonable?'

He uncrossed his legs. 'I think you need to have a good think about the dynamics of your relationship.'

'What do you mean, the dynamics?'

He stood and removed his car keys from the table. 'The dynamics. The bearing that one of your actions – whether conscious or unconscious – has on the other.'

'You're not going? Phillip, you've made me feel … dirty. Like I'm at fault. Don't leave it like this, we need to talk.'

'No.' He held up a hand. 'I think it's best we spend some time apart. Take some time to consider what I've just said.'

The walls behind him seemed to be zooming out of focus. 'There isn't anything to consider.'

He looked towards the doorway. 'We both need some time to assess the situation.'

'We're meant to be taking Holly to stay in your holiday house in the Lake District next week. Her birthday treat.'

'I'm not sure I feel comfortable about that any more.'

She gestured at the ceiling. 'But Holly. We've been building her up to it for weeks.'

'I'm sorry, Alice. I don't think it's a good idea.'

'She's been really looking forward to it.' Something struck her. She found herself getting to her feet. 'This isn't about Nathaniel Musoso?' There! She saw it – a spark of anger in his pupils. 'I didn't mean to question your clinical judgement. Is that what this is all about?'

'Not at all.' His mouth was tight. 'This is about your husband acting like a stalker. I need to get going. It's very late.' He moved towards the door, avoiding her eyes.

'Will you call me?' She stepped closer. 'This is all … I'm confused. I don't understand why you're doing this.'

'I'm not doing anything, Alice – other than pointing out some things you need to reflect upon.'

The pale and delicate curls fell like snow, joining the layer of shavings on the flagstone floor. Oliver Brookes held the sculpture at arm's length, turning it one way then the other. To capture the hooked lip properly, more needed to come off the underside of the salmon's mouth. He was about to pare some more wood away, but a low hum caused him to pause.

He inclined his head towards the radio, wondering whether it was interference. The reception was fine, the sound of piano music crystal clear. The noise, he realised, was more distant, but getting louder. He placed the near-complete sculpture to the side, stood and looked out of the half-open front door. A point of light, far brighter than any star in the canopy above it, was bobbing towards the shore. The beam swept off to the side and he glimpsed three silhouettes in the small boat.

Voices, obscured by the noise of the outboard.

He thought about stepping back into the tiny cottage and locking the door, but something told him it would be useless.

The engine cut and the torch was directed down at the water. He could see one of the men tilting the engine forward so its propeller was lifted clear of the water. Their words were now audible.

'Soon as it touches the sand, you jump out with the rope.'

'I know! For fuck's sake.'

A twang to their accent. Bristol, or thereabouts. There was a soft crunch as the prow of the boat bit into the sand.

'Now – go on!'

'We're still in the sea. My trainers will get wet.'

A gentle wave broke against the back of the boat, causing it to rock. 'Get in the fucking water and pull us in.'

'Wankers.'

The man hopped into the shallows, the other two laughing as he yanked the vessel forward a couple more feet. His mates jumped straight onto the sand and they all dragged the boat up the beach.

'He's there. In the doorway.'

The torch was directed at him for a moment. 'So he is.'

'My trainers are bloody soaked.'

More low laughter as the three of them began making their way across the sand.

Brookes walked down to his front gate. 'Evening.' It was, he realised, several days since he'd last heard his own voice. The torch was shone into his face and he raised a hand to shield his eyes from its glare.

'Give us all your fucking ducks.'

'Pardon?'

A hand connected with his chest, causing him to stagger back. The gate was kicked open. 'The ducks, you twat.'

'Which ducks?'

Two of them stepped across to the giant mobile.

'He's put holes in them all. For the string.'

The torch shone back in his face. 'You looked inside them, Grandad?'

'I took the plugs in the bases out. To thread the string.'

'What about any notes? Was there paper in any of them?'

'Paper? No.'

The other two had now uprooted the mobile and dragged it

across to the light spilling from his front door. Both men were in their early twenties. The one with a skinhead and leather jacket spoke up. 'Just shake them. If there's a note inside you feel it rattle – she folded them really tight.'

Methodically, they ripped each duck from the mobile, shook it then threw it to the side. After a couple of minutes the mobile had been stripped bare.

'Nothing,' the skinhead spat.

'You got more in there?' the man with the torch demanded, shining it at the stone cottage.

'No.' Brookes looked at the leader's profile. Heavy cheeks and greasy hair flattened against his head. The torch was one of those heavy-duty metal things. More like a policeman's baton.

The beam swung towards the front door. 'Have a look, boys.'

The other two men marched inside. Objects started to crash around, the tinkling of piano music abruptly cut. The torch turned back on him. 'Give us any notes and we'll stop trashing your pad.'

'I have no notes!'

One of them appeared in the doorway, holding up a wooden seagull with outstretched wings. 'Ark! Ark! Ark!' he shouted, before throwing it into the darkness.

The man with the torch leaned closer. 'If they find anything, I'm going to smash your teeth down your throat.'

The sound of breaking china. Plates, cups. Clattering saucepans, cackles of laughter. The two men reappeared. 'Not a thing. He hasn't even got a telly. Fucking peasant.'

The man with the torch cursed. 'Nothing?'

'Apart from this.' The one in the leather coat held up a bottle.

My Laphroaig, Brookes thought, looking at his precious bottle of single malt.

'That'll do. For the boat ride back.'

The torch was shoved under his chin, bright light streaming upwards. He squinted and the roof of his world turned red. The insides of my eyelids, he thought.

'Any more ducks wash up, you keep them safe for us. We'll be back, all right?'

Brookes watched in silence as they ambled back down the beach, passing the bottle between them. They shoved the boat back into the water and soon the engine restarted. The vessel glided off across the bay.

He took a deep breath and examined the tips of his fingers. Tiny tremors ran through them with each thump of his heart. He walked back to his cottage and looked inside. The armchair was on its side, the radio lying next to it. Wooden creatures had been swept to the floor, birds ripped from the ceiling. Fragments of broken crockery were visible on the kitchen floor.

He righted his armchair, lowered himself into it and glanced about his property once more. What were they looking for? Pieces of paper, according to the man with the torch. Inside the ducks. Just shake them, the skinhead had said. If there's a note inside you feel it rattle – she folded them really tight.

A memory surfaced. After the young minke whale had made it back out to sea, he'd picked up a duck washing around his ankles. The very first one he'd seen. Something had rattled inside it. He'd assumed it was a droplet of water or two.

Raising himself back out of the seat, he stepped from the cottage and waited a moment to be sure the boat had gone. Then he made his way to the stone shed at the end of the garden. The spade and bucket were still inside the door. He slid the bucket out, spotting the duck inside, next to the hurricane lamp. He lifted it up and shook it. Something light and insubstantial fluttered against the sides. Hooking a fingernail under the plastic plug, he prised it out then cupped a hand beneath the duck and gently shook it again. A tightly folded piece of paper fell into his palm.

He opened it out. By turning to the side, light fell from his cottage across its surface. Tiny, immaculate handwriting filled the page.

My name is Amira Jasim, age 22, former resident of Baghdad, Iraq. I am writing this letter in English to declare to the world that, on the fourteenth of July, I paid $6,000 to board a ship in

*the Pakistani port of Karachi. This money was to buy me passage
to Great Britain. Last night I, and many others like me, were
abandoned. If we are to die here in the sea, the captain of the
Lesya Ukrayinka is a murderer for he did not turn back for us.*

Brookes squinted in the half-light. There was another paragraph
to go and he could barely make the words out. Carefully folding
the note in half, he made his way back to the cottage.

Nineteen

'More letters,' Rick announced. 'Have you seen the report?'

Jon paused in the act of taking his jacket off. 'And good morning to you, too.'

Rick waved a hand, attention still on his newspaper. 'Sorry. Morning. They say they've got the lot.'

'Who?'

'The *Express*. Every letter, including what they reckon is the final one. The only one still to be found now is the very first. Ten grand, they're offering for that. They're printing them all over the next few days.'

'So which ones are in this morning's edition?'

'Numbers six, seven and eight. Oh,' he glanced across their desks, 'what was the score with Yashin's place?'

Jon removed the keys to the flat from his jacket and sat down. 'Stripped bare. And not because of Murray and Gardiner. They only recovered nine items. I reckon the bloke didn't spend more than his first night there. He's good at folding bedding, though.'

Rick looked vaguely confused. 'Bedding?'

'His blankets. They were … it doesn't matter. What I want to know is where he's been staying since. They were screened in Liverpool ten days ago, so he's been holed up somewhere.'

Rick shrugged. 'He must either know someone or he's got hold of some cash, somehow.'

'Yes,' Jon replied, an image of Mykosowski in his head. He toyed with the ziplock bag containing the keys. 'Have you spoken to Alice recently?'

Rick turned back to his paper. 'No. Why?'

'She hasn't called you this morning or anything?'

'No.' He looked up, wariness cause him to stretch out the word. 'What's happened?'

Jon scratched at an eyebrow. 'Nothing. We had a bit of a run-in. Late last night.'

'I thought you were looking over Yashin's place?'

'I was. But then I swung past our house afterwards.'

'That must have been after ten at night.'

'Around then.'

'Why?'

Jon looked sullenly at his in-tray, then reached out a hand. 'Seen Buchanon yet?'

'Nope.'

Jon read the uppermost piece of paper. 'That's because he's upstairs already.' He held the bit of paper up. 'They're expecting us.'

'Who is?'

'Buchanon and the Chief Super.'

'Chief Superintendent? What ...' He snapped a finger. 'MI5.'

Jon nodded. 'I said we'd get dragged in, didn't I? We'd better head up there.' He gave a mischievous look at the paper on Rick's desk. 'Once you've read me the first of the new letters.'

Rick was on his feet. 'You are joking?'

'Go on. How long can it take?'

Rick bowed his head. 'Letter six.'

Our second day at sea is almost finished. The winds are growing again and dark clouds fill the sky. I am terrified of what the night will bring. The eastern men have got a bottle one had hidden. Ali says it is the same spirit they drank when in the container.

They are now drunken, their stomachs are empty, they are thirsty and exhausted. Night makes all our fears bigger. The waves are much stronger and the eastern men have started shouting. They believe we will all die in the storm. They are waving at the plastic barrel – they want the food.

Jon sat back. 'First two lines of the next?'

'Buchanon and the Chief are waiting for us.'

Jon raised his eyebrows. 'Come on. Just the opening.'
'Fuck's sake.' Rick looked down again. 'Letter seven.'

The storm only lost its strength when the sun rose above the horizon. With the day, I could see the horror on everyone's face. Last night our raft became a place of madness.

'That's it, OK?' He set off across the office. 'Though I have to say, mate, what's coming next is bloody dynamite.'

Upstairs, Jon surveyed the small brass placard. Chief Superintendent Gower. My, my, he said to himself, I'm finally going up in the world. He knocked twice.

'Come in.'

Gower's gravelly voice, Jon thought. Unmistakable. He opened the door to see Buchanon sitting off to one side of a large desk.

Behind it was the giant of a man in overall charge of the Serious Crime Division, of which the Major Incident Team was just one component. 'Morning, gents. Take a seat.'

Jon led the way across the large room, giving his immediate boss a quick nod. 'Sir.'

Buchanon's expression was grave. 'Jon.'

Once they were seated, Gower placed his hands on the desk, interlinking fingers that bristled with patches of greying hair. 'So what have you two been doing, blundering into the set of spooks?' He let the question hang, before grinning broadly, the gap between his front teeth drawing Jon's eye. 'I gather you were accosted at Euston station?'

Jon sat back, relieved at the other man's famously relaxed attitude. 'It was a bit odd. I thought they were after pickpocketing us. Made a right tit of myself trying to warn Rick.'

Gower's eyes were twinkling with amusement. 'Well, you weren't to know. I'm just glad you didn't lay one of them out.'

Jon's mind went back to the Cheshire Cup some six years before. He had captained Greater Manchester Police's rugby team to victory in a hard-fought final at Macclesfield's ground.

During one of many off-the-ball incidents, he'd knocked out the opposition's number eight. The punch had been in plain view of the main stand, and was witnessed by every senior member of Manchester's police force. Once the match was over and he'd raised the cup, Gower had sought him out and congratulated him on the quality of the punch.

'No,' Jon said. 'They whipped out their badges pretty quick.'

The Chief's voice turned serious. 'Well, I'm afraid they're using their weight with this one.'

Jon felt a sinking feeling. 'Meaning what, sir?'

'It's their operation and they want it to stay that way. The shipping owner, Myko-whatsisname, is the subject of many days' surveillance. Your visit wasn't appreciated. Apparently, they observed the entire thing from a room in premises on the other side of the Thames.'

Jon remembered working his way along the giant windows of Mykosowski's office. Strange to think, he mused, the whole thing was being watched.

'It's serious stuff, Jon,' Buchanon interjected. 'If you'd actually followed protocol and taken the trouble to inform the Met you were heading into London to question the guy, they would have told you to steer well clear.'

'Why are they watching him?' Rick asked. 'The MI5 officer wouldn't say.'

'They're not divulging much,' Gower stated. 'It relates to a shipment coming out of the Middle East. Obviously not Turkish Delight.'

'Possibly an arms shipment,' Buchanon added. 'The section of MI5 involved is JTAC.'

'The Joint Terrorism Analysis Centre − where they assess international terrorism?' Rick asked incredulously.

Bloody hell, Jon thought. Was some kind of bomb attack being planned?

Gower gave an appreciative nod. 'Correct, DS Saville.'

'Which involves personnel from both the police and security services,' Rick added. 'So why are we being shut out?'

Gower shrugged. 'Who knows. Everyone's very touchy in

the current climate. I have to instruct you to back off, though. Sorry, lads.'

Jon sat up. 'What about SOCA? Can't we plead an involvement through them?'

'The case is deemed to involve issues of national security and counter-terrorism. So it's MI5's area, not the Serious Organised Crime Agency's,' Gower answered. 'Which places it beyond my reach.'

Jon glanced at Rick, then Buchanon, in exasperation. Both men met his eyes with resigned expressions. 'But, sir,' Jon turned back to the Chief. 'We have three bodies up here. I'm lead officer.'

Buchanon held up a hand. 'It's not going to affect our syndicate's clear-up rate, Jon. These are exceptional circumstances.'

I don't care about the whiteboard, Jon thought. Bollocks to it. I want to catch the bastard who's killing people. He searched for another angle. 'The dead men probably have families. Kids, maybe. People who'll need to know what's happened. We have an obligation here.'

Gower sighed.

He's wobbling, Jon thought, pressing his point home. 'Plus, we've got a psychopath killing pretty much as he pleases. On our patch. A prime suspect whose prints and DNA will, I'm certain, be found at the crime scenes. Christ, the MI5 people told us garrotting is his preferred MO.'

'Jon, calm down,' Buchanon said. 'You work for my syndicate and this investigation gets put on hold. End of story.'

'They know who he is,' Jon said. 'You realise that? They've got a file on him. They have his bloody name.'

'I know. My request to search Interpol's and Europol's fingerprint databases bounced back with a referral to MI5.' Buchanon's voice was cold.

Jon tapped a finger on the arm of his chair. The doors were all slamming. There was no way forward. 'What about if more evidence about our prime suspect comes to light? We're expected to hand that on to MI5 like good little plodders?'

'They aren't overly concerned with these murders, Jon,' Gower announced. 'Finding the cargo is what interests them.

This Yashin person is wanted purely in connection with what he might know about that. I imagine if they find him, we'll be able to add the murder charges to whatever else he's been up to.'

'So I can continue with our investigation?' Jon's look bounced between his senior officers.

Gower stared at Jon for a moment as he considered the request. 'Tie up your local enquiries only. Report anything you find to DCI Buchanon and we'll wait for more word from London.'

'In the meantime,' Buchanon added. 'I need you on other cases.'

Jon glanced about in disbelief. 'So, in reality, you want us to mothball an investigation into three murders?'

Gower closed the file on his desk. 'Yes.'

Jon slumped with his legs thrust straight out, one foot banging repetitively against the side of his desk. 'Unbelievable. Fucking unbelievable.'

Rick shrugged. 'Out of our hands.'

Jon thought about the smug-faced MI5 officer. The little prick. He really did have the clout to pull the plug on my case. He banged his foot against the desk harder.

'Give it a rest, will you?' Rick scowled.

Jon crossed his ankles and leaned his head on the chair's back-rest. 'Well, I'm in no hurry to pick anything else up. Read us the rest of those letters, will you?'

'Oh yeah,' Rick replied, reaching for the paper. 'Right, letter six was dusk, second day on the raft. The Chinese or whoever they are had drunk a bottle of spirits and were demanding all the food.'

Jon laced his fingers across his stomach in readiness for the next revelations.

'Letter seven.' Rick snapped the pages of the newspaper tight and started to read.

The storm only lost its strength when the sun rose above the horizon. With the day, I could see the horror on everyone's face. Last night our raft became a place of madness.

Before night came, an army of waves advanced on us, each lifting us high then throwing us down. The eastern men began to gulp from their bottle, screaming at the sea. Then the one mad with pain from the jellyfish tried to take the drum of food. All order vanished immediately.

We beat them back, but night made it impossible to see. The raft was rearing up and down when they attacked us again. Only their voices let us tell them apart. Lightning showed me the crewman breaking one of their necks. They threw Khadom from the raft. I tried to reach his arm, but the sea carried him off. Again the eastern men retreated.

They stayed at the end of the raft and we didn't know what they would do next. My imagination created such terrible fears. Lightning revealed they were undoing the ropes which secured our raft, trying to kill us all. We attacked them. Fingers dug at my eyes. Water pushed me from the raft and I held a rope. I felt someone slide over me, his screams moving far away.

Ali dragged me back and we stayed close. Whenever the wind dropped, we could only hear one of the eastern men. Hours passed and the need to sleep was so strong. I knew to stay awake, but my eyes could not remain open. I dreamed of our garden in Baghdad, helping my mother to gather pink roses from our bushes. If Ali did not hold me, I would have fallen into the sea.

Daylight revealed only eight of us. Ali, Parviz, Jíno, the old couple from China, myself and the crewman. Qais and Khadom are gone and so is the brother of Parviz, Mehdi.

The back of Ali's leg has been badly bitten. Also, the old lady's arm is injured and her husband talks to himself all the time.

At the other end of the raft only one eastern man remains. He is lying with his legs in the water, weeping and begging forgiveness.

The drum containing all the dates and the bottles of Coke is gone – lost during the night.

Parviz just spotted the eastern man pulling at the ropes once again. They threw him from the raft and he sank without a fight.

Jon lifted his head to stare at his partner. 'This is a bloody horror story. What does the next one say?'

'Letter eight,' Rick lowered his eyes.

This, our third day at sea, has been all pain. The sky is cloudy but the wind is warm. Now our numbers are seven, the raft floats so only larger waves wet us. The sea has made the skin below my knees swell and it causes the wound on Ali's leg to burn. I only wish to lie down.

Salt has also turned all our hair and clothes to cardboard. Thirst and hunger are constantly with us. When food was given out, Jíno and I ate our biscuits slowly, like mouses. The men swallowed theirs quickly, hoping to make their stomachs feel full. All of us licked every dot from our fingers.

We drift, without control, sometimes slowly turning. Everyone's eyes are closing and heads falling to the side. The only sound is water at the sides of our raft. How can there be no ships?

When the sun was low the old man suddenly cried out. He had seen one of the lifeboats, far away. We all looked. There are still many ducks around us, but no one could see a boat. He became most angry.

I also have seen things today. A harbour, its wall lined with the ships that sailed along the Tigris. What is dreaming and what is real are changing places in my head. The weak cannot survive. The arm of the old lady is bad – she holds it like a baby and she no longer knows where she is. The boy is full of despair, and I can only hug him to me. Parviz stares at the sea. This desert of water we are trapped in.

The crewman and Ali have such energy. All day they have secured the ropes the drunken men made loose. Maybe it is work that keeps them strong.

I fear the night and what it brings. My mind makes terrible pictures when it has nothing to see. The wind has stayed away and I pray there will be no more storms.

He looked at Jon. 'How grim is that?'

'Doesn't bear thinking about. How could nothing spot them?'

His mind raced forward. 'You said the *Express* reckons they've got the final letter?'

'So they claim.'

'Well, surely that must mean they didn't survive. If a ship found them, they wouldn't be calling it the final letter. Sounds too much like the end, to me.'

'We'll just have to wait until tomorrow.' Rick folded the paper and placed it to his side.

'So, gentlemen, here's what you've got.'

Jon looked at the incident room's allocator as he approached their desks. In his hand was a printout. 'Fast-track actions were completed by Parks's syndicate who were on shift last night.'

'What is it?' Jon asked, wearily raising a hand.

'Attack on a cannabis factory,' the allocator responded, lowering the paper into Jon's fingers. 'Big house in Didsbury.'

Jon screwed his eyes shut and rubbed the knuckles of his free hand against them. Bursts of purple filled his head. 'Why isn't Narcotics on it?'

'Body in the upstairs bedroom. Blunt trauma wounds to the head.'

'Nationality?' Jon opened his eyes and watched the bursts of colour fade to green then yellow.

'South-east Asian.'

'Vietnamese?'

'Prior experience would suggest so.'

'Here illegally?'

'I wouldn't like to wager otherwise.'

Jon sat up. The dead man would have been the farmer, paid a nominal sum by the gang who'd actually rented the property. His job would have been to cultivate the crop of cannabis plants and take all responsibility should the police discover it. What his job description wouldn't have included was having his head stoved in when a rival gang decided to raid the house.

'Witnesses?'

'Nope.'

'Any decent forensics?'

'The house was stripped bare, the entire crop taken.'

'Bollocks.'

The allocator smiled. 'Another hard-to-do murder goes to Spicer and Saville.'

Jon sat up in his seat. 'Yeah. Cheers, mate.'

The allocator paused in the act of turning away. 'Actually, you might have something to go on.'

'What?' Jon asked, placing the piece of paper on his desk and scanning the top lines. Incident number. Name of officer that called it in. Time of arrival at the scene.

A scrap of paper landed across it. 'Phone number of the man in the house opposite. He saw a four-wheel drive vehicle parked outside the house in the early hours. A group of men were piling bin bags into the boot.'

'Really? Did he clock the registration?'

'No. But he recognised the make. Nissan Navara. Those bloody great things with a huge loading compartment at the back.'

Jon nodded. 'I know. For people who have mistakenly come to believe they're living on a half-million-acre cattle ranch out in America.'

The allocator chuckled. 'Can't be too many of those things on the road.'

'Maybe not.' Jon turned his computer on then logged on to the Police National Computer's database of stolen or abandoned vehicles. He selected the overnight numbers for the north-west and started searching the list on the off chance the vehicle had only just been stolen for the raid. Audis, BMWs, a Subaru, Hondas, a Lexus, a few Mercedes. Another Audi. His eyes stopped halfway down. 'Rick! Guess what's been dumped on the forecourt of the Avis place by Piccadilly station?'

'Don't tell me: a stolen Navaro? Surely we can't have that kind of luck.'

'No. A red Mini Metro. Registration ends in the letter X.'

'The car we parked next to out in Runcorn?'

'Precisely,' Jon grinned, standing up and reaching for his jacket. 'And if he dumped it on the forecourt, chances are there'll be CCTV footage.'

'Hang on.' Rick glanced nervously towards Buchanon's office. 'What about this cannabis farm?'

'Fuck that. I'm sure the murder victim won't mind waiting for us.'

'But, we've been told, Jon. The Chief Super himself—'

'Said to tie up any local enquiries,' Jon said. 'You coming?'

Alice pointed to the desk by the water cooler. 'Is this free?'

A woman with multicoloured beads at the ends of her braided hair paused from stacking files in the cabinet next to it. 'Think so.'

'Great.' Alice placed her handbag on the carpet, sat down and turned on the ancient-looking computer. As it slowly cranked itself to life, she looked around the office of Refugees Are People. Men and women were bustling around, gathering up documents for clients waiting in the interview rooms that ran the length of the main corridor.

Once the screen settled down, she opened up Google, typed in 'Royal Liverpool University Hospital' and clicked on the website. The UK's largest Accident and Emergency centre. Clicking on the tabs for wards, she scrolled down to P. Psychiatry provided by another specialist unit. Damn. She scrolled back up to C then selected Casualty. Psychiatric clinic provided as part of the Casualty Unit. That'll do for starters, she thought, picking up the phone and keying in the number.

It rang for a full minute before the call was answered. 'Casualty.'

'Hello. I'm phoning from a charity called Refugees Are People, over in Manchester. I'm trying to trace the records of a foreign national currently in the mental health unit at Sale—'

'You've come through to the nurses' station. I'll try to put you through to the front desk.'

The line cut to a beeping noise before a woman with a foreign accent came on. 'Hello?'

'Hi,' Alice said, trying to place where she was from. Russia, maybe? 'I'm phoning from a charity called Refugees Are People, over in Manchester. We work with the mental health unit at

Sale General. I'm trying to trace the records of a foreign national currently on the unit. The person was transferred from the Royal Liverpool.'

'What is the person's name or NHS number, please?'

'We don't have that information. The case file is missing.'

'You have no name?'

'Just J. Smith.'

'When was Mr Smith transferred from—'

'It's a fictional name. John Smith? For people whose identity is unknown.'

'I'm sorry. I do not understand.'

'I assume the staff at the MHU at Sale General gave the patient that name until his actual records show up. He was transferred from your hospital about six days ago.'

'I will have to search. There are many admissions here.'

'I realise. Could I leave you my name and number, please?'

'Certainly.'

'It's Alice Spicer. You can reach me at this office or, better still, on my mobile.' She dictated both numbers to the woman at the other end of the line. Please don't just put this request to the bottom of the pile, she thought, worrying how long it would be before a decision was made to shunt the poor soul off to Yarl's Wood detention centre. Knowing the pressure for beds, it would be sooner rather than later. 'Could I have your name, please? In case I need to ring back.'

'Yes. It is Yulia.'

'Julia?'

'No, Yulia. It is Russian. And my second name is Volkova. Shall I spell it?'

Twenty

Jon looked along the street. It ran past a massive square warehouse that had been turned into an apartment hotel, then continued towards Ancoats. The end of the building further on was covered by a black poster with white lettering. H.A. Howard & Sons. Day & Evening Wear. The poster was mottled with age, corners peeling back. He wondered how long ago the company went out of business. From the direction the Metro was facing, it had come from Ancoats. 'The vehicle's registered owner lives in Blackley. I wonder if our man's been based around there,' Jon mused.

'He could have driven it from further afield,' Rick replied.

Jon surveyed the Avis office's small forecourt. It was crowded with glossy Audis, BMWs, Range Rovers and a couple of Porsches. The battered old Metro looked completely out of place. 'Awfully posh cars,' he stated.

'Our prestige models,' the young staff member said. 'Budget ones are located at our sister site, five minutes away.'

'So,' he glanced at the nametag on her tunic. 'It was here when you turned up for work this morning, Maria?'

'Yes. At half past seven,' she replied, bands of sunlight catching in her long mane of black hair.

Jon glanced at the bodywork of a nearby Porsche and saw the same shimmer there.

'It's completely blocking this entrance,' she continued. 'We can't get any cars on this side of the forecourt out. Stolen, is it?'

'Yes,' Jon replied, stepping round the vehicle to examine the crumpled rear panel. 'It's our man's.'

Rick was peering through the side window. 'Doors are unlocked.'

Jon bent forward to survey the litter strewn across the back seat. Crisp packets, chocolate wrappers, empty bottles of milk-shake. 'He's got a sweet tooth.'

'And a big appetite, assuming it's all his,' Rick murmured.

'If it is,' Jon said, eyes on the neck of an empty bottle. 'We could have DNA to add to his fingerprints.' He straightened up and turned to the office. 'Please tell me those things actually work.'

The lady looked at the two cameras mounted on the front corners of the low building. Both were trained on the forecourt. 'With these cars parked here overnight? Absolutely.'

Jon sent a silent thank you to the blue sky above. 'We'll need last night's tapes, in that case. I'll give you a receipt. Rick? Can you call in a crime-scene unit?'

'When will the car be moved?' Maria asked.

Jon snapped on a pair of latex gloves. 'Right now, if you want.' He opened the driver's door, released the handbrake and, with one hand on the wheel and the other on the window frame, rolled it clear of the entrance.

Rick drew the video room's curtains against the glare of the sun. 'It's always so hot in here,' he complained, resting a hand on the radiator. 'No wonder. This bloody thing's on full.' He checked each end for any way of turning it off. Nothing. 'Maintenance. What a waste of space they are.'

Jon pulled his chair closer to the screen. 'Open a window then.'

'I would if the things in here weren't all locked.' He loosened his tie and sat in the next seat.

'I thought you liked the heat.'

Rick shot him a questioning look.

'You're always going on sunbeds.'

'Ha bloody ha. This tan's from surfing, mate. One hundred per cent natural.'

'My arse.' Jon sat back, remote in his hand. 'All set?'

'All set.'

He pressed play, guessing the succession of still images were separated by intervals of about two seconds. Repeatedly pressing fast-forward, he brought the speed up to times thirty-two. The time record in the upper right-hand corner moved swiftly forward. Crowds of early-evening commuters filled the screen, freezing for an instant before blurring out of sight. 'Like watching an episode of *Ben Ten*,' Jon whispered.

'What?'

'*Ben Ten*. It's this kids' programme Holly loves. The boy in it can change into one of ten monster things. One has super-speed. You know, there one second, gone the next. She loves it.'

'When have you got her again?'

Jon thought about the previous night's confrontation. 'I'm not sure. Weekend after next, hopefully.'

'I can't wait for Saturday. We've decided on taking Zak to Scarborough. Apparently you get some nice surf there.'

Jon snorted. 'And who'll be looking after the little fella while you and Andy are out catching waves?'

'We'll take it in turns.'

'You'll be marching up and down the beach, trying to balance him on a manky old donkey he'll insist on riding.'

'He's too young for that.'

'That and trying to wipe melted ice cream off him. Sand'll get stuck to him and he'll start to itch. Surfing. You'll be lucky.'

'You're a miserable sod, aren't you? It's worked fine down in Cornwall.'

Jon shrugged, eyes fixed on the screen. Late evening came on, the numbers of people appearing in the images suddenly picking up as eleven o'clock approached. 'Last trains home. People heading into the station.'

The street grew quiet once again, the headlights of passing taxis making the screen temporarily flare. Midnight passed by and Jon pressed the remote, bringing the speed down to times sixteen.

'Sometime in the next seven hours.' A fox appeared at the edge of the picture and vanished. 'I saw him the other night.'

'Who?'

'The fox.'

'Where?'

'Out the window at Carmel's. He was following his owner.'

'It had an owner?'

'Yeah. He was scoping cars for anything to nick.'

'The fox?'

'No, the ... forget it.'

'You're losing it, mate.'

A dark blur suddenly obscured the view of the forecourt. 'What the ...?' Jon hit pause. 'A moth.' He speeded up again and the insect disappeared.

At twelve minutes past five, headlights began to approach. The footage skipped forward and suddenly a vehicle was parked across the forecourt's entrance.

'Back!' Rick snapped.

'I know, I know,' Jon replied, pressing the rewind button. He let the succession of images jump back, and when the glow from the car's headlights began to fur the edge of the screen, he pressed play. The car itself appeared. The next still showed it parked across the entrance.

Jon felt himself hunching forward, finger ready on pause.

The car door half open, the top of a man's head visible in the gap. Next image, he was standing by the side of the car, wearing jeans and a dark turtleneck top, its sleeves rolled up to his elbows.

'It's him,' Jon stated, studying the man. His shoulders were rounded with muscle, but there was a slight scrawniness about his neck, as if he'd just recovered from a bout of illness. The next image showed him removing a sports bag from the rear seat. Then he was mid-stride across the forecourt. Jon spoke from the corner of his mouth, not wanting to look away from the screen. 'What do you reckon – five foot nine or ten?'

'Five ten easily.'

'And what? Twelve, twelve and a half stone?'

'About that, yes.'

So, Jon thought. You're the fabled killing machine. He reflected on his own size and strength. I'm at least six inches taller and about three stone of muscle heavier. If you were up against me on a rugby pitch, you would definitely come off worse.

But the following image caught Yashin looking directly up at the camera. The menace seemed to surge off his face like a wave of heat and Jon felt his tongue go loose in his mouth. He had the urge to look away, instinct telling him not to catch the man's eye too long. There was a poise about him. It reminded Jon of the fluid way dancers or gymnasts moved. Speed and flexibility. No, Jon thought. I'm not sure I'd like to meet you on a rugby pitch, after all. He felt a tapping on his upper arm and turned to Rick. 'Mmm?'

'You were miles away. I was saying, he really should see someone about his anger issues. He's got a face like thunder.'

'Anger?' Jon tried to smile. 'Rage, more like. Early coronary for him, at the rate he's going.'

'Cutting across the forecourt like that, he's heading for the station. Probably through the side entrance where all the smokers congregate.'

'You're right. Know what? I feel we've been here before.'

Rick nodded. 'Butcher of Belle Vue. That case must be four or five years ago, now.'

'And at that time of the morning, we know there's pretty much only two places you can catch a train to.'

'The Intercity to London or the Express to Manchester Airport. Think he's left the country?'

Jon hesitated. Normally, the thought of a suspect making it out of Manchester left him wanting to stamp his feet with frustration. But this man ... maybe it was better if he had crawled back to where he came from. 'Possibly,' he said cautiously. 'We'd better check the CCTV from Piccadilly station.'

Twenty-One

The CCTV suite inside Piccadilly station smelled of old coffee. The light on the percolator glowed red in the dim surroundings and Jon wondered when the pot had actually been brewed. 'Mind if I grab a coffee?'

'Go for it,' the man sitting before the bank of screens replied. 'Not sure how long it's been sat there for. I only drink tea.'

Jon stepped over to the machine, filled a waxed-paper cup and took a sip. A sharp, bitter taste filled his mouth. Probably yesterday, he thought. 'Rick, want one?'

His partner eyed him suspiciously. 'What's it like?'

'Not bad.' He couldn't keep his mouth straight.

'Yeah, right.' Sarcasm filled Rick's voice.

The security officer glanced at Jon. 'Rank, is it?'

'Like the scrapings off a badger's arse.'

The man grinned as he turned back to the screens. 'What time are we looking at, again?'

'If you start at ten past five. He probably entered the station by the side doors near the Virgin Trains desk.'

'No problem.' The man pressed a couple of buttons and scrutinised the console's centre screen. 'Camera fourteen covers that entrance. Here we are. Not much footfall at that time of the morning.' He punched the time in and the recording started at exactly ten past five.

'Impressive,' Rick stated, taking the spare chair. 'Is it digital?'

The man's fingers were on a little joystick. 'Yeah. Top notch, it is.'

At fourteen minutes past, they spotted a figure approaching. The outer doors parted and the man calling himself Yashin appeared, one elbow raised, arm bent back on itself, the sports bag slung over his shoulder.

'That's him.' Jon took another sip and waited for the roof of his mouth to shrivel.

The man froze the picture and zoomed in on Yashin's face. 'Jesus, what does he do for a living? Steal wheelchairs off disabled grannies?'

Rick smiled. 'Nasty-looking bastard, isn't he?'

The officer leaned forward. The Russian's mouth was slightly open, exposing the jagged line of lower teeth. 'Ugly as. You want his face on a printout or emailing anywhere?'

'Both, if that's all right.' Rick placed a business card next to the man's keyboard. 'That address, please.'

The officer saved the image to a file in the tool bar at the side of the screen. 'Continue?'

'Yes.' Rick sat back.

Feeling light-headed with caffeine, Jon placed a hand on the backrest of Rick's chair. He glanced at the oily surface of the coffee. One more sip, he told himself.

The footage on the screen resumed and Yashin moved out of the camera's field. The security officer switched to a different camera, this one mounted much higher. 'There he is. Screen left.'

Yashin made straight for the third set of sliding doors leading to the platforms themselves. 'Looks like he's made this journey before,' Jon said.

The security officer switched views again. Now they were looking directly down on the doors. Yashin strode into view.

'He's getting thin on top,' Rick murmured.

'Platform seven,' the security officer announced. 'The five twenty to London.' He switched to a camera positioned far down the platform which looked back to the terminal. Yashin made his way past the first-class carriages and boarded the train about two-thirds of the way along.

'Had his tickets already,' Rick said, looking back at Jon. 'We could try and see if he paid by card.'

Jon swilled the remains of the coffee round. 'Forget it. He'll be using cash – it leaves no trail.'

'Good point.' Rick looked at the clock on the wall. 'Wonder what time that train gets to London.'

'It's less than two and a half hours, these days. Eight, or just before,' the security officer stated.

'Does Euston have a similar system to this?' Jon nodded at the bank of screens and the dozens of people captured on them.

'Not this good – but they'll be able to pick him up again.'

'Great, cheers.' Jon took the final sip, grimacing like it was a shot of neat whisky. 'That's me bouncing off the walls.'

'I can't believe you just drank that.' Rick shook his head, turning back to the screens. 'He's off our patch.'

Jon looked back at the main console, realising he could now feel the blood pumping through his ears. The Virgin train was pulling out, carriage after carriage gliding from view. There you go again, he thought. Always one step ahead.

'Where do you think he's heading for in London?' Rick asked.

'Who else is involved in this thing that lives down there?'

'The shipping owner.'

Jon nodded. 'The shipping owner. Someone's been giving our man funds to operate with, too. Train tickets that time of the morning can't be cheap.'

'We'd better get this to Buchanon then.'

Knowing the information would be passed straight on, Jon didn't move. Furnishing that smarmy MI5 officer with information, he thought. How bloody infuriating.

'We are passing this on, aren't we, Jon?'

A rapid series of beeps. Jon pulled his mobile from his pocket. 'DI Spicer.'

'It's Catherine. From the incident room at Grey Mare Lane.'

Jon racked his brain. One of the civilian support workers. 'Hi, Catherine.'

'Hi. You asked me to look into the payphone records for the two buildings where those murder victims were housed.'

'Yes. What've you found?'

'There was a call from Hedley Court in Oldham to the London number you flagged up.'

'Myko Enterprises?'

'That's right. It was called on Saturday the twenty-first at nine forty-three in the evening. Duration of the call was five minutes forty-two seconds.'

Jon felt himself beaming. We are closing in on this bastard. 'Good work. We'll be back in soon.' He cut the call and raised a thumb triumphantly at Rick. 'Victim two, the one found in Oldham. Tsarev. He also phoned the shipping owner's office.' He looked at the empty platform on the screen and pictured the Virgin train pulling into London. 'What I'd give to speak with that Mykosowski again.'

The records of Myko Enterprises' ships were spread across Rick's desk. 'Nothing from St Petersburg in the last month.'

'And even if there had been,' Jon responded, 'it wouldn't be approaching the west coast of Britain from a northerly direction.'

'Why?'

He pointed to the world atlas he'd borrowed from Buchanon's office. 'Look. Coming from St Petersburg, you go through the straits of Finland, Sweden, Denmark and Norway. But then why go north, round the tip of Scotland and down past Ireland? The distance is greater and you've got sub-arctic weather conditions up there. It's why the Jocks are such a miserable bunch.' He gave Rick a quick grin. 'Far quicker to go south towards the English Channel.'

'So, it's unlikely the murder victims were on a ship travelling from St Petersburg.'

'Which other ships of his were in the area when the fishing boat was found?'

Rick consulted his pieces of paper. 'Of the ones I've got here, three. The *Baden Star*, en route to Bergen, Norway. The *King Olav III*, heading south to Barcelona.' He pondered the last printout then put it aside. 'This one is, I think, out of the time frame. It was heading to Felixstowe then on to the States. But it docked at Felixstowe six days before the Russians were even found.'

Jon nodded. 'Probably. What was its name, anyway?'

'The *Lesya Ukrayinka*.'

'OK, let's go with the *Baden Star* to begin with. It seems to fit best.'

'DI Spicer.'

Jon looked round at his senior officer's bark. Buchanon remained in the doorway of his office for a moment then stepped back inside without another word.

'He was not happy,' Rick whispered, throwing Jon a questioning look.

'Nope.' Jon walked across the incident room, catching a few ominous glances as he went. 'Sir?' He leaned his head and shoulders across the threshold of Buchanon's office.

'Come in and close the door.'

Once it clicked shut, Jon turned round. I have a horrible feeling what this will be about, he thought.

Buchanon was studying a sheet of paper. 'Arkville Road, Heaton Moor. An incident was reported there at ten thirty last night.'

Jon stood where he was, arms hanging at his sides.

'A dark blue Mondeo with a registration I don't need to remind you of. One male occupant got out and threatened the female driver of a Nissan Micra. The Mondeo had been parked opposite number thirty-seven, but attempted to drive off when the female occupant of that house came out.' He drilled Jon with a hostile look. 'The driver of the Mondeo then appeared to verbally threaten the male occupant of the house. Oh sit down, for God's sake.'

Jon took a seat. 'Who rang this in?'

'The driver of the black cab. I told you, DI Spicer, to leave it. Do you ever bloody listen?'

'Sorry, sir.'

'What happens when your wife – I assume it was her you were having a slanging match with?'

Slanging match? Jon thought. I didn't say a bloody word. He nodded.

'What happens if your wife files an official complaint?'

Jon shrugged. 'You suspend me?'

Buchanon looked at the printout once again and shook his head. 'Sometimes, I think you actually try and fuck things up for yourself. What a mess.' He put the piece of paper to the side and the anger seemed to go out of him. 'What's going on with Alice? She's not prepared to allow you back?'

There was a weariness in his voice, as if this was a conversation he'd grown tired of long ago. Jon thought about the officers in the incident room outside. He knew of at least ten others struggling to keep their marriage afloat. 'No.'

'And how's your daughter doing?'

'She's taken to wetting the bed again. Her behaviour at school has gone downhill. She's quiet. Far too quiet.'

'I'm sorry, Jon. I really am. At least the psychiatrist, Braithwaite, hasn't called in a complaint, yet. I assume it was him you were having words with?'

Give him time, Jon thought. 'What would you like me to do?'

'Carry on. But promise me, you'll keep away from your old house.'

'I promise.'

Buchanon sighed, doubt on his face. 'What's been happening with the cannabis farm murder?'

Jon glanced down. 'Well – we started a search for stolen Nissan Navaras on the PNC. But I found that stolen Metro instead.'

'The one from Runcorn?'

'Yes. It had been dumped outside Piccadilly station. We've got Yashin boarding the early-morning train to London. There's a SOCO taking samples from the car. I reckon we'll get a DNA sample from one of the bottles he'd been—'

'Pull him.'

'Pardon?'

'I'm not authorising any more resources for that investigation. Pull the scene of crime officer, seal the car and get it impounded. Write a report on Yashin's movements for me and I'll send it down to MI5.'

'But, sir – we'll ...' He caught the look in his boss's eye. 'OK.'

'Have you taken a full statement from the man living opposite the cannabis farm?'

'Not as yet.'

'Door-to-doors on the houses the syndicate on cover didn't have time to knock on?'

'No.'

Buchanon sat back. 'Well, there's your schedule for the rest of the day.' He turned to his computer screen and began to type.

'Sir.' Jon made for the door.

'What was that about?' Rick asked, looking across the desks as Jon sat down.

'Me and my career.' He made a swirling motion with a forefinger. 'Going down the pan.'

Rick's eyes moved to Buchanon's office then returned to Jon. 'Come on. He was almost shouting in there. What's up?'

Jon looked at his partner, suddenly tired of the subterfuge. He dropped his voice. 'Late last night I was parked outside Alice's. The nosy old cow who lives opposite saw me sitting there and rang the house.'

Rick pressed his forehead against the heel of his hand. 'What the hell were you doing there?'

'Waiting for that shifty bastard Braithwaite to show his face. He's been leaving the house in the evenings and driving over to Fairfield Street.'

Rick raised his head. 'You've been following him around?'

'Too right I have.'

'Christ.' He frowned. 'Fairfield Street near Piccadilly?'

'Exactly. Where the working girls tout for business,' Jon replied, realising his way to alert Alice was sitting opposite him.

'What's he been doing there?'

'So far, just sitting in his car and watching them.'

Rick turned away, tapping his fingers for a couple of seconds.

Jon watched him. I can almost hear what's going through your head, he thought. 'I don't reckon Alice has any idea of what he's up to. She probably believes he's driving straight home.'

Rick inserted the tip of a thumbnail between his lips and started working his lower teeth against it.

'She won't believe it if I tell her,' Jon continued. 'All I could do was keep following the bastard and hope to catch him in the act. But now he's on to me, he'll be more careful. Rick, the arsehole is sleeping in the same house as my wife and daughter.'

'All right!' Rick banged his palm down on the table. 'I'll let her know what you've just said. How many times has he driven over there?'

'I've followed him three times, so far. Plus I saw him once when I was picking up a curry for me and Carmel.'

'And he's definitely scouting for girls? Not just ... going for a drive?'

Jon cocked his head to the side.

'OK, OK, I'll speak to her. There's probably a perfectly normal reason, though.'

'When?'

'When, what?'

'When will you speak to her?'

'Tonight.'

'Cheers, mate. If I could deal with it myself, you know I would.'

Jon splashed more of Carmel's rum into the tumbler and let himself sink down in the armchair. His feet ached and he kicked off his shoes. Immediately the air began to cool his socks. Feels good, he thought. Even better with a sip of this stuff.

To his side, The Pogues CD got to 'Dirty Old Town' and he pointed Carmel's remote, inching the volume up a notch. He reached for his thin briefcase and slid the folder of photos and scrawled notes out. Vladimir Yashin. Jon sipped again, holding the liquid in his mouth, letting the warmth spread deep into his gums as he stared at the man's face. Where, he wondered, were you born? What were you like as a child? Images of a windswept Russian town appeared in his head. A young boy skulking in the ruins of a derelict building, hurling broken bricks at a cat trapped in the corner. Trudging home to a drab apartment and a father who sat immobile with a bottle of vodka. Did he beat you? Did he hammer your love of killing into you?

He placed the images from the CCTV to one side and looked at the copy of the photo taken at the screening unit. He held the photo nearer then reached down to the floor lamp and switched it on. The printout was slightly grainy and Jon held it so close to his face he could see the very pixels making up the man's pupils. He examined the gaps in between them. What, he thought, are you?

An oblong of light appeared in the dark window before him. He turned to see Carmel, wearing a vest top and knickers, in the doorway of the bedroom.

'Sorry,' he said. 'I'll turn it down.'

She waved a hand, padding barefoot across the room before perching on the armrest. 'What are you up to?'

He angled his head back, taking in her slightly puffy eyes and twisted strands of hair. 'Just work stuff.'

'Who is he?'

'A suspect. Nasty piece of work.' He slid the photos back into the cover and looked at her reflection. 'Want a sip?'

She looked down at the glass he was raising. 'No. Is he connected to that case from the other day? The asylum seeker?'

'Yes. But I can't discuss it, Carmel. You know that.'

Her head turned. 'You've always got this CD on the go.'

'Have I?'

'Always.' She half stood and reached across him to pick up the case, her hair tickling the top of his head.

He raised his face so it played across his eyes and nose. The strands smelled faintly of coconuts and he suddenly wondered how many days it was since they'd shared a proper conversation. He cursed himself. I've been treating you like shit.

'*Rum, Sodomy and the Lash,*' she murmured, sitting back on the armrest and scrutinising the cover image. 'It's such a disturbing painting.'

Jon slid his hand against the small of her back. He began a gentle rubbing motion, eyes closing as he did so. 'The music's not, though. I don't know why they went for that cover.' He heard her opening the CD case and, a moment later, he felt the muscles beneath his palm harden.

'You still love her, don't you?'

He kept his eyes closed, the memories swirling in his head. 'Who?'

'"To Alice, the girl I kissed on a factory wall. I'll love you always."'

Oh no. He remembered the inscription he'd written to her on the inner sleeve, even though he knew the album would probably end up as part of his collection. The song started winding down and he felt the CD case land in his lap.

'You sit here night after night playing that bloody album.'

He opened his eyes as a drum started its lively beat. Turning the music off, he looked up at her. 'Carmel—'

'No, don't.' Arms crossed tight against her breasts, she stood up. 'It's all you ever listen to, sitting here late at night.'

'It happened to be at the top of my box when I opened it up. That's all.'

'Obviously.'

He heard a sniff and saw her fingers picking at the seam of her vest top. When he reached forward to place a hand against her hip, she stepped away.

'What are you actually doing here?'

Jon looked around. 'What do you mean?'

'Why are you living here, with me?'

He realised, with dismay, that she was about to start a dissection of their relationship. 'Come on, Carmel. What sort of question is that?'

She stared back at him, lips set tight.

Knowing he was going to have to give a proper answer, he raised himself up. 'Carmel, work's a nightmare at the moment. But it won't be for ever. We'll go for that meal, start enjoying ourselves again.'

'You still love her, don't you?'

He slumped back and looked at the CD. 'I don't know. My life's been turned upside down. I don't know what I feel.'

'Yes or no. Do you love her?'

'Of course I do. She's the mother of my daughter.'

'No, not your family. Do you still love her? Is that where you'd rather be? With her?'

He kept his head bowed. I can't summon the energy, he thought. Denying, pretending, lying. 'Yes.'

'And there's me thinking ...' She took a sharp breath in. 'You shit.'

The anger in her voice made him look up. Tears had filled her eyes and an inkling of how badly he'd judged the situation began to dawn.

'I did everything I could to make this work. I tried to make your daughter feel at home – show you how good I am with kids. I was even stupid enough to think that, one day ...' She raised a hand and wiped furiously at her eyes.

'Oh, Carmel.' Guilt, likes waves of nausea, washing out from his belly. 'I didn't think you were ... we've never talked about having kids.'

'I'm thirty years old! You think all I want from life is to swan about around Manchester? Did you?'

Half-heartedly, Jon held out a hand towards her. Have I made a mess of this. He wondered what he could say to make her feel better. No, he decided. No more pissing around. She deserves the truth: nothing less than that. 'I'm so sorry, Carmel. I've got a family already.'

'A wife that doesn't want you,' she spat. 'And I now see why.'

'It's my family,' he asserted quietly, hand dropping back down, eyes lowering with it. The silence stretched out then he heard her footsteps walking away.

'Get out. Take that CD out of my machine. Pack your stuff and get out.'

He said nothing, staying perfectly still until the bedroom door shut. Do I go over? Knock? Try to apologise? He took another sip. What's the point? You don't really want to be here. Slowly, he lifted his head and looked at the ghost in the glass. Nice one, mate. You really fucked that up. They stared at one another for a while longer then he fished his phone from his pocket and selected a number. A groggy voice eventually came on the line.

'What?'

'Rick,' Jon whispered. 'Any chance I can crash on your sofa?'

'When?'

'Now?'

'Now?

'Yeah.'

'Carmel?'

'Finished.'

His partner sighed. 'Come on. I can let you know why Braithwaite's been driving over to Fairfield Street as well.'

Twenty-Two

Jon walked down the steps of the renovated warehouse where Rick's apartment was located. It had rained heavily in the night and the dark asphalt of Whitworth Street glinted in the morning sun. Curls of steam rose from the kerbs and the city felt like it had been given a new lease of life.

'Just nipping into Olive, they'll have this morning's *Express*,' Rick announced at his side. 'The next five letters are in it – numbers nine to thirteen.'

'You and those letters,' Jon replied. 'You're obsessed.'

'And proud to admit it,' Rick called over his shoulder, heading to the delicatessen at the corner of the building. 'And, of course, you're not at all interested in hearing what they've got to say.'

Jon shrugged. 'I'm parked at the back.' He wandered round to the rear of the warehouse. The far side of the little car park was bordered by the Rochdale canal. Follow that far enough, he thought, and you'll get to Pomona Docks where Dad used to work. He pictured Alan unloading cargo from ships that had travelled to Manchester from around the world.

His mind went back to the conversation he'd had after getting to Rick's, a box balanced across his forearms, a bag hanging from each shoulder. His colleague had spoken to Alice and raised the subject of Braithwaite. Alice had promptly let rip, accusing Jon of stalking the man. It was Jon's fault, she'd asserted, that Braithwaite had decided to cool things off.

'He's leaving her?' Jon had asked, trying to damp down his delight.

'Just taking a step back, by the sound of it. And don't look so pleased, mate,' Rick had replied. 'Alice is furious with you. She said Braithwaite had only been searching for a patient. She's

206

trying to decide whether to let her solicitor know what happened.'

'Her solicitor?' he'd asked. I was hoping she hadn't actually got herself one. Christ, she really is going to end our marriage. Divorce. That word, he thought, carries such weight. Like the sound of a funeral bell. 'What do you mean, a patient?'

'Some rich kid. The daughter of one of his patients who left home and ended up on the game.'

'Lying prick,' Jon had replied.

As he stepped on to the cobbles, he became aware of a slight grittiness beneath his shoes. He looked at his car: it was covered in a light, reddish, sheen. Frowning, he extended a finger and ran it down the rear windscreen. Powdery sand. He looked at the other cars and realised they all had a similar coating. Footsteps approached.

'This is going to be good,' Rick said, paper in one hand. 'Is it unlocked?'

Jon pointed the key fob and the locks pipped. 'Seen this sand?'

Rick regarded the vehicle. 'Oh, yeah. They mentioned that on the radio.'

'Mentioned what?'

'It's from the Sahara. Storms down there launched it up into the atmosphere then winds carried the clouds north. It's to do with all this hot weather we've been having.' He dabbed a finger on the roof and then circled it against his thumb. 'Like red talcum.'

'More like a five-quid car wash,' Jon grunted. 'I should send the bill to wherever the stuff came from.' He opened the driver's door, slung his briefcase on to the back seat and got in.

'You do that,' Rick said, climbing in the passenger door. 'Just address it to "The owner of the Sahara Desert, Africa". I'm sure he'll pop a cheque in the post.'

Jon shot him a look as he started the engine.

Rick opened up the paper as the vehicle rumbled backwards across the cobbles. 'Right, here we go. Letter nine, the one found in Lyme Regis that ends with the crewman seeing a boat.'

'Shall we skip it? We know what it says.'

'No – I want to go over it again.' He smoothed the page and started to read.

Last night was free of storms. The old lady moaning and her husband talking to himself disturbed us all. In the blackness, the boy saw balls of fire floating above the sea. He believed they were witches. To calm him, I said they were ships, searching for us. I heard Parviz praying.

At dawn, the old Chinese man told us he was getting help. He stood up, but I was too weak to reach out. He stepped from the raft and was gone.

Our numbers are now only six. Ali said to use the pallets from the ends of the raft to make a higher area in the middle. The man with the throat scars agreed.

Jon felt his upper body jolt. Throat scars. His mind jumped back to the previous night when he'd been studying Yashin's mugshot in minute detail. The image was slightly grainy and Carmel's flat had been dimly lit, but, thinking about it now, he thought he could remember something wrong with the man's skin, just above the top of his turtleneck. No, Jon said to himself, surely not.

'You all right?' Rick asked. 'Not left something in my flat?'

'No,' Jon replied, relaxing his shoulders and joining the slow-moving traffic on Whitworth Street. 'Carry on.'

Rick turned back to the paper.

Clothes and some plastic bags have been laid across, so little water passes through. At last, after four days, we can lie down without getting wet.

Hunger has woken us all. Cruel and sharp, it never tires. After our noodles, Ali and I lay down and talked of how Abu Nawas Street was before the Americans came. Strolling along beside the river, choosing a restaurant to sit and eat muskof. The smell of the fish as it roasted slowly beside the coals. Amba, the spicy mango sauce, and sweet, smoky tea, flavoured by the pot being left on the glowing coals. Such memories!

Ali spoke of bache, the lamb flavoured by dried lemon pieces. I spoke of sipping yoghurt, mixed with water, salt and ice. He answered with watermelon, cool from the fridge and I begged him to stop.

At sunset, a family of dolphins surrounded us, chasing under our raft, leaping from the sea. They are the masters here and we are nothing. When they left, I cried. Who will save us?

Jon glanced at Rick. 'What does the next letter say?'

Rick gave a wry grin. 'I thought you weren't interested.'

'Come on, stop fucking about.'

'OK, OK – ready?'

The crewman has just seen a boat!

When he shouted, I did not believe it was real. Then others saw it too.

It is the life boat that was washed overboard. Excitement passed through us like electricity. Everyone had suddenly the strength to wave and shout.

They saw us and paddled closer. After some time we could hear their voices. Four men, all from the crew. The man with the throat scars shouted back to them. I recognised the language – now I know he is Russian. I decided to keep it secret that I understood his words.

Unable to quite believe what he was hearing, Jon looked at Rick again.

His partner glanced up. 'What?'

Needing more time to absorb the implications of what he suspected, Jon said, 'This woman is sharp. I like her – keeping quiet that she speaks Russian. Good move.'

Rick nodded, then continued to read.

The men in the boat were happy to see him, but they looked at us like we are dogs. It is strange no one from the containers is with them.

When the life boat was close, the man with throat scars swam across. His friends pulled him in and I was afraid they would leave us. They talked for a long time, but I could not hear what of. Then they paddled next to us.

Using English, the man with throat scars explained the lifeboat has no food, but two large bottles of water. They have a compass in the handle of a knife. A thing no more in size than an old dinar, but it can save us all. They will tie our raft to the boat, then use their oars and our plastic sheets to make a sail and steer us east. They say we will find ships in that direction.

The man with the throat scars said he will keep the drum with the food safe in the boat. I had not the strength to argue. Later, when they passed over our rations, we could not wake the old woman to eat.

For the first time, I told Ali about my life in Baghdad. I described our garden and the rose bushes my mother so loved. I told him of my job as an interpreter. How, since I was a little girl, I liked other languages. How Daddy used to get me English and Russian newspapers. How I improved until I became a gold student. How proud of myself I was to do the job.

When the Americans came, the Russian oil company I worked for had to leave. Like many, I thought at first the Americans had come to help us. I worked for the Exxon Mobil Corporation, helping their people assess how our oilfields might be developed. Then I was offered a higher-paid job, working for the CPA. So much money to be spent on reconstruction! But the office was run most poorly. Files everywhere, Americans leaving for their country, new ones taking over their jobs.

I had so much more to say, but Ali did not have the strength to stay awake.

'The CPA,' Rick murmured. 'That's the interim government, isn't it? The thing the Americans set up to run the country.'

'Maybe they can work out who she is, then,' Jon answered. 'How many translators can there be?'

Rick shrugged. 'All I know is their identities are kept very secret — for their own protection. They don't even use their real names when doing their work. Anyway,' he licked his lips, 'things are looking up. Letter eleven?'

Jon couldn't stop his mind from reeling. 'Go for it.'

Last night there was no wind. There were stars and I could see the sleeping faces of Ali, Parviz and Jîno. Sounds were so clear I could hear the whispers of the crewmen. They were talking about the ship and why it left us. They spoke of what is hidden below its deck in a container. What I heard made me so angry for how our country has been ruined.

'She knows what was on board the ship,' Rick said, letting out a low whistle before continuing with the letter.

The four from the life boat wanted to throw off the line and leave us. Only the man with scars – their leader – stopped this. I dare not tell the others what I heard.

The stars are different here. In the summer, we would sleep on the flat roof of our house. The jasmine from our garden would fill the air, and if a breeze came, the palm tree would whisper gently.

Ali woke and we began talking of how things were when the Americans first came. We were so full of hope. But things did not get better. Everything ground down to nothing. Soon, only bad people were free to drive at night. Because I worked for the Americans, I was a traitor, a spy, deserving of being killed. No one could know my real job. My husband, Younis, would drive me in his taxi to the Green Zone, I hiding under a blanket on the floor. Once near the first security check, I would leave the car and walk. Then, in the evening, he would be there to pick me up. It wasn't life, never knowing if someone will knock the door in the night and enter your house. To sleep I had to start taking pills. In the mornings there would be the dead bodies on the streets, men with their hands tied behind their backs. Children walking round them on their way to school, the American soldiers just driving past.

Ali told me about Al Sarafia, Baghdad's most beautiful bridge. The Americans said it was a terrorist truck bomb which collapsed it. But how was it destroyed in two different places and why did so many people hear their helicopters nearby before the explosion? Ali said their missiles destroyed that bridge. Why? His cousin is an engineer. His firm calculated it could rebuild the bridge for six million dinars. But the firm which the CPA gave the contract to charged three times that amount.

When the sky grew light, we found the old Uighur woman was dead. Jino was given her food, but he is so thin, I fear he also will not live much longer.

Just to roll her body into the water made Ali and Parviz's breathing heavy. We all are now so weak. Parviz says very little.

The food grows smaller. Three mouthfuls of water, two sweets and a square of dry noodles. Parviz is sure the crew are cheating us. He stares at their boat, but the crew are lying down, out of the sun. We still wait for wind.

Jon took a right on to Fairfield Street, spotting a single working girl in the shadows of the railway bridge at the back of Piccadilly station. He couldn't help glance about for Braithwaite's Saab even as Rick started speaking again.

'Letter twelve. Another of the ones that turned up the other day. Want to hear it again?'

Jon nodded, his sense of certainty gaining strength.

Afternoon. The sea just broke into activity. Tiny fish, fleeing from a dark shadow below. Many leaped onto our raft in panic and we fell on them, squeezing our cheeks full. More we wrapped in clothes. I saw Ali chasing one with his fingers, many tails sticking from his lips. I pointed at this and we laughed together at our luck.

Once we had eaten, Ali and I lay back down and talked of food once more. It's all we can think about. Ali described tashreab – the rich, tomato sauce poured over two pieces of flat bread. I spoke of sha'ar benat – how the soft, pink lumps would melt in my mouth.

Ali told me they have this too in Great Britain. It is called candy floss. I am so desperate to make a new life there, to not be afraid all the time. I know they read Arabian Nights to their children. At Christmas they even have plays about Aladdin. Ali says they also keep pigeons, in cages on roofs, like at home. We smiled at memories of the birds, rising in the evenings over

Baghdad, the whistles as the old men called them back.

I miss the sounds of birds. The bulbul's song. The Americans cut down all the trees, saying their enemies could hide in them. Their tanks tore up the pavements and knocked down all our traffic lights and street signs.

The edges of where Ali was bitten have grown angry and the wound bulges out.

Rick didn't look up. 'Where are we?'

'Just coming on to the Ashton Old Road. The nick's one minute away.'

'We've got time. Letter thirteen.'

The fish have given strength to Parviz's anger. As it grew dark, he grabbed the rope and tried to pull us to the life boat, demanding water. This was too hard, so he leaped into the sea and swam to the boat.

He tried to climb in, but the crew members have cut open his arms and head with the knife. He is with us again, but the blood from his head will not stop. He is talking to his brother who we lost in the storm.

Jon slowed, eyes on the rear-view mirror as he turned into Bell Crescent. 'That's it?'

'Yup.'

'Well, he's dead.'

'Reckon so,' Rick replied, scanning the rest of the page.

They drove the last few hundred metres in silence. As Jon swung into the police station car park, Rick closed the newspaper. 'The last part of the article was some kind of psychologist. He says she's now writing the letters as a form of therapy. Trying to make sense of what's happening to her by putting it into words.'

Jon felt the curl of his lip as the words came out. 'Some head doctor's always on hand to offer their valued opinion.'

Rick unclipped his seat belt. 'They're publishing the last six tomorrow. Says there are more revelations to come.'

Jon turned the engine off. 'Rick, don't laugh when I say this.

But we've got a bunch of Russian-speaking crewmen, who've been abandoned at sea.'

'Yes,' Rick replied, reaching for the door.

'The one who appears to be in charge has scars all over his throat.'

Rick's hand seemed stuck to the handle.

Jon carried on. 'Every photo we've got of our man, he's wearing a turtleneck. But, I think you'll find that if you look closely at the mugshot from the screening unit, there's something wrong with his skin. Just above his collar.'

'You're saying our man – Yashin – is the crewman in these letters?'

Jon pursed his lips for a moment before replying. 'Yes.'

Rick turned his head to the building. 'Let's go in. I want to see the photo.'

'I've got it here.' Jon swivelled round, plucked his briefcase off the back seat and opened it up. 'Shit! I've left the folder at Carmel's.'

Rick opened the door. 'Originals are in the file.'

They marched across the incident room, taking in the weary faces of the syndicate who'd been on cover that night.

'Mind if we open a window?' Jon announced. 'It reeks in here.'

'The smell of masculinity, son,' one of the other detectives replied, stretching his arms out and yawning, belly straining against his trouser belt.

'Alpha males,' another added, standing up and scratching at the few wispy strands still clinging to his scalp. 'Proper men.' He bent forward to retrieve his jacket, letting out a loud fart as he did so.

Jon surveyed the empty pizza boxes, sandwich wrappers and empty cans filling the bin in the corner. 'Go and get some sleep, for fuck's sake.'

Rick had succeeded in opening the window nearest to their desk by the time Jon reached Buchanon's office. 'Morning, sir.'

'Jon.' Buchanon looked back down at the sheets of paper on his desk.

'Any word from MI5?'

'Not so far.'

'Nothing? Not even an acknowledgement?'

'An email received message came back. One of those automated receipts.'

Rude bastards, Jon thought. 'We might have something more.'

Buchanon's eyes lifted. 'You're still working that case?'

'No – it was something from this morning's paper, that's all. A possible connection. We're just double-checking it.'

'OK. Bring it through if you're on to something. Then I want progress on the cannabis farm murder.'

'Sir.' As Jon approached his desk, he could see Rick opening a folder. His colleague held a printed sheet closer to his face, staring intently at it.

'Am I right?' Jon called out.

Rick sat down. 'You are. The tips of thin lines. Fuck me.'

Jon took the photo and examined it. Oh, my God. 'It's like some sort of bodged operation.'

'More like someone tried sharpening a scalpel on his throat. We'd better let Buchanon know.'

Jon scowled. 'You know, the arrogant tossers down in London haven't even thanked us for letting them know about Yashin's movements. Now they're getting this given to them on a plate, too.' He bunched a fist and brushed his knuckles back and forth across his lips. 'They won't even tell us his real name.'

Rick sighed. 'What can we do? Nothing. Get over it, mate.'

'We could speak to the captain of the fishing trawler who picked them up. I'd like to know if there was any sign of the raft with the asylum seekers. That letter said it was linked to the lifeboat by a rope.'

'Don't forget the *Express* is publishing the final six letters tomorrow. They could well tell us a lot more.'

'Good point. You get on to their news desk, switchboard, whatever. Explain we really need to know what the next letters say. I'll ring Marlow at the screening unit in Liverpool and see if he's got the details of the fishing trawler.'

Rick nodded towards Buchanon's office. 'What about the murder we're meant to be working on?' he whispered.

Jon waved a hand. 'We can start on that in a bit.'

'Holly! Breakfast is ready.' Alice placed the plastic bowl on the kitchen table. The stubby tip of a Weetabix protruded from the milk like a submarine surfacing. She stood with hands on hips, one ear cocked towards the doorway. The sounds of the television continued. 'Holly! Come through now or there'll be no more telly for the rest of the day.'

A couple of seconds later, her daughter appeared in the corridor, one shoulder pressed against the wall as she toyed with the remote control. 'I don't want any.'

Oh no, Alice thought. She's going to start playing up. Since the incident out on the road, Holly had almost stopped eating. Alice couldn't help glancing at the kitchen window. Yet another set of sheets was hanging out to dry in the back yard. And I haven't even mentioned that her birthday trip to the Lake District is probably off. 'I'll put some honey on.'

'I'm not hungry.'

'There's no ice cream when we go to the park, then.'

The comment caused her chin to lift.

'Come on,' Alice encouraged. 'I'll bet you'll be hungry once you start eating.'

Holly pushed herself clear of the wall, but stayed where she was, one toe pointing in at the other.

'Come on, Holly,' Alice urged. 'You make me sad when you don't eat.'

Her daughter edged forward reluctantly. Once she got to the table, Alice smoothed a hand over the little girl's blonde hair. 'You know, if you want to talk to Mummy about anything, I'll always want to listen.'

Holly climbed onto her chair. She opened her mouth, but seemed to change her mind about speaking.

'What, sweetie? Did you want to say something?'

'Why didn't Daddy tuck me in?'

Alice felt her stomach lurch. 'When?'

'When I woke up. You were outside shouting. I was crying but he drove away. Why did he drive away?'

'Sometimes grown-ups get cross. Your daddy and I were having an argument.'

'Is he cross with me?'

Alice bent down to caress her daughter's cheek. 'No, sweetie, of course not. Daddy isn't cross with you.'

'But why did he drive away?'

'Well, it was for the best.'

'What does that mean?'

'It was better he didn't come in. We were both very cross. That's why we were arguing. But we're not cross with you, OK? We love you.'

Holly stared down at her cereal in silence.

Alice felt sick. How do I explain to her what's going on? Her mobile started to ring and she straightened up. 'OK? No one is cross with you.' She picked her handset off the shelf above the radiator. The word ANONYMOUS filled the screen.

'Hello?'

'Hello. Alice Spicer?'

That Russian accent. Alice felt her heartbeat pick up. 'Is that Yulia?'

'Yes.'

'Thanks for calling.' She stared at the wall, eyebrows raised hopefully.

'I have some information for you, but not a clear answer.'

'OK.'

'There was a referral to your hospital on the twenty-second. The patient arrived in A and E and was assessed by the duty psychiatrist, but we had no beds.'

'Hence the referral,' Alice concluded. 'So you have the missing file?'

'There never was one.'

'Sorry? How could the patient have had no notes? Where did he come from?'

'This is what's confusing. The patient we referred was female, not male.'

'Female?'

'Yes.'

'But the name is J. Smith—'

'Yes. Jane Smith. The house officer here at our hospital gave her that name because we had no other.'

My God, Alice thought, picturing the frail form in the private room. The large eyes, the long lashes, the delicate cheekbones. Of course, with no hair, she was able to pass for a feminine young man. But what was she doing in a male-occupancy room? She almost clicked her fingers: no female beds had been available. 'Where did she come from then?'

'The screening unit.'

'What's that?'

'Near the waterfront here in Liverpool. Where people who want to claim asylum have to go. To have their screening interview.'

'But when she arrived, she was virtually catatonic. She still doesn't speak.'

'Which is why she was sent to us.'

'And you shipped her straight on to here.' Alice thought for a second. 'So, who brought her to the screening unit? Surely that person had her notes?'

'I spoke to the house officer – he remembers her being brought in. She arrived in a taxi and the man driving it said he'd come from a hospital in Plymouth.' She pronounced each syllable of the city as if they were separate words.

'Plymouth?'

'Yes, Plymouth. Do you know it?'

'It's a city on the south coast. A taxi? Why would a taxi drive her all the way from Plymouth to Liverpool?'

'I do not know.'

'Are there any other screening units apart from Liverpool?'

'One. A place called Croydon.'

'Down south,' Alice said. 'It's near to Gatwick airport – not far from the likes of Dover. Why wouldn't the taxi have taken her there?'

'I do not know.'

Alice took a long breath in. This was bizarre. 'OK, thanks very much for your help, Yulia.'

'That is fine. I hope you have luck finding those notes.'

'So do I,' replied Alice, wondering, again, how long it would be before they decided her bed should be freed up for someone else.

Twenty-Three

'Hello, madam. My name's DI Spicer. We're making enquiries about the incident that occurred across the road, night before last.'

'You mean at number nine? Oh, Archie.' The woman stepped aside, then bent down to pick up the toddler who had appeared between her ankles.

Jon noted she was in bare feet, toenails perfectly painted. As she perched the little boy in the crook of an elbow he spotted the Fat Face logo on her fashionably faded top. She brushed strands of light brown hair from her tanned face and peered across the leafy avenue. 'I thought the new owners were doing it up. You know – getting it ready to rent out.'

Jon's gaze was on the toddler who was now playing with the wooden toggles at the neck of his mum's top. 'Did you ever speak to them?'

'No. They looked Chinese. They'd turn up at really odd times, ferrying stuff into the house. Then it all seemed to go quiet. The curtains were permanently drawn. Is it true,' she placed a palm on her son's head, 'you know. A person inside was ...'

'That's correct. Do you know what type of vehicle it was the people drove?'

'Not really. A van, one time. Something expensive-looking as well. A Lexus, maybe. Silver.'

Jon jotted the information down. 'Were they all male?'

'Yes. In their twenties, early thirties, I'd guess.'

'And on the night of the incident. Did you hear or see anything?'

'No – not until the police cars showed up in the morning. What actually happened?'

'We're still establishing that. It looks like some sort of a feud. A private matter.' He pocketed his notebook. 'Thanks for your help, Ms ...?'

'Randall. Mrs Randall.'

'And if you – or your husband – think of anything else, please give me a call.' He handed her a business card, looking at the little one once again. 'How old is he?'

She smiled. 'A year and a half. Aren't you, Archie?'

Jon grinned. 'Keeps you busy, I bet.'

'Oh, he certainly does.'

'Thanks for your time.' He strode back up the garden path, seeing Rick emerge from the driveway of the house opposite.

His partner shook his head. 'Out. Probably at work.'

Jon nodded. 'Yeah, only a couple of mums in on this side.' He surveyed the quiet street. 'Looks like we'll have to come back this evening. Did the paper call you back?'

'Not yet.'

Jon glanced at his watch. Almost one o'clock. Marlow had provided him with the name of the man who owned the fishing trawler. An answerphone message had said he was out at sea, due back late morning. As they set off back to his car, Jon tried the number again, breathing a sigh of relief when it was answered.

'Hello?'

Jon could discern the man's Welsh accent above something clanking away in the background. 'Is that Lee Davis?'

'Yes.'

'Detective Inspector Jon Spicer, here, Greater Manchester Police. Do you have a minute?'

'Hang on.'

There was movement and the background noises abruptly fell away. Now Jon could hear the shrieks of a seagull. 'What's this about?'

'The Russians you found drifting in a lifeboat thirteen days ago.'

The man didn't respond.

'There were four of—'

'I remember.'

'Where, exactly, did you find them?'

'About twenty-five miles out from St Bride's Bay.'

'Where's that?'

'Pembrokeshire, Wales.'

Jon frowned. He'd assumed the men had been dropped off closer to Liverpool itself. 'You head that far south?'

'If that's where the fish are.'

'The men were in quite a state, I gather.'

'Terrible. Starving, they were. Very unlucky not to have been spotted sooner. There's Irish ferries crossing that stretch all the time during the summer. Mind you, a boat like theirs, it was so low in the water, anyone could have missed it.'

'How long would you say they'd been in it?'

'Several days. As I said, they were starving. Almost too weak to eat. They only managed soup, at first. When we gave them food they were like dogs eating it.'

'Was there any sign of other vessels in the area?'

'Commercial vessels?'

'Anything. Lifeboats, dinghies, rafts. Even debris in the sea.'

'No.'

'Just four starving Russians in a lifeboat.'

'Just four starving Russians in a lifeboat.'

'OK. Thanks for your help. I may need to call you again.'

'No problem.'

Jon was just returning his phone to his pocket when it started to ring again. He looked at the screen. A mobile number. His eyes swept the houses lining the quiet residential road. Maybe someone's remembered something from the night the Vietnamese was murdered. 'DI Spicer.'

'Hello, sir. This is Victor Labon.'

Jon closed his eyes. Victor Labon. Where've I heard that name?

'You paid me five pounds for the loss of credit to my telephone.'

Labon! The man from the block of flats over in Runcorn. The one whose mobile the Russian, Andriy Bal, had borrowed. 'Mr Labon, let me call you straight back.'

He hung up, selected last received call and pressed the return button. 'Hello, Mr Labon. Better we talk on my phone's credit, not yours.'

'Thank you. I have some more information for you.'

'Fire away.'

'I am sorry?'

'What information do you have?'

'That Russian man who used my mobile telephone. He also sent a text message. I have just found it in my sent messages store.'

'Really? What does it say?'

'It says this: Lesya left me. Now in the UK. Do not reply, Andriy.'

'That's all?'

'That is all. He sent it just before he made the phone call. At twelve minutes past four on the twenty-first. I have looked up the international dialling code – it is for Russia. Would you like the number of the phone he sent the message to?'

Jon couldn't help smiling. This guy was a dream come true. 'Yes, please, Mr Labon.' He wrote the number down. 'Mr Labon, would you mind giving me your Home Office reference number? I'll get on to your case owner and make sure he's aware of how helpful you've been. Maybe it will have a bearing on your claim.'

'Thank you. I would appreciate that.'

Once he had the information, he turned to Rick. 'We've got a contact number in Russia.'

'Who for?'

'The one who was using the name Andriy Bal. He sent a text just before calling Mykosowski.' Jon glanced at his notebook. 'Lesya left me. Now in the UK. Do not reply, Andriy. Seems like the Christian name he was using was real.'

Rick's eyes narrowed. 'Who left me?'

'Lesya. Probably his wife?'

Rick raised his eyebrows. 'No bells ringing?'

'What do you mean?'

There was a glitter of excitement in Rick's eyes. 'The *Lesya Ukrayinka*.'

'Who?'

'One of Mykosowski's ships. The *Lesya Ukrayinka*. It docked in Felixstowe, I think. Then was heading for the States. Boston, Baltimore. Somewhere beginning with a B.'

A wave of energy went coursing through Jon. This, he thought, is what I get up for in the mornings. This fucking feeling, right here. 'Do you remember where that ship had come from?'

'No, but it'll be on that shipping register website.'

Jon pipped the car's lock. 'Let's go.'

Oliver Brookes' hips ached from the long trek. When the zigzagging path had reached the top of the cliff, he'd looked back down on his secluded bay, watching the bands of white materialising in the sea a few metres off the beach. The wind carried the sound of the waves as they expired on the sandy expanse. A pulse, he thought. Slow and steady. He examined the sand's smooth surface; not even the faintest groove remained of the channel he'd dug.

He wondered about the note he'd found in the duck. Amira Jasim. Could what was written on the scrap of paper actually be true? Since reading it, he'd found himself scanning the ocean more often. Searching, he wondered, for what? Debris? Plastic barrels? A raft, sunburned and skeletal people clinging to its timbers?

A small shudder went through him as he pictured the internet terminals in Combe Martin's tiny library. Just the thought of tapping into technology like that again. Memories of multiple screens appeared in his head, the hours he'd spent tracking the flow of numbers, pouncing on some fluctuations, ignoring others. But he had to know if the *Lesya Ukrayinka* actually existed.

Holding the sound of the ocean in his head, he plodded his way inland, crossing clearings of grass in the heather that had been trimmed neat as any lawn. Sheep fled at his approach. Occasionally his way was barred by enormous webs stretching between gorse bushes that dotted either side of the trail. He'd bend down to seek out the spider that had weaved it, marvelling at the colourful markings on its bulbous body. Then he'd skirt round the bushes to leave the creature's web undisturbed.

The high street of Combe Martin was clogged by holiday-makers' cars and he looked at the shiny machines with dismay, remembering his time in London and the sense of confinement that had had such a crushing effect. Passing a small newsagent's, his attention was drawn by the A-board on the pavement outside. The headline talked of a flotilla of rubber ducks.

Once inside the library's doors, he stood still. Soft sounds. Someone tapping lightly on a keyboard. The rustle of a news-paper. A muffled cough. He looked towards the computer terminals on the right, walked over and sank gratefully onto the padded seat. After logging in, he went straight on to the internet, typed in the words *Lesya Ukrayinka*, and pressed enter.

Passing over the initial hits for sites about a Ukrainian poet, he quickly spotted an entry for a shipping company called Myko Enterprises. He clicked on the site and read through the poorly phrased text. After a couple of minutes, he pressed 'back' and typed in another company's name. Once he'd written the number down on the back of his hand, he logged off and went over to the payphone in the library's porch.

He slotted in a few twenty-pence pieces, keyed in the number on the back of his hand and waited for the call to be con-nected.

'Mayweather Maritime Securities. How may I help?'

'Hello. Do you have a Peter Durwood working there?'

'I'll just put you through.'

The line rang twice.

'Peter Durwood.'

'Peter, it's Oliver Brookes.'

A second's silence.

'Oliver! My God, he lives!'

'How are you, Peter?'

'Same old, same old. What about you, old fellow? Is it true? A fisherman's cottage? Somewhere in the West Country?'

He smiled. 'Your sources are as good as ever.'

'Well, I do my best. My God, I can't believe it's you. It must be four years, at least.'

'Nearer six.'

'Six? Well I never. A fisherman's cottage. Sounds idyllic. What's it near?'

'Nothing, really. It's on National Trust land. I have it on a rolling ten-year lease. A short distance from a little place called Combe Martin. Where I'm calling from.'

'You really did it. Got out. Made a clean break.'

'It was that or go mad.'

'Tell me about it. Things are crazy here in the City.'

'Not tempted to get out yourself? You must have put aside some nest egg by now.'

'One more year, then I'll probably jump ship.'

'You were saying that when I was still there.'

The other man chuckled. 'So, what do you do with yourself all day long?'

'Not a lot. A bit of wood carving. Watch the ocean. Whistle to seals.'

'Seals?' he laughed. 'You must keep an eye on the markets, surely? Old habits die hard.'

'You know what? I don't.'

'Didn't you hear about Brian? He was bought out last year. An Indian operation. They paid sixty-five million for his company, so the reports said.'

'No, I didn't.'

'Still read the *FT*?'

With every comment, he sensed more greatly the gulf that now separated him from that world. The ebb and flow of capital. Buying that currency, converting it to another, selling it on. Never actually anything to hold in his hands, to run his fingers over. How meaningless it all now seemed. 'Listen, Peter. Believe it or not, I'm on a payphone.'

'Bloody hell, Oliver. You really have gone back to the Stone Age.'

'Could you check out a shipping company for me? What kind of freight it specialises in. Annual turnover. Who owns it – shareholders or otherwise. That kind of detail.'

'No problem. What's it about?'

'Something washed up, that's all. It's piqued my interest.'

'You can't resist, can you? Same old Oliver at heart. What's the name?'

'Myko Enterprises.'

'Got it. Give me the rest of the afternoon?'

'Fine, thanks. How about I call you tomorrow morning?'

'No problem. Let me give you my home number.'

After hanging up, Oliver stepped back into the library and approached the table of newspapers. The pink pages of the *Financial Times* stood out against the other dailies and he sat down to take a look.

A story on page five caught his eye. Yellow ducks being washed ashore along the coast of south-west Britain. Rumours that the *Daily Express* was now offering twenty thousand pounds to secure the first in a series of notes someone had been placing within the plastic toys.

He pulled the paper closer and started to read.

The lift doors opened on the fourteenth floor of Waterloo Tower and Valeri Salnikov stepped out, taking a final bite of a Mars bar as he did so. Looking at the plant pot on his left, he spotted the Bounty wrapper he'd left there after his last visit. Scrunching up the Mars bar wrapper, he dropped it in as well. The thin plastic immediately began to stretch out, as if making itself comfortable on the dusty pebbles at the yucca plant's base.

Brushing his palms together, Salnikov swallowed his mouthful then made his way down the corridor to Mykosowski's office. Instead of buzzing the intercom, he turned his head and listened at the door. Mykosowski's voice was faint on the other side. First giving out orders then switching calls to book a slot on a golf driving range.

You really have no idea, Salnikov thought, stepping back to gauge where on the door the lock mechanism was located. He raised his right knee and shot his foot out so the heel of his shoe connected with the correct point. The door flew open and he stepped quickly inside, swinging it shut behind him.

Mykosowski was halfway to raising a cup to his mouth. For a

second, he stared in open-mouthed confusion. Then, seeing who stood before him, the colour vanished from his face. He threw the cup aside and jumped to his feet, looking wildly about.

Salnikov observed him in silence, wondering briefly whether the other man was actually going to jump at the plate glass windows in an attempt to get away.

Instead, Mykosowski darted to the corner of his office where he dragged a golf club from the bag propped against the wall. He raised the iron above his head, breath coming fast and shallow.

Salnikov's head tilted slightly to the side, amusement showing in his eyes. He padded silently across the carpet, coming to a halt just within Mykosowski's striking distance. He bent both legs slightly, raising his hands to stomach height. 'Come.'

Mykosowski took a few more breaths, eyes bulging as he gauged his options. The tension went from him and the club was lowered back down. 'The Americans.'

Salnikov gave a single nod. 'The Americans.'

Mykosowski's shoulders dropped lower. 'But they said ... they said—'

'Whatever they said, you should not have believed them. You're about to die, Slavko. You must decide how fast you want it to be.' His eyes flicked to the golf club.

Mykosowski's fingers uncurled and it fell to the floor with a thud. He tried to take a breath in but his chin abruptly dipped, lips coming apart as he retched lightly. He swallowed and raised his eyes. 'What do you want to know?'

'Everything. When did you make the call?'

A tremor passed through him. His voice rose. Pleading. 'If ... if I tell you everything, can I live?'

Salnikov shook his head. 'If you tell me everything, I'll make it so you don't suffer.'

Shaking now, Mykosowski stared at the other man. Then his head jerked to the side and a mouthful of steaming coffee erupted from his lips.

Twenty-Four

'I can't believe the *Express* hasn't called you back.'

Rick grunted at Jon's comment, forefinger hovering a milli-metre from his computer's screen. 'There you go – the *Lesya Ukrayinka*. It left Felixstowe on Monday the eighteenth. Went via Rotterdam and is due to arrive in Baltimore ... let's see. Christ, later today.'

'Which just gives us time,' Jon said, 'to get word to the US authorities.'

Rick nodded. 'And they can intercept whatever's in that con-tainer before it's even unloaded.' He started to stand. 'Let's tell Buchanon.'

'Hang on. We want to be watertight on this. Especially after that business with Mykosowski. Where had it travelled from?' he asked, leaning over Rick's shoulder and trying to make sense of the table. Different national flags formed a colourful end column, followed by the ship's name, the type of vessel it was and its weight in tonnes. After that, the boxes just contained meaningless words and numbers.

Rick scrolled across, finger tracing the *Lesya*'s entry. 'The port of Umm Qasr, Iraq.'

'Iraq?' Jon pictured the MI5 officers who'd closed in on them at Euston station. 'What was the section of MI5 involved in this?'

'JTAC. The Joint Terrorism Analysis Centre.'

Jon looked back at the screen. 'How far back can you trace the ship's route?'

Rick continued scrolling. 'Karachi, Pakistan. It left there on the fourteenth of July and before that it was docked at Shenzhen, China.'

'China,' Jon murmured. This was it. We're finally getting to the heart of the thing. 'This business with the rubber ducks. They were originally manufactured in China, weren't they?'

'Yes.' Rick began tapping a biro against the edge of his desk. 'This is all fitting together. Aside from the cargo, the *Lesya* was carrying illegal immigrants – bringing them up from Iraq and other places. Then something happens off the British coast; a group of them end up in the water, along with the Russian crew, or whoever they are, and thousands of those ducks.'

'Pretty much how I had it. Keep going.'

Rick thought for a moment. 'According to the letters, the raft drifts for a few days before the crew on the lifeboat turn up. Throat scars transfers to his mates. Then the lifeboat and raft get separated. The Russians are found by the fishing trawler. Then, some time after, the ducks start being washed up along the south-west coast.'

They looked at each other for a few moments.

'I reckon we're almost there,' Jon replied. 'But how did they all end up in the sea in the first place?'

'A storm. That's what the early letters went on about, didn't they?' Rick opened up a new tab on his computer. 'This site has all the letters in chronological order. First one's yet to be found. Letter two, here we go, a raft of wooden pallets. "This we held on to during the storm. Surrounding us are the yellow ducks. There are many thousands of them." Letter three ends in another storm. "Ali and the man with throat scars have made a mast with some long pieces of plastic and the mirrors are tied to the top."'

Jon looked at the rest of the office. Colleagues were talking on phones, leafing through paperwork or typing away. None had the slightest inkling of what was unfolding feet away from them. This moment, thought Jon. Savour this moment. He took a deep breath, feeling his scalp tingle. 'It's him. She is talking about our man.'

Rick scrolled down. 'Letter five. "The man with throat scars guards the drum. All day we drift ..."' He skimmed forward. "The wind is moving us north."'

'North,' Jon murmured. 'Hang on.' He pulled his mobile out and keyed in a number. 'Mr Davis? It's DI Spicer again. I spoke to you earlier about the Russians you picked up? Yes. A quick question, for you. If they'd drifted for several days, where would they have drifted from? Would they be just going round in circles, or what?' He listened for a few seconds. 'Yes, I've heard of the Gulf Stream. OK. OK. Connected to this high pressure we've been having lately? And depending on wind speeds. Storms? Right. That's great, thank you.' He flipped his phone shut. 'He reckons they could have originally gone into the water as far south as the Bay of Biscay.'

Rick blinked. 'Off Spain. One of the early letters described Portuguese men-of-war, remember?'

'He also said it's notorious for storms. Freight ships frequently have to steer out to sea to avoid them. If they went overboard during a storm down there, the Gulf Stream would have carried them in a north-easterly direction towards the British coast. Depending on wind, they could have taken about a fortnight to drift this far.'

Rick leaned across and grabbed the world atlas off Jon's desk. Using his biro, he pointed to Iraq. 'Umm Qasr, up through the Suez Canal, round Gibraltar and along the Spanish and French coasts to the English Channel.'

Jon's head was bobbing in a series of nods. 'Know what, mate? We've cracked this thing.'

'What I don't get is this: why didn't the *Lesya* go back for them? Isn't that one of the fundamental rules of the sea? If people are in trouble, you drop whatever you're doing and go to help.'

'The cargo. Whatever MI5 has been tracking. The master wasn't prepared to jeopardise its delivery, even for people going overboard.'

Rick sat back. 'That's a chunk of his crew and, what, thirty passengers? And he's prepared to make that sort of decision. What the hell is on that ship?'

'Maybe we'll be told, eventually. In the meantime,' Jon said, 'we'd better get this to Buchanon.' He held a hand out. 'We've nailed it, mate. We've absolutely bloody nailed it!'

Rick shook his hand. 'Good work, partner.'

Jon looked wistfully to the window. 'Know what I'd give to get that slimeball Mykosowski in an interview room so I could see his face when we ran all this past him?'

Rick wrinkled his nose. 'What you'd give? I don't know what twisted fantasies go through your head. A night with Angelina Jolie?'

Jon thought for a moment. 'You'd have to do better than that.' He looked at the doors. 'Oooh, I'm going to get so pissed tonight.'

'Hang on – let's see Buchanon first.'

Jon's surge of elation suddenly lost strength. 'This is all our work. And it's just going to be handed on a plate to those pricks in London,' he muttered.

Rick placed his palms on the desk and stood. 'Come on,' he announced. 'The longer we sit on it, the harder it will be.'

Jon thrust his hands into his pockets. 'It makes me sick.'

Rick attempted a smile. 'Let's get it done. We can be in the pub in no time.'

'I bet we don't even get a thank you,' Jon complained, following Rick towards Buchanon's office. 'And another thing: they don't give a shit about our murders. And they certainly don't give a shit about the dead refugees.'

'Maybe. Maybe not.'

Jon gave a snort as Rick knocked on Buchanon's door before pushing it half open. 'Sir? More on the dead Russians.'

Buchanon put his pen down and crossed his arms. 'Really? And the cannabis farm?'

'We've completed door-to-doors in the street,' Rick replied. 'A couple of vehicle descriptions are worth looking into.'

'Sir,' Jon cut in. 'What we have on the Russian murders is urgent, to say the least.'

Buchanon waved them to the chairs on the opposite side of his desk. 'So, you've made no meaningful headway tracing that Nissan Navara?'

'Not so far,' Jon announced, registering Buchanon's cold stare.

'What have you got then?' Buchanon uncrossed his arms and turned to Rick.

'This morning, we pointed out how our prime suspect could well be the man with throat scars referred to in the letters published this morning by the *Express*.'

'Yes. That information has been sent to JTAC.'

'Any response?' Jon asked.

Buchanon shook his head. 'Not as yet.'

'Well,' Rick continued, 'we believe we now know the name of the ship they came from.'

'Are you sure?' Buchanon sat up. 'That would be any journalist's wet dream.'

'I had considered seeing what the papers might pay for it,' Rick said light-heartedly. 'It's called the *Lesya Ukrayinka* and it's registered to a shipping company called Myko Enterprises.'

Buchanon's lips slowly peeled apart. 'Are you sure?'

By the time Rick had finished, their senior officer was staring at the Border Agency photo of the man calling himself Vladimir Yashin. Eventually, he looked up. 'Credit where it's due, lads. Bloody good work. Bloody good work.'

Jon caught Rick's smile. I'd be happy, too, he thought, if I didn't think Buchanon is about to take all the credit for this himself.

'OK, I'm alerting Gower immediately,' Buchanon continued. 'While I make the call, I want you two to bring through all your background material. After that, I want to see something happening with the cannabis farm murder.'

Rick's smile faltered.

'You've been neglecting it too long. Now, go. Get me the other files you have.'

Back at their desks, Rick looked at Jon with disbelief. 'Back working the cannabis farm job?'

Now it was Jon's turn to attempt a smile. 'As I said, I'm going to get so pissed tonight.'

'Think I'll bloody join you,' Rick muttered, gathering up the information Buchanon had asked for.

When they re-entered the DCI's office, he was still talking on the phone, smiling as he did so. 'No problem, sir. As I said, the ship is actually due to dock later today. Baltimore, yes. Absolutely. OK, speak to you soon.'

As he hung up, Jon could see a proud glow in the man's cheeks. Nothing like a pat on the back from upstairs, he thought.

Buchanon pointed to the corner of his desk. 'It can all go there, thanks.'

Once they'd put the paperwork down, Buchanon sat back. 'Rick, can I have a minute with DI Spicer?'

What now, thought Jon.

Rick turned round without a word and walked to the door. Once it had shut behind him, Buchanon turned to Jon. 'The progress you've made on this case doesn't make saying this easy.' He held up a form. 'This turned up in the internal post earlier on.'

Jon eyed the sheet suspiciously. 'What is it?'

'A memo from the PSD.'

Jon sent a glance up at the ceiling. The Professional Standards Department. 'Braithwaite.'

'Braithwaite,' his senior officer echoed, voice heavy with feigned surprise. 'Imagine that. He submitted a complaint against you this lunchtime. He's really gone for it – even including a supporting statement from his wife.'

Jon's head dropped. Shit. 'What's he claiming?'

'You know what he's claiming.'

'And he's prepared to account for why he's been frequenting an area known for prostitution?'

Buchanon lifted the sheet of paper and began to read. '"On several occasions over the last few weeks, I have attempted to locate a patient of mine. The young lady has left the home of her parents and is believed to be working as a prostitute in the area around Fairfield Street in the city centre."'

'Yeah, right,' Jon sneered. 'And does he give the patient's identity?'

'Lucinda Waddell. Daughter of Guy Waddell.'

'Who's he?'

'The Conservative Member of Parliament for Altrincham.'

Jon felt himself sag. 'Is Waddell prepared to confirm that?'

'As long as it remains in confidence.'

'That's me fucked, then. What happens next?'

'I've spoken to Braithwaite.'

Jon looked up. 'Really?'

Buchanon placed the form back on his desk then pushed it away, as if an offensive smell was rising off it. 'I don't need this in my syndicate. So I nipped it in the bud. I persuaded him the best way to deal with this is by local resolution.'

Jon straightened his shoulders. That meant the Independent Police Complaints Commission wouldn't be involved. It also meant no formal disciplinary proceedings could result from the investigation. Result.

'Don't look like you're off the hook, Jon. Braithwaite might not realise you can't now be dragged over the coals officially, but if you think he'll be happy with you getting a slap on the wrist, you're wrong. The man was livid.'

Yeah, Jon thought, recalling Mrs Braithwaite's look of annoyance when he'd appeared at her door uninvited. The cheek of such a thing.

'He wants something to be done,' Buchanon continued. 'He wants you punished. Now, I managed to divert him, to some extent. Pressures of your personal situation, et cetera. A lapse in judgement.'

Jon nodded, making an effort to keep his mouth shut. Pressures of my personal situation? I could be enjoying the happiest day of my life, he thought, and I still wouldn't trust that fucking stick-insect crawling around inside my house. 'Thanks, sir.'

'I also explained that there have been several complaints from residents living in the vicinity of Fairfield Street. I mentioned that its use by prostitutes is something we're aware of.'

'So I was there as part of an operation?'

'I let him make his own connections.'

'He accepted that?' Jon asked, surprised the man had been palmed off that easily.

'It's a plausible story,' Buchanon replied, 'but no, he probably didn't. Luckily for you, he doesn't want to bring attention as to what he was actually doing there.'

Of course, Jon thought. That would risk his Tory MP friend's little secret getting out.

'But as I said, he still wants to see you punished.'

Jon nodded. That's typical. His entire life has probably been spent getting his own way.

'So, as far as he's concerned, you'll be going on a course or two. Ones that offer advice on improving professional conduct, that sort of thing. I also told him you'll be on quarterly appraisals for the next two years.'

'Was he happy with that?'

'No.'

'No? What else does he want? A letter saying sorry?'

Buchanon stared back.

'No,' Jon groaned. 'Don't say I've got to apologise to the prick.'

'His wife, actually. For the distress you caused her.'

'Distress? That hard-hearted bitch isn't capable—'

'Christ, Jon,' Buchanon snarled. 'I've dug you out of a shit pile of your own making. And all you can do is argue. Unbelievable. You will write her a letter. You'll state, without going into any specifics, that your actions were inexcusable. You will state that you deeply regret any distress caused. Got that?'

Jon lowered his eyes. 'Yes, sir.'

'Good. Now clear out of my office.'

Twenty-Five

'What was that about?' Rick asked despondently.

'Where do you want to start?' Jon replied, lowering himself into his seat. He remembered his file notes on Yashin and un-clipped the catches of his briefcase.

Rick raised his arms and linked his fingers behind his head. 'Nice to feel appreciated.'

Jon started searching for the folder, hand stopping when he realised the stuff was still at Carmel's. All he could find was the printout with the phone number and directions for Myko Enterprises. Placing the sheet of paper on his desk, he wondered sadly how Carmel was. He brought up her number and pressed green, but the call went through to answerphone. Probably ignoring my calls, he thought, glancing at Braithwaite's office. Tough, you won't be getting all the case notes straight away. He looked again at the sheet on Mykosowski's company, mind going to all the work they'd put in. Feelings of frustration begin-ning to grow, he looked at his phone positioned to the side of his monitor. His fingers twitched. Sod it. 'You might want to nip out and get some food or something.'

'Why?'

'I'm calling Mykosowski.'

Rick's eyes widened. 'What? Don't be so bloody ridiculous.'

'Don't worry, I'm not going into specifics. A few open-ended questions. A little rattle of his cage.'

'Jon, we're off the case,' Rick whispered. 'Why not just march in to Buchanon's office and call him a frizzy-haired fuckwit to his face?'

'As you said, we're off the case. They'll be waiting for the *Lesya* when it sails into Baltimore. But we could have had

Mykosowski – and through him we could have found Yashin. I can't stand the thought of that oily-haired wanker sitting in his flash offices, surveying the Houses of Parliament and thinking he got one over on us.'

'You can't bear to lose, can you?'

'No.'

'Even if it jeopardises your career.'

'My career? Gower's got a soft spot for me. I won't get sacked over this call. It might not do my prospects of promotion much good, but I'll stay part of this department, you'll see.'

'So, just to prove a point you'll …' He threw his hands out. 'You're right. I'm off to run some errands in town. I'm not having anything to do with this.' He got up and started heading for the doors.

'We weren't given a fair go, Rick. That's my point in this.'

'Whatever.'

Jon swivelled back round and picked up his phone. What shall I say to him? Work it out on the line, another part of him replied. He keyed in the number and his call was picked up almost immediately.

'Myko Enterprises.'

Jon pictured the woman somewhere in the basement of the building. The company names must flash up on her console, he thought, letting her route endless calls through to the myriad businesses above. 'Slavko Mykosowski, please.'

There was a slight hitch in her voice. 'One moment.'

The line made a series of clicks. After a few seconds, a new voice came on the line. 'Who is speaking?'

Jon frowned. It was a clear, English accent. 'I'd like a word with Mr Mykosowski.'

'Who is this?'

'Who is this?' Jon repeated back.

'Why are you calling this office?' The voice was young, familiar somehow. 'You're in Manchester. I can see your dialling code.'

Suddenly, Jon was back in Euston station, talking to the MI5 officer on the balcony of the pub. He thought about hanging up, but realised it was too late. 'Officer Soutar, it's DI Spicer, here. Greater Manchester Police.'

'Spicer? What the hell are you doing calling this number?'

Jon sat back. 'We've just received some fresh evidence about Myko Enterprises. I ... I needed to confirm a detail with Mykosowski before passing it on to your good selves. What's going on?'

'You were instructed to make no more contact.' Soutar spoke away from the phone. 'It's OK, carry on.' Immediately several voices began speaking in the background. 'Detective,' Soutar continued, 'do you always ignore orders so blatantly?'

'What are you lot doing there? Is he under arrest? Did you get the information we sent you about—'

'I received it. Mykosowski isn't under arrest. He's dead.'

'Dead? When?'

'The last few hours. I'm looking at him right now.'

'Garrotted?'

'No.'

'What, then?'

'We're not sure. He's lying face down in the middle of the office. There's no sign of any struggle, apart from the lock to his office being forced. The pathologist thinks it's a possible broken neck.'

'Well, at least you're not having to work with all the windows open.'

'Pardon?'

'Usually, they crap their pants as he garrottes them.'

'You're assuming this is the work of the man you're looking for?'

'We've got him on camera boarding a train to London early this morning.'

'I gather.'

Don't mention it, Jon thought. It was no problem letting you know. 'Any sign of him now?'

'What do you think?'

'I thought you had the office under surveillance?'

Silence.

Ouch, Jon thought. Someone fucked up. 'You realise we've got the name of the ship the murdered Russians were on? It's registered to Myko Enterprises.'

'When did you get that?'

'Just now. Our Chief Super is probably on the phone to your boss right now.'

'What's its name?'

'The *Lesya Ukrayinka*.'

'I'll give you this, Detective. You're a tenacious bastard, aren't you?'

Jon felt his mouth open and shut. 'You knew the ship's name already?'

'It's been tracked ever since it left Iraqi waters.'

Jon hunched forward. 'One of the letters in the paper this morning mentions the Russians were talking about something hidden on the ship. You knew all along that cargo was on it?'

'We're in discussions with the *Express*. Those letters are now putting this entire operation in serious jeopardy.'

No wonder they weren't returning Rick's calls, Jon thought. 'I spoke to the owner of the fishing trawler who found the crew.'

'What trawler?'

'The three dead Russians and the killing machine. They were picked up by a fishing trawler off the coast of Wales a fortnight ago. I spoke to the captain of the vessel. Oh, and one of the murder victims – Andriy Bal – texted a number in Russia. We haven't had much time to look into it, but the number's registered with Delta Telecom, whose coverage includes the St Petersburg area. That's where Andriy—'

'Hang on.' Soutar's speech became muffled and Jon strained to hear what was being said. 'Detective?' His voice was clear once again. 'Where are you in Manchester?'

'Grey Mare Lane – we work out of this station.'

'Sit tight. We'll be there in less than two hours.'

Jon glanced about. 'You're coming here?'

'That's right.'

'Shall I let my boss know?'

'I would. He'll probably like to hear all about the *Lesya Ukrayinka*, too.'

'You mean you're going to—'

'Yes, Detective. And that includes the real identity of Vladimir Yashin – the killing machine, as you like to call him.'

Jon had started to get up when his phone rang again. Sinking back in his seat, he lifted the receiver. 'DI Spicer.'

'Jon, it's Richard Milton.'

'Richard. How's things? Are we heading up Chart Toppers, yet?'

'With what I'm about to tell you? We are the uncontested number one. Not eating lunch, are you?'

'No,' Jon replied, realising he was starving. The only breakfast cereal at Rick's was organic muesli: he'd settled for toast.

'Good. You must have been tracking the rubber duck letters?'

'Yup.'

'So have I. Our three dead Russians. You realise they all showed signs of prolonged exposure to the sun alongside rapid weight loss?'

'Richard – we're pretty certain it's them.'

'Who?'

'The crewmen described in the letters. Other things have come to light which appear to confirm it.'

'Bloody hell – I knew it!'

'What did you find?'

'In the autopsy, I bagged up their stomach and intestinal contents.'

'I remember you saying. It could give a clue to where they'd come from.'

'Correct. Well, I had some time the other day, so I had a rummage around. Stomach contents weren't much use and all three had evacuated their bowels as they died. But, I found a hard compressed ball in the lower intestine of all three.'

Jon took a breath in. 'Why do I get the feeling this is going to be utterly gross?'

'It's meat, Jon. It often sits in the lower intestine for extended periods. I thought pork. But it's not. The tests have just confirmed that it's human.'

Detail of the Géricault painting flashed in his head. The desperation on the faces of the survivors. The corpses sprawled around them on the raft. The barren sea stretching to the far horizon. 'Oh my God,' he whispered. 'Which of the poor bastards did they eat?'

'Derriford hospital, Plymouth.'

'Admissions, please.' Alice said, pacing back and forth across her kitchen.

The line beeped and an elderly sounding man with a West Country lilt spoke. 'Admissions.'

'Hello. My name's Alice Spicer and I'm calling from Refugees Are People – the charity based up in Manchester. We help out with foreign nationals who have no friends or family.'

'Yes – I've heard of you. Hello, Alice.'

'Hi. I'm trying to trace the patient notes for an asylum seeker we have up here. Currently, she's on the mental health unit at Sale General. All we know about her is that she arrived in a taxi that had originally come from Plymouth.'

'When did she arrive?'

'On Friday the twenty-second. She was originally taken to the immigration screening unit in Liverpool. Because of her mental state, they referred her on to the Royal Liverpool hospital but, due to a lack of beds, she was shipped over here.'

'In a taxi, you say?'

'Apparently. I wondered why no ambulance.'

'Not for that size journey – assuming she wasn't hooked up to any medical equipment.'

'No, she wasn't.'

'OK – I'm looking through referrals now. Far fewer names than admissions. How old is this woman?'

'Early twenties, probably. Middle Eastern appearance.'

'Let's see … nothing for that Friday. Are you OK waiting while I check the days either side?'

'No problem.'

'Right you are.'

She listened to the man's tuneless humming, the occasional pom-pom punctuating the drone. Keeping the phone cradled against her ear, she reached for a cup and turned the kettle on. The water had started to boil when he spoke again. 'Nothing, I'm afraid.'

That can't be right, Alice thought. 'How about adolescents? Are they categorised differently?'

'No. Everyone goes on to this central database.'

Alice gritted her teeth. The trail can't go cold now. Please. 'Well, are you Plymouth's main hospital? Could she have come from somewhere else?'

'There's always the MDHU. They keep separate records to ours.'

'MDHU?'

'The Ministry of Defence Hospital Unit. We're home to Europe's largest naval base here. They closed its hospital back in the mid-nineties and opened the unit here. It has its own facilities, for things like intensive care, physiotherapy, infection control. Shall I put you through?'

'Please.'

Twenty-Six

Shaking his head, Rick took a bite of his olive bagel then looked at it with a slightly queasy expression. 'Horrific. You hear about that kind of stuff, sometimes. Wasn't there that case where the plane crashed in the Andes?'

Jon nodded. 'A rugby team from Uruguay. Quite a few survived, including some medical students. They ended up eating the dead passengers until the snow thawed enough for them to trek back out. I saw the film.'

'According to the *Lesya*'s itinerary, if our lot went overboard off the Spanish coast, they drifted for nearly two weeks before that trawler found them.'

'Plenty of time to run out of food and start getting really desperate,' Jon replied.

Rick regarded his bagel again then placed it on the corner of his desk. 'I can't wait to hear what this is all really about. Who's coming, then?'

Jon balled up his sandwich wrapper and pinged it off the inner edge of his bin. He heard it roll to a stop on the bottom. 'He didn't say. Obviously the smarmy one with the fringe, Soutar, but I'm not sure who else. You should have seen Buchanon's face when I told him.'

Rick's eyebrows lifted. 'Must have been worth a photo. When do they get here?'

He glanced at his watch. 'Any minute.'

'You're a lucky bastard, mate. I wasn't sure if you'd still be here when I got back.'

'Just as well I rang you to bring me back a sandwich, then.'

Rick held out a palm. 'Three quid, now you mention it.'

'Three? For a ham and pickle sandwich? I keep telling you,

that gourmet sandwich bar is a total rip-off. Gregg's. That's the place.'

Rick pointed at his bagel. 'Do they offer this stuff in there? No.'

'That's not proper bread.'

'So what is it?'

'I don't know. Mostly air, by the look of it. I bet you prefer Polo mints, too.' His phone started giving off single rings. Internal call. 'Jon speaking. OK – let them through, I'm coming down.' He hung up. 'They're here! Give Buchanon a shout – I'll see you in the main meeting room.'

He bounded down the stairs, hearing a southern accent in the corridor below. Rounding the final flight, he saw three people looking up at him. Soutar and two other men, both tanned. The taller, blond one was in his late thirties and was wearing a dark jacket, pale blue shirt and crumpled chinos. Jon's eyes went to the second. Younger, Hispanic-looking, also wearing chinos, but with a white T-shirt beneath a green windbreaker.

'Gentlemen,' Jon announced, trotting down the remaining steps with his hand out. 'Welcome to Manchester.'

Soutar's BlackBerry went off and before taking the call, he turned to the other men. 'This is him. DI Spicer.'

The blond-haired man's eyes were pale blue. Grasping Jon's hand, he smiled, the whiteness of his teeth singing out. 'Greg Mueller. Detective, you've been making some impression with your colleagues down in the capital.'

His American accent was quite strong – elongated vowels preventing Jon from deciphering how much sarcasm was in the comment. There was a cultured air about him. If Soutar is Oxbridge, Jon thought, this guy is Ivy League. 'Thanks.' He turned to the other man and saw something in his eyes. The same type of glance he got from members of the opposition just before a rugby match kicked off. Calculating, adversarial. Jon held a hand out and the other man delayed a moment before raising his own.

'Carl D'Souza.'

'Detective Inspector,' Soutar said, returning the device to its leather holder. 'These gentlemen are with the CIA.'

CIA? Jon tried to keep his expression casual. 'Are you just over?'

'A few days ago,' Mueller replied. 'We're staying at our embassy in London. Damn sight more comfortable than Iraq, where we've been these last few months.'

Jon thought of the *Lesya*. Soutar said the vessel had been tracked since it left Iraqi waters. Dying to ask if the cargo had been successfully intercepted, he gestured with his hand. 'We're in the main meeting room, next floor up.'

When he opened the door, Rick and Buchanon were already inside. Once introductions were over, everyone took a seat.

'So,' Buchanon announced, 'I've had Detectives Spicer and Saville tying up local enquiries on this.' He uncapped a pen and looked across at his officers.

Taking the cue, Jon slid photocopied sheets across to the three newcomers. 'Since sending you down the information about the movements of the man calling himself Vladimir Yashin ...' He paused, catching the look that bounced between Soutar and CIA agents. Irritation that he still didn't know the man's real name made the back of his neck prickle. 'I then received a call from a man who had lent his phone to the third victim, Andriy Bal.'

'That was the call that led you to Mykosowski, right?' Mueller interjected.

Jon gave a nod. 'The man called me back to say a text message had also been sent on his phone. We've made initial enquiries.' At the head of the table, he saw Buchanon narrow his eyes. 'The number is registered with a Russian mobile network called Delta Telecom. It mainly serves the north-west region of Russia, including St Petersburg, where the victim claimed to be from.'

'What did the message say?' Soutar asked, attention going to his BlackBerry as it pinged again.

Jon referred to his notes. '"Lesya left me. Now in the UK. Do not reply, Andriy." From that, we were able to place the murdered Russians on the *Lesya Ukrayinka* – a ship registered with Myko Enterprises.' He paused to allow the visitors a chance to divulge what the cargo actually was. Still they volunteered nothing. Jon continued. 'And from the description given in the letters found in these rubber ducks, and the Border Agency mug shots, we surmised our prime suspect is the crew member with the throat scars.'

'Have you the number of that mobile?' Soutar asked, reading something on his BlackBerry.

'Yes. You want it?'

Soutar picked up a pen and nodded. Once it was written down, the MI5 officer started typing a message in on his keyboard. 'Carry on.'

Jon looked at him for a moment. You really are an arrogant prick. 'We then contacted the owner of the fishing trawler who picked the Russians up. By his estimation, they could have been adrift for almost a fortnight.'

'On what basis do you assume that?' D'Souza asked.

'It being a storm down in the Bay of Biscay that caused them to go overboard in the first place,' Rick replied. 'From there, ocean currents and prevailing winds would have carried them in a northerly direction – mostly outside of any shipping lanes – until reaching British coastal waters.'

Mueller smiled appreciatively, eyes twinkling. 'Anything else you've got for us?'

'That's about it,' Jon replied. 'Except for a call from the pathologist who conducted the autopsies. Each of the dead Russians had a chewed-up ball of human flesh caught in the lower intestine.'

'Are you serious?' Buchanon asked.

'I am, sir.' Jon turned to the other three men. 'You don't seem particularly surprised.'

Soutar shrugged. 'We've read the final letters. The ones that will be in the *Express* tomorrow.'

Mueller rubbed at the tear duct of one eye, corner of his mouth rising as he did so. 'Is it DCI Buchanon?'

Jon watched his senior officer incline his head.

'You got a great pair of detectives, here.'

'They're not bad.'

Jon wanted to laugh.

'Cost us a very expensive piece of satellite equipment, though.'

Soutar's voice was cold. 'And perhaps the entire investigation.'

Buchanon glanced momentarily at Jon. 'How so?'

Soutar placed his briefcase on the table and entered the combination for the lock. 'How much do you know about the reconstruction process in Iraq?'

Jon remembered Alice's outraged reaction to accounts of the National Museum being looted of its treasures while American marines guarded the nearby Oil Ministry with tanks. Electricity blackouts, failing sanitation, a lack of clean water. She had said the country's infrastructure had been annihilated by the invasion. 'It could be going better?'

'That's one way of putting it. As Agent Mueller will concur, colossal amounts of money have been earmarked – mainly for building projects. Colossal amounts of cash have also been vanishing.'

'When you say colossal, what do you mean?' Rick asked, sitting forward.

'You heard of the CPA?' Mueller asked.

Jon remembered it being mentioned in one of the letters from the raft.

'Once Saddam's regime was toppled,' Mueller elaborated, 'Iraq needed to be rebuilt. Schools, roads, hospitals, power stations, bridges. Shock and awe took out all sorts of stuff and the Coalition Provisional Authority was in charge of allocating funds.'

Rick cocked his head. 'Which is run by America, is it not?'

Mueller nodded. 'We're talking billions in cash. Hundred-dollar bills, shrink-wrapped in plastic, piled on pallets and then flown in on cargo planes. Two billion per flight.'

'Two billion?' Buchanon murmured.

'Correct,' Mueller nodded. 'This money was then handed on to various bodies. Problem was, there was no proper accounting system in place.'

'How much missing money are we talking, then?' Rick asked.

'We're aware of $8.8 billion – but it's hard to keep count. Could be over $20 billion according to some estimates.'

'Simply vanished?' Rick's face was disbelieving.

'We prefer to say it's unaccounted for.'

'Whose money is it?' Rick's head was shaking. 'Where did it come from?'

'Much of it is Iraq's own funds. Oil revenues and cash left over from the oil-for-food programme run by the United Nations. After that, it's mainly come from the UN and American tax-payers.'

'But surely the CPA has some idea where it's gone?' Buchanon asked.

'All we know is money went to a whole variety of govern-ment departments – including the Iraqi Defence Ministry – and myriad private contractors.'

Jon thought about something else mentioned in one of the letters. The contract for rebuilding Al Sara-something bridge. What had she said? The CPA paid a company three times the amount that was needed. She'd also said the circumstances sur-rounding the explosions which destroyed the bridge in the first place were dodgy.

Rick sat back. 'Incredible. Which private contractors?'

'There are dozens, hundreds, out there handling all sorts of aspects of the reconstruction. It's big, big business.'

Soutar placed a hand on his briefcase. 'Now, about three months ago, our security forces in Basra received a tip-off about a consignment of US dollars being transported overland to the Iraqi port of Umm Qasr. Members of the Special Forces man-aged to get close enough to tag it with a satellite tracking device. The money was then placed in a container and loaded onto a ship, but we didn't know in which container. All we could do was sit back to see where it went.'

'The *Lesya Ukrayinka*,' Jon said.

'Hang on,' Rick interrupted. 'This operation you've been conducting. It's got nothing to do with some kind of arms ship-ment?'

Soutar smiled condescendingly. 'No, it hasn't. The *Lesya* is a tramp ship with no fixed itinerary. It travelled up through the Suez Canal, through the Straits of Gibraltar and round the

Spanish coast, diverting from the shipping lane on the fourth of August to avoid a major storm in the Bay of Biscay.'

Rick looked at Jon. Well, at least we got that right, his glance said. Jon winked in return.

'It then proceeded along the English Channel, docking in Felixstowe on Friday the eighth. It remained in the dock for ten days while repairs were completed. During that time, containers were off-loaded, but not the one with the satellite tracking device inside.'

Rick rubbed at his brow. 'Can I get this right? This is all about some looted dollars?'

Soutar nodded. 'That's right. Just a few looted dollars.'

Jon registered the man's mock breeziness and glanced warily at his partner.

There was now a note of caution in Rick's voice as he asked, 'How many dollars?'

'From the number of bales counted by our special forces guys, we estimate around eight hundred and fifty.'

'Eight hundred and fifty what?'

Soutar looked back, expression neutral. 'Eight hundred and fifty million dollars.'

'Really?' Rick's voice had gone up a notch.

Jon sat back and crossed his arms. Incredible. This entire thing, everyone who's died: it was all about money.

'The vessel then posted notice that it was making a delivery to Rotterdam before continuing to Baltimore, USA. When we knew the embezzled cash could be heading out of British waters and towards the States, we alerted our counterparts in the CIA.'

Rick looked at Mueller. 'Do you know who's awaiting delivery for the shipment in the States?'

'That information is classified,' Mueller replied curtly.

'Unfortunately,' Soutar continued, 'you gentlemen then chose to question Mykosowski about his apparent connection to a murdered crew member from the *Lesya*.'

Jon stared uneasily at the MI5 officer. 'You're getting to your satellite tracking device.'

'We lost the signal within hours of your visit to London. We presume it was jettisoned overboard, along with the cash.'

Jon blinked, then turned to Rick. What did he just say? Rick was looking like a schoolboy who had just been told he was about to be expelled. Jon turned his head to Mueller, who was now studying something beyond the window. Feeling slightly queasy, Jon tried to swallow.

Buchanon cleared his throat. 'Did you just say the money went overboard?'

'Now somewhere at the bottom of the Atlantic.' Soutar's voice was brittle with fake cheer. 'A big clap for Detectives Spicer and Saville.'

Jon sat perfectly still. He opened his mouth to speak, but his throat felt like sandpaper. Peeling his tongue from the roof of his mouth, he said, 'How do you know it went overboard?'

Mueller spoke up. 'The *Lesya* had just entered American waters when the signal was lost. One of our naval vessels intercepted it, the master and crew were placed under arrest and the ship taken to a secure port to be searched. The money is no longer on that vessel.'

Jon thought about his bank account. A couple of hundred quid, tops. Probably not worth offering to help pay it back.

'If we had any idea,' Buchanon started to bluster. 'But there was no alert from SOCA. We couldn't have known.'

Soutar raised a hand. 'We realise lines of communication could have been clearer. To take a charitable view, the storm is the real culprit. If the crew members hadn't gone overboard with all those bloody ducks.'

And the small issue of a few dozen refugees, Jon thought.

A bit of colour had returned to Buchanon's face. 'What will your next actions be?'

Soutar directed a questioning glance at the CIA officers. Mueller gave the smallest of nods. 'We need to find your man,' Soutar said. 'He's trying to take out anyone with any knowledge of that cargo and its intended recipients. First his three colleagues, now Mykosowski.'

'What about the ship's master?' Jon cut in. 'He must know something.'

Soutar's BlackBerry started beeping and he turned away from the table to take the call. That bloody thing, Jon thought, wanting to hurl it against the wall.

'He died,' Mueller announced. 'En route for questioning.'

'En route?'

'A suspected heart attack, mid-flight.'

'Couldn't he ...' Jon paused. 'There was no way to keep him alive – just until reaching a hospital on the mainland?'

'He was en route to Egypt.'

'I don't understand. Why fly him to—'

'He'd been rendered,' Rick interjected. 'Am I right? He was en route to an Egyptian prison?'

Jon looked at his partner, realisation dawning. No wonder the poor bastard's heart gave out. The prospect of being tortured.

'So we need Vladimir Yashin, as you know him,' Soutar announced, turning back round. 'And we think we've got a way to lure him out.' He looked at the other men. 'The author of these letters being found in the rubber ducks. From conversations she overheard while on the raft, it appears she also had a good idea where the cash was headed. Possibly a whole lot more, besides. She is the last loose thread.'

'Is she alive?' Rick asked.

'Having read the last letters being published tomorrow, we don't think that's possible. But with a small alteration to her final note, we can make her alive. In the same way the Russians were rescued, so can she be. All that's needed are two words at the end of the last letter: "a ship".'

Jon looked at the windows, realising the sky was now growing dark. Finally a refugee is acknowledged, he thought. But only as bait for the person they want.

'We'll then announce she's in a hospital near here while her claim for asylum is being processed,' Soutar added.

'When?' Jon asked.

'Tomorrow. That was what my last call was about. It's all set up – the hospital will release a statement announcing her presence tomorrow at nine. Once the *Express* has made its sales from the last six letters – they want to wind up the story before some other big exclusive in Sunday's edition. She's going to be in the,' he glanced down at his BlackBerry, 'Manchester Royal Infirmary. After that, we wait for Salnikov to appear.'

Instantly, Jon sat up. 'Salnikov? That's his name?'

Soutar reached into his briefcase and took out a file. 'Valeri Salnikov. Here's who you've been chasing, Detective.'

Twenty-Seven

Alice knelt in silence on the floor of Holly's room, one elbow propped on the bed, her fingers wrapped in her daughter's gradually loosening grip. She gazed down at the little girl's face, studying the flawless skin and marvelling at its ability to absorb the night light's soft glow. Holly's eyes had stopped moving about behind her closed lids and her breathing had slowed and deepened. Alice slid her hand free from her daughter's fingers and they curled in slightly. The petals of a closing flower.

She was finally asleep, though for how long, Alice couldn't say.

Sometimes it was a matter of minutes before she woke again, a nameless sense of disquiet causing her to sob and whimper. Holly could never say what the dreams contained; but it was plain they left her feeling frightened and anxious.

Careful to make no sound, Alice climbed to her feet and tiptoed from the room. On the landing, she paused, eyes drawn to her own bedroom door. She recalled Jon's ability to spring up, whatever the hour, instantly alert to their daughter's needs. There comforting her before she was even fully awake. Alice slept so deeply that, with him no longer in the house, the first knowledge she had of anything being wrong was often when her daughter appeared at the side of the double bed, cheeks wet with tears. More and more often, she simply beckoned her daughter under the covers and they spent the remainder of the night together, two slender forms clinging to each other on the bed's wide expanse.

In the kitchen, she flicked the kettle on and looked around. The house felt so empty and quiet. She glanced at the corner of the room where Punch's basket once lay and tears stung her eyes. What has happened to us all?

Her phone started to ring and, for a second, Jon's face appeared in her mind. Then she pictured Phillip, perhaps calling from his house, ready to sort things out. She didn't recognise the number displayed on the screen. 'Hello?'

'Hello – is that Mrs Alice Spicer speaking?'

The words were well spoken. Brusque, even. 'Yes,' Alice replied warily, fearing some kind of sales call.

'Mrs Spicer, sorry to call you so late in the evening, but I've only just received your message. My name is Patrick Seakins, a Principal Medical Officer in Her Majesty's Navy.'

'My message?' Alice mumbled, trying to make sense of what he was saying. 'I've never heard your name before. Patrick Sea—'

'Call me Beach. Everyone else does.' His voice had softened slightly and now she could detect something that sounded very much like excitement. 'Sorry, I've got ahead of myself. You didn't personally leave a message for me. You made an enquiry at MDHU Derriford, here in Plymouth.'

'God, yes.' Alice raised a hand and swept her hair back. 'I did. About a young female—'

'We found her. It was us who brought her ashore.'

'We?'

'I work on a Trafalgar Class submarine, HMS *Triumph*. We were on exercise in the Atlantic. At one point we switched our sonar from passive to active and the operator detected a small object on the surface above us. We went to periscope depth to see what it was. We couldn't believe it. He'd detected a raft – with a young woman on it. I'm certain she's the one you have up there.'

Alice sat down, eyes squeezed shut as she tried to process the information. 'You found her out at sea on a raft?'

'That's correct. How is she?'

'Alive, still confined to bed, often being fed intravenously because she shows no interest in food. There are concerns about her liver, apparently. But she'll survive; she's obviously a fighter.'

'Absolutely. To have made it through what she did: it was obvious she'd been drifting for quite a while before we found her.'

'I'm concerned about her mental state,' Alice responded. 'She hasn't been able to speak since arriving.'

'The same with us. Has she put on any weight?'

'A little. The staff have been trying to spoon-feed her solids.'

'When we found her, Mrs Spicer, she was hours from death. Her body had started shutting down – severe dehydration. To a degree I've only ever read about.'

'You're called Beach, did you say?'

'Yes.'

'What do you mean, she was on a raft? Was she alone?'

'Yes.' His voice was suddenly guarded. 'It was ... I won't ever forget the sight of her on that raft. Wooden pallets – that's all it was. Lashed together with children's skipping ropes.'

Alice had to place a hand on the kitchen table, the sense of the floor lurching was so strong. 'Do you not read the newspapers?'

'We docked just over an hour ago. I've been at sea this past week. We've had no outside contact in that time. Of course I've seen the papers, now. It's her – she wrote those letters. I would bet my life on it.'

'But I don't understand. Why did she end up here?'

'I'm piecing it together, too. We brought her ashore and I had her placed in infection control at the MDHU. I'd put her on a drip onboard the *Triumph* and started her on a course of antibiotics. She weighed just over six stone when we lifted her from that godforsaken thing.'

'Then what?'

'I don't fully know, yet. We had three days ashore then went back out on training exercises. There was some confusion as to what we should do with her – once she was well enough to be moved. Beds on infection control are hugely expensive. I know questions were being asked as to where that money was coming from. I presume the decision was made to refer her on to that place for refugees.'

'The screening unit in Liverpool?'

'I thought it was East Croydon?'

Alice raised her eyes. That's where her notes must have gone: East bloody Croydon.

'So she arrived with you how long ago?' Beach asked.

'Seven days,' Alice sighed. 'She was too ill to be interviewed by the Border Agency. And Liverpool had no psychiatric unit beds free, so they shunted her on to the mental health unit at Sale General. A taxi dropped her off, but without any case notes.'

'After everything she'd been through – a taxi just dumped her at the hospital?'

Alice could hear the anger in his voice. 'I'm sorry to say, but, yes.'

'And she's been there ever since?'

'Yes. No one had a clue about her.'

'Well, it's her, Mrs Spicer. I know it. Young female, early twenties. Much of her hair missing.'

'Yes – some nurses thought maybe she was Indian or Bangladeshi. Is there nothing else you can tell me?'

'Yes. When I examined her, I found something written on her hand. I wasn't sure if it was her name: she didn't ever speak.'

'What was it?'

'Amira.'

'Amira?'

'That's it.'

'Nothing else?'

'I'm sorry. No – there was! She was clutching this miniature bottle of perfume. Tiny thing made of glass. All curved edges. I had to prise it from her grip. It went into the washbag we gave her.'

'Washbag?' Alice thought about the woman's room on the MHU. The bedside table and the single bag inside it. I didn't search through it properly. She stood, ready to drive back to the hospital there and then. Holly. Looking at the clock, she realised her mum was out, so couldn't babysit. Tomorrow. First thing after dropping Holly off at school. 'That's it, then. There really was nothing else on the raft?'

'Nothing worth mentioning.' He sounded guarded again. Upset, too? 'Nothing to identify her. The raft was – it wasn't pleasant.'

'What happened to it?'

'It was used for target practice. Best that way.'

She wanted to know more, but something in his voice dissuaded her from asking anything else. 'Can I get you on this number? I'll go and see her in the morning. Check for that bottle.'

'Please, call me. I know it's her, Mrs Spicer. I really do.'

'Thanks for ringing. We'll speak again tomorrow.' She pressed red then placed the phone on the table. My God! She pounded her feet in a series of little stamps. I know who she is – I may even know her name! She looked at her phone then started circling it round and round, desperate to tell someone. Mum was out. Jon? She dismissed the idea. Perhaps Phillip? Suddenly, she remembered the lady at the hospital in Liverpool. Yulia. The Russian woman who'd been so helpful working out the connection to Plymouth. Alice toyed with the idea of ringing her. Eight thirty at night. Her office would probably be closed, anyway. Alice lifted her handset, unable to resist. After six rings, an answerphone clicked in. Alice recognised the woman's accent.

'Hello, this is a recorded message. The admissions office of the Royal Liverpool University Hospital is now closed. We open again at nine o'clock in the morning. If you wish to leave a message, please do so after the tone.'

As soon as the beep ended, Alice began to speak. 'This is a message for Yulia Volkova. It's Alice Spicer speaking, from RAP in Manchester. Yulia, I think I've found out her name. She's called Amira. Call me when you get this message.'

Twenty-Eight

'Valeri?' Jon asked incredulously.

Muller raised a finger. 'You want to tell him he's got a woman's name?'

Smiling, Soutar opened the file. 'This information comes from multiple sources, and some of that provided by the Russian security services is open to question. However, we know this much.' He laid his hands to either side of the printed sheets. 'Valeri Salnikov served in the regular Russian army for less than three years before he was selected to join Spetsnaz. I presume you've heard of this part of their armed forces?'

'They're like the SAS, aren't they?' Rick asked.

'Essentially. Spetsialnoye Nazranie, or troops of special purpose, were a closely guarded secret for many years. When Salnikov joined in the early eighties, we think they numbered about thirty thousand. Their primary, wartime role, includes deep reconnaissance of key targets and the demolition of strategic points such as bridges. We believe Salnikov went into an anti-VIP company whose specialist role was to seek out and kill important political and military leaders.'

Mueller grunted. 'Assassinations.'

Jon glanced at Rick. 'The garrotte.'

'That's one technique,' the American answered. 'And highly effective, too. Apparently Salnikov was deployed to Chechnya where he was busy using his favoured technique before being captured. We're unsure of his whereabouts for the next few years – but it seems he spent some time as a prisoner of the Chechnyans. As payback, they used the garrotte on him, repeatedly. But they were careful to never quite kill him.'

'The scars covering his throat,' Rick said.

'That's right. We're not sure how or when he escaped. But to survive what he did – well, he's a tough cookie.' Mueller tapped a finger against his temple. 'Though I think a few wires have come loose, if you know what I'm saying.'

Soutar turned a couple of pages. 'Then came the nineties. The coup in Russia and its period of economic decline. Like the rest of the country, the special forces faced crisis. Neglected, underpaid – and soon demoralised. Salnikov left to use his skills in the private sector. Many members of Spetsnaz did. He knows explosives, communications, surveillance, close combat. He's been taught other languages, including English. And he's been trained in the use of just about every type of firearm on the planet. He's ice-cold under extreme pressure and he's clever.'

'You heard of the System?' D'Souza suddenly asked, placing his forearms on his knees and looking directly at Jon.

'No.'

'It's a Russian martial art. But there's no rituals, no belts, none of that stuff. It's more like organised street fighting. Close-range style, using wrestling manoeuvres, elbow strikes, kicks to the knee joint, quick fists to the face or genitals, choke holds. Anything goes – pulling hair, if it helps.'

'He's trained in that?'

'Anyone who made it into Spetsnaz had to go up against a series of three or four soldiers who were already in – and they had to still be standing after twelve minutes of combat. You just wouldn't get that in any Western army: it would be banned. Hospitalisations, the occasional death. Salnikov, we gather, ex-celled.'

Soutar flipped another page. 'After leaving Spetsnaz, we think he worked as a bodyguard for senior executives in one of the country's newly formed private oil companies. There's evidence he started spending a lot of time in Iraq from the mid-nineties onward. Russian oil companies had extensive agreements with Saddam Hussein's regime.'

'Until the invasion,' Rick said, a smile of understanding on his face. 'Then they're all booted out and the likes of Shell, Exxon and BP come in. I've read about this. What are they trying to call the contracts? Technical service agreements, that's it.'

Soutar nodded. 'The Russians leave. But Salnikov doesn't.'

'So who did he start working for next?' Rick asked.

'We've linked him to several assassinations of prominent fig-ures in the new Iraqi administration.'

'What sort of figures?'

'A couple of Shia politicians. A Kurdish business leader.'

'So, he's working with the Sunnis?' Rick asked. 'Remnants of the old regime. Trying to destabilise things?'

'He's certainly got those connections. Maybe he was at first. But we believe he'll work for whoever's prepared to pay enough for his services.'

'Plus,' D'Souza said darkly, 'he's implicated in a roadside bomb in Baghdad that killed three US marines.'

Jon pictured crowded, dusty streets, flanked by breeze-block houses baking under a merciless sun. Churning, oily smoke and the mangled remains of military vehicles. Woman shrouded in dark cloth screaming, abandoned sandals and pools of blood soaking into the sand. 'And now he's bringing that carnage here.' Jon's voice was quiet. 'My God.'

'So you see,' Mueller sighed. 'We want him pretty bad.'

Jon frowned, turning to Soutar. 'Isn't this a British investiga-tion?'

Soutar looked at his CIA counterpart. 'There are agreements in place between our governments.'

'Don't tell me, if we catch him, he'll be rendered, too?' Jon said accusingly.

'He'll be taken into our custody, yes,' Mueller responded, looking embarrassed.

'And then where will he go?'

Mueller shrugged. 'I'm unable to say.'

Jon blew out breath. 'This is so wrong. If we catch him, it's on our soil. I can't believe we'll simply hand him over.'

'To vanish into some black prison in Eastern Europe,' Rick added.

Jon turned his head. 'Black what?'

'CIA interrogation facilities. They've got them dotted around the world. Countries where the regimes aren't quite so accountable.' He looked at the CIA agents. 'I've read about them, too.'

'Seems you read a lot,' D'Souza replied, lips barely moving.

'Enough to know the invasion would never have taken place if Iraq's main export was carrots.'

'Hey.' D'Souza's grin was cold. 'Britain stood shoulder to shoulder with us, remember? So don't start lecturing me, Detective.'

'Gentlemen,' Buchanon cut in, flashing Rick a warning look. 'Agents Mueller and D'Souza are our guests here. And if it's been decided he goes into US custody, he goes into US custody.' He looked at Soutar. 'This has all been cleared for tomorrow?'

'It has,' Soutar replied, closing the file.

'Any other assistance we can give, please say.'

'Thank you.' The MI5 officer glanced at the door. 'Is there a lavatory I can use?'

'Yes. Rick, could you show Officer Soutar?' Buchanon got up and extended a hand to Mueller and D'Souza. 'I have some other matters I need to deal with. Pleased to meet you. And good luck.' He paused in the doorway to glance at Rick and Jon. 'Gents, my office, eight thirty tomorrow, please.'

Rick followed him out, Soutar just behind.

Mueller sat back and began to jiggle one knee up and down. 'Listen, I'd be pissed off, too. You Brits have stuck by us. How our government's playing things – well, it's no way to treat an ally.'

'Yeah, well. Seems we can't do much about it.'

'We've been reading your file.' This from D'Souza.

Jon paused in the act of getting up.

The agent chuckled. 'Those boys in MI5 were getting pretty damned pissed with you.'

'Really.' Jon sat back down. 'They never said.'

D'Souza grinned at his sarcastic tone. 'I see you captained Greater Manchester Police's rugby team. Open-side flanker.'

'Yup,' Jon replied warily, wondering how much the other man had read about him. 'You know about rugby?'

D'Souza nodded. 'As a student, I played for the Keelhaulers.'

'The who?'

'I went to the Californian Maritime Academy, part of the State University. The student rugby team's known as the Keelhaulers.'

'I thought it was all basketball and baseball over there.'

'Mostly, but rugby gets a bit of a following, too. Not much of one, granted. But there are leagues and competitions. We won the Pacific Coast Championship.'

'Good to hear.' Jon leaned back in his seat. He assessed the other man. Too small for a forward. 'What position were you?'

'Scrum half.'

That figures, thought Jon. Nasty little terrier's position. Sniping at gaps, snapping at heels. Not ready to give the man any credit, he sighed. 'Out with the girly backs.'

The American stared for a moment then gave a mock salute. 'The girly backs. Not doing the ... what do they call it? The hard yakkas you forwards do.'

Hard yakkas. Jon grinned at the Australian term for winning ground in the opposition's territory, every inch bitterly fought. 'That's them.'

'Well, you've been doing the hard yakkas up here, too,' D'Souza responded, looking across at the closed door and lowering his voice. 'I realise Soutar's a bit abrasive. Touch of the officer class about him.'

'You're not wrong.'

Mueller spoke up. 'You've been making things happen up here. You've got the ground-level knowledge we need.' He removed a business card. 'The number of my cell is on that. If you hear anything, call me. It won't go ignored, trust me.'

Jon took the card, grateful to be acknowledged at last. 'OK, cheers.'

'And Jon?' Mueller's face was now deadly serious. 'This Salnikov? Sounds to me you can take care of yourself on any rugby pitch, and I know you've worked some tough cases, taken down some very bad guys. But he's not the same. Did we stress that enough just now?'

'You did.'

'Good. You went after him – which took balls. But,' he shook his head, 'there's only one way to deal with this guy. And that's from a safe distance.' He raised one hand and pulled an imaginary trigger.

'He'll be shot?'

'We want to question him, but once he realises he's trapped, I can't see it ending any other way. Someone like Salnikov? He doesn't do prison – especially after what happened to him in Chechnya. He'd rather go down fighting.'

Jon glanced at the men's jackets, wondering what might be concealed beneath them.

After showing the three men out, Jon stood on the top step. Time to head home. An image of his front door appeared in his head and he quickly snuffed it out. Rick's sofa, he thought. That's where you're sleeping tonight. He remembered his colleague's comments about Alice involving her solicitor. Taking in a breath, he wandered across to his Mondeo. Once inside, he removed his phone, stared at it for a minute then keyed in Alice's number. 'It's me.'

'Oh. What do you want?'

Her voice sounded so clear. He closed his eyes and imagined looking at her. She was probably sitting at a slight angle on the sofa in the telly room, legs curled beneath her. Bare feet, tracksuit bottoms and her faded pink training top that was beginning to fray at the neck. What she always wore when just sitting around in the evenings. He gazed out the window. A row of dark vehicles stared back. 'Is he there?'

'No. What do you want?'

'Don't do this, Ali. Don't involve a solicitor in this.'

'Jon, there's no point in trying to discuss with you—'

'There is. We can sort this out.'

'We've gone over all this before,' she sighed. 'It's pointless.'

'You want me to change. I will change.'

'You can't change.'

'Give me a chance. I'll show you.'

'It's not in your nature. You're incapable of changing.'

'I've said, I'll give up the job, if that's what it takes. Maybe if I was in something less intense. Dealing with murders; it takes over.'

'Jon, you are that job. It's like oxygen to you.'

'No. You and Holly – you're my oxygen. You two.'

'Jon.' Her voice had softened a fraction. 'It's not just the job. It's about your need to battle – to fix something in your sights and defeat it. You'll be doing that no matter what you do. At least in the police, it works to your advantage. I don't want you to leave it – it suits you down to the ground.'

'I don't need to be battling things.'

'Really?'

'Yes.'

'I think you do.'

'Well, you're wrong.'

She snorted. 'So, what are you doing now?'

'I'm ...' Shit, she's got me.

'I just want a normal life, Jon. A husband who I know will be there.'

'I'm there for you. I'll always be there for you. If you ever need me, you know that.'

'You weren't!' Cracks had appeared in her voice. 'When I was in that hospital. You weren't there, were you? Trying not to let Holly see my ...'

'Alice.' He closed his eyes again. Here we are again, he thought. Back at the one thing I can never put right. He imagined his wife in that airless room when the sonographer said their unborn baby was dead. Holly sitting in the corner, wondering why Mummy suddenly couldn't speak. 'If I could change anything, you know that would be it.'

'You left me on my own in there.'

'You know there wasn't anything I could do.'

'I know.' Her voice had dropped to a whisper. 'The job puts you in these positions. I know that.' She sniffed. 'I'm talking everyday things, too. Watching the telly. Shopping. Boring stuff.'

'And you get that with Braithwaite.'

'I get routine. Yes, he works ordinary times of the day. Things are ... they're normal.'

'Slumped in front of the box, your life slowly ebbing away. Since when have you gone for dull?'

'Not dull. Normal. There's a difference. We're able to plan things – even just going for walks, I'm not always dreading that phone call. You, working late, working weekends. "Alice? I've got a runner. Not sure when I'll be back." How many times have I heard that? How many times have I had to try and cheer Holly up when Daddy does another no-show?'

'So you get normality. Great. Do you love him?'

'He's kind. He considers others – I'm not answering your questions. God! Do you love Carmel?'

'We're not seeing each other any more.'

A second's silence. 'Why?'

'It just wasn't working. I love you, Alice.'

'Forget about me. We need to move on with our lives.'

'It's not only our lives though, is it? Think about Holly.'

'I am thinking about Holly! Thinking about Holly is why I asked you to leave.'

'And now look at her.'

'What?'

You know what, he thought. I can hear it in your voice. 'Look at her, Alice. This has turned her life upside down.'

'She has routine. A solid base. Two people who she knows will be there for her.'

Jon felt the bile at the back of his throat. 'He's not her dad. He can never be her dad.'

'So that's your justification for stalking him, is it? You know what? She actually gets to see him! He reads her bedtime stories. So don't you dare try and use Holly in this.'

'Use her? How am I using her?' He heard the anger beginning to infect his voice, too. 'You're not thinking of her interests. This thing is wrecking her!'

'Don't you raise your voice at me!'

'Well, isn't it?'

'It's not wrecking – I'm not getting into this.'

'Yes, you are. Admit it. Holly is ...' He paused. The line had clicked and he moved the phone away from his ear to see the screen. Don't you hang up on me. He pressed redial. Engaged tone. Fuck! He threw the phone onto the seat beside him and started slamming the heels of his hands against the steering wheel.

Once the anger had subsided a little, he sat back and pressed the tips of his fingers against his temples. Why? Why are we unable to talk this through? He tried to replay the conversation in his head, vainly attempting to work out when it had flared into an argument. Too many issues. This whole thing with us is a bloody minefield.

Back up in the incident room, the syndicate on night cover were gathered in one corner watching a football match playing out on a little TV.

On the opposite side of the room, Rick was at his desk, eyes roving over the screen of his computer monitor. The light was off in Buchanon's office. Jon looked at his watch. Almost ten. He sauntered over to Rick. 'You not got a home to go to, either?'

His partner glanced up. 'Ha bloody ha. You drove me in this morning, remember?'

'Oh, yes. Tell you what; I'll give you a lift if I can crash on your sofa again.'

'No problem.' He clicked through to a new screen.

'What are you looking at?'

'Stuff about those missing billions of dollars.'

'Yeah?' Jon drew up a seat. 'What does it say?'

'The figures are incredible.' He flashed Jon a quick grin. 'Makes the eight hundred and fifty million tossed from the *Lesya* seem like peanuts.'

Jon placed a hand over his eyes. 'Don't. You realise when that gets round this place, we'll have the piss ripped out of us for months?'

Rick was scrutinising the screen. 'Once the Americans were

in control, Lukoil, the Russian oil company, was given the heave-ho. The US administration is now pushing for Production Sharing Agreements to be given to five Western oil companies. Basically, they're no-bid contracts giving access to Iraq's largest oil fields for a thirty-year period. Elements in the Iraqi parliament are desperately trying to oppose them.'

'I've never seen any reports about oil contracts. What about the weapons of mass destruction? Didn't Blair say that's why we invaded?'

'Yeah, right.' Rick laughed. 'They don't let this stuff about oil appear as headline news, mate. You have to dig a bit for it. There's more. Hundreds upon hundreds of contracts went to US firms to rebuild the areas their own air force bombed to smithereens. This article mentions firms that have links to people at the very top of American government. That Cheney bloke? His old company, Halliburton, was given a contract worth up to seven billion without any bidding process. And that was before the country was even invaded.' He tapped the screen. 'And the missing money? Fraud investigations into some of America's largest firms cannot be discussed in any way.'

'Why?'

'Gagging orders put in place by the Bush administration. Discuss the allegations in public and you'll be arrested.'

Jon sighed. 'It always seems to come down to it.'

'What's that?'

'Greed. From the school bully ripping off lunch money to these big boys out in Iraq. Just a bunch of money-grabbing bastards.'

Rick closed the screen down. 'Well, you know what they say about money. The root of all evil.'

'Yup.' Jon stood. 'Can't argue with that. So, tomorrow. Buchanon's office, eight thirty.'

Rick grimaced. 'What's that about?'

'Why MI5 showed up here, I should think.'

'Oh, Christ. You rang Mykosowski's office, didn't you?'

'Yeah – but Soutar? He agreed to say that he rang me about that fishing trawler – wanting to know more details.'

'When did you arrange that?'

'On the stairs on the way up to the meeting room.'

'Crafty git.'

Jon spread his palms. 'Just covering my arse.'

Rick scowled. 'You know, I've got holiday booked from tomorrow. Heading over to Scarborough, remember?'

'Not till after that meeting, you're not. When are you picking up Zak?'

'Andy's collecting him at ten.'

'You can be back home for then.'

'And when am I supposed to pack?'

'Tonight?'

Rick huffed.

'Anyway,' Jon smiled. 'Think about tomorrow's papers. The last six letters and the announcement she's been found.'

His partner's eyes showed a mix of trepidation and excitement. 'Not sure if I want to know how grim things got.'

Twenty-Nine

Oliver Brookes opened his front door and stepped out into the cool morning air. Off to his left, a seagull let out a series of mocking screeches. He regarded the placid sea stretching away to a hazy horizon. Sunlight was cutting through the crags at the top of the cliffs behind him, mighty shafts of light angling across the bay, thistledown silently drifting through them.

Stiffly, he walked down his garden path and out on to the beach, aiming for a brightly lit patch of sand before the tidal line of seaweed. As he stepped further into the sunlight, he felt its warmth across his shoulders, then his buttocks, and finally the backs of his legs.

He turned round and raised his hands, eyes closed to the immense glow. Once the coldness had been forced from his body, he lowered his chin and took the piece of paper from his pocket. After cautiously unfolding it, he read the tiny words yet again.

My name is Amira Jasim, age 22, former resident of Baghdad, Iraq. I am writing this letter in English to declare to the world that, on the fourteenth of July, I paid $6,000 to board a ship in the Pakistani port of Karachi. This money was to buy me passage to Great Britain. Last night I, and many others like me, were abandoned. If we are to die here in the sea, the captain of the Lesya Ukrayinka is a murderer for he did not turn back for us.

His eyes moved to the second paragraph.

The other man who must face justice is Mr Scott King of the Coalition Provisional Authority in Baghdad. When I showed him evidence of how the money meant for rebuilding my nation is being stolen, he passed my identity to militia. They killed my husband, Younis, and I was forced to flee before they came for me.

He looked at his cottage at the base of the cliff, thinking it would still be in shadow by the time he reached Combe Martin. Refolding the message, he placed it back in his pocket and started for the narrow path that led up from the secluded bay.

Alice buzzed the intercom of the school's front door then waited for the lock to click. 'Come on, Holly,' she said with forced cheer. 'You can play with all the lovely toys. Martha and Eve will be inside. Don't cry.'

Holly continued to whine and sob, arms wrapped tightly round Alice's leg. Forcing back the lump in her throat, Alice buzzed again. The lock released and she pushed the outer door open, picking her daughter up as she did so. 'You know, Mummy will be back very soon. Now be a big girl, please, Holly.'

She carried her to the doorway of the reception room, where a member of staff was waiting. Alice gave her a pained look and the woman nodded in understanding.

'Holly? Can you help me get out the play dough? We're making models this morning.'

Alice held her daughter over the stairgate forming a barrier across the lower part of the doorway. Holly's cries grew louder. 'Mummy will be back soon,' Alice said, feeling the hoarseness in her voice. As the member of staff prised Holly away, Alice felt like a piece of her was being peeled off, too. 'I love you.'

The member of staff was pointing into the room, as Holly stretched her arms out to Alice. 'Look! Martha's here. Let's she if she can help us.'

Alice made for the exit, taking a couple of deep breaths as soon as she was outside. Once the ache in her chest had subsided, she reached for her phone. 'Hi, Martin. It's Alice here.'

'Morning, Alice. Everything OK?'

'Yes.'

'You sound flustered.'

'It's Holly. I've just dropped her off at pre-school club. She's going through these separation anxieties – it's not easy leaving her.'

'Take the morning off, if you need to.'

'No. She has to learn I'm not leaving her for ever. Listen, I'll be a bit late, if that's OK. I wanted to pop in to see that patient in Sale General's MHU.'

'The missing case file one?'

'That's right – I think I might be getting somewhere with it.'

'Fine. See you later.'

'See you later.'

Jon stepped out on to the top step of the renovated warehouse and took in the sun-drenched street before him. 'This heatwave is going on for ever,' he yawned.

'That's what I want,' Rick replied, slipping on a pair of wraparound shades and trotting down the steps. 'See you round the back.'

Jon removed his car keys. 'Where are you rushing ... oh, yeah. Newsagent's.'

'That's right,' Rick called back, jogging towards the deli at the corner of the building.

Jon made his way down the steps then along the side of the building to the car park at the rear. He'd just reached his vehicle when Rick reappeared, a couple of papers in his hands. 'Trouble,' he announced.

'What?' Jon replied, opening the driver's door and getting in.

The other door opened and Rick slid into the passenger seat. He removed his sunglasses. 'How the hell did they get hold of this?' He turned the *Manchester Evening Chronicle* so Jon could see the front page headline.

BRITAIN'S DEADLIEST MAN?

Jon's eyes went to the main image: the Border Agency mugshot of Valeri Salnikov. 'What?' He whipped the paper from Rick's hand and read the opening paragraph:

Is this man behind a spate of gruesome slayings currently baffling Greater Manchester Police? In the past few days, three men have been found murdered in accommodation put aside for asylum seekers. Each one is thought to be a Russian national. All had been garrotted with such force their heads were almost severed.

Leading the hunt is DI Spicer of the city's Major Incident Team. Sources close to the investigation reveal that DI Spicer has been struggling to identify the mystery man. The image below captures DI Spicer in front of the police station on Grey Mare Lane where the MIT are based. More details about the slayings on pages 5 and 6.

Jon examined the shot. It was of him showing Soutar, Mueller and D'Souza out of the station the night before. Bloody hell, whoever took it must have been parked up on the road right in front of them. His eyes returned to the top of the page, picking out the small panel below the headline.

By Carmel Todd, Chief Crime Reporter

He let the newspaper sag between his knees. 'She's fucking done me.'

'How do you mean?'

'No!' He made a fist and ground his knuckles against the centre of his forehead. 'The cow has done me.'

'What are you on about?'

Jon let his hand fall on to the page. 'The case notes I left in her flat.' He tapped Salnikov's mugshot. 'This photo and loads of notes. Bits and pieces I'd jotted down about old throat-scars here.'

'Oh shit, Jon.'

He dropped the paper on to the floor between them. 'I asked for it.'

Rick sat back, tapping his fingers on the copy of the *Express*. 'Buchanon will know by now.'

'Yup,' Jon said grimly, starting the engine. 'I am well and truly in it.'

'It could have come from somewhere else. Border Agency, maybe?'

'Be serious, mate.' He reversed, then swung the car on to Whitworth Street. 'Come on, then. Let's hear the last letters.'

Rick glanced down at the copy of the *Chronicle*, shook his head then turned to the other paper. 'OK, here we go,' he announced, opening the front page. 'Letter number fourteen.'

Morning, our sixth day at sea. No cloud or wind again. Writing these words now takes me many hours. I have tied the pen to my wrist so I cannot drop it. The sun is strong and my lips are covered in flakes of salt. Awake I can think only of a cold drink. All we have is our urine.

The crewmen have taken down the sail and made a roof to hide from the sun. They ignore my requests for food. I have tried to eat clothing, but the taste of salt is so strong. There is leather on one of the women's bags, but my teeth cannot tear it. I chewed on some small pieces of wood.

Ali and Jino are now awake. Ali had kept a few fish and these he shared. Parviz remains asleep. There is no new blood coming from his head.

Shouting on the life boat. They have water! The man with throat scars has found another man stealing it. In the struggle, the boat nearly turned over. The one with throat scars held the other from behind and pushed the knife deep into his neck. Then he threw the dying crewman into the sea. The man tried to swim to our raft, but sank.

I do not know if the man with throat scars is good or bad. Why did he not agree to cut the rope which connects us?

'Fucking hell, does this guy do anything else but kill people?' Jon asked.

'Things are getting desperate. Chewing on leather, trying to eat wood.'

Jon nodded. 'And we know what Milton found in the dead Russians' lower intestines.'

Rick rolled his shoulders as if preparing his muscles for a task. 'Next?'

'Yup.'

Ali has searched the raft again. Inside a bag, he has found a tiny, curved bottle of perfume. It smells of roses. Jíno likes it very much. He presses it to his nose for many minutes with his eyes closed. He is so young, I do not want someone so young to die.

We cannot wake Parviz.

At sunset, the man with throat scars brought the boat close and passed across sixteen dates and a little water. His face is also burned from the sun and blisters cover his lips.

He said there is nothing more and he pointed to Parviz. He said he is going to die and we should roll him from the raft – then we will have more dates and water each.

Jon scooted round a bus that had pulled over to pick up passengers. 'You know, it's been confusing me. Why didn't throat-scars leave the refugees when the lifeboat turned up? That's what his mates wanted to do.'

Rick fiddled with the catch of the glove compartment. 'There's a bond between them, now. Survivors. He can't leave them.'

'Come off it, mate. He's left them to roast on the raft. The guy doesn't feel emotion. He just stuck a knife in the neck of one of his mates.'

'That bloke was stealing water.'

'OK, point taken. He does have emotion; when someone jeopardises his chances of survival, he kills them.'

'What are you getting at?'

'He'll do anything to survive, right? Anything. Including keeping that raft attached to the lifeboat, even though it must have been slowing them down.'

'I don't follow—' Rick stopped. He looked at Jon in dismay. 'You mean he's keeping the refugees alive for ... no way.'

'You heard what Milton found in their lower intestines. Read the next letters.'

Alice stepped out of the lift and looked at the front desk of the MHU. The heads of the receptionist and security guard were bowed over a small radio that had been placed on the counter. Some sort of news item was being read out.

'Morning,' Alice announced.

The security guard looked up and quickly waved hello.

She walked slowly across, trying to make out what they were listening to. The bulletin ended and the receptionist sat back. 'In the MRI. I can't believe she's in the MRI. That's a quarter of an hour drive from here, at most.'

'Who?' Alice asked.

'The rubber duck woman. The one who's been writing the letters. It turns out she's in the MRI, the BBC just announced it.'

'What do you mean, she's in the MRI?'

'A ship found her. She was brought ashore in Liverpool and taken to the MRI.'

'How do they know it's her?'

'I don't know. She told them? It didn't give details.'

Alice's eyes dropped. 'That can't be right,' she murmured. 'Did they say what she's called?'

'No.'

Alice found herself looking at the woman's copy of that morning's *Express*. The last six letters were inside. 'Mary, can I borrow your paper, please?'

'Of course.'

'Thanks. OK if I take it through to the ward?'

'Bring it back, though. I do the crossword at lunchtime.'

Once the security guard had checked her, the lock on the outer door was released and she stepped into the airlock. Six quick strides took her to the inner door. Damn it! No one at the nurse's desk. She pressed the buzzer as her sense of claustrophobia increased. Come on, come on. A nursing assistant appeared in the corridor, walking from the direction of the telly room.

Alice buzzed again and he stepped over to the desk, clicked the lock and continued into the nurses' room. Alice stepped into the deserted corridor. Four holes were in the wall, all that remained of Constable's *Hay Wain*. Trouble at the mill, Alice thought, striding quickly down the corridor. A tall, black-skinned woman was standing in the doorway to one of the women's bays. Ethiopian? Sudanese? The woman's thin arms were hanging at her sides and

Alice could see dozens of scars dotting her forearms. Cigarette burns? She realised with a shock that the woman was pregnant.

The stretch of corridor with the private rooms was also deserted and Alice hurried to the end door, eyes settling momentarily on the name tag. J Smith. She peered through the little window, relieved to see the young woman was still in the bed, lying on her back, staring at the ceiling. She had been hooked up to a drip once again. Gently, Alice opened the door and stepped into the little room, unable to stop herself glancing at the bedside cabinet. 'Hi.'

As usual, the young woman didn't react.

Alice stared at her sunken cheeks, the dry patches on her scalp, the welts that remained on her lips. She stepped over to the bedside. 'I've brought you some dates. I read you have over four hundred varieties in Iraq.'

The young woman's large eyes shifted, settling on Alice for a moment before moving away.

'And fruit juice. Apple and orange, freshly squeezed.'

No reaction.

Alice placed the items on the bed. 'Is it OK to take a look in your cabinet? I think you've got something in there.' She crouched down and pulled at the little door. The metal latch opened with a ping. On the middle shelf was the dark blue wash-bag. She slid it out, turned it round and saw the letters MDHU on the zip's tag. Christ, no one even thought to enquire what they stood for.

Perching on the edge of the bed, she pulled the zip open. 'I think I might know who you are,' Alice murmured, peering inside. A toothbrush and toothpaste. A tube of lip salve. Since she'd last examined the bag's contents, someone had added a pack of sanitary towels. It'll be a while before her body recovers enough to need them, Alice thought, pushing everything to the side, fingers probing into the corners. A small, rounded object. She took it out and held it up. A curved perfume bottle. Alice unscrewed the tiny cap and sniffed. Roses. She felt tears in her eyes as pictures formed of what the other woman had gone through.

Movement in the bed. Alice looked over her shoulder. The

young woman had averted her head, nostrils flaring in and out. The scent! Alice quickly replaced the cap, realising how smell evoked memories.

'Can you hear me?' she whispered.

The other woman kept staring at the wall.

'Is your name Amira? Am I talking to Amira?'

A tear welled up at the corner of the woman's eye and Alice felt her own cheeks suddenly become wet. She reached out to cup the other person's cheek. 'It's OK. Everything will be OK, now.'

The woman remained motionless and Alice looked at the tiny bottle in the centre of her palm. My God. Whoever's in the other hospital, it's not the person who wrote the letters. The paper was lying next to her thigh and Alice unfolded it. The headline read THE FINAL CHAPTER?

Alice turned to where the letters were printed.

'OK.' Rick adjusted his seat belt to a more comfortable position. 'Letter sixteen.'

Ali did it in the night, while Jino slept. The lump of wood he used he threw far out into the sea. Then we rolled his body over the side, I am ashamed to say.

This morning we had one date each and kept the last two for the boy. I think Ali needs him to live as much as I. He has so few years, to die here would be a terrible thing. We hold clothing over him to make shade.

The sun is directly above, so strong the air is dragged from our mouths. When Jino woke, he could not eat his dates. He didn't notice Parviz had gone. We gave him drops from the cap of our bottle. It is nearly finished.

There are small fish living in the water below our raft. I can see them through the gaps in the wood. I know we should try to catch them, but I am so tired I cannot think how.

I want to sink down into the cool sea and sleep for ever.

My legs and feet no longer sting.

The silence of the ocean makes my ears hurt.

We are so hungry we searched the raft again. In a small gap I found a tiny tube of toothpaste. A dot on the tongue has a magical effect – thirst vanishes. We rubbed some on Jino's teeth and his eyes opened, but he did not see us. He whispered to his mother.

The end of the day is near and I have not seen the crewmen. Have they really no food or water?

Above there are no clouds, all around smooth sea, dotted with smiling ducks. How can there be no ships?

With the sun low in the sky, Jino began to moan. He tried to stand, calling for his mother, for food. We only just stopped him falling into the sea. This dying boy.

In the boat, I saw the one with throat scars, his eyes far back in his skull, all his teeth showing. He watches, only watches.

At sunset Jino's legs started to kick. He sat up, then fell to the side. I hugged him and he made small noises, then all his body shivered. His last breath left him while he slept. I cannot let him go.

I told Ali why I had to leave Baghdad – the invoices I found in the CPA offices from American companies for work they could not have done. Millions of dollars. I gave the documents to my boss. Later that day, my family rang to say my husband, Younis, had been taken. When the kidnappers called my phone, the man said I would see my husband next morning, when I found his body on the street.

I said I knew Americans, that they would help me. The man laughed. He said the Americans had told them about me, about how Younis picked me up from the Green Zone. That, if I hadn't been working late, they would have taken me, too. He said they knew where I lived.

I left behind everything. My lovely family and friends. My memories. I hired a car and drove to the border because, if I stayed in Baghdad, I would not be alive.

'Christ,' Jon said. 'It sounds to me like whoever she gave those invoices to in the CPA sold her out. If she'd only have given his name.'

'The boy died,' Rick whispered. 'I'd really hoped ...' He sighed. 'Right, letter seventeen.'

This, our eighth night, was full of dreams about how Baghdad used to be. I heard the market, the man selling oranges and lemons. The crowd brushing against me.

My eyes opened on the empty sky above. The sun like a hammer. I splashed sea water on my cracked lips and then I saw. The boy is gone.

Ali woke and we ate the last two dates. He says he did not move the boy. There are whispers in the boat.

We hide from the sun beneath clothes and pass the toothpaste and perfume between us. Mint then roses, mint then roses. We are now unable to stand.

Movement on the boat. A crewman is making a line of thin strips in the sun. It is meat and I know what happened to the boy. I cannot tell Ali.

The sun's heat is now weak.

On the boat, I can see their fingers reaching for the flesh.

Jon looked out of the car window. Two women were walking along the pavement, chatting happily away. Three young men stood in the doorway of an office, dragging on cigarettes. Something was said and they burst into laughter. They passed a grocer's, baskets of fresh fruit and vegetables arranged on the pavement in front of it. An old lady held up a lemon and sniffed it. A young boy finished some crisps and then let the empty packet drift from his fingers. A travel agent's – the poster in the window shouting about cut-price cruises to the Caribbean. Life went on as normal.

'You were right,' Rick stated. 'He was keeping them as food.'

'Doing what he has to do. He knows they're drifting well outside the shipping lane. No way of telling when they'll get any wind.'

'Even so – could you do it? Could you eat human flesh?'

They passed a butcher's, racks of ribs hanging in the window. A remark popped into his head. Something someone said about Western civilisation being nine meals away from anarchy. He thought about the recent oil scare, how rumours of lorry drivers blockading the Stanlow oil refinery had led to queues instantly forming at petrol stations across the north-west. People emptying supermarket shelves of bread, refusing to give a single loaf to other shoppers. 'We're all cannibals, mate. Given the right circumstances. Come on. Let's get the last letters over with.'

Rick was silent for a few more seconds then looked down at the paper across his lap. 'It says these ones were written in Arabic. She's reverted to her mother tongue.'

Day nine? Pinned to this place by the sun. No movement, no sound. I can only lie here and write. The sun does not hurt my skin.

Ali's wound is black and smells most strongly. When he stirred I tried to speak. My tongue is not my own. It is grown large and hard and it knocks against my teeth. No words come. My saliva is thick and it tastes very bitter.

I lifted my head and much of my hair remained where I lay.

Ali's face is collapsing. His teeth show all the time. His nose has withered and the skin inside is black. His eyes do not close. He stares at me, panting.

There is little urine left. A few drops to wet our lips.

My fingers are so clumsy. I have dropped the toothpaste. It fell into the water and sank.

Movement on my face. Is the air moving? Small lines wrinkle the water. Gentle wind. I tell Ali but he cannot feel it.

Their whispers carry to me. The meat has rotted and this night they will take one of us.

When it is dark, I will try to throw off the rope.

'She didn't survive this, surely,' Rick whispered.

Jon kept his eyes on the road ahead, saying nothing.

'Second to last letter.' Rick cleared his throat and continued reading.

Morning. The tenth day? The wind still blows and their boat is now far away.

In the night, I heard their curses. The oars splashed, but they had no strength to reach us.

Clouds drift over me. I can see the sail of their boat, the wind is taking it to the horizon.

Ali's skin is now grey, with red patches. He is trying to speak. I will wet his tongue with the last drops.

I held his head. Before he died, he said I must break one of the mirrors on our mast. I am to cut his flesh so I may live.

A little rain fell and I licked some from the plastic. I can hardly write these words.

Rick stopped reading and Jon saw his Adam's apple was trembling.

'That's it?'

'Just the last letter, now. All of five lines.'

My tongue is so huge, I can hardly breathe. This is the only sound.

Blood is coming from my eyes.

Wind stronger.

I will not eat him but wait for death.

A ship!

They drove the last few minutes in silence. 'She's dead, then,' Jon finally announced. 'They all died out there.' He was surprised at the level of anger inside him. For some reason, he thought, I expected her to survive. He pulled into the police station car park. 'Her eyes were bleeding. That must be end-stage starvation. When your body has consumed so much of itself, you start bleeding inside.'

Rick folded the paper. 'I feel ill.'

Jon swallowed. 'You want someone to pay for this, but who? The ship's owner is dead. Who'll pay? If only we had a bloody name. Her boss in the CPA, that would do for starters. Get him in custody, threaten him with one of those CIA prisons and he'd start spouting information in no time. Or the name of the company that cash was going to.'

Rick sighed. 'The CIA won't give that up. Protecting their own, saving the administration a major embarrassment.'

'Which leaves Salnikov,' Jon murmured. 'And from what Mueller said, the guy will never let himself be taken alive.'

Once Alice had read the final letter, she placed the paper to one side and shut her eyes. She kept very still, waiting as the urge to weep slowly sank back. Gradually, she turned to look at the young woman. What do I do? Who do I tell about you?

She imagined the media attention when they realised the frail and damaged thing at her side was who really wrote those letters. Perhaps they could trace her family back in Baghdad, if they were still alive. Get someone over here to be with her. Her mother. A sister.

Her phone started to ring and she took it out of her pocket. The call was showing up as anonymous. 'Hello?' she whispered.

'Hello, Alice. It is Yulia speaking. I just heard your message!'

'Yulia.' Alice stood and moved to the far side of the room. 'It's her,' she said, examining the perfume bottle in her hand. 'It really is.'

'That is wonderful. Is she OK?'

'Not really, no.'

'They are saying the woman in the Manchester Royal Infirmary is her. This is not correct, though?'

'No. It's the MHU at Sale General. I've no idea what's caused that mix-up.'

'I thought so. I hope you do not mind, but I rang a gentleman who knew about her. He asked that, if I heard where she was, to contact him.'

'Who – a relative?'

'No, a Russian man. He had also been on the same ship. He knew her name – he gave it to me. Amira Jasim. I didn't think it could ever have been the lady writing the letters—'

'That's her surname?'

'Yes, Jasim.'

'Yulia,' Alice whispered, 'it was a Russian man who did all those terrible things on the raft. Some kind of naval soldier.'

'Oh, no,' Yulia replied. 'This man worked for a trade union. He said they were friends.'

Feeling slightly uneasy at what Yulia had done, Alice asked, 'Where is he?'

'I do not know.'

'Is he still in Britain?'

'I think so. He said he will try to visit.'

Thirty

As Jon entered the main room, the receiver looked up and gave him a tight-lipped look of regret. Jon glanced to his side where a cluster of officers were poring over the front page of the *Chronicle*. On the other side of the room, Buchanon's door was open. The boss was in.

'Rick,' Jon said. 'Perhaps I should go in on my own.'

'He asked for both of us.'

'Yeah, but that was before this.' He nodded at the officers reading the paper. One of them raised his head, caught his eye then quickly looked back down.

'If he wants me to leave his office, he can say so,' Rick replied. 'But I'm not hiding out here.'

'Fair enough.' He turned to his partner. 'And thanks, mate. I know being paired up with me isn't the biggest boost for your career.'

'Bollocks to that. I'm learning all the tricks I need from you.'

'Yeah – like keeping clear of bloody journalists.'

They paused at their desks, the urge to go through the usual routine strong. Jon turned on his computer, but didn't sit down to start sifting through his actions tray as he normally would. Rick placed his sunglasses in the top drawer then tapped the back of his chair, leaving it pushed in.

They regarded each other and Jon nodded. 'Come on, then.' He walked over to Buchanon's door, knowing most people in the room were surreptitiously watching. 'Sir, eight thirty meeting?'

'Come in. Shut the door. I take it you've seen this?'

Jon glanced at the copy of the *Chronicle* on his senior officer's desk. 'Yes.'

'Can you account for how she came by this information?'

'I think she looked through one of my files.'

'How? Does she have a free run of this office?'

'It was in my briefcase. I must have left it in her flat.'

'Her flat.' Buchanon raised his eyes to the ceiling. 'You're in a relationship with her?'

'We've been seeing each other. Nothing too serious.'

'Nothing too serious?' Buchanon scoffed. 'I asked you to hand in all information you had regarding those murders.'

'I realise, sir. It was just the one folder – I meant to retrieve it, but it's been impossible to get hold of her recently.'

'Gosh, she hasn't been returning your calls?' Fury flooded his voice. 'Maybe she was busy – putting this story together.'

'Yes, sir.' Jon looked at the empty chairs to the side of Buchanon's desk. I don't suppose, he thought, you'll be offering me a seat.

'And on the subject of the Russian case. What prompted the visit from the MI5 officer? I was handing my report in to the Super, when the thought occurred.'

'He called me, sir. They were looking for more details about how the four Russians were found. I had the number of—'

'The captain of the fishing trawler. Yes, yes, detective, I spoke to Soutar.' His voice dropped. 'Do you think I was born yesterday?'

'Sorry?'

Buchanon waved a hand. 'Don't try and play me, Spicer. Soutar might have agreed to back you up, but I don't believe he called you. He hasn't replied to anything I've sent, so why would he suddenly ring you direct? What I think, is this.' He placed his elbows on the table. 'You couldn't leave the case alone, could you? The fact all your work was being taken without any acknowledgement really pissed you off. So you kept picking away. Also, you lied to me about keeping clear of the psychiatrist and you lied to me about your relationship with that crime reporter.'

'Sir, I don't believe it's necessary I tell you who I might be seeing.'

'It is when you leave evidence about an ongoing murder investigation in her flat!' He slammed a fist down on the paper. 'The bloody head crime reporter for the *Chronicle*. Jesus, Spicer. Did the thought not even occur?'

'We had an argument. I didn't ever think she'd get back at me through this.'

'You're both off duty now. Correct?'

Rick nodded.

'Right, I'll be taking over as SIO on this case. Saville, I'll see you after your break in three days' time. DI Spicer, take the weekend off – while we try to clear up this whole mess. All calls from the media – and I'm sure there'll be many – will now be referred direct to me. You make no comment.'

'The *Chronicle* names me as the lead officer.'

'Well, the *Chronicle* got it wrong. I am. If, as a result, they infer you've been removed from the case for some reason, that's their shout.'

Jon went to cross his arms then dropped them back down, realising the stance would have seemed aggressive or defiant. Buchanon stared at him, a challenge in his eyes. Jon looked away, shoving his hands into his pockets as they curled into fists. He analysed his options, trying to see any way to counter Buchanon. There was nothing. 'I'm suspended?'

'No, you're not suspended. But consider yourself out of my syndicate. I don't want you.' He looked down at the paperwork before him.

Jon and Rick exchanged a glance then made for the door. Out in the main room, a couple of detectives were hanging around near their desks.

'What's the score?' one whispered.

'Any room in your syndicate?' Jon replied, seeing the message light blinking on his phone. He paused in the act of picking it up. What was the point? 'Need a lift home?' he asked Rick.

'Cheers,' his partner replied and they started walking for the doors. 'If you're moving syndicates, I'm coming with you.'

Jon sighed. 'Maybe you're best staying put. I only balls things up.'

'Nah.' Rick shook his head. 'I've had enough of that crinkle-haired cock, to be honest. By the way, you're welcome to stay in my flat as long as you want.'

The light breeze was funnelled down Combe Martin's high street, blowing Oliver Brookes' thinning hair back as he approached the library doors. He paused on the pavement to check he had sufficient change in his pocket. As he did so, excitement tickled his spine. The old pleasure of unearthing information, making links, anticipating events.

A young-sounding lady answered the phone. Funny, Oliver thought. I don't remember Peter having any children. 'Is Mr Durwood there, please?'

'Hang on, I'll get him.'

His old associate came on the line within seconds. 'Oliver! How are you?'

'Fine, thanks. Who was that on the phone just now?'

'Helena, my wife.'

'Helena?'

'Peggy and I parted company year before last, I'm afraid.'

'Ah. Sorry to hear.'

'Well, life moves on. Now, what are you on to, here? You're up to something, Oliver, you old dog.'

Brookes' eyes narrowed. 'How do you mean?'

'Oh, come, come. You ask me to look into Myko Enterprises, particularly the owner. A Mr Slavko Mykosowski, as it happens.'

'Yes.'

'So I start a data search then make a couple of calls,' he lowered his voice, 'only to learn the man in question has just been murdered.'

Brookes felt himself blink with surprise. 'Someone killed him?'

Durwood's voice remained quiet. 'Clinically, by all accounts. He was found on the floor of his office. Apparently his neck had been cleanly snapped.'

'Well, that's ... a shock. What sort of company is it?'

'Dodgy, to use one word. Very dodgy, to use two. Head office listed as being in Odessa, the Ukraine. Mykosowski conducted most of his business from London, but had all sorts of satellites and subsidiaries dotted round the globe. He offered a tramp service. Are you familiar?'

'Non-scheduled shipments, aren't they?'

'That's right. Any time, any place, anywhere, to quote Mr Rossiter. Or was it Joan Collins? You understand, though. Myko Enterprises would take anything. One rumour has it that's included the odd shipment of decommissioned Soviet army hardware to the Sudan. Probably boxed up as engineering equipment or some such.'

'It's that easy?'

'If port staff are in your pocket and it's got the blessing of the country's powers-that-be, of course.'

'Could Myko Enterprises have been smuggling people, too?'

'Why not? People are just another form of cargo, in that sense.'

'So he's dead.'

'And it's not the regular police looking into it. There were loads of plain-clothes officers at the scene.'

'Who?'

'MI5, apparently.'

'Interesting.'

'Indeed. I don't know what you know, Oliver, but be careful, won't you? Ever since it all went computerised, they've got better and better at tracking these things. Any sudden switches in stock.'

Money, Brookes smiled. You think I'm trying to make money.

'OK, that's much appreciated, Peter.'

'My pleasure. And if you're ever in town ...'

'Will do.' Brookes replaced the receiver, but his hand stayed on it as his thoughts drifted away. The *Lesya Ukrayinka* was happy to see its human cargo go overboard. Other letters found indicated over twenty had died. Mykosowski is then murdered. Was there a connection? There was if he made the contents of the letter in his pocket known. He pushed his way through the inner doors and sat down at the newspaper desk. Someone else was reading the *Express* and, from the front page, Brooks could see the headline announcing that the final letters were inside. He flicked through the other papers, but they were only going over old ground.

At the computers, he logged on and went straight to the homepage of the BBC news service. My, my, my, he mouthed to himself. Breaking news was about the author of the letters being found. He read the brief paragraph. Manchester Royal Infirmary. He returned to Google and searched for Manchester newspapers. Top of the list was the website for the *Manchester Evening Chronicle*. He clicked on it. Lead story was about a spate of murders, each victim's head having nearly been severed. Professional jobs: just like the owner of Myko Enterprises, he thought. All the victims were Russian nationals. He scanned through to the end of the report. A detective called Spicer was leading the investigation.

Brookes brought up the website for Greater Manchester Police, noted down the number and walked back to the payphone. 'Hello, could I be put through to the Major Incident Team, please? Yes, there is a particular detective I'd like to speak with. He's called DI Spicer.'

The phone on Jon's desk began to ring. A civilian indexer, filling her cup at the water cooler, glanced over. That must be the eighth call in the last half-hour. Her eyes settled on Jon's empty chair. Where was he? His computer was on, he must be around somewhere. She stepped over and picked the receiver up. 'DI Spicer's phone.'

'Could I speak to him, please?'

'He's not at his desk. Can I take a message?'

'Yes. It's in regard to the murder of three Russians.'

'OK.' She grabbed a pen and Post-it note from Jon's desk-tidy. 'Go ahead.'

'Well, I have a letter. Er ... when will he be in?'

'He's around somewhere. Possibly in a meeting?'

'OK. I'd prefer to just leave my name and number, if that's OK.'

'Of course.'

'It's Mr Brookes and he can reach me on ...' He squinted at the phone then read out the numbers in the panel above the buttons. 'It's a public payphone, but I can wait an hour or two for his call.'

'Lovely. I'll leave the message out for him.' She stuck the Post-it note to the base of Jon's keyboard then returned to her desk.

Alice sat on the bed, one hand resting on the young woman's beneath the bedclothes, the other turning her mobile phone over and over. She sneaked another glance at her. You poor thing. The things that those final letters described ... Alice tried to close down the images before they became too vivid. What horrors. Looking back at her phone, she took a breath in. 'Amira, I'm just stepping outside, OK? I only need to make a phone call. I'm not leaving you.'

The young woman's gaze alighted on Alice's face and she gave a small nod. Alice closed the door with a gentle click then went into her phone's address book.

'Hello?'

'Officer Seakins? It's Alice Spicer, here. We talked—'

'Yes, Alice. Is it her?'

'Yes. I'm holding the bottle of perfume from her washbag in my hand. Have you read the letters in this morning's paper? She actually mentions the bottle.'

'I knew it was her.'

'I'm not sure what to do. I haven't told anyone, yet. I've just been sitting with her, stroking her face. She understands everything I'm saying.'

'You must tell whoever's in charge.'

'I know. But I don't want her to go through the stress of her identity becoming known.' She felt the question welling up and was powerless to stop it. 'Did you say you'd read the final letters?'

His voice sounded guarded once more. 'I have.'

Bowing her head, Alice closed her eyes and pinched the bridge of her nose with her fingertips. 'I'm sorry, but I have to ask. When you found her, what had happened to the man's body? Was it still ... were there signs of, you know ...'

She heard him breathing for several seconds before he spoke. 'You need to plan very carefully how to handle this. You're right, when the press learn where she really is, a huge amount of attention will be focused on her.'

Alice opened her eyes, realising he'd avoided the question. 'I know one of the consultant psychiatrists here. I'll let him know the situation.'

'That sounds like a sensible move. Well, Alice – good luck. I'm sure we'll speak again. One day, when it's practical, I would like to see her again.'

'Right, yes.' She glanced about her, making sure the corridor was empty. 'Officer – I mean Beach,' she took a breath in, 'had one of the mirrors on the raft been broken?'

'Alice, things happen at sea. Things that are best not spoken about on land. Take care of her, Alice. Goodbye.'

She stared at her feet for a few seconds. Did that mean Amira had survived by eating Ali's flesh, or not? Unable to decide, she dialled Braithwaite's number. 'Phillip, it's me, Alice. Can you talk?'

'Yes. Have you given some thought to what I said?'

'Phillip – I need to ask you something.'

'If it's about the complaint I made, I only did—'

'You know the patient, J. Smith. The one in the MHU?'

Braithwaite paused. 'What about her?'

'You knew she was female?'

'Yes, why?'

'It doesn't matter. I think I know who she is. I do know who she is.'

'Alice, are you calling about the issues that we raised the other night?'

'What? No, I'm not. Phillip, the young woman is her: the one who wrote the letters.'

'Which letters?'

'The ones in the ducks.'

'Alice.' Irritation washed through his words. 'I had the radio on earlier. They already know her whereabouts. She's a patient in the MRI.'

'That's a mistake. She's here, on the mental health unit.'

He sighed. 'Alice – I have a patient waiting outside. Why don't you have a word with the sister or charge nurse? Let them know about your concerns.'

'Phillip, I need your help. This needs to be managed properly, she's so vulnerable.'

'Alice, the person who wrote those letters is in the MRI. I don't know who the woman on the unit is, that's why she's referred to as J. Smith.'

'She's called Amira. For God's sake, Phillip. I spoke to the medical officer at the naval hospital in Plymouth she was sent from.'

'You're becoming aggressive again. I've really got to go.'

'Please, Phill—' The line was dead. She lowered her hand, digging the corner of the phone against her thigh. What a wanker, she cursed. What a total and utter wanker. She opened the door to Amira's room. 'Hey. I said I was coming back, didn't I?'

Jon stood on the balcony of Rick's flat, staring across the city. The ornate towers of the Palace Hotel shimmered above the surrounding buildings. Off to the right, the harsh angles of the Beetham Tower stabbed up at the hazy sky. What an eyesore, he reflected. Holly's made better-looking towers with her bloody Lego.

His mind went to arriving at the flat. Andy had already collected Zak from his two mums' house and had got the car ready. Jon thought back to his doubts when Rick had announced he was donating sperm to the lesbian couple. But hearing the little lad's laughter as Rick and Andy had set off with him made it obvious the boy was happy. Far happier, he concluded sadly, than my own daughter. His eyes roved back to the south, settling on a spot he guessed was close to the house he once lived in.

How have I ended up here? He stepped back inside and examined the tray of bottles to the side of the door. Tequila. That'll burn. He unscrewed the lid and swigged direct from the bottle, relishing the fire that flooded his throat. With the bottle hanging from one hand, he paced round the empty living area, idly looking at photos of Rick, Andy and the little boy. The three peeping over the top of an upturned surfboard, posing next to a knee-high sandcastle, sitting on a sea wall eating ice cream. Jealousy, like a worm stirring inside his stomach. He turned the telly on. A stream of sound and images, he thought, something to deaden my mind.

The news came on and he lowered himself onto the sofa, taking another swig as he did so. Jesus – the throng of cameras on Oxford Road outside the MRI was ridiculous. Cordons had been erected and the reporter was pointing at the upper level of the main building, excitedly announcing that the intensive care unit was on the third floor. The mystery woman was believed to be in a private room somewhere on that ward. Jon scanned the background. Apart from a couple of uniforms at the main entrance, there was absolutely no police presence. He spotted Carmel chatting to some other hack and raised the bottle to the screen. Nice one, girl. You got the last laugh on me.

He sat back, trying to imagine how they'd have staked out the ward. Would there be a real officer posing in the bed? MI5 officers posing as orderlies? Snipers on the surrounding rooftops? Keep guessing, he told himself, raising the bottle to his lips another time. You are well and truly out of this one.

His mobile went off. 'Rick.' He tried to inject some cheer into his voice, but his jaw felt slack and heavy. 'You don't sound like you're in the car.'

'I'm not. I forgot my bloody sunglasses – swung by the station to pick them up.'

'Oh, right. What's going on there?'

'Buchanon's in with Gower. He's holding a press conference at noon, apparently. Get this, he's trying to contact the two CIA agents.'

'How come?'

'That *Manchester Evening Chronicle* shot of you showing them out of the front doors? A witness from the first murder rang in to say it was D'Souza he saw in the vicinity of Marat Dubinski's flat. I swear, Buchanon's hair has scrunched up even tighter with the prospect of having to interview and eliminate the Yank from an investigation he's in Britain to assist with.' Rick chuckled for a moment. 'Anyway – there's a note on your desk. Message to call some guy.'

'Who?'

'An Oliver Brookes.' He adopted the mechanical tone of someone reciting written words. 'Information on the Russian murders, calling from a payphone. I recognise the area code: Devon.'

'Payphone?'

'Yup. Probably a head case, but one thing's for certain: no fucker here is going to bother ringing him. You want the number?'

Jon sighed. 'Go on, then. It'll give me something to do.'

Thirty-One

The alarm obliterated the echo of Phillip's final comments in Alice's head. Startled, she looked to her side, as if Amira could confirm whether it was a test. The young woman's eyes turned to her questioningly. Alice raised a hand to indicate everything was OK, then waited. A minute passed and the two-tone wail showed no sign of stopping. When a staff member hit a panic button, the alarm was a rapid series of beeps. This was different. I hope that's not for real, she thought. 'I'll go and check what's going on. I won't be a minute.'

She stepped out into the corridor and immediately heard a low moaning from round the corner. The woman with cigarette burns was hunched on the floor, hands clamped over her ears. A nursing assistant was trying to get her to stand. From the bay further along, patients were being led towards the exit.

'Is it a test?' Alice asked, raising her voice above the din.

'No test!' the assistant replied. 'Some idiot probably burnt their toast on a floor below. Can you give me a hand?'

Alice glanced over her shoulder. 'Who's doing the single-occupancy rooms?'

'They're next. Bays first in an emergency.'

She crouched down to hook an arm under the woman's.

'OK, on three,' the nursing assistant instructed. 'One, two, three.'

Together, they lifted her to a standing position. But as soon as their grip relaxed, the woman's knees buckled.

'I'll get a wheelchair,' he cursed. 'Hang on.'

At the end of the corridor a staff member was locking up the meds room. Male patients began to appear from the direction of the telly area. Tony Garrett caught sight of Alice and lifted both arms triumphantly. She almost expected him to start bellowing 'England!', but he began to sing instead. 'This is the end!'

'Quieten down, Tony,' a male nurse ordered, tugging at the man's elbow.

He shook it free and pointed to the exit. 'The Doors, isn't it! Do you get it? The Doors!'

'Yeah,' the nurse replied. 'And you're walking through them.'

Garrett pulled his tracksuit bottoms higher and followed the other patients into the airlock. 'Come on baby, light my fire. Hey, Danny, you got any ciggies on you?'

The nursing assistant reappeared with a wheelchair and they hauled the woman into it. 'What about the private rooms?' Alice repeated, wincing at the volume of the alarm directly above their head.

'Get this lot out first!'

An old woman wearing a cream-coloured nightie wandered out from the bay next to them, silver hair like traces of a cobweb that had drifted down onto her head. 'Can you hear the organ? It's such a wonderful, wonderful sound!'

'You get her,' the assistant growled, pushing the wheelchair towards the doors.

Alice put an arm round the old lady and had got her to the nurses' desk when a low boom sent a tremor through the building. The lights flickered momentarily and the sprinklers suddenly kicked in.

'What the hell was that?' Alice called to the nurse with a clipboard standing by the doors, trying to check patients' wristbands before ticking their names off the list.

'I don't know!'

The old lady held her palms up to the fine droplets raining down. 'Cascades of notes! Cascades of notes!'

The door to the nurses' room was flung open and the charge nurse – a muscular man originally from Nigeria – stepped out. His face was grey with shock. 'That was an explosion. I could see from the window – the side of the building's been blown out.'

Alice swept dripping strands of hair from her eyes. 'Go through

297

there.' She directed the woman to the doors then turned to the charge nurse. 'The private rooms.'

'Haven't they been cleared?'

'No! Jane Smith – she's still back there.'

'OK, you wheel her out. I'll check the others.'

The nurse with the clipboard called over, hand moving down the list. 'You're getting Jane Smith?'

'Yes!' Alice hurried back up the corridor, feet sliding on the shiny floor as she tried to round the corner too fast. She stumbled forward, reached Amira's room and opened the door. The bed was empty, fine spray drifting on to it from the sprinkler in the ceiling. She stepped back and looked along the corridor. Deserted. Back in the bedroom, she checked behind the door then inside the little wardrobe. Where was she? The bedside stand holding the drip caught her eye. The tube stretched down and then ran under the bed. Getting onto all fours, she saw her there, curled in a tight ball. 'Amira, we need to get outside. There's been some sort of explosion. Come on, I'll help you.'

Amira wriggled desperately towards the wall. 'It's him. He's come for me.'

Alice's hand froze in midair. Christ, now she decides to speak. 'Who?'

'The man with throat scars. It is him.'

Alice felt a shiver of fear pass through her. Get a grip, Alice, she told herself. That's absurd. 'Amira, it's a fire alarm. Come on.'

'He's coming!'

Alice lay down, reached under and was able to place a hand on the other woman's upper arm. 'Amira? We have to get out. I'm going to pull you towards me, OK?'

The door opened and the alarm grew louder. Amira started shrinking away and Alice heard the charge nurse call that it was clear. The door clicked shut again.

'No!' she shouted. 'I need help in here.' Bloody hell. She grasped Amira's arm more firmly and other woman suddenly stopped resisting. Alice pulled her across the smooth floor. She

298

can't weigh much more than Holly, Alice thought. 'Can you stand?'

There was now a far-off look in Amira's eyes and she failed to reply.

She's gone, Alice thought. Back into her shell. Alice scooped her other arm under Amira's legs and just managed to deposit her back on the bed. Quickly, she checked the drip was still intact, folded the damp blankets back over her and then lay the drip stand alongside the younger woman. 'OK, we're going outside.'

She grabbed the handrail at the end of the bed and pulled. The thing didn't budge. Squatting down, she searched for the wheel locks, drips falling from her eyebrows. She flipped the levers up and was about to pull the bed once more when the dull thud of another explosion caused the floor to vibrate. Jesus! She stepped over to the window, but it only overlooked the roof of a single-storey building. A traffic cone lay there, next to a dead pigeon. By craning her neck and looking to the side, she could make out a couple of nurses running across a small car park, the air above them dark with billowing smoke.

Alice dragged the bed to the door, opened it with one hand and wheeled Amira out into the corridor. She found herself squinting at the alarm's intensity. No sign of the charge nurse. She swung the bed round and started pushing it forward. At the corner, her step faltered; the nurse checking names at the exit had also disappeared. They've bloody gone without us. At least the sliding doors were still open. Seconds later, she was at the nurses' desk, reaching over it and pressing the exit button. The doors at the far end of the airlock remained shut.

'Shit, shit, shit,' Alice cursed, looking fearfully into the twelve-foot-long tunnel. She pressed the button again. Nothing. OK, she told herself. Keep calm. 'Amira, can you walk? If I help you, can you walk?' No reply. 'OK, that's OK.'

Alice wheeled Amira's bed so it was halfway through the first set of doors and glanced nervously at the mechanism set into the ceiling. Please, do not decide to shut yourself. Taking a deep breath, she strode rapidly to the other end of the airlock.

Payphone in Devon, Jon said to himself. I've got to be bloody desperate. He keyed in the number, half surprised when it actually started to ring.

'Hello?'

A well-spoken voice. Posh. Jon frowned. 'Is that Oliver Brookes speaking?'

'It is.'

The guy didn't sound like a gibbering loony. 'My name is DI Spicer, from the Greater Manchester Police. You left a message for me.'

'I did. It's to do with the murders you're investigating.'

Was, thought Jon. 'You're calling me from Devon, is that right?'

'Correct.'

'About murders in Manchester?'

'Yes.'

'How did you get my name?'

'From the internet. A report in the *Evening Chronicle*.'

'Right. So, what can you tell me?'

'Well, it's going to sound rather odd.'

Here we go, Jon thought, closing his eyes. Did God speak to you by any chance? 'What's your address, sir?'

'I don't have one as such.'

Why me? Jon thought. Why do I always get them? 'You're of no fixed abode?'

'No. I live in a small cottage. But it doesn't have a postal address. It's on the beach, you see. The post office in Combe Martin holds any letters for me.'

'Right.' Jon reached for the remote and started flicking through for some sport. 'I'm all ears.'

'A few days ago, several of those rubber ducks – the ones that have been in the news, yes?'

'Yes.' Jon sat back, eyes on the screen.

'Several were washed up on my beach. Or the National Trust's beach, more accurately. There was a letter in one.'

'Really? A letter?' A Super 14 match was starting in ten

minutes. Waikato Chiefs versus ACT Brumbies. Nice.

'It was numbered one. I believe it's the first in the series written by the Iraqi woman.'

'That would be the letter the *Express* has been offering twenty thousand pounds for?'

'I'm not concerned about money.'

'Good for you.' Jon continued flicking through the channels. 'What did it say?'

'Not much. But it mentions her name and the ship that abandoned her.'

Gosh, thought Jon. This is when you tell me it was the *Titanic*. 'And what was the ship called?'

'The *Lesya Ukrayinka*.'

The remote almost fell from Jon's fingers. He struggled upright, placing the bottle of tequila on the coffee table. 'Have you still got this letter?'

'Yes. I'm holding it in my hand.'

'Please read it to me.' A news report had come up on the television. Something about an explosion at Sale General Hospital. Bloody hell, Jon thought. That's where Alice goes to help out.

'OK. As I said, it's marked with a one. Then it says, "My name is Amira Jasim, age 22, former resident of Baghdad, Iraq. I am writing this letter in English to declare to the world that, on the fourteenth of July, I paid \$6,000 to board a ship in the Pakistani port of Karachi. This money was to buy me passage to Great Britain. Last night I, and many others like me, were abandoned. If we are to die here in the sea, the captain of the *Lesya Ukrayinka* is a murderer for he did not turn back for us.

'"The other man who must face justice is my boss, Mr Scott King of the Coalition Provisional Authority in Baghdad. When I showed him evidence of how the money meant for rebuilding my nation is being stolen, he passed my identity to militia. They killed my husband, Younis, and I was forced to flee before they came for me."'

Jon stood and walked over to the desk with Rick's computer on. I've got the name of her boss in the CPA! He picked up a pen and piece of paper. 'Sir – I'd like to see this letter.'

'I'll gladly post it to you.'

'No.' The last thing I need, he thought, is it disappearing in the post. He looked at his watch. How many hours to Devon? Five? Six? 'I'll drive down.'

'Well – if you're sure.'

'I am. How can I find you?' He jotted down the other man's instructions. 'OK, Oliver, so if the library at Combe Martin is closed by the time I arrive, you'll be in the Focsle Inn.'

'Yes.'

Jon hung up then started looking round. Where the bloody hell did I put my car keys?

Alice peered through the windows of the doors leading out into the lobby area. No one was there. Glancing at the panel above the lifts, she saw a couple of dashes flashing on and off where a floor number was usually displayed. Oh, Jesus. She hammered on the doors. This was ridiculous, she told herself, trying not to acknowledge the feeling of panic gathering strength inside her. 'Is anyone there!' she yelled, painfully aware the alarm easily drowned out her cries. I need air. She turned round, ran back to the inner doors and wheeled Amira out into the unit. The phone, of course. I can ring security. She stepped round the nurses' desk and picked it up. Dead line. Twisting round, she reached for the door handle of the nurses' room. Locked. No! This isn't happening! In desperation, she hit the staff emergency button on the wall panel. The rapid beeping seemed trivial alongside the fire alarm's incessant screech.

Fire escape. Where the bloody hell is the fire escape? Other end of the corridor, next to the isolation room. She jogged back along it, seeing only blackness through the wire-mesh window. This door is alarmed, angry red letters announced. She realised the blackness was smoke, thick against the glass. Grasping the bar with both hands, she shoved it open. Smoke engulfed her and she immediately started to choke, just able to make out the enclosed metal stairwell before she had to swing the door shut once more. I couldn't climb down there myself, let alone with

Amira. Sweeping her soaking hair back, she turned round and returned to the main exit.

'OK, Amira,' she announced. The muscles of her throat felt constricted and she tried to swallow. 'Let's find somewhere clear of these stupid sprinklers.' She wheeled the bed towards the telly room, trying each door on her right. Meds room locked. Staff room locked. Visitor room locked. She crossed the corridor and tried the games room. It opened. She looked in. Chairs and two small tables for playing cards were positioned before a table-tennis table that was missing its net. No sprinkler in the ceiling. Once the bed was inside, she closed the door and the alarm's volume dropped. Immediately, she walked over to the window and looked out. Another wing of the hospital filled the view. She regarded the locks on the reinforced windows, realising the keys would be in the nurses' room.

After trying to wipe her hands dry on Amira's wet sheets, she pulled her mobile out. Who the hell do I call? The fire brigade must surely be here by now. Police? They'll need instructions to locate us, she thought, picturing the hospital complex. Phillip. He'll know what to do. The moment he answered, she started speaking. 'Phillip! It's me, Alice. We're trapped in the MHU.'

'I beg your pardon?'

'The fire alarms have gone off. An explosion. They evacuated the unit, but me and Amira were left behind. The bloody airlock doors are jammed and I don't know how to open them. Can you get over here?'

'Alice, just get out of there. Immediately.'

'I can't! Someone needs to release the outer doors.'

'Use the fire escape.'

'The smoke is too bad – it's right above the fire.'

'There's a code for the airlock. A panel to the side of the doors which let you out into the lobby.'

'You mean inside the airlock?'

'Yes – for exactly the situation you're in now.'

'What's the code?'

'Hang on, it's in my notebook. Wait a second, it's here some-where.'

Come on, come on, Alice thought, eyes on Amira's immobile form.

'Got it. One nine seven zero. Think of it as the year – nineteen seventy.'

'Thanks.'

She pulled Amira's bed back to the door, bracing herself for the din as she opened it. The sprinklers were still going and the floor was now awash with water. Alice swung the bed out, repositioned it halfway through the airlock's first set of doors again and walked quickly to the other end. There it was, a small panel. She flipped the cover open. Please, please work. One by one, she keyed in the numbers. As the doors leading into the lobby slid open, the inner ones closed, clamping on each side of Amira's bed. Alice looked with horror as the mechanism started to judder. Suddenly, they reopened and the outer ones slid shut. She looked from one set of doors to the other and groaned with exasperation.

Finger trembling, she keyed in the numbers again. This time, the inner doors didn't close as the outer ones opened. Alice bounded to the other end of the airlock. As she gripped the railing at the other end of Amira's bed, the inner doors slid across, trapping it once again. Alice started yanking with all her might and the bed began inching forward when her feet slipped out from under her, shins crashing against the bed's base. The outer doors closed once more. Christ! She scrabbled to her feet and, with the doors continuing to judder against the frame of Amira's bed, hobbled back to the panel. She keyed in the code but the outer doors stayed shut. She tried again. Nothing happened.

'Phillip, can you hear me?'

'Just. Where are you?'

'In the airlock. The door mechanisms are linked. As the outer ones open, the inner ones close!'

'Yes,' he replied impatiently. 'But it gives you several seconds to get out.'

'I can't. Amira's bed is wedging open the inner doors. I think it's messed the mechanism up. I've tried the code again – it's not working.'

'Pull the bed into the airlock with you and try it.'

Alice pictured the inner doors closing on them and felt nauseous at the prospect. 'What if the code still doesn't work? We won't be able to get out.'

'OK, try it again and if the outer doors open, get yourself out.'

'Leave Amira?'

'Yes – so you can summon help.'

'I'm not leaving her.'

'It's the only way.'

'I'm not leaving her.'

'For Christ's sake, woman, do it!'

'I'm not leaving her! You've got to help me.'

'I'm at my clinic in Hale. It's over a half-hour drive.'

Alice pressed a palm against the window looking into the lobby.

'Look,' Phillip said. 'I'll call the hospital, OK? God knows how busy the switchboards will be, but I'll try and get word to security.'

The judder of the doors against Amira's bed wouldn't stop and Alice felt light-headed, as if the oxygen in the airlock was growing thin. 'Just bloody get here!'

'Alice.' His voice was stern. 'You're being irrational.'

'Will you come?'

'It will serve no purpose.'

She could see him there, leaning back in his leather chair, surveying the rows of certificates on his wall. 'Well, Phillip, fuck you – fuck you and your superior fucking attitude, you colossal fucking prick!'

She pressed red, ran back to the bed, clambered across it and, bit by bit, pulled it clear of the whining doors. They immediately reopened as if daring her to step back through. Yeah? Alice glared at them. Fuck you, too.

By the time she'd wheeled Amira back into the games room, she was gasping for breath. Sinking down onto her haunches, she stared at her phone's tiny screen. Fighting back sobs of anger, she scrolled down, selected a number and hit the call button. 'Jon?'

'Alice – I'm in a massive rush. Can I—'

'Help me, Jon.'

'Alice? Are you OK? Is that a fire alarm? What's wrong?'

Suddenly she began to cry, tears coursing down her face.

'Alice! Where are you? Tell me where you are! Alice!'

She pressed the back of her head against the wall and the words tumbled from her mouth. 'I can't get out, Jon. We're trapped in here.'

'Who? You and Holly? Are you at home?'

She dragged in air through her nostrils. 'The MHU at Sale General.'

'Who's with you?'

'An Iraqi woman called Amira. There's been an explosion. We can't get out.'

'Amira? You're with a woman called Amira?'

'We're trapped. The place is on fire and she said the man with throat scars is coming for her and everything's starting to get to me—'

'Slow down! She said the man with throat scars is coming?'

'I told a lady over in Liverpool about Amira. She then rang a Russian man to tell him where Amira is. This is all starting to really scare me, Jon. Please, hurry.'

Jon cut the call and Alice's mobile number faded from his screen. Jacket! Where is my jacket! I left it by the sofa. Finally, he spotted it hanging on the back of Rick's front door. Frantically, he started patting the pockets, eyes going back to the television in the corner. Suspicions were on an electrical fire in the room used to store the hospital's oxygen tanks. That's no fire, he thought. That's Salnikov.

His fingers closed on the CIA officer's card. Thank Christ for that. He slammed the door shut behind him, keyed in the number then started racing down the stairs. God, he thought. I'm half pissed. 'Greg? It's DI Spicer. You're at the wrong hospital!'

'Jon, what was that?'

'Wrong hospital. The woman who wrote those letters is called Amira Jasim. She's in Sale General.'

'How do you know that?'

'No time.' Unable to check his momentum, he careered into the wall of the first landing, bounced back and carried on down the next flight of stairs. 'You and D'Souza, get there with all the back-up you have.'

'Where is this place?'

'Five minutes, with your sirens on. Greg, you've got guns, haven't you?'

'Yes.'

'Please, get there.' Another landing. He kept hold of the banister, almost wrenching his shoulder out as he swung himself round. 'My wife just rang. She's with her, Greg. There's been an explosion, the hospital has been evacuated, but she's trapped on the Mental Health Unit with the Iraqi woman.'

'An explosion?'

'It's Salnikov. He's there. Word's got to him of the Iraqi woman's exact location.'

He heard a sharp whistle, then Mueller shouting off to the side. 'Carl! Get us a car, now! Jon? We're on our way. But you're sure it's her?'

'Positive.' The lobby came into view and he jumped the last six steps, legs almost buckling beneath him as he landed. Someone was coming through the doors. 'Move!' Jon shouldered the man aside. Whitworth Street, the normality of it surreal.

'Jon, leave it with me. Do not go there. I repeat, keep away.'

'Sure,' Jon replied, snapping his phone shut as he sprinted towards his car.

He first glimpsed the column of smoke while still five minutes away from the hospital. 'Oh Christ,' he murmured, accelerating along the Chester Road, gritting his teeth and praying no vehicle would emerge from a side road as he hurtled across junction after junction. Three ambulances with their lights flashing passed him going the other way, and with each one his sense of dread mounted.

Finally, the flyover for the M60 came into view, and seconds later he was slowing down just enough to veer on to Dane Road.

A mass of fire engines were gathered at the main entrance to the hospital, the ground floor corner of which was belching smoke. Dozens of patients, mostly in their night clothes, were gathered at the far end of the car park. Dumping his vehicle on the pavement, he hurdled a low fence and ran towards a police car in the midst of the other emergency vehicles.

'DI Spicer, Major Incident Team.'

The uniformed officer glanced at his badge and nodded.

Jon looked back at the main building. Smoke was like a veil across the front of it. He tried to scan the upper windows. She's in there somewhere, he thought. And so is Salnikov. 'Has a group of men just gone in? Plain clothes, like me?'

The officer shook his head. 'My boss said no one's to go in. Not until the senior fire officer says it's safe to do so. There could be further explosions.'

Jon looked wildly off to both sides. 'What about the Armed Response Unit? Is it here?'

'Armed Response? It's just the officers on the road, me and the two Community Support Officers over there. We haven't called for Armed Response.' He lowered his voice. 'Sir, have you been drinking? I can smell alcohol.'

Jon frowned. Where the hell were the bastards? They should have got here by now. He looked at the building once again. Fuck this, he thought, breaking clear from the cordon of vehicles to sprint across the expanse of yellow hatching covering the tarmac in front of the main entrance. Once through the doors, he slowed down, scanning the departments listed on the wall behind the deserted front desk. MHU. Sixth floor.

Alice backed away from the window in the women's bay which overlooked the car park. It was no good. The rising smoke flowing silently across the outside of the glass was too thick. Like being in a plane, she thought, as it plummets through cloud towards the earth. Ears now numb from the siren's continual wail, she splashed her way back to the corridor. Please, Jon. Hurry. The airlock was directly in front of her as she made her way towards the games room. She paused in mid-step. Was that someone in the lobby? It was! She raised a hand, tentatively beginning to wave as a man started forcing the outer doors apart.

Water was cascading down the steps, streams of it falling into the stairwell as Jon sprinted up the last flight, lungs now heaving with the effort. He reached the door for the sixth floor and spotted a wet handprint on its surface. Pushing it open, he peered into the lobby area. Fine droplets rained down from the sprinklers set into the ceiling. He saw a security desk, wrinkled sheets of paper clinging to the counter. A sodden copy of the *Manchester Evening Chronicle* on the floor. He saw the entrance to the unit itself and felt a jolt pass down his spine. The outer doors were wide open. Perhaps someone's already let her out, he thought, walking over to it on tiptoes in an attempt to reduce the splash each step made. As he entered the airlock itself, he tried to focus on hearing anything during the minuscule amount of time between the alarm's two screeching notes. Impossible, the hiss of the sprinklers was too loud.

He ducked his head through the inner doors. Two options. Follow the corridor straight ahead or turn immediately to the left. What had Alice said? The games room. Opposite a visitor room. He looked at the signs on the nearest doors in the corridor to his left. Medication room. Staff room. Visitor room.

He removed a fire extinguisher from its metal bracket on the wall and the cold metal felt good in his hands as he crept along, eyes fixed on the door to the games room. A man's voice. He peeped through the window. Alice! He gripped the handle and pushed it open, raising the fire extinguisher up like a giant club. Greg Mueller and Carl D'Souza were standing next to her, both of them at the end of the bed with the girl in. D'Souza was half turning, hand already in his jacket. Jon saw the man's eyes were almost popping out of his skull.

'Stop – it's me!' Jon lowered the extinguisher and looked at his wife. 'OK?'

She nodded and he turned back to the CIA agents. 'Where's your support?'

D'Souza lowered his hand, eyes cutting to the corridor behind Jon.

Mueller gestured to the window and announced, 'On their way.'

'You're on your own?'

'Yes.'

'Christ, then let's get out of here.'

Mueller exchanged a glance with D'Souza then nodded. He looked back at Jon. 'I'll cover the corridor. Carl will help you.' He brushed past Jon and positioned himself on the opposite side of the corridor, back to the visitor room.

Jon turned to Alice. 'Right, you hold the door open. Carl? It'll be quicker if we just carry her out between us.'

The CIA agent nervously ran a hand across his mouth, turned to the bed and then looked back at Jon. 'No. We wheel her out.'

'Seriously, Carl, it'll be faster to carry her.'

'I'm not carrying anyone. If Salnikov's here, I want both arms free.'

'Who?' Alice asked, glancing nervously at the two of them.

'Just someone,' Jon replied, placing the fire extinguisher on the floor and then stepping into the room so the door swung shut behind him. The volume of the alarm immediately dropped.

'Is he talking about ...' Alice's eyes went to Amira, '... who I think he is?'

'I'll explain later,' Jon replied. 'Help me sit her up and I'll carry her over my shoulder.'

He moved past Carl, who stepped back to the door and peered anxiously out of the window. Alice folded back the covers and Jon found himself staring at Amira's near-skeletal form. Oh, he thought. Everything you've survived and you're hardly bigger than a child. He knelt by the side of the bed, reaching for one arm so he could drape it over his shoulder. 'Carl, open the door.'

The CIA agent stepped back towards the bed, staring at Amira.

What the fuck are you doing? Jon thought, turning to Alice. 'Lean her forward so I can get my shoulder under her.' He had just started to brace himself to lift her up when a thud came from the corridor outside. The loudness of the alarm suddenly increased. Craning his neck to the side, he saw the door opening. A man in full surgical gowns stepped swiftly inside. The gap between the man's face mask and cap was narrow, but Jon recognised the eyes immediately. Salnikov.

Thirty-Two

Jon's eyes went to D'Souza. Before he could even shout, the CIA agent was reaching into his jacket, shoulders starting to turn. His hand emerged with a gun and he began to swing his arm round, straightening his elbow as he did so.

Salnikov's legs suddenly buckled and, for a moment, Jon wondered if a shot had already been fired. In a flash, the Russian jumped sideways like a crab. The pistol went off and the window in the door shattered. One hand on the carpet to steady him, Salnikov whipped his right foot out, connecting with D'Souza's knee. The joint gave out and the CIA agent's balance was lost.

Jon was trying to shrug Amira back off his shoulders as Salnikov rose up, lifting both hands above his head to catch D'Souza's gun arm before sweeping it down towards the ground. The momentum of the move spun D'Souza towards the bed and Jon saw the look in the other man's eyes. I'm going to die, it said. The pistol went off again, bullet firing straight into the floor.

Then Salnikov was twisting D'Souza's arm up behind his back. Jon heard cartilage snapping and D'Souza's mouth was opening in a gasp when the central part of his chest burst outwards. Another retort and the man's collar bone exploded. As he started to drop, Salnikov kept his grip with one hand, controlling D'Souza's descent. His other hand appeared with the pistol. He held it to the base of D'Souza's skull and pulled the trigger again. D'Souza's upper jaw disintegrated and Salnikov let him fall face first to the carpet.

Amira landed back on the bed and Jon sprang up to step in front of Alice.

Salnikov levelled the gun on Jon. 'Back.'

He looked to his side. Two chairs and a small table.

'Back!' Salnikov shouted, bringing his other hand up to cup the base of the pistol's grip.

He felt Alice's fingertips digging into his arm as he retreated, aware that he was now pressing her up against the wall. They were trapped. 'An Armed Response Unit is coming,' Jon said shakily, unable to understand why it hadn't accompanied Mueller and D'Souza to the scene. 'They'll be here any minute.'

'I doubt that,' Salnikov replied, pulling the surgical mask down. Jon saw the mass of scars above the pale green cloth. 'Now, kneel.'

Oh no, Jon thought. Not like this. We can't die like this.

'It's him.' Alice's voice was ragged with fear.

He tried to tuck her in behind him, glance going to the fire extinguisher on the other side of the room. I have no way of stopping this man, he thought, estimating the distance between them. Ten feet? If I jump at him, could I pin him down long enough for Alice to escape? He knew the distance was too far. Abruptly, the alarms in the building fell silent.

'On your knees,' Salnikov whispered. 'I will not hurt you.'

Holly's face appeared in his head and a moan escaped him. My sweet child, we'll never see you again. He looked at the table once more. A shield. If I grab that, could I rush at him? He looked back at Salnikov, but his eyes were drawn to the black circle of the gun barrel now pointing directly at his face.

Salnikov slowly shook his head. 'On your knees,' he hissed.

Knowing he had no other option, Jon lowered himself down. Next to him, he felt Alice doing the same. He'll take a step closer, Jon thought. Just to make sure. As soon as he does, that's when I'll grab the table.

Alice had started to sob and he said, 'Close your eyes. Just close your eyes.'

He readied himself to snatch at the table leg just inches from his grasp. But rather than move in for the kill, Salnikov crouched over D'Souza's corpse. Gun still trained on Jon, he started searching around in the American's jacket with his other hand. Their eyes met and Jon felt only coldness. He realised he'd stopped breathing.

Salnikov's pointed lower teeth showed as he smiled. 'You are lucky.'

Jon blinked. This is it, he said to himself. If I don't move now, we're dead.

'He would have killed you.' Salnikov removed something from D'Souza's inner pocket. Jon glanced at the other man's hand. A wire-like loop, small wooden handles at each end. 'The garrotte would have been ineffective with three of you. He would have shot you then claimed it was me.'

Air finally rattled into Jon's throat. What was the bloke ranting about?

Salnikov placed the garrotte on the floor. 'Your name is Spicer?'

Jon didn't dare move.

'You've been looking for me. I know. We passed on the stairs of Andriy's apartment.' He nudged D'Souza with the toe of one foot. 'As soon as that khokol, Mykosowski, phoned with the locations of my three colleagues, this man caught a flight up here and killed them.'

Among all the thoughts racing around inside his head, something that Rick had said stood out. A witness had asserted he'd seen D'Souza in the vicinity of one of the murders. He looked at the CIA agent's corpse. Why had the bloke got a garrotte in his jacket? And why had he stepped back to the bed as I was about to lift Amira? Jon swallowed. 'You didn't kill the Russian crewmen. That's what you're saying?'

'The only person I killed,' Salnikov replied, 'was Mykosowski, for betraying Marat, Yegor and Andriy.'

Jon glanced at the garrotte again. 'It was D'Souza?'

'That's his name? When I first rang Mykosowski – after the trawler took us to Liverpool – he immediately called the Americans. They contacted D'Souza and his friend – who then caught the first flight they could out of Baghdad. They arrived eight days ago.'

'The Americans?' Jon said slowly. 'You mean the people in America waiting for the shipment of cash?'

Salnikov nodded. 'That money was sacrificed the moment your people told them it was on its way.'

'My people? Who?'

'MI5? Whoever it was who rang the CIA to say the cargo was heading for Baltimore on the *Lesya*. Once the people involved knew the cash was being tracked, they contacted Mykosowski and told him to get rid of it.'

No, Jon thought. This can't be true. 'The CIA was stealing that money?'

'People within the CIA,' Salnikov stated. 'People with connections to these two, here. Helped by people in the CPA and by people working for American businesses out in Iraq. Many people are getting rich from the invasion.'

Jon's knees were beginning to ache, but he still didn't dare make any kind of movement. 'You're saying people in the CIA ordered the money to be thrown from the ship?'

'That's what Mykosowski told me. He received a call telling him to get rid of the money.'

Jesus, Jon thought. Soutar said that, once MI5 knew the *Lesya*'s next stop was Baltimore, they alerted their counterparts in the CIA.

Salnikov carried on speaking. 'Mykosowski then called Kaddouri, master of the *Lesya*, and ordered him to dump the cargo overboard.'

Who now is dead, Jon realised. An apparent heart attack while in CIA custody. And I thought it was our visit to Mykosowski that had led to the money being jettisoned. He could feel himself frowning.

Salnikov narrowed his eyes. 'You are wondering how I know all this?'

Jon gave a nod.

'Before I snapped his neck, I made Mykosowski tell me everything. It was when I refused to kill Marat, Yegor and Andriy, that's when Mykosowski passed their locations to this man.' Without looking down, he landed a kick on the back of D'Souza's ruined skull. It rocked slightly. 'He made the murders look like my work. He promised Mykosowski that, when I was caught, no one would ever see me again.'

'Rendition orders,' Jon stated.

Salnikov looked at Amira then turned to Alice. 'She will live?'

'Yes,' Alice whispered.

'You must get her warm. She is shivering.' He weighed up Jon. 'Do not move.'

Jon remained motionless, one arm still forming a shield across his wife.

Salnikov stepped to the end of the bed. He laid a hand on the bump that was Amira's foot and she shrank away. 'We did what we had to out there, Amira. All of us. When the *Lesya* left us, we did what we had to. You understand that?'

Slowly, her brown eyes turned to him.

'There was no other way we could survive,' Salnikov whispered.

Jon felt he should lower his eyes: the man was practically pleading. A flicker of some kind of understanding passed between them. Lower jaw still set tight, Amira looked away, breaking eye contact with the Russian.

Salnikov turned back to Jon. 'You must protect her. She knows the truth about that ship.'

She knows a lot more than that, Jon thought, picturing the letter in Oliver Brookes' possession.

'I must go. You will not try to stop me.'

Jon shook his head. 'You have the gun.'

Salnikov adjusted his grip on it. 'Wait here. No more oxygen tanks will explode.'

'You caused all that?'

He nodded. 'I didn't know if this was a trap. It was the only way I could be sure. Do not let the Americans near her.' He walked backwards to the door, raised the mask over his face then slipped out into the corridor.

As soon as the door shut, Jon turned to Alice and wrapped his arms around her.

She pressed her face into his chest. 'That was him, wasn't it? The man from the letters.'

'Yes.' He helped her up. 'Come on, let's get her out of here.'
He placed a hand on the bed. 'Amira? It's going to be easiest if I
just pick you up. Is that OK?'

She regarded them both for a moment. 'With your help,' she
said in a quiet, firm voice, 'I would prefer to walk.'

Alice nodded. 'Of course.'

Supporting Amira between them, they walked her, complete
with drip stand, out into the corridor. They passed Mueller's life-
less body and continued slowly through the airlock and into the
lobby. Jon paused to look out of the window. Far below them,
firefighters with breathing apparatus were making their way back
to their engines as others were running hoses towards the building. Ambulances and police cars lined the main road and the car
park was busy with patients and hospital staff. A figure in surgical
gowns came into view. For a second, Jon contemplated banging
on the window to try and alert those below. Instead, he watched
as Salnikov walked quickly across the tarmac, merging with the
people milling about. He passed behind a row of ambulances and
Jon didn't see him again.

Epilogue

Jon watched as Holly, giggling with delight, placed a tennis ball into the bowl-shaped end of the plastic handle. Once it was in position, she raised it above her head and tried to flick it forward. The ball was only thrown a few metres across the grass but Punch bounded after it anyway, stump of a tail wagging furiously.

His gaze travelled beyond the pair, taking in the rearing hill-sides dotted with oak trees that, from a distance, resembled frozen explosions of green. Higher still were pastures flecked white with sheep and then the craggy crests straining at the cloudless sky. The sun was nearing their jagged tips, its heat starting to fade. Beside him on the bench, Alice turned her head to nestle the back of it in the hollow of his shoulder. He lowered his chin, savouring the smell of her hair before looking out across the sparkling waters of Windermere.

Swallows were out feeding, flying just above the lightly ruffled surface in their search for airborne insects. He tracked a single bird as it veered this way and that, wings snapping at the water like a pair of thin jaws. As he watched it, a memory of a previous holiday spent up in Scotland returned. 'Remember the time on Skye? We'd stopped for a rest on top of that hill. You'd just unscrewed the flask when that fighter plane buzzed us?'

Alice laughed. 'I thought it was a swallow at first, didn't I? Racing through the air towards us.'

'Until it closed that last mile in an instant, getting bigger and bigger and bigger. The sonic boom as it went over our heads? Jesus.'

'And I jumped so much, I got tea all down my trousers.'

Jon chuckled, replaying the image of the plane as it sped on across the bay, the pilot tilting each wing in acknowledgement of the prank he'd just played.

They continued to watch the birds and when Alice spoke again, Jon could tell she was smiling. 'And that time we went to Egypt. You saw all those swallows lined up on the wires between the rickety-looking telegraph poles ...'

'And felt cheated,' he continued. 'I know it's stupid, but I still have that same sense of ... I don't know. It was weird seeing them there. I thought they were ours to enjoy. It hadn't even occurred to me where they might disappear every winter.'

A cluster of Mirror dinghies was out in the middle of the lake and Jon could hear the snap of their red sails and thrum of rope as the first ones rounded an orange buoy. 'Well, she got her birthday trip to the Lake District,' he said. 'Are you glad we came?'

She reached up to squeeze his hand. 'Of course. Glad we came. Glad Holly's so much happier. Glad about everything.' He felt a little shiver go through her. 'It frightens me, you know. Thinking how close we came ... how near our marriage was to ...'

'Hey.' He pressed his cheek against the top of her head. 'We're through it, Alice. It's behind us.'

She squeezed his fingers again. 'And I'm so glad it is.'

'Me, too.' He stretched his legs out, crossing his ankles and taking in a deep breath. This is the life. Especially, he thought, because my letter of apology was enough to appease Braithwaite. I wonder what Parks will be like? The only DCI in the Major Incident Team prepared to accept me into her syndicate. Brave woman.

'There was more in the papers,' Alice said quietly.

Jon suppressed a sigh. The story had turned into a media feeding frenzy. He thought of the desperate attempts by journalists to obtain Oliver Brookes' identity. The old man wasn't interested in claiming the reward for Amira's first letter; but preserving his anonymity had still been some feat.

'I had a flick through when I was buying the ice creams from that newsagent earlier on,' Alice continued. 'Another subsidiary of that American company's been implicated.'

Jon thought about Amira. Once Denmark had offered her asylum so she could live with an aunt and sister already there, her progress had, by all accounts, been excellent. The fact she was able to recall company names on the invoices she'd handed to Scott King was even more impressive. Confronted with the evidence of his corruption, the man had promptly offered to give up everything he knew. Rick had taken a call from Soutar the other day. The MI5 officer had said it was like falling dominoes; a chain reaction involving company after company. Rick had grinned at first but, as the enormity of the scandal sank in, the smile had faded from his face.

'Who knows,' Alice continued. 'Maybe they'll even lift those gagging orders. Then, some of Bush's closest cronies could face prosecution.'

'Send the lot to Guantanamo Bay,' Jon sighed, mind going to the forensic evidence from the crime scenes of the three murdered Russians. D'Souza's hairs had been recovered from two of the flats and residents in the building where the second murder had occurred had also picked his photo out. Fibres of silk from the man's garrotte had also been recovered from all three victims' throat wounds.

Jon guessed the CIA agent had posed as some sort of official. It was the only way he could have got the Russians to sit still while he manoeuvred himself behind them.

Mueller and D'Souza. Jon shook his head. At first the American authorities had tried to say they were some kind of renegades. Bad apples, acting alone. But freelance journalists had revealed that, after leaving Yale, Mueller had enrolled with the CIA while fellow graduates had joined the very company whose oil-drilling machinery had supposedly been in the container which actually held the stolen cash. The non-existent equipment was en route, the documentation had claimed, for repairs back at the corporation's American headquarters in Baltimore.

Before America attacked Iraq, Mueller had applied to work in an advisory capacity as the logistics of reconstructing the country after the coming invasion began to be calculated. D'Souza, it transpired, had enrolled in the CIA after a stint in the army. The man had been trained in a variety of anti-terrorism techniques, though, for the moment, the CIA was refusing to elaborate further.

The sad fact remained, they weren't aberrations: it was becoming more and more clear that embezzlement involving private companies in collusion with US officials had taken place on an industrial scale. Not wanting to sour his feelings of contentedness, Jon pushed the thoughts from his head.

'Howzat!'

He looked over his shoulder to where the triumphant shout had come from. A father and his two sons playing cricket. His gaze drifted across their picnic blanket then on to where the mother and daughter were standing in the shallows of the lake, saris hitched up over their ankles.

'What shall we do tonight?' he asked.

'I don't know,' Alice replied. 'Not eat in the hotel, anyway.'

He grinned, recollecting the plates of bland lasagne they'd struggled through the evening before. The woman serving them had been so proud of her creation, they hadn't dared to complain. He thought about their little bungalow in the hotel's grounds. He and Alice were still in separate beds, as they were back in their home in Manchester, but that wasn't a problem. What was important, he reflected with a smile, is that my family is together again. 'Come on, then,' he announced.

Alice sat up so he could get to his feet. Something was floating at the water's edge, tiny waves doing their best to deposit it on the gravel shore. He stepped across and looked down. A wooden fork, rounded at one end, two blunt prongs at the other. He bent forward and plucked its bobbing form from the crystalline water. 'How about fish and chips?' he asked, walking over to the nearby bin. 'We haven't had that in ages.'

Author's note

This novel required me to research far more than I have ever done before. You might be interested to know about some of my sources.

Thankfully, I've never had to face near-starvation on a raft. Instead, I read two compelling and harrowing accounts informed by people who have:

Wreck of the Medusa by Alexander Mckee

In the Heart of the Sea by Nathaniel Philbrick

Mainstream Western media has been as pitiful at reporting the catastrophic consequences of the invasion for ordinary Iraqis as the Allied forces have been in keeping count of the numbers of civilians they've obliterated. Fatalities that have occurred as a result of the invasion and subsequent occupation now exceed one million.[1] (More, incredibly, than the number who died in the Rwandan genocide.) Many times that number have been forced to flee the country as refugees.[2]

Numerous blogs describe the carnage and upheaval; I found 'Baghdad Burning' particularly well written. You can read it for yourself at: http://riverbendblog.blogspot.com. The author has posted nothing since October 2007.

All the facts and figures relating to the theft of money intended for the reconstruction of Iraq are, at the time of going to print,

1   ORB Survey, January, 2008 (www.opinion.co.uk).
2   United Nations High Commissioner for Refugees (www.unhcr.org).

accurate. It is a crime that has led Congressman Henry Waxman, chair of the House Oversight and Government Reform Committee (2007 to 2009) to state that the stolen billions, 'may well turn out to be the largest war profiteering in history'.[3]

His view is backed by an anonymous American businessman active in Iraq, who stated, 'I believe the real looting of Iraq after the invasion was by US officials and contractors.'[4]

To date, no major US contractor faces trial for fraud in Iraq. Gagging orders still prevent the public discussion of seventy allegations.

For an explanation of why America was prepared to take on the costs – both financial and human – of invading Iraq in the first place, I recommend Naomi Klein's *The Shock Doctrine: The Rise of Disaster Capitalism*.

---

3   BBC News, 'BBC Uncovers Lost Iraq billions', June 2008.
4   *Independent*, 'A fraud bigger than Madoff', February 2009.

Acknowledgements

Writing this book was possible only because a variety of people were willing to share their experiences and expertise with me. The manuscript itself was initially knocked into shape by Stephanie at Gregory and Company then further improved with the help of Jon and Jade at Orion.

The descriptions of everything from rescuing stranded whales to the realities of the invasion for ordinary Iraqis were based on information kindly provided by the following people:

Faye at British Divers Marine Life Rescue (www.bdmlr.org.uk)
Chris at the UK Border Agency
Julia at Refugee Action Manchester
Jonny Mac (for his insights into police case file preparation)
Dan (for a glimpse into life as a nurse on a mental health ward)
Beach and Steve (for all the naval stuff)

and finally,

Nasreen, for describing to me so vividly how her country has been torn apart.

I would also like to thank the Authors' Foundation whose grant enabled me to carry out so much of the necessary research.